My Thousand & One Nights

Middle East Literature in Translation

Michael Beard *and* Adnan Haydar, *Series Editors*

Selected titles from Middle East Literature in Translation

The Committee
    Sonallah Ibrahim; Mary St. Germain and Charlene Constable, trans.
A Cup of Sin: Selected Poems
    Simin Behbahani; Farzaneh Milani and Kaveh Safa, trans.
Disciples of Passion
    Hoda Barakat; Marilyn Booth, trans.
Fatma: A Novel of Arabia
    Raja Alem, with Tom McDonough
Granada: A Novel
    Radwa Ashour; William Granara, trans.
In Search of Walid Masoud: A Novel
    Jabra Ibrahim Jabra; Roger Allen and Adnan Haydar, trans.
Moroccan Folktales
    Jilali El Koudia; Roger Allen, ed. and trans.
The Night of the First Billion
    Ghada Samman; Nancy Roberts, trans.
Nightingales and Pleasure Gardens: Turkish Love Poems
    Talat S. Halman, ed. and trans.; Jayne L. Warner, assoc. ed.
Sleeping in the Forest: Stories and Poems
    Sait Faik; Talat S. Halman, ed.; Jayne L. Warner, assoc. ed.
A Time Between Ashes and Roses
    Adonis; Shawat M. Toorawa, ed. and trans.
Women Without Men: A Novella
    Shahrnush Parsipur; Kamran Talattof and Jocelyn Sharlet, trans.

My Thousand & One Nights

A NOVEL OF MECCA

Raja Alem & Tom McDonough

SYRACUSE UNIVERSITY PRESS

First Edition 2007
07 08 09 10 11 12   6 5 4 3 2 1

Originally published in Arabic as *Sîdî Wadhâna* (Beirut: n.p., 2002).

The paper used in this publication meets the minimum requirements of American
National Standard for Information Sciences—Permanence of Paper for Printed Library
Materials, ANSI Z39.48–1984.∞™

For a listing of books published and distributed by Syracuse University Press,
visit our Web site at SyracuseUniversityPress.syr.edu.

ISBN-13: 978-0-8156-0866-0
ISBN-10: 0-8156-0866-7

Library of Congress Cataloging-in-Publication Data
'Alim, Raja'.
   [Sidi Wahdanah. English]
   My thousand and one nights : a novel of Mecca / Raja Alem and Tom McDonough.
— 1st ed.
      p. cm. — (Middle East literature in translation)
   ISBN 978-0-8156-0866-0 (alk. paper)
 I. McDonough, Tom.   II. Title.

PJ7814.L53S5313 2007
892'.736—dc22   2007014596

Manufactured in the United States of America

Contents

RAJA ALEM is the author of seven novels, many plays, and collections of poetry. She lives in Jeddah, Saudi Arabia.

TOM MCDONOUGH is the author of a novel, *Virgin with Child*, and a story collection, *Light Years*. His cinematography won an Academy Award for the feature documentary *Best Boy*. Raja and Tom's first collaborative work was *Fatma*, published by Syracuse University Press.

Introduction

The Woman Who Invented Zero

TOM McDONOUGH

> We've all arrived at a very special place—spiritually,
> ecumenically, grammatically.
>> —Captain Jack Sparrow in *Pirates of the Caribbean*

I first met Raja Alem in 1997, in the Arabian port city of Jeddah. Like all
Saudi women venturing outside the privacy of her home, she was wearing
an *abaya,* a long black shroud that covered her from head to toe. Raja had
published seven novels in Arabic, as well as several plays, poems, children's
books, and quite a bit of journalism. I gathered that her reputation in contemporary Arabic literature was similar to Nabokov's in ours: masterful,
erudite, witty, and somewhat dangerous, with a pre-photographic confidence in the supremacy of words. She was accompanied by her identically
dressed sister Shadia, a painter who had recently won a competition to
design the decorations for the tail fins of Saudi Airlines jets. So far as I
could tell from the little of them that was on view, the sisters were in their
thirties, tall and graceful. They radiated a droll, tense intelligence, in the
manner of prisoner autodidacts.

My wife and I had been invited to teach in Jeddah by the USIS cultural
attaché, whom we'd met while working a couple of years earlier in Morocco. Saudi Arabia has the makings of a great Club Med destination, but
unlike Morocco, it is very much a closed country. Unless you're a Muslim

pilgrim or a diplomat or an oil worker or a pliable journalist or an Indonesian servant, you can't just apply for a visa and go there. If you do manage it, your movements will be severely limited. When my family and I landed in Jeddah, we were preceded at customs by a black man carrying a French passport. The inspector slashed open his luggage with a saber.

Raja, Shadia, and my wife and I shared a hookah at a restaurant overlooking the Red Sea. The breeze was a twitch of heat. The sisters urged us to extend our stay; they proposed to show us around the Rub al-Khali, the Empty Quarter, a desert the size of France. Flying over it on the way in, it struck me that great religions tend to arise in vast wastelands—there *has* to be more to our lives than this, this nothingness from horizon to horizon, hour after appalling hour.

I told the sisters that I had no interest in suffering further. They regarded me sternly. I looked back at them, trapped into saying precisely what I was thinking: "There must be something attractive about captivity."

Raja whispered an interpretation of this remark to Shadia, and as she did, a different scent came off her, an intimate, flowery alarm. Shadia understood English as well as her sister, but she was the edgy one, suspicious of foreigners, of everyone. Raja was regal, sustained by a lofty shyness. Yet she was marvelous at promoting the illusion that she knew me well and that we shared a long history. I'd known her for an hour. The first and most important questions—Who is this person? Is she (he) to be trusted?—had already been settled.

I flew back to the States with the manuscript of a novel Raja had written in English. Her ambition was to break away from the very limited audience for Arabic literature; a novel, no matter how classy the author's reputation, typically sells only a few hundred copies in the Middle East. Her strategy, which had been concocted more or less in isolation, was to draft in Arabic and rewrite in English, the world language, and so find her way to a wide audience, to a hot Mercedes (pathetically, for a Saudi, she was being chauffeured around in a '70s Oldsmobile), and to the kind of freedom that fame can bestow. But she knew that her command of English was not up to her own literary standards. "I don't know how I *sound* in English," she said as she handed me her manuscript. It was the one time I would hear sadness in her voice.

I skimmed the manuscript on the plane. Though Raja's prose was off-key and not always comprehensible, it was clear that she was the genuine article—a serious writer with a compelling vision. As soon as I got home, I rewrote the first fifteen pages, making wild guesses where I got lost, and faxed them to her. Raja faxed right back, delighted. Parenthetically, she mentioned that she'd started embroidering my initials in Arabic on a bolt of black velvet, and asked me to supply her with my mother's unmarried name, an ingredient necessary for the completion of the Bedouin spell she was casting to ensure the success of our project.

Raja's spell bathed me in the unexpected glow of good luck. I'd come to Saudi Arabia as a cinematographer who had written a couple of books; the professional voyeur in me felt thwarted by the closedness of the society. Also, I was miserably aware that my own culture had reached a point—sometime in the early 1980s, I think it was—where more cheesy pictures had been disseminated than honest words had ever been written, and that the weight of these images was stifling the adventure of discovering, or even conceiving of, any culture apart from TV. A suffocating new oppression had settled over all of us: there seemed room now for only one way of seeing, one god, one fulfillment. I needed to see inside the strange land that had struck my soul a glancing blow. Collaborating with Raja was a way to do it, to get inside. Clinically speaking, mine was clear-cut case of *ripae ulterioris amore*—the lure, as Virgil calls it, the love of the further shore.

Haza Haza Haza, the first book Raja and I worked on together, was a romantic adventure set in seventeenth-century Mecca. Her panorama (I wouldn't be too quick to call it a plot; more about this later) included a blind, love-struck dervish, several doomed princesses, a beautiful slave girl with magical powers, shape-changing wizards, run-amuck witches, crazed calligraphers, sexual intercourse with scorpions, and, needless to say, scheming eunuchs.

My agent was ecstatic. "How soon can you get her over here?" he asked. "When can she start touring?" As it turned out, he was the only other white person on the planet who thought he could make commercial sense of the book. Raja and I put it away and started working on another. This one, *Fatma,* got published. It is an eerie, occasionally beautiful novel, always passionate, though slight in comparison to her other work. I suspect that *Fatma* was the first of Raja's books to get published in the West because its general theme conforms to Western expectations of fiction from the Middle East: "Abused Arab Woman Tells All." (For nonfiction, the formula is: "What Arabs Think, Why They Think It, and What, If They Were Really Nice People, They Ought to be Thinking.") Raja is an original, her work is an acquired appetite. My guess is that her books are fated to be published in English in reverse order of their strangeness and forcefulness.

We have kept at our collaboration for almost ten years now. Since meeting in Jeddah, we've seen each other twice, for a total of perhaps six days: once when Raja and Shadia passed through New York City on their way to visit a relative undergoing surgery in Atlanta, and then at a literary festival in Toronto, where distinguished male litterateurs trailed the exotic sisters around like puppies.

We have learned to be amused by one another; we have come to understand that the species of translation we have adopted is the perfect blend of intimacy and distance. We have gotten to know each other perhaps too well, like a couple married for fifty years, finishing one another's sentences, anticipating every reaction, savoring the inspiration and adoration, the nagging, the flat-footed jokes, the interdependence, the coy deafness, the tender tolerance, the evasions, the micro-divorces, the astonishing strengths. Like most marriages, our collaboration began with naive expectations and a sense that we were exchanging vows, a belief that this was a step that could change our lives and the hope that our fates might become plural.

Yet whatever glamorous claims might be made for it, translation remains the orthodontics of literature. Writing about our collaboration in a diplomatic, novocained way does not get to the heart of the matter, which is that there is no bridging the gap, no healing the wounds between Raja's world and mine, no glossing over the centuries of insult. Our mutual histories are more than normatively vicious.

But maybe things are not so terrible. Because neither, between Raja and me, is there war. There is, every now and then, a mirage of perfect meaning.

Since 9/11, so much of America has been about pretending to win. However credulous or incredulous one is supposed to be nowadays, I believe certain things now that I felt too safe to believe as a child. One of the things I believe is that as long as Raja and I are translating, her people and mine may have something to do besides going to war for embarrassing reasons.

Oh yes, the work itself . . . We do about five pages at a time. Working from her English draft, I send her my version, along with queries. She responds. In the beginning we ran up enormous fax bills; lately we've been using email. We chat about the weather, we exchange family bulletins and saucy Internet jokes. We use teasing salutations ("Dear Rising Oil Prices . . . " "Dear Tom of Arabia . . . ").

What with one thing and another, a book takes us about six months. Here's an example of how it goes. First, a paragraph of Raja's English:

> She treasured you, and captured you in this undying image: dedicated rising on a blue mountain, and a china gate, facing a rebellious black guarding slave, with a Sheik meeting you at the gate, clad in a night or the most dark gowns, sending you into a hall way built of the Yemeni onyx inlaid with gold, reaching a grove inhabited by infinite creatures, each praising the Mighty Creator or King of the kings, facing divans in each a setting raised around a fountain cornered with transfixed lions, in which a circle of wise sheikhs are setting surrounded by books and golden magnifiers, on which traces of incenses fingerprints are invisible, used books, living books, imprinted with the touches of the students of magic, all awaiting your appearance, receiving you drinking of your knowledge with the utmost curiosity.

Which turned into:

> I adore you, Jummo; I always have. I picture you in a single unvarying image: climbing a blue mountain, focused to the point of ferocity, approaching a gate made of shiny red tiles. You are

confronted by a surly Ethiopian slave. The sheik who rescues you seems to be wearing night itself—surely the crushing darkness of his aura can't be accounted for merely by his pitch-black robe.

The sheik ushers you toward a hallway made of onyx inlaid with gold. You come to a meadow populated by billions of strange creatures milling around in rooms that face one another. All the creatures are singing songs, different songs, softly. The rooms are raised a few inches above a fountain with lions crouched in each corner, bearded chins resting on forepaws. The fountain itself bubbles at the center of a circle of learned sheiks surrounded by books and gold-rimmed magnifying glasses on which faint traces of the fingerprints of perfumed hands are rapidly fading. The scholars are enclosed by a still wider circle of books that are reading themselves, books walking and talking, books aglow with the ministrations of student magicians. All these things and people and animals are intensely curious about you, Jummo, impatient to meet you. To taste you.

The alteration I most notice, three years after rewriting this, is that I glossed over Raja's "praising the Mighty Creator or King of the kings." I can't remember my reasons for doing so; probably they were not very smart. Plus I moved the paragraph from its original place in the manuscript to another place hundreds of pages away. In short, I chop-shopped it. By conventional standards of translation, this is meretricious. But Raja and I are what passes these days for grownups, and it suits us to adapt the original with the idea of moving her vision transparently from one culture to another. We are not, in this enterprise, precisionists. Permit me to take refuge in the words of Walter Benjamin:

Translation does not find itself in the center of the language forest but on the outside; it calls into it without entering, aiming at that single spot where the echo is able to give, in its own language, the reverberation of the work in the alien one.

I came across this citation in an essay by the poet and classical scholar Anne Carson, who has herself been known to play it fast and loose with her translations of Sappho.

Arabia, like Ireland, is mostly a country in a movie.

The 1947 movie *Sinbad the Sailor* is based in its elastic Hollywood way on episodes from the original *Thousand and One Nights*. In those days it was fashionable to start a period movie with a title card written in old-fashioned script. The idea was that you were about to tunnel through to a time before the movies, before even the printing press, a calligraphic time—a time like, say, the Crusades.

> *O Masters, O Noble Persons, O Brothers, know you that in the time of the Caliph Harun-Al-Rashid, there lived on the golden shore of Persia a man of adventure called Sinbad the Sailor . . .*

Douglas Fairbanks, Jr., plays the clever Sinbad. Anthony Quinn is the cruel, swarthy sultan. He threatens to gouge out Douglas Fairbanks, Jr.'s eyes. Fairbanks flashes his dazzling piratical smile and winks at Maureen O'Hara, the red-haired harem girl. Further outraged, the Sultan says he is going to pry off Sinbad's fingernails, expose him on a cliff, rip him apart with wild horses, slice him to pieces and feed the scraps to his bushy white Wolfhounds.

"Words—mere words!" says Fairbanks, and nimbly executes one of his back flips to freedom.

You have, of course, seen Peter O'Toole swanning around in *Lawrence of Arabia*. Have you seen *Hidalgo*? Mustang pony ridden by boozy cowboy (Viggo Mortenson) outruns Arabian thoroughbreds in a marathon race across the Empty Quarter. Cowboy sobers up, frees slaves, and captures heart of cruel, swarthy sheik's doe-eyed daughter.

May I submit, with all due solemnity, that this slapstick comes close to conveying the archetypical hero of non-Western narrative? *The Thousand and One Nights* of the Arabs and the Popul Vuh of the Mayans, to cite two examples, do not defer to the solo messianic heroes and heroines favored by Europeans. They go for picaros, tricksters. Gabriel García Márquez is said to have learned many of his tricks from Cervantes, who learned many of his tricks from Arab story tellers in Andalusia, who learned many of their tricks from . . .

In the 1860s, when Sir Richard Burton's translation of *The Thousand and One Nights* was published, the book was regarded as so far beyond the orbits of mature Western narrative—this was the heyday of Charles Dickens and George Eliot—that it was consigned pretty much to the realm of children's fantasy. (Raja gasped in shock when I mentioned this to her.)

The Old Man and the Sea can be read as a children's book, too, as can most of Marilyn Robinson's *Housekeeping*, for that matter. Children are easily frightened, but they are not flustered by tragedy. On coming to the end of *The Old Man and the Sea,* my seven-year-old son requested one change: instead of the shark eating the marlin, how about the marlin eats the shark? That's the kind of notion Raja might entertain.

At the heart of Western narrative is the secular belief in questions and answers, the conviction that our creaturehood can be profitably investigated. What shapes Raja's world? Design rather than investigation. Her stories are braided strands.

In her introduction to *Middlemarch,* George Eliot speaks of "Saint Teresa of Avila, foundress of nothing." No one has ever been able to attach a convincing reason to this haunting remark. Think of Raja as the woman who invented zero. Her narratives, like the stories in *The 1001 Nights,* are told in the voice of an innocent—a wise innocent, to be sure. Sometimes she preserves her innocence through allegory. Her storytelling strategies may be at variance with ours, but the concerns are much the same as those of our canonical *romans*: How dangerous is love? How lethal are women? Can spiritual labor keep up with the ever-increasing demand for immortality?

Raja's *My Thousand and One Nights* is highly regarded by readers of Arabic, who know it as *Sidi Wadhana,* which means, approximately, *Sir Death.* One of the reasons the book is so loved in the Arab world is because it is a pilgrimage to a Mecca that no longer exists. The Mecca that Raja grew up in during the 1970s was a medieval city; its modernization lay in an unimaginable future. A Victrola makes an appearance on the very first page of *My Thousand and One Nights* and later, very briefly, we get a glimpse of cigarettes and a Jeep. Everything else is centuries old, changeless.

Raja was raised in her grandfather's house, on a slope overlooking the central mosque of the holy city. Her grandfather was the Sheik of the Zamzam Water Carriers. Zamzam is the well in Mecca's sacred mosque, and also the name of the healing waters that flow from it. Her grandfather was, in effect, the superintendent of water supply in a large desert city, where water is a miraculous substance, venerated and feared, never taken for granted. In a vault in the basement of his house, her grandfather kept a collection of ancient maps and charts of Mecca's subterranean waterways, bound into books whose covers were inlaid with silver. Raja became a writer the night she crept downstairs and sneaked a look at his beautiful, mysterious maps. "Words became my water," she said in one of her emails, "my secret supply of life."

Old Mecca went into its death throes in November of 1978, when a squad of insurgents lead by a man who claimed to be the *madhi,* the savior of Arab civilization, smuggled automatic weapons into the holy mosque. Raja and the other women of her family watched the siege from the shuttered balconies of the women's quarters in their house, stoically evaluating the imported French commandos' sickeningly efficient application of force. A short while later, their house, their eccentric pleasures, their secret passageways, and their intense but expansive beliefs would be gone, replaced by high-rises of rebar and cinder block.

During the oil boom of the 1980s, the holy city was bulldozed and entirely rebuilt, extinguishing an intricate culture whose resources and feuds were sorted out according to neighborhood codes rather than merciless geopolitical forces. Which makes a good case, so far as Raja is concerned, for the theory that the driving force of artistic endeavor is forsakenness.

It is hard for us Anglophones to approach this book without expecting to learn something about "the Arab Mind"—as if it were possible to define the consciousness of six hundred million diverse people and tether it, like a cartoon balloon, to the head of a generic veiled woman. We may in fact learn a thing or two about the Arab Mind, but the issue at hand is, how does Raja do what she does?

She is in no way embittered. I would venture to say that we would be embittered, given similar circumstances. Obviously, thresholds of embitterment vary; for example, the music of South Africa, before and after apartheid, has always been the merriest in the world. Raja does not kid herself, but her vision is easy on people. She aspires not so much to English fluency as to a universal voice, a tone that transcends dictionaries, like Billie Holiday, Bob Dylan, or Cesaria Evora. Maybe this is how captivity sounds. The sound of honesty sustains her.

Raja is esteemed as a musical writer in one of the most musical languages. She has a singer's purposeful ambivalence about lyrics: a given word means what she wants it to mean when she means what she wants it to mean. In America, this is jazz. In classical Arabic, it's good writing. In recognition of this and in deference to the incantatory tradition of Quranic recitation that means so much to Raja, I've done my best to make the book sound right when read aloud. The late Norman O. Brown, one of the last celebrity humanists, suggested that the artifact of our culture that most resembles the Qur'an in sonority and wildness of language is *Finnegans Wake*—except the Qur'an is not just for lit majors.

The possibilities of English, to a writer whose mother tongue is English, feel limitless. Everyone's mother tongue feels infinite. So follow me here: If one's mother tongue is infinite, then great works written in other languages exist in separate galaxies. Ergo, translation is a subgenre of science fiction. (Beam me up, Raja . . .)

Or, if you happen not to be of a pop-techy bent, then translation is a visionary craft along the lines of miracle-working, or a mystery like Transubstantiation, a mesmerizing impossibility. And if Raja is the captive, then I am the fool air-guitaring Arabic.

◆   ◆   ◆

Let us now praise invisible editors. If hope (and hopelessness) are immeasurable, there is no way adequately to thank two people whose constancy made the publication of this impossible book possible. Nevertheless, we thank Mary Selden Evans and Michael Beard, editors so dedicated and shrewd that one can't help continuing to believe in this quaint line of work.

Cast of Characters

ABDUL HAI: the father of Mohammed al-Maghrabi.

ABU SHARRAB/SOCK MAN: a man of learning; Jummo's suitor after her divorce.

AL-HOSN: Nara and Sheik Mohamed al-Baikwaly's adopted son.

AL-RIBEANYA: a widow and celebrated singer.

DAY AL-LAYL: younger brother of Zohr and Krazat al-Yosir.

DUBLOLA: a neighbor woman.

ESHA THE ONION: a homeless madwoman.

FATMA MOSLIYA: the widow of Sheik Abdul al-Magharbi and Zohr's paternal grandmother; later in the story, the family matriarch.

HAMIDA KHAJA (HAMIDA THE WISE): the semimythological leader of women from mountains of Nowaria, descended from the Nymphs of Waq.

HANIM: Mohammed al-Maghrabi's cat, and a spirit from the underworld.

HANNAH: the oldest daughter of Nara and Sheik Mohamed al-Baikwaly.

HASSAN AL-BASRI (HASSAN OF BASRA): a legendary alchemist, gold-smith, and adventurer.

JOMAN: the older sister of Zohr and Krazat al-Yosir.

JUMMO/DUMBOSHI: the middle daughter of Nara and Sheik Mohamed al-Baikwaly.

KHADIJA: Nara's mother. Early in the story, Khadija reigns as family matriarch.

KHAIRIJA: the daughter of Safiya and cousin of Zohr.

KHATIM AL-HIJAZI: a wedding singer.

KRAZAT AL-YOSIR and ZOHR: the granddaughters of Nara and Sheik Mohamed al-Baikwaly and nieces of Jummo. Zohr is the putative narrator of the book; about halfway through, briefly, Krazat takes over the storytelling.

MA'AMOOM AL-NEYABI: briefly, Jummo's husband.

MEYAJAN: the assistant of Yakut Khan/Big Ruby.

MOHAMMED AL-MAGHRABI: The son of Fatma Mosliya, husband of Hannah, and father of Zohr.

MOQAENA SAFIA: a wedding stylist.

MUSROOR: a playboy neighbor.

MUSTORA: Musroor's lover, then wife.

MYJAN: a young man from a respectable middle-class family, and Jummo's suitor.

NABEE JAN: the older brother of Zohr and Krazat al-Yosir.

NARA: the wife of Sheik Mohamed al-Baikwaly.

QAHTAN: a Bedouin boy, playmate of Jummo in Taif.

RAHMA: al-Hosson's wife.

SAFIYA: a neighbor lady.

SALIH: the ne'er-do-well son of Abdul Hai.

SAMEER and HYAT: Hannah's children, who died in infancy.

SAYED HASSAN: a prominent traditional healer.

SHEIK MOHAMMED AL-BAIKWALY: family patriarch and sheik (chief) of the Zamzam Water Carriers.

SIDI WAHDANA: Literally, Mister Death, or Sir Death. Sidi Wahdana is a harbinger of death and, sometimes, a spirit-guide. He often manifests himself as a dervish. Throughout her life, Jummo has a special relationship with Sidi Wahdana.

SITEE FAHEEMA: a Meccan power broker and the city's foremost midwife.

SONBOK: Meyajan's uncle, Sheik of the Pharmacists.

TRONJA: Fatma Mosliya's female slave.

YAQUT KHAN/BIG RUBY: widow of the Sheik of the Textile Merchants. A wealthy woman, one of the most powerful merchants in Mecca.

ZAINUB KABLIYA: the pretty, lute-playing girl next door.

ZUBAYDA: the youngest daughter of Nara and Sheik Mohamed al-Baikwaly.

My Thousand & One Nights

1. The Gramophone

Jummo puffs into the incense burner, inflaming the embers of aloe and musk, dizzying herself on the fumes. She tries to turn off the gramophone. Two, three, four times, her fingers slip on the wooden switch. She crosses to the mirror and takes off her clothes. Piece by piece she peels the curtains from the theater of her body; she stands shining, a naked radiance split by the black cord circling her waist. She cocks her head to sculpt the sinews of her neck. Amulets jingle against her belly. She inhales. She exhales. Her stomach stays flat. She's sweating with the effort of trying to see her body whole and clear. Her reflection feels offended. Her nipples look innocently upward.

In the shadow cast by the lip of pale flesh just below her navel, Jummo begins to draw with a kohl liner pencil, following the rules for traditional tattooing, sketching a dark, straight line, then another. And another and another, shaping four connected triangles. She smiles: the tattoo looks like a medieval fortress. In the rightmost triangle, she sketches a sprig of basil. In the other triangles she writes the names of all three loves of her life.

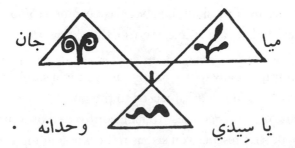

She puts the finishing touch on the sprig of basil. The heavily scented soul of the plant rises higher. Jummo sighs the name of her first man: Mayjan. *My-jahn.*

In a corner of one of the other triangles she draws a set of heavy eyebrows whose stare digs eyelessly into her skin. She exhales the name of her second lover: *Sidi Wahdana.*

Mayjan materializes on Sidi Wahdana's tail, where he digs a narrow but very deep hole in the O of Jummo's loneliness, ensuring that no one else can have her.

In the third triangle a black snake slithers, hissing and tunneling.

The tattoo tightens like an animal her stomach. She squeezes her eyes shut. Her knuckles blanch, her thumbs cramp. She jabs the kohl pencil into her belly, drawing blood. The blood vaporizes into a mist of water and basil. The droplets shiver across her body. She gasps, she covers her face with her hands, she can't stop shaking. She ducks away from the mirror, away from the brazen gaze of her men. She clasps her amulets against her hips, switches the gramophone off at last, dives on the bed and passes out face down, hands pressed against her belly, smothering the life pulse quivering there.

"Oh look, look, this is really something!" Zohr stifles a giggle. "Jummo just got herself pregnant!"

Zohr and her sleek sister Krazat are peeking at Aunt Jummo.

Krazat looks down at her right hand. On her palm she sees a replica of the triangular animals tattooed on Jummo's belly.

Zohr, the whiter sister, winces at the flames she feels in her stomach. She runs her finger over the drawing on her sister's hand. In Jummo, another flame flares sympathetically. The little girls sense that Jummo is afraid that the flames of her own passions are about to become visible. But of course they want them to become visible. And so, they know, does Jummo.

I adore you, Jummo; I always have. I picture you in a single unvarying image: climbing a blue mountain, focused to the point of ferocity, approaching a gate made of shiny red tiles. You are confronted by a surly Ethiopian slave. The sheik who rescues you seems to be wearing night itself—surely the crushing darkness of his aura can't be accounted for merely by his pitch-black robe.

The sheik ushers you toward a hallway made of onyx inlaid with gold. You come to a meadow populated by billions of strange creatures milling around in rooms that face one another. All the creatures are singing songs, different songs, softly. The rooms are raised a few inches above a fountain with lions crouched in each corner, bearded chins resting on forepaws. The fountain itself bubbles at the center of a circle of learned sheiks surrounded by books and gold-rimmed magnifying glasses on which faint traces of the fingerprints of perfumed hands are rapidly fading. The scholars are enclosed by a still wider circle of books that are reading themselves, books walking and talking, books aglow with the ministrations of student magicians. All these things and people and animals are intensely curious about you, Jummo, impatient to meet you. To taste you.

It never occurred to any of us, Hannah's children, to pay any attention to the ancient trunk with the silver-inlaid sides. It was the only thing my mother inherited from her sister Jummo. The trunk entered our house unlocked and sat there for years, eliciting little curiosity and less sympathy. It lived quietly under the kitchen stairs until one day, as I was passing obliviously by, I caught the scent of an otherworldly perfume and felt an urge to start poking around in the trunk.

It was then that I discovered the fortune Jummo had left my mother. Tucked inside an embroidered bundle I found a collection of amulets strung on a strip of camel hide. My mother identified the wrapping as the last piece of embroidery her sister had done. Gently, reverently, I set the amulets aside, not wanting to disturb their spirits.

I opened a letter lying at the bottom of the bundle. A cloud of coal dust puffed in my face and settled back down on the paper, dimming the words written in henna dye. In a nervous attempt to tidy things up, I tapped the letter with my middle finger. The words responded by mixing with the coal dust and puddling in grease blots, rendering themselves unintelligible. Had Jummo actually written this letter? And if so, to whom? I could smell the kohl and henna she'd been so fond of. What feelings had she wanted to reveal by using these special inks?

I asked my mother if Jummo had been able to write in her mother tongue, the language called al-Khazr, which is spoken by people from Uzbekistan.

"Not a word of it!" said my mother with the heat reserved for revelations about her sister. "She was illiterate. Even more illiterate than me!"

Her gaze drifted down to the letter, settling on the blots of coal dust. She blinked. "The eye of Sidi Wahdana!" she gasped, struggling to keep her eyes from capsizing.

Sidi Wahdana . . . Sidi Wahdana . . . the scariest dervish in all of Mecca. Sidi Wahdana . . . Sidi Wahdana. . . .

I've been looking for you, Jummo.

My innocence, my girlhood—I've been looking for them, too.

Just outside, a stiff breeze ruffles the date palms. The fountain's spray cowers under the gusts. I see a band of young virgins, soaked to the skin; they are lovely beyond imagining. They scatter across the dunes, chased by dust devils (dust devils being the camouflage most favored by stalkers of virgins).

You remember the old hag who put Sidi Wahdana on your trail? Remember how she showed you (and the witch was quite clear about it, considering the kaleidoscopic nature of her revelation) how many graves lined the road to your lovers' beds?

There you are, my infidel friend, crawling out of the secret compartment on the dark side of Jummo's trunk! So it's you my fingers keep tripping over whenever I leaf through the time-yellowed pages my aunt ripped from a copy of *The Thousand and One Nights* so she'd have something to write on.

"Write" I say . . . in her fashion. With each page I flip, I picture Jummo's fingers looking for something, for the one or two written words she knew, circling them with her eyeliner, tearing out the pages with the circled words on them, folding the pages, folding them again, shuffling them and rearranging them into a book of her own.

Not much of a book, you say? Well, wait till you've learned how to read it, as I have. Here, let me give you a hint: The circles Jummo made around her words are shields. When you shatter the shields, you have in cracked the containers of time.

I've been looking for you, my friend, ever since I first saw the trunk. The moment I saw it I knew it was you, and only you, I could tell my aunt's story to. My innocence, my youth—I've been looking for them too, so I can hold them in my hands the way I used to many years ago.

After what feels like a thousand nights, I've come to my senses. I'm sending you Jummo's wrinkled old letter, her amulets, the animal talisman she drew on her belly, and one of her lovely gold rings. I'm hoping that their language, the sticky language of solid personal objects, might touch you.

Open to me now, infidel friend, *kaffir*, faithless reader, as I am opening to you.

2. The Dervish

Because Jummo thought it possible for my sister and I to sin only with men, she went to great trouble to defend us against shady male characters. Constant vigilance, she said, was the keystone of security. But my first sin was a woman.

The women of Mecca used to be called by nicknames derived from their surnames. Sindiah, for example, was short for Fatma Sindi. Some women had names that hinted at eccentricities or special talents. One lady, a neighbor notorious for her shrewdness and sharp tongue, was called Moosiah, after *moos*, meaning razor. Moosiah liked her nickname because she liked razors; in her hands they were versatile appliances. She shaved the hair off her temples, back to behind her ears, leaving her ears uncovered. This caused a lot of gossip in Mecca. We lived in a city that worships beauty in women so long as it is displayed in classical, conservative fashion.

Now Jummo—Jummo, the middle daughter of my grandfather Mohammed al-Baikwaly—her nickname was Dumboshi. Which had nothing at all to do with her real name. People wanted to soothe Jummo's excitable soul, so they started calling her Dumboshi, a sobriquet that stuck with her for the rest of her life. This nickname was a net cast over a woman generally thought to be a domineering bitch.

In certain respects, I suppose, my approach to storytelling is like the name changing that goes on among the women of Mecca. I have to admit that the comparison is fragile, and we certainly don't want to make a major point of it, not right now. Allow me to observe, however, that the practice of name-switching bears a resemblance to the stammering many writers experience when starting a story that threatens to swerve toward a subplot strewn with genies . . . w-w-w-which way to t-t-t-turn?

The moment my dark sister and I opened our eyes on our women-dominated world, we found ourselves at war with grandfather Mohammed al-Baikwaly's daughters, Jummo foremost among them. It was an endless campaign of clandestine, take-no-prisoners battles.

Krazat and I were neither the oldest nor the youngest children in the family; we were not, as they say in Mecca, the ripest of the grapes. And despite the fact that my father called me Zohr, meaning Moonlight Most Clear, and was smitten by every little thing I said and did, no one on my mother's side of the family shared his infatuation. Maybe this was because I didn't choose to direct my charms toward anyone but him. In any case, my aunts were irritated rather than impressed by my lofty lunar rank. They lavished their affections on our older sister Joman and our brother Nabee Jan, the firstborn male, neglecting those of us who came later.

This balance of power changed when my sister and I got older and came to have more influence in the family, particularly after Joman withdrew into marriage, with all its restrictions, all the heavy doors that opened and closed according to the whims of her husband, who, being a husband, could deign to be generous or jealous, depending on his mood. What finally happened was that the reins of power were handed over to me and Krazat, if only because it became clear that we were not about to hand them over to a man.

This was the situation in which I made my fatal move, or series of fatal moves.

My aunts wanted to control that moony spirit of mine that so enchanted my father, and to brighten the darkness lurking inside my sister.

If anything, my father's reinforcement of our position (funny—once I get started on this topic, I just can't stop talking in military terms) only inflamed my aunts' antagonism toward us, since he was regarded as the Outsider. He would always be the Outsider, the Other, and none of my aunts ever dreamed of dropping their guard in his presence; instead, the ladies turned the enormous arsenal (oh!) of their frustrated dreams and smoldering ambitions against him. Still, my father loved my mother with all his heart, and he enjoyed being close to her sisters and their circle of women friends. His strategy was to play the Invader, beaten back by bristling defenses and outright defiance. I see now that this tactic was a sort of gallantry. My sister and I were his undercover agents.

My sister is a painter. When she caught sight of the name of Sidi Wahdana, Mecca's most notorious dervish, inscribed on the cover of Jummo's letter, she went wild.

"It's from Jummo!" she said with a startled, love-struck gasp. "Give it to me!"

"No, never! It's mine, it's a messenger, it's Jummo's story! No!"

"I just want to touch it with my brush." Krazat was begging. "I just want to feel it. I want my brush to have some fun—you know, trace it, see how it feels. It's like an emotional thing."

I may be fond of the desperate way in which Krazat expresses herself, but this doesn't change the fact that I'm stingy when it comes to things I love, especially little things. I cut her off: "No living soul can have any contact with Sidi Wahdana."

At sundown, as usual, Mother served white coffee with almonds. The scent of cardamom filled the house. Everyone passing by—workmen, beggars, anyone at all—was welcome to have a cup. People sipped Mother's coffee with their eyes uptilted, as if savoring it were an activity akin to tasting the Infinite.

"Yes, oh yes . . . " Krazat hissed, crunching a bit of almond between her teeth. "This coffee is ssssurely a *sssign*. Yesss . . . it is a *sssign* that that the name wants to belong to *meeee*."

In Mecca, and especially in our house, white coffee signifies a special occasion. This, along with the fact that there is a side to my sister so sinister that none of us dare contradict her, not to mention the fact that she possesses complete assurance about predicting the future by means of signs, dreams, coincidences, and wild guesses—all served to increase the fear that, to her, our deepest secrets were open books. So I abandoned the name of Sidi Wahdana to my sister's tender care.

Ali, who has been with us since he was an infant, is being slaughtered on the order of my father. His blood is puddling under the window on the south wall of my room. My father hired a specialist to do the terrible deed. Warm blood, friendly blood, blood rich with so many memories, so much laughter, is being painted all over the corners of our house.

This ritual sheepicide marks the end of the third week of my mother's illness. For all that time she has been covered with nasty burn blisters all over her snow-white skin. Now, after the bloodletting, snowy whiteness has swallowed the fever blisters, and Mother is once again as white as she ever was, white as on her wedding day.

White . . .

No—don't turn the page yet, infidel friend! I want to give you something. Here it is—the map, the Map of Living Skin.

It's very fragrant and it comes with the usual fiery accessories, including a trigger. Keep this map. Whenever you need help, whenever you find yourself in trouble, summon the spirits of the map's incense, think of me, and I will come to your rescue.

3. The Donkey Sheik's Son

What does Jummo's nickname Dumboshi mean? I don't really know for sure, none of us ever did. It was meant to be a secret. One day we woke up and there it was, drifting along, cool as a cloud caressing the belly of the eastern sky. We liked the scuff of the name on our tongues. We vaguely understood that it hinted at a dark sort of irony, and there was in the thumping sound of it—Dumboshi . . . Dumboshi—an echo of the Forbidden, of an obscure something that held out hope of escape. Dumboshi . . .

We would never have had the slightest inkling of the meaning of this nickname if it hadn't been for the incident involving the son of the Donkey Sheik.

Not very long ago in Mecca, every trade had a sheik, or chief, in charge of the workers. There were plenty of camels and horses wandering around the holy city, but transportation was handled mostly by donkeys. The sheik in charge of transportation was known as the Donkey-Wranglers' Sheik, or Donkey Sheik for short.

One morning the son of the Donkey Sheik was spotted running up and down the street directly under my grandfather's house. He was a tall young man, skinny as a spear. And buck-naked. Clearly he had fallen under the spell of the wild spirit of the horned gazelle, who controls Mecca's flash floods. There could be no other explanation: the boy was hurling himself against the old doors lining the street and attempting, with the aid of no tools but his front teeth, to pry off their antique brass knockers, carved lions, crowns and crescents.

He succeeded in detaching several knockers. These he tossed skyward, and when they reached a point about an arm's length above his head, they stuck to one another as if magnetized by the force of his madness, paused for a rattling moment to arrange themselves into an aerodynamically suitable shape, then dropped back down into his hands.

The son of the Donkey Sheik was accompanied by several donkeys. From time to time he would dance toward them and place on the head of a bewitched beast one of the magnificent doorknockers. Before long he was surrounded by a circle of crowned donkey kings. He hooted and danced with the blackest donkey of all, a jennet pony, a superb specimen from Andalusia.

Dormers plinked open all up and down the street. Ladies peeked out, holding their breath. Krazat and Jummo and I watched from the seventh floor of my grandfather's house. Our bodies, pressed together, felt confidentially warm. We kept pushing against one another, trying to get a broader view than the narrow window would allow. My older brother, Nabee Jan, opened the dormer next to ours, hoisted himself onto the ledge, and hung far out. We, the decorous girls, made sure to keep a few slats of shutter between ourselves and the crazy goings-on below.

I remember Jummo's laughter, the sharpness of its ringing as she scuttled from dormer to dormer, soaking up the insanity, fluttering from one vantage point to another, anticipating everything, capturing subtleties no one else could catch. At each dormer she adjusted her arms and legs as if dancing at a mysterious but intimately precise distance with the mad boy and his animal entourage. Her clacking of shutters matched their clattering hooves.

My grandmother Nara suspected Jummo might be up to some mischief. She followed the scene nervously, muttering and trying to restrict her view to the contortions of the boy directly beneath her, worried that her eyes might wander to the grand *majlis,* her sitting room. My grandmother's nickname, Nara, meant Small Fire. Everyone had forgotten her real name, including my grandmother herself, who was by nature inclined to keep dangerous things confined. She was an eager explainer.

"The poor boy's father," she proclaimed, "has a helper from Yemen. This Yemenite has big ambitions. He's the one behind this *dumboshi.*"

The Yemenite helper, Nara went on, wanted to eliminate all rivals standing between himself and the right to inherit the job of Donkey Sheik in the municipality of al-Shobaika. Since the mad boy was the son of the current Donkey Sheik, and since he was his father's heir apparent, it was only natural for Nara to suspect the ambitious assistant.

Jummo added a spooky detail that sealed the verdict: "The Yemenite is just using the tried and true way of getting rid of rivals—the method known as Ashokta wa Anokta."

Eyes widened, eyes squinted. Ashokta wa Anokta meant, literally, the Way of the Dot and the Line. It was a talisman, a magical device used by Africans living in Mecca. The popular name for it was *dumboshi.*

Grandmother Nara shuddered, melting her maidenly stiffness. "For the love of God! Can't somebody please just cover that lad's nakedness!"

The boy jumped and came crashing down between the legs of the handsome Andalusian without disturbing the crown on the pony's head. From high up, where all of us were standing, it looked like he was pumping his naked loins in our faces.

"Oh, for the love of God . . . " Nara's voice, addressing herself, was tight with horror and pity.

No one dared make a move to help the crazy boy; that would have meant getting close to him.

He kept grabbing the doorknockers with his teeth. The crown of door ornaments on his head was taller now, and the grandeur of his invisible kingdom truly immense. I couldn't take my eyes off the blood dribbling from the corners of his mouth.

The show went on and on and on. The lad repulsed the thick-armed men who tried to subdue him. Other men, very strong and densely handsome in white silk belts, stood on the sidelines, stiff as military flags.

At last the Donkey Sheik himself appeared. He was accompanied by my grandfather, Sheik Baikwaly. My grandfather walked toward the crazy boy like a man confident that stone walls would crumble before him. The boy jerked and yelped and hurled himself so high that he came near crashing against one of the top-floor dormers.

My grandfather launched into one of the esoteric recitals for which he was famous. He chose a formula with the power to tame even the wildest beast, a talisman composed by none other than—yes!—the celebrated Haj Atellmesani of Morocco. Slowly, word by thundering word, he approached the boy until he got close enough to whisper—and then his words were lost to everyone, I swear, except the boy and me. This was his refrain:

"How can a believer carry on like a horny infidel?!"

The boy was still jumping, but lower now . . . lower, lower . . . Finally he stood still, transfixed by my grandfather's eyes, those deep, dark, whirl-pool eyes that sucked the words he was trying to say deeper and deeper into his soul until, just as the words seemed drowned in the depth of his feeling, they erupted toward the light and gushed from his lips: "*Nozulan, nozulan, nozulan*—down, down, down . . . "

The boy sank to his knees. My grandfather knelt beside him. On the palm of the boy's right hand he drew the Ring of Solomon. The Ring's seven horns flashed, momentarily blinding three curious bystanders who came too close. In each of the Ring's horns was a letter of the alphabet. My grandfather breathed life into *fa, jeem, sha, tha, kha,* and *za.* In the middle band of the ring he engraved: *This is the one we brought back from the dead.* He placed the Ring precisely in the center of the boy's palm. On a splinter of blue kindling he scratched: *A hell we have prepared for the unjust, surrounded by a moat. Scorch the faces, scorch the faces, scorch the faces!* He dipped the kindling in a can of tar and waved it under the boy's nose. The boy's eyelashes fluttered. My grandfather, relentless as a siege machine, kept reading directly to the boy, at his body, battering it with verses from the chapter about geniis in the Qur'an. Fumes of benzoin and mastic clouded the street, rose to the dormers and crept into the women's quarters, raising goose bumps on the ladies' arms.

Sheik Baikwaly kept on reciting. The boy's spine twitched, his shoulders quaked. The donkeys scattered and clattered down the street. The black Andalusian clopped toward the boy, sniffing his purple sweat. The boy's chest was flecked with blood. The Andalusian began walking in a tight circle, like a child lost in the dark, pausing occasionally to examine the boy's body, which was stretched out now on the paving stones. The Andalusian crumpled his forelegs and knelt down next to him.

My grandfather stopped reciting. He ran his fingers through the Andalusian's sweaty mane and plucked out a wad of black amber. He rubbed it between his thumb and forefinger while reciting another verse, summoning clouds and thunder from the sky. With a flash and a crash, they expelled multicolored demons from the evil amber ball. A cold, wicked wind came up, chilling us, and the stench of sulfur puckered our nostrils. The demons flapped away, screeching as they collided with dormers down the street.

The Donkey Sheik's Yemenite helper, Nara hastened to explain, had inscribed a magic formula on the wad of black amber gum and stuck it in the Andalusian's mane. So whenever the boy came close to the pony, he lost his mind.

With all the excitement going on, we paid little attention to what my grandmother was saying. But one of the words she used, *dumboshi*, kept coming up whenever we had occasion to deal with mysterious occurrences or the bewitchment of one of our neighbors. Gradually we came to understand, in the dimly fascinated way in which one understands the weather, that Jummo, the aunt with the huge collection of amulets and the nickname *dumboshi* hovering about her, was quite possibly a creature of the magical kind. At the very least, she was a woman who instinctively welcomed invaders of all sorts, whether they be winds, strange lights, or Soldiers of the Unknown.

4. Sheik Mira's Sermon

"Sidi Wahdana!" Sheik Mira cried.

The Sheik had made himself comfortable in the curbside sitting area furnished by the mayor of the municipality called al-Shamia. It was customary for the mayor of every municipality in Mecca to provide a public sitting area in the street outside his office. This outdoor sitting room was an arrangement of high-backed couches quilted with red damask, each wide enough to accommodate four men. Here, amid the tall red couches, civic issues were settled, political strategies debated, news discussed, wars declared, truces and marriages arranged, annulments adjudged, and other momentous decisions arrived at.

"Sidi Wahdana!" Sheik Mira cried again. He had spotted the Donkey Sheik's son. "Sidi Wahdana!"

Everyone looked at the mad boy, then at the Sheik. Sheik Mira was one of the Long-Lived Ones. It was not so much that was he very old (though his mortal years were beyond counting) as that his life seemed palpably to be getting longer and longer and longer. People attributed his longevity—indeed, his near immortality—to his habit of imbibing Zamzam, the sacred water from the well of Mecca's Grand Mosque.

Zamzam, the saying goes, is for whatever you drink it for. Sheik Mira drank Zamzam in the belief that none of Time's sharp horns would ever jab him. Wherever the horns of Time popped up, whichever way they turned or twisted, however slyly they slipped back into darkness, drinking Zamzam rendered the Sheik's reflexes too swift to allow his venerable flesh to be skewered, or even nicked. Thus the sheik believed, thus he drank. And thus he went on living, living, living.

"Sidi Wahdana!" he cried again, gesturing in the direction of the mad boy, who was twisting in one of his fits. "Sidi Wahdana!"

Everyone recognized the ancient dervish. There were many in the crowd who could identify his face as that of Sidi Wahdana, the dervish who orchestrated the endless wars afflicting Arabia. His presence created no panic precisely because escape was not an option; Sidi Wahdana was a fact of life.

"Sidi Wahdana . . ." the mayor of al-Shamia intoned, leaning forward and clearing his throat in preparation for serious sermonizing. The mayor was a small man with a shiny nose and stooped shoulders, but when he spoke in that deep, grave voice of his, he seemed to rise above his tall red chair without taking the trouble to stand. "Sidi Wahdana, yes . . . oh yes, Sidi Wahdana's voice is a death rattle, his gaze a command to martyrdom. When his dark eyes fall on a soldier, the soldier knows it's time to utter God's name—or die an infidel's death. Never has there been a deathbed, or a birth-bed, where Sidi Wahdana has not been present. To the newborn child he appears kindly, showing only the whites of his eyes and bestowing on infants the perfect innocence that allows them to enter this world oblivious to its evils and limitations. But beware, oh yes, beware when the eyes of Sidi Wahdana go dark! Moan then, and wail; taste the bitterness of your loss. For death is near, and the streets will be choked with funeral processions. Yes.

"Yes, oh yes, Sidi has many faces, and all his faces are good omens. But beware the pupils of Sidi's eyes! Stay away, if you can, stay clear of their blackness. Because that is where death fates are written. There, in the pupils of Sidi Wahdana's eyes, that's where every name of everyone who dies is written, and there you can read, clear as clear can be, the identity of whoever is about to die, and the exact moment of his death. You can even see the look on his face. Every time the sun rises, and every times the sun sets, the record is refreshed with a new list of names. Ah yes, Sidi Wahdana . . ."

The mayor pronounced the name with utter neutrality, smoothly, breathing without effort, without heaviness or stress on any syllable. The slightest emphasis would have provoked the dervish to drop his mask and expose his terrible power.

"God preserve each and every one of us from that eye! This earth of ours receives the sheaves of paper that fall from the Book of Life in

Heaven. Whenever a paper falls from that great register, there is a name written on it, and as it falls the letters of the name rearrange themselves to spell Death, and the instant your name-paper hits the ground, a grave opens for you in the cemetery of al-Maala. Then there is nothing more to be done except to call on Ezrael, the angel of death."

The mayor bowed his head. In a hushed voice he uttered God's name, wrapping himself in the sound. Scarcely anyone thought that the mayor, who was about to marry his fourth wife, stood in need of divine protection. Still, he hadn't gotten where he was by taking any chances.

Sidi Wahdana made frequent appearances in the Hijaz, the settled western region of Arabia, where the tribes had been feuding for as long as anyone could remember. The dervish knew exactly how many drops of blood would be shed by the combatants before the kingdom of the Hijaz fell. He was often seen strolling through the valleys. On the dreadful day of the massacre at Taif, for instance, many soldiers saw him marching shoulder-to-shoulder with them, just before he gathered the most valiant of the fallen warriors and dumped them into the dozens of mass graves he'd dug in advance. At al-Hada, he left the troops to bury their own heroes. Since then he'd not been seen, not on the roads nor in the houses of Mecca where he'd always been such a welcome guest, thirsty as Meccans were for diversion during extended dry seasons.

The Donkey Sheik's son got wilder every day, traveling further into the Unknown; he'd become a complete stranger to sanity. During his seizures, he would appear under my grandfather's dormers and look blankly up at the pigeons flapping on the eaves, shrieking over and over: "*Ya hai, ya hai . . .* You Who Are Alive, You Who Are Alive . . ." He cried and cried until he passed out and collapsed under the hooves of his pretty black Andalusian.

To me it seemed he was simply pleading for permission to live.

Nara and her daughters recognized his cries immediately. They hurried to the dormers, and there they sat silently (and somewhat sinfully) watching the boy quake like the flame of a breeze-blown candle.

"Sidi Wahdana has entered him," Nara whispered. "See how the dervish possesses him in the blink of an eye, in less time than it takes his body to hit the ground. It is written: whoever meets Sidi never recovers, never finds rest till he sheds his mortal skin."

Jummo laughed. "Your Sidi is death, death—nothing but death. People die. And no one ever returns from the dead, that's all there is to it."

Nara glared. "Don't . . . don't you dare, Dumboshi . . . don't you dare ever cross Sidi Wahdana. Don't you dare—even if you don't believe!"

"Oh, don't worry about me," Jummo replied. "Are you absolutely sure there's no road back? Maybe *I'll* come back after *I* die."

The words cut Nara's believing heart. She pinched Jummo high on her inner thigh, her favorite spot for private punishment. "Don't be a fool," Nara said. "Silly, spiteful fool! This is fate we're dealing with here. If you think you can jump on the back of a wild horse, you're going to get thrown. You want to hurt yourself, be my guest. But leave us decent people in peace."

Jummo looked up, challenging Heaven to speak on its own behalf. Her silence, and Heaven's, left Nara with nothing to do but seethe. Nara the explainer could not bear her fears to be nameless and unknown. Her knees wobbled.

"You Who Are Alive . . . none but Him . . ."

A shaft of sunlight fell through the high window and sliced Jummo's bath water, as she poured it, into bright wiggly strands. She sagged voluptuously, letting the mad boy's words wash over her, through her. He shrieked. She sighed. The sunlight, warm and piercing, lapped her neck and breasts. Her skin went pebbly.

"No God but Him . . ." she said in a shaky voice.

She stood up. She bent over and reached for a bucket of ash-water to wash her hair with. Ash-water was effective in cleansing hair and soul of bitterness and mean-spiritedness, as well as ordinary dirt. It was commonly used to straighten the braids of virgins, which tend to kink and frizz when subjected to life's harsh experiences. The water increased the energy emanating from Jummo's hair, lending it streaks of the fire faintly remembered by the ashes that had purified the water. She stretched. Her upstretched body was as perfect as something drawn—a lily, perhaps, or a tournament bow.

5. Sidi Wahdana Calls on Jummo

To Grandmother Nara's way of thinking, the incident of the Donkey Sheik's son was linked to the day Jummo got her first period. At that time they were living in my grandfather's old house, a tiny, one-story affair. The entire structure amounted to little more than two vestibules opening onto a small yard with a *nabk* tree, which Nara, who had advanced from nervous opinionating to outright pedantry, insisted on calling a lotus jujube. One of the vestibules, the one with a crudely carved wooden door, was designated as an inner sanctum for the exclusive use of Nara and her three daughters; here they slept and lived their private lives. The other room was for Sheik Baikwaly and his men friends. It was off-limits to the ladies of the house, most especially at night, when the men gathered to play music and sing.

That day started early, Nara remembered. Sheik Baikwaly had left before dawn for morning prayer in the grand mosque. The women were woken at first light by a banging on the wooden door.

"May God grant us every drop of goodness in this hour!" Nara said, rising from her mattress on the floor. She slipped into her wide skirt with the hourglass waist, wrapped her hair in a flowery white sash, arranged the white *mihrana,* the comb-with-wimple, and shuffled to the door. Hannah and Zubayda followed at her heels. Jummo yanked the quilt over her ears to keep the knocking out of her head.

Nara opened the door.

"Generous masters . . ." croaked the blind man. " . . . a sip of rosewater for the poor . . ."

Jummo's snicker corrupted the morning's calm.

Something unearthly slipped past the beggar and entered the little house. A feeling of profound loss entered with it, freezing the hearts of Nara and the girls and the beggar in a brittle tableau.

The beggar blinked. The milky film on his blind eyes flashed, focusing on Jummo. She had gotten up and was standing in the doorway opening on the small inner courtyard. She was wearing only a white vest and her long white Syrian underpants. Slowly she swayed, ever so slowly, amplifying her whiteness, widening the eyes of the women. And the blind beggar.

Nara signaled Zubayda, her youngest daughter, to go inside and fetch water. Nara had learned some time ago how important it was to be prepared for beggars who came calling at odd hours with odd requests. They must always be treated respectfully, because more often than not they were pilgrims who had left their homes and loved ones and traveled great distances to the Holy City. Over the years Nara had encountered a few pilgrims who'd made outlandish demands, and because of the way her mind insisted on tidying things that lay beyond the borders of her everyday experience, she had devised a simple formula for dealing with strangeness in general and pilgrims in particular: The stranger the request, the more attention should be paid to the one making it. When confronted by a beggar with an air of gravity, her rule was to act straightforwardly, without reservations—certainly not, as Jummo was doing, with humor.

Zubayda returned to her mother's side carrying a bottle of scented water and a *tazza,* a copper goblet. The rim of the goblet was inscribed with verses from the Qur'an praising God's throne; these words were especially effective in warding off evil spirits. Zubayda poured the fragrant water into the goblet and handed it to the beggar, whose eyes stayed fixed on Jummo's whiteness.

Suddenly, as if responding to a silent request, Jummo moved soundlessly to her father's trunk, removed a bundle, walked to the door where the beggar was waiting, and said to him: "You requested the Sheik's best clothes, sir?"

She swept the frosty dew off the threshold with her bare hand, set the bundle down, untied it, and started cataloguing its contents. The irony in her voice required the beggar to give his assent to each item. "Black topcoat? . . . silk turban? . . . silver dagger? . . . gold belt?" At the conclusion of this litany Jummo burst out laughing.

The beggar recoiled as if punched. He staggered backward into the street and fell down, spilling the goblet, which clattered some distance before getting snagged under the hooves of one of the milkman's cows. The cows charged, mooing and stampeding down the street to the accompaniment of hundreds of cooing pigeons and the clanking of lanterns. Dozens of people clustered around the unconscious beggar.

"God save us all," the milkman said. "That girl's laugh is louder than the devil's." Jummo's laughter died on her lips.

Nara recited the verse inscribed on the goblet: "You who are alive, You who never sleep, whose eyes never blink when we are in need . . . " She refilled the goblet with water and sprinkled the beggar's face. At the touch of a single drop, he groaned and exhaled, relaxing against the hard ground, which was so thirsty that the blots of water disappeared the instant they plopped on it. His eyes opened wide. His pupils reshaped themselves quickly, and very dark pupils they were, a glossy sort of amber-black whose shine spread like a scent till every man, woman, child and beast in the street recognized the unmistakable meaning behind the beggar's gaze: death. Before anyone had time to even gasp, he was gone, leaving them all in breathless amazement.

So Sidi Wahdana came knocking at my door? Nara muttered. *He came to me in need? What did he want? I mean,* really *want?*

Nara enjoyed talking with herself, even if she could seldom come up with answers to the questions she asked. Had she satisfied the beggar's needs? Had she missed her chance at getting some good luck? Was that too much to ask—a little luck? He *had* taken the bundle. Or at least the bundle wasn't on the threshold anymore. Was that a good sign? Or was it ominous? Hard to say for sure.

The facts were these: first, the beggar was gone, along with his ambery black eyes, and second, Jummo got her first period the same morning. By the time the sunrise had become more than a glow, she was a woman. Nara could hardly contain her cries of joy. But she did, because she didn't want to make the neighbors jealous. Her two other daughters got their first periods that same day, too. Nara knew, and Great-grandmother Khadija agreed, that this was extraordinary. Yes, the family's fortunes were soaring. Oh yes.

6. The Proposal

Great-grandmother Khadija wiped away her happy tears and mumbled a verse about shooting stars and good luck. At sunset she went around the house spreading mastic incense, sprinkling holy water, and lugging her black incense burner from one corner to another, drawing a tight circle of guardian spirits around her beloved daughter and granddaughters. Every drop of holy water and every whiff of incense were intended to calm Sidi Wahdana's restless soul.

When darkness fell, Nara distributed *ludo* candies, reverently kneaded confections of sugar and garbanzo beans, to everyone in the neighborhood. The tiny *raski* raisins on top of each piece of candy guaranteed that the Evil Eye would keep its distance.

Seven days later the man of the house, Sheik Baikwaly, received a proposal: Mohammed al-Maghrabi, a gentleman from one of Mecca's finest families, asked for the hand of Hannah, his eldest daughter, in marriage. Al-Maghrabi was a true "son of Istanbul"—an "Istan-bull," as the wealthy merchants, religious leaders, and sophisticates who lived in the neighborhood of al-Shamia were called by admiring Meccans. Al-Shamia was in effect one vast balcony overlooking the grand mosque. Home to the city's elite, it was often called the Istanbul of Mecca. People couldn't help remarking, in proudly circumspect whispers, that this happy turn of events—al-Maghrabi's proposal—was a direct result of Sidi Wahdana's recent visit.

Sheik Baikwaly, however, was not a man to take anything for granted. He stayed up all night studying the astrological charts relevant to the marriage. He wanted to be absolutely certain that his daughter's union with al-Maghrabi would bring nothing but good fortune. He set about reading the stars in the customary way: every star had a name, every name had a spirit. Every letter of every name had a spirit, too, and these were consulted as well. The stars were living things, since they, like humans, were made of fire, water, earth, and wind. It was the relationship of these elements that determined whether or not any two people would be able to live harmoniously or wind up going to war with one another. If the stars were unfavorable, the couple would fight till they extinguished one another's stars. Or the marriage would simply continue numbly, like so many other things in life that must be, but be miserably. This was the future that Sheik Baikwaly was trying to chart by consulting the stars.

He thought it best, in order to do the job thoroughly, to travel to the Spring of Zubayda, an ancient well constructed by the wife of the Caliph

Haron al-Rashid to supply water for the desert in the eastern quarter of the Arabian Peninsula. In preparation for this expedition, he spent several hours in one of the lightless tunnels that channeled water deep inside Qubais, the mountain of Mecca. Tonight he would be navigating The Forbidden Zone.

Ordinary mortals did not dare venture into these dreaded tunnels, not unless they were expert guides with detailed knowledge of the magic formulas required for the task. The very best guides were those in charge of cleaning the tunnels and removing blockages that accumulated over years of darkness and silence. Al-Baikwaly was well qualified; before becoming Sheik of the Zamzam Water Carriers in the Holy Mosque, he had been Sheik of Mecca's Water Works. When it came to water or anything to do with the tunnels and aqueducts supplying water to the Holy City, there was no one more highly regarded than Sheik Baikwaly.

Accomplished as he was, he was confronted at every turn by the tunnels' guardian spirits, by colossal serpents and tar-black bats, not to mention the monsters that assaulted the imagination of anyone who dared enter the tunnels.

Wrapped in a goatskin inscribed with a top-secret talisman known as the Secret of All Secrets, he came at last to the watery center of Mecca's heart. On a suitable outcropping, in darkness more absolute than blindness, he wrote the names of his daughter and her suitor in several different combinations, crowning each one with the names of the mothers of the prospective bride and groom: Hannah, Nara, Mohammed al-Maghrabi, Fatma, and so forth. The spirits—the inner energy—oozed out of the names and took the shape of dazzling stars.

The anxious father watched Mohammed al-Maghrabi's four-pointed star dissolving into Hannah's five-pointed star. Duel or diffusion, it was difficult to say precisely what was going on between the two of them, but whatever it was, it went on all night. At one point, the groom's four-pointed star bulged and overflowed and melted the five-pointed star in its fire—his penetrating hers, as it were—and her five-pointed star sparkled with the sweetest water, and this water liquefied his fire; his heat was dissolving in her honey, bubbling over with signs of life, children, and all sorts of good times.

Al-Baikwaly sat contentedly reading the signs. So far as he could tell, the evening's astrological events boded well for the proposed marriage. He rested, satisfied. When he could detect not one star in all of God's sky blinking with warning or hesitation, his satisfaction deepened.

He slipped off the goatskin on which the Secret of All Secrets was written and stepped into Noah's Eye, a tunnel with implausibly smooth walls leading to the top of Mount Qubais. There he dove into Zubayda's Spring, only to surface a few moments later at the Zamzam well in the Grand Mosque. By now happiness had lent an athletic buoyancy to his step and he fairly leapt out of the water, convinced that Hannah's liquid star would dominate the fiery star of her fiancé, Mohammed.

The very next Sunday—and a splendidly warm, sunny day of the sun it was, truly an auspicious, semidivine day—Mohammed al-Maghrabi came in person to ask for Hannah's hand. The timing did not escape al-Baikwaly's notice. By the Sheik's calculations, the date of the young man's visit—astrologically speaking, Sunday was a day of good fortune—confirmed that there was bound to be a passionate intimacy, a perfect oneness, between the soon-to-be bride and groom.

As far as Nara was concerned, the real reason, the thing behind the upcoming marriage, was Sidi Wahdana's appearance on her doorstep. No two ways about it—Sidi's visit foretold good fortune. Great-grandmother Khadija, however, expressed reservations; what made her even more cautious than usual was Jummo's unpredictable talent for questioning the unquestionable and touching on matters better left untouched.

"Suppose you were to give me away as the bride," Jummo suggested, nakedly earnest. "Just suppose. I'd teach those Istan-bullies a thing or two."

Jummo would not let go of the notion that Mohammed al-Maghrabi was marrying a woman without a name. She had her own interpretation of the elaborate rules of courtesy that prevailed in her conservative corner of the world. She knew it was forbidden to mention the name of an unmarried female in public. She assumed that when a man asked a family for the hand of a daughter in marriage, it was taken for granted (because the name of the lady in question could not be mentioned) that he was talking about the oldest daughter. To Jummo's way of thinking, this meant that the man was really marrying the family's name and good reputation, compared to which the nameless daughter was merely a cipher. In short, any unmarried female in the family would serve the purpose.

"That Istan-bull Mohammed is in love with a nobody," she informed her great-grandmother.

"Shame on you, girl," said Khadija, covering her smile. "We are talking about matrimony here. Who said anything about falling in love?"

"Love, marriage—whatever . . . the issue is with whom! Your name is the key to your soul, grandma; that's why people in Mecca don't say the name of an unmarried lady to a stranger. Because if you know the name, you own it, and if you own the name, you have a legal right to the whole body and from there it's only a short step to repeating the poor lady's name and possessing her completely. So why don't we just say to Mohammed's family, maybe we'll give you Hannah . . . or maybe Zubayda. I bet you anything they wouldn't know the difference, except maybe they'd wonder how come they got that tan skin of Zubayda's instead of the snow white skin of what's-her-name."

"God forbid!" Nara cut in. "What's gotten into you, girl, talking such trash? I'm speaking to you too, Khadija! Look at the way our daughters are walking into marriage—talking about it just like men do!" Khadija smiled. Not just at her granddaughter's naiveté, but also at her granddaughter's and her daughter's shared need to smother and control what could never be smothered or controlled.

Nara saw her smiling. She sat down and sighed over the awful things Jummo's outrageous attitude foretold about her family's prospects. "What are people going to say about us? What will they think when they hear you talking about fiancés like they're just *qreens*, just studs, like nothing was at stake besides servicing your . . . your . . . your lust? What do you think's going to happen? I'll tell you exactly what's going to happen: talk like that stirs up the Underworld, it always does. The geniis will come and get you, just you wait and see. Shady characters love that kind of talk, make no mistake about it."

Jummo scampered to the topmost branch of the *nabk* tree. There she sat for a long time looking down on the cluster of women fussing over the fancy hand-sewn clothes they'd made for the wedding, spreading them out on shiny pebbles in the courtyard. Salama the dressmaker took three yards of exquisite Syrian silk between her teeth and with three firm yanks, three flashes of her experienced dentures, she sliced the fabric into three identical pieces to make three *shirwals*, three soft silken underpants, for the bride. Three.

And the ribboned silk belts were so beautiful, Jummo was thinking, so strong—so big—they could wrap themselves completely around the mountains of Mecca. She made a sincere effort to stop thinking this way. Ever since that creepy beggar's visit, Nara had been running out of patience with her. One word, one little word from Nara, and she'd be down out of the *nabk* tree like a rocket. The women had strictly forbidden her to lay a finger on the bride's presents till she finished her period. But her blood was still flowing, she could smell it. Now *there* was a bad omen—a trousseau touched by a woman having her period! But Jummo had been running all over the place anyway, touching everything, pestering everybody, thinking every second about the silly edicts of prohibition that made her even more furious than the teasing of her sisters, Hannah and Zubayda. Now, in her hiding place high up in the tree, feeling bright and brave and jittery as a smart little star, sucking on a dry jujube leaf and licking her lips, passionately, sinfully, she summoned the forbidden words to the tip of her tongue: "Beggar! Stupid old beggar!"

Her smile widened. Nara had expressly forbidden her to let her mind go down this road. But a road is a road and it needs to be followed. "The beggar . . . " Jummo said again, letting her mind go, the image beginning to take shape, " . . . the stranger who snatched al-Baikwaly's bundle . . . "

A turtledove landed on her shoulder. She sat as still as she possibly could, willing the branch she was sitting on to be still, too, for fear of frightening the bird away. The turtledove, hopping its sacred dance, fluttered and gently brushed Jummo's cheek with the tips of her high, pretty tail, tickling her. Jummo tried not to giggle, but the bird brushed her again and she burst out laughing and everyone looked up from the yard in time to see to the turtledove flap her golden wings and fly away, leaving only her eye, the irresistible eye of a beggar bird, peering into Jummo's heart and begging for a sip of perfumed water.

7. The Girl Next Door

Jummo wasn't the only one preoccupied with the intricacies of marriage and anonymity. The bridegroom's own mother, Fatma Mosliya, was worried sick that her son might be falling into a trap by getting engaged to a nameless woman. *So my lovely boy winds up proposing to a total stranger?* she kept saying to herself. Fatma Mosliya started out being curious about the bride-to-be; it wasn't very long before she came to regard her as a rival.

She prayed for guidance, certain at dawn that Sidi Wahdana would make an appearance at dusk, convinced by twilight that he would appear before dawn. But Sidi never showed up. So Fatma spent her sleepless nights obsessing about the girl's looks, her coloring, her posture, the way she plaited her hair. About none of these things did she have a shred of information. Finally she sent for Sitee Faheema, the famous midwife, the one and only woman who knew everything there was to know about every human being in Mecca.

"Mosliya—darling!" Sitee Faheema exclaimed. Her eyes were of unequal size. The left one was constantly smiling. The right one, which was smaller, seemed pensive because it kept wandering off on its own, keeping its distance. The effect was intermittently artistic. "Ah yes," she said, "that clan of al-Baikwaly—they come into this world drenched in darkness. So let me just tell you: the young lady's hair has got to be darker than the devil's—pitch black!"

"Yes, yes; of course, of course," Fatma Mosliya said. "Now please tell me about her skin, the color of her skin is what I need to know. The skin is the lantern of the soul, and I want to know: is her lantern lit? Or is it all burned out?"

The midwife lowered her eyes to consult the latticework of henna tattoos on her hands. She turned her palms up and adjusted her voice to an ultra-confidential purr. "Oh Fatma, these two hands, all tattooed with henna, these are the very same hands that delivered each one of Nara's daughters. I can assure you that all the little girls crept into this life as light and white and delicate as baby rabbits—you know, those rabbits from Nowaria?"

Fatma cocked her eyebrows in appreciation of the Sitee Faheema's reference to the rabbits native to the mountain of Nowaria, near Mecca—for Nowaria was also the place where the fair-skinned Khazar women like Nara and her daughters came from.

"But who knows?" Sitee Faheema continued. "We're all familiar with the wind that blows through Mecca now and then—that's right, darling, I'm talking about al-Simoom, the hot wind that can change adorable little bunnies into ogres, the breeze that can scorch the whitest fur into ashes dark as coal! Yes, oh yes! Can I guarantee the girl's whiteness? No, darling, I cannot! This much I can tell you, though: if Nara so much as suspects that you are the least bit curious about these matters, she will turn herself into a veritable dragon to defend her daughters: they might as well be invisible." The midwife turned her hands palms down, as if closing a book. "I'm ashamed to have to tell you this, darling, but I missed my chance to do a thorough checkup on Nara's daughters. But now with Salma, Naiab al-Harem's daughter, well that was a different story. I disguised myself as a laundry woman—hah! I went to her house and helped out ironing the piles of clothes the family took with them on their summer trip to the mountain of al-Shafa. One day's ironing and I knew everything there was to know about little Salma . . ."

Fatma Mosliya sighed philosophically. This woman's a raving egomaniac, she thought. She dismissed the related, more disturbing idea that Sitee Faheema knew much less about herself than she knew about other people. "Yes, dear midwife—our own flesh and blood turns against us. The very child that's nurtured in our womb, he becomes our enemy. God knows how much I've prayed for my son not to be led astray, not to be fickle, not to make us all miserable by marrying . . . by marrying . . . by marrying some . . . some *colored* girl!"

The truth was that Fatma, like every other mother in al-Shamia, wanted her son to marry the girl next door. The girl next door was Zainub Kabliya. Zainub played the lute, a pretty little instrument made of aloe wood. Her charms, framed in the dormer of the house directly across the street, had an irresistible glow. There was a precocious quality to her singing that made her renditions of the *umbawe shilat*, the sweet old songs from Yunbua, more refreshing than the yowlings of the house-slaves who aspired to the status of professional entertainers.

"Oh, Fatma . . ." Sitee Faheema said, reading her client's mind.

Fatma was remembering one of the songs Zainub liked to sing: *"A cloud just passed by, carrying water and singing its dream to thirsty hearts . . ."* Zainub had such a surprisingly happy singing voice. And so husky! Oh, it was so nice to be serenaded—and it would be nice to continue to be serenaded—by a charming daughter-in-law. Yes, Fatma quite enjoyed sitting queen-like by her window, idly adjusting the shutters, nodding and exchanging cups of ginger-scented *sahlab* with adoring neighbors—so close, so cozy, so comfortable it seemed they were sharing a living room suspended in air. And Fatma would answer Zainub's serenades song-by-song in a warm, generous voice famous for its soulfulness.

> *"Oh lightning flashes from the Holy City's holiness . . ."*
> *"My heart is back home, I'm getting lonelier . . ."*

How nice. So why couldn't her lovely nice son pay more attention to nice girls closer to home, girls from his own neighborhood? If only he'd stay home long enough to listen to Zainub singing: *"Ya-lee-la . . . oh pigeons landing on our roof . . ."* with the sweetest little Yemeni accent . . . *"ya-lee-la, ya-lay, ya-lay . . ."* Oh, damn that boy, damn his hot blood! *Ya-lee-la* . . . that moron, that insensitive slob! *"Oh pigeon skimming over the stream . . . ya-lay . . . over the stream, ya, over the stream . . . oh pigeon . . ."*

The echoes of Zainub's singing drifted into murmurs, into plaintive questions. Where was her handsome suitor? Where was he going? When would he come back? Why? Where? Why? Who with?

Stubbornness was the spine of Nara's strength. She saw to it that her daughter Hannah was kept shrouded in veils of suspense. To all inquiries, no matter how diplomatic or oblique, she replied: "If this fancy man of Mecca wants my daughter, let him have her—but with respect, sight unseen!"

8. The Wedding

Jummo spent all day and night before the wedding perched on boxes of dates and little green apples stacked in the yard. First thing in the morning, Sheik Baikwaly's servants arrived from the orchards of Taif with crates of fruit. The dates came all the way from Medina, the only city serene enough for the Prophet to make his home in. There was cardamom, too, from the spice market in central Mecca.

Jummo occupied herself ordering the other girls around. She worked in an inspired frenzy, instructing one and all about the intricacies of stringing apples and dates into necklaces, about how to the connect the fruits with little wrinkled balls of cardamom dipped in silver. The necklaces, heaped together in the flickering light, panted. Because the very next day they would be kissing the neck and breasts of the bride.

It was a long day. Jummo adjusted her headband of silvered fruits and cardamom and shook the sparkling tail dangling down to her ankles. After a bit of practice she was able to tiptoe around like a nymph and skip in time to the lute music wafting from Sheik Baikwaly's quarters—until great-grandmother Khadija spotted her, gripped her head between her hands (how warm they were!), wedged her shoulders between her rock-hard thighs, and solemnly recited protective verses from the Qur'an.

Later, Khadija had a private word with Nara. "Don't let that little girl get too wild," the old lady said sternly. "She's the type that if you let her step out of line, she'll have the Evil Eye on her in a minute."

That night Khadija read the same verses of protection over the bride's wedding dress, which was spread out in the women's quarters. The glittering gown had been unpacked from a trunk belonging to Abdul Khaliq, the uncle-custodian in charge of all the treasures, wills, and documents pertaining to Khazar family properties in the Holy City. Sheik Baikwaly, the sole heir, had inherited everything from his grandfather, the Supreme Sheik of the Khazar Sheiks and Master of the Secret of All Secrets.

In Mecca, no bride was ever denied the opportunity of making a great display on the eve of her wedding. Every wedding that took place in the sacred circle of the holy city was a grand affair, every bride was a queen.

Extravagance made perfect sense in a city encircled by life-threatening desert. Mecca's location was a punishing stipulation in the metropolitan contract with life that kept everyone in a state of high anxiety. Except when there was a wedding; then people turned liquid and merry as wine. Every strongbox opened, everyone made a contribution to the celebration. Wedding dresses were refitted, jewelry and presents and furniture were laid out for poor people, and heaps of free food were delivered to the house where the reception was held.

The night of Hannah's wedding, there was the unmistakable scent of amber in the air; the spirit who was Sidi Wahdana could not have been far away. All around the *rika,* the bride's great chair (a throne, actually, as large as a small room) the air shuddered with subtle perfumes, scents more rare and elusive than never-ending happiness.

Hannah's *rika* was a *rika*; words are merely words. Picture this: the bride on her throne, submerged in necklaces of apples and dates and silvered cardamom, her ears outlined by crescents of pearls, her breasts hugely padded and studded with diamonds and emeralds trading winks and glints with the precious stones sewn into her gown, the gown itself flickering, illuminating the bride and the entire room so dazzlingly that the strands of blindingly white pearls heaped in her lap seemed, in comparison to her brilliance, mere shadows. The bride—how slender she was! —swam in a jangling sea of light, scattering envious glances like frightened fish.

Jummo dashed here, dashed there, stooping to adjust the hem of the bride's gown wherever it looked less than preternaturally straight, trilling all the while in a high voice. No one trilled like Jummo. Her voice was piercing, literally piercing; it penetrated everyone who heard it, shot through them like a spear, pinning them to the spot. So many things about Jummo were like that: her laughter, her raunchy jokes, the jangling of her golden bracelets; she rang like a bell.

People stared at the animal hennaed in red and black, writhing from the tips of her fingers, all over her hands, and ending just before it reached a malignant-looking mole halfway up her right arm.

"That little girl is like hot sand!" Great-grandmother Khadija whispered in Nara's ear. "No, wait—make that *feverish* sand!"

Nara frowned. She had no idea what Khadija was talking about.

"I warned her last night," Khadija continued, "about dyeing her hands with henna before she's finished her period. When a girl has her period, her whole body's upset by menstruating spirits. There's an acid taste to her skin, the same as the taste of Satan's gallbladder. Strange thing, though—it repels passion but it attracts souls and sucks the evil blackness out of them."

On Henna Night, the night before the wedding, the night when the bride's feet and hands were tattooed, Jummo sneaked away while everyone was sleeping. In defiance of every known rule of wedding decorum, she secured a great gob of henna paste for her own use. When Great-grandmother Khadija woke up in the morning and got a look at Jummo's hands, she went into shock.

"I warned you, young lady! I warned you about using that dye before your period's over. You know what's going to happen now? The demon's going to stay with you until the dye fades away!"

Jummo could not have cared less; she was quite matter-of-fact about her defiance. Last night, without any great effort, she'd sneaked away from her great-grandmother and charmed Moqaena Safia, the stylist who'd been brought in to supervise the beautification of the bride. She had no trouble persuading Moqaena to part with her secrets about what to do with her hair, how to highlight her eyes, how to arrange her jewelry, and what henna tattoos were guaranteed to take everybody's breath away. Jummo spent the morning hours daubing the dye paste into branches spotted with animals that flowered from palm to wrist to halfway up her arms.

Moqaena wrapped her hands in sheer silk to intensify the colors of the henna and help it set. Jummo squinted slowly and fell asleep. Her slumber gave life and voice to the tattooed animals. As the darkness and silence of night deepened, the mute beasts shed their polite skins and took on the ferocious will to prevail so typical of things that are authentically alive. Their essences seeped under Jummo's porous young skin, possessing her, mingling the dark, bloody core of their beings with hers.

In the morning, when she washed the excess paste away, the itch of the animals' intrusion changed into a pleasurable numbness that stayed with her, reminding her, with a tingling in her private parts, that she and the animals were one. It felt good to share herself in this way.

All during the night before the wedding, Moqaena Safia glanced back and forth between Jummo's tattooed animals and the decorations on Hannah's face. Moqaena suppressed a wicked smile. Jummo's tattoos tickled her. Their sheer animality was a revelation. Moqaena may not have been entirely up to date on the latest wedding protocol, but she suspected Jummo was doing something—possibly several things—wrong. She admired the girl's talent for getting away with things. Only small things, maybe, but in the flare Jummo had for designing her own tattoos there was more than a hint of cutting loose, of abandoning herself to the Unknown. The vivacity of her tattoos caught the attention of the girls from al-Shamia. Fatma Mosliya, the mother of the groom, pursed her lips as if sucking on a lemon, and shook her head. Her jowls wobbled with disapproval.

"The girl's a savage," she said. "Like an African or something. Those Khazar ladies, have you noticed how fluent they all are in the language of wild animals? Have you noticed? *I* have."

Fatma thanked God for having the decency to make her new daughter-in-law an exception to the Khazar family's rule; obviously, Hannah was a well-behaved young lady.

The Shamia women lined up in a row, side-by-side with the Khazar women, so they could watch the bride make her entrance on the shoulders of her male relatives. The women of al-Shamia felt they were looking at a frieze on an enormous Far Eastern drinking fountain miraculously brought to life, an ancient mosaic excavated and restored, bubbling with life-giving water. Their formerly low opinion of the bride faded; no longer was she a coarse interloper who'd stolen the flower of al-Shamia's young manhood.

The bridegroom entered with his escort of women relatives.

"Way-*loo!*" the black singers sang. "This little filly looks so fine in our tent, God Himself must've given her that shape . . . Way-*loo*! Our Adam prepared gifts and perfume and went out looking for . . . Way-*loo*! Our bridegroom comes wearing a black crown. Way-*loo*! They're out trapping turtledoves for him. Way-*loo*! The bridegroom's painted our doorways with gold, poured gold into our bowls. Way-*loo*! All the judges tip their turbans to him, and all the wise men, too."

Young girls lined up where the bridegroom was about to walk and prepared for the ritual of pinch-and-pinprick—a little pinch, a little pinprick, and they would be guaranteed good luck in finding a marriage partner.

Mohammed came closer. The girls rolled needles and pins between their fingers. Mohammed, entranced by the heavenly Hannah, approached the reception hall and the throne of the bride. She raised her eyes and gave him her fatal look, lowering her lashes. Mohammed staggered and reached for the arms of the women walking beside him. They caught him and broke into joyous song, invoking God's name: *Bism Al-lah Al-Rah-man Al-Raheem* . . .

What had Mohammed seen in the eyes of his bride? The overpowering passion that awaited him, the sheer threat of it? How could a look so powerful come from a child so sheltered, from a girl who only hours ago had been ceremonially bathed as a new bride, who had just stepped out from behind the curtains of embroidered Indian muslin and put on her hennaed veils? How was it possible for her body to carry such a charge, this body that had just been dipped in starch to protect it from prying eyes?

Mohammed was dazed. With each step toward Hannah he felt a fresh tingle. It was his bride he was feeling, the blunt womanly fact beneath the magical henna patterns, the force behind her seven curtains of shyness, the weight of the curtains themselves, and the heaviness of her lowering lashes, their irresistible, intoxicating enticement—this was the charge, the deadly power, the deceptively innocent exterior disguising a lethal invitation to sleep, to sleep, to sleep . . . luring him across the room of inquisitive faces.

Things trembled, things flashed—the black singers' drums, the bowers of jasmine draped across the bride's colossal *rika*, the mirrors inlaid on top of the towering archways. The shuddering embraced the mixed-up rhythms of sensations swirling around the room—high notes layered on low notes, sustained thumps, exalted passions climbing over bitterest grief. Each note was a shriek announcing another omen good or bad, piling one on top of another, shattering the hearts of the people gathered round with too much joy, too much sadness, too much . . .

Too much. Tears and sweat beaded on Hannah's cheeks, dribbling like pearls on her face and her finery. Ever so lightly, Mohammed stepped on her chair. The chair tilted. Her right foot stepped on his bewildered toe. She drew it back. She'd been schooled in this lightning-quick ritual by the old women of the Khazar family. Its purpose was to ensure that her star would rise higher than Mohammed's; her throne would ascend to great heights in his kingdom. "Step on his feet!" someone had advised in a low voice, and the other women repeated the instruction. "Be sure your throne's in his heart!" With oil of musk they'd traced talismans of coquetry and domination on her cheeks.

The formidable old women of the Khazar family were gratified to see how beautifully their brave little girl carried everything off. She will have good fortune, they agreed. No question about it.

Mohammed managed to exhale. Every fiber in his body strained toward the spot on his foot where Hannah had stepped so swiftly, so firmly. His vision was cloudy, blurred as if by wine. He was aware only of the heaving energy beside him, around him, inside him. He felt her fierceness, the authority she'd asserted simply by stepping on that little spot. He was a man enthralled, like most men, by the elementary moves of a woman's body. Was it the same for women, he wondered, dimly hoping his question would unite him with her. Were women so easily swayed? No—a hazy smile of pleasured incomprehension ruled his face—the curves of a woman's body . . . and women are all curves, aren't they? . . . the curves hide secrets I'll never understand. . . . but such ignorance is truly bliss . . . because Hannah's body is a language unto itself, a language of secrets, holding endless conversations with the Unrevealed. Mohammed blinked. It was like the strike of an eagle's talons, he thought, the tap of Hannah's foot—astonishing, unforgettable, instantly forgotten.

He spent the rest of the evening discretely trying to make contact with her foot again, convinced that it held the key to conquering her. No matter how hard he tried, though, her foot remained out of reach. This clue, the key he needed to solve his problems, had vanished, leaving him blind to all the other beauties of Mecca, even though there seemed no end to the procession of astonishing females parading back and forth in front of the bridegroom, dressed in veils so sheer they were practically transparent, their beauty forbidden to every man except on his wedding night—and now all of them were Mohammed's, his alone to savor. (The cornelian amulet worn by his bride, a miniature apple carved from the twig of a dogwood shrub, ensured that his delight would be only in looking.) The Khazari chorus sang:

> *Oh bridegroom's homeland, left behind . . .*
> *Left so he could seek our favors . . .*
> *Leaving family and friendly women far away . . .*
> *Seeking our hand, seeking our favors, seeking . . .*

Their piercing voices infuriated the Shamiah women, paralyzing them with jealousy. The singing continued until midnight, when the bride's procession disappeared in the general direction of al-Shamia.

That night, as the cavernous rooms of Mohammed al-Maghrabi's home closed in around the seabird bride of the al-Khazari, he had the odd sensation of feeling lost. He spent what remained of the dark hours floundering in the briny wake behind his seabird—who was also a bird made of fire, or a bird made of mercury, or some substance that couldn't be gripped and chewed between his teeth. She was a creature he could not consume. His need to possess her turned to anger.

There was really no way, this side of outright assault, to have her without stoking the rage in his heart, without teasing the brute anger that fed the shapeless flames of frustration and melted every certainty he'd ever known. She was getting wilder and wilder. Exhausted, al-Maghrabi gave up trying to capture the unholdable, the unpossessable.

Then he remembered an old trick used by falconers.

He locked his bride in a dark room, himself along with her, and while she was blinded in this way, he meditated on the secrets of her soul and the hidden pathways she'd kept closed to him. For an entire week he never left the side of his seabird. He stayed close as her own shadow, worshipful as an idol in the inmost temple of her soul, and from this intimate vantage point he kept feeding her, one piece at a time, bits of his heart, which aroused her all the more, made her pull closer and lunge toward him as if draining the very elixir of life from his spine.

At last she was satisfied. The longing in the pit of her heart, the timeless yearning for the *nabk* tree of her left-behind home, was quenched. The seabird bride of the al-Khazari found the strength to leave her old nest forever. She was ready now to face a new life with her *qreen*, with her husband-lover.

Mohammed gazed at her with a connoisseur's eye. In no time at all she had become skilled as the most experienced falcon. High, high over him she would soar, then swoop down, talons bared. There was nothing in him—no tender feeling, no delicate dream—that she did not pounce on and clutch to her own whims and wild desires. He became her captive.

She turned the falconer's trick on him: she sewed his eyes shut and bound his hands. She explored his body, opening eyes older and more profound than the ones she'd sealed, uncovering a sense of sight that specialized in the smallest, most evanescent, most exquisite tastes and gossamer nudges, the shudderings of cobwebs. He was sealed in her amber, bound by the swift beating of her wings, imprisoned by the breathless fluttering of her feathers on his skin.

They were breathing slowly now, synchronously.

Then came the tranquility that follows the hunt.

9. Big Ruby's Big Party

Yaqut Khan, the wife of the Sheik of the Textile Merchants, sent out invitations for a party in honor of the bride's first excursion away from her husband's house. Yaqut Khan (or Big Ruby, to translate colloquially) was eager to ingratiate herself with Sheik Baikwaly. To accomplish this she staged an elaborate demonstration of respect for her new in-laws.

For the site of her celebration she chose the Garden of al-Ashraf, the loveliest citrus grove in the municipality of Nowaria. With its beautiful rose beds and elegant gazebos, it was *the* location for Mecca's fashionable gatherings and musical soirees, a place where local virtuosi serenaded their favorite flowers and sang classical songs inspired by rippling water. Roses rambled everywhere, many of them rare hybrids imported from Medina. Dozens of slaves were assigned to care for them, since they were inclined to wilt whenever the scorching al-Simoom began to blow, at which time the slaves hung nets of wet gauze over the flower beds, keeping them moist till the hot wind subsided. When the air turned suffocatingly still, they fanned the roses with huge palm fronds. It was the slaves' sacred duty, during the cool hours of morning and evening, to pluck the roses and squeeze nectar from their petals. This syrup they poured into the pond in the center of the garden, scattering the petals across the water. The pond rippled like a giant rose in the midst of the fragrant green lemon trees standing all around it; its surface reflected a sky shivering in one of the Seven Heavens.

The caravans carrying Big Ruby's guests started arriving at dawn and never stopped. In the shade-glow under the trees, diamond brooches gleamed on regal bosoms; flashing gold reflected the lemony sun as it climbed in the chattering sky. Fine Persian carpets were strewn about with splendid randomness, their dark patterns smoldering in the shade. Some ladies took refuge in the calm shelter of the gazebos, attended by slaves who brushed the heat aside with palm-leaf fans, pushing cool breezes made cooler by sprinklings of water.

Jummo was swanning around in a green dress that eclipsed the bride's rosy glow. All eyes were drawn to her; she seemed to be sparkling. Little girls clustered around her and climbed trees and tossed lemons into the pool and dumped them on the Persian carpets and ran around squirting lemons and flinging rose petals at the slaves, who went imperturbably about their tasks.

They worked in dark, flimsy shacks next to the stables where donkeys were bred and hired out for grand processions in Mecca. It was the slaves' job to decorate the beasts with silver rattles and necklaces, and feed them leaves from lemon trees to enhance their intelligence. Thus groomed, the donkeys stood ready to play their part in religious celebrations such as the birth of the Prophet and the enormous pageants that traveled across the desert to the Prophet's birthplace and burial site.

The slaves kept their eyes cast down; it was not for them to savor the beauty of forbidden females. Jummo noted their submission. She stepped closer to the donkeys. She jumped on the back of the wildest and glossiest black one, the one without a saddle. Jummo rode off, trampling the Persian carpets and beds of clover. Behind her clopped a caravan of donkeys ridden by little girls.

At the edge of the lemon trees she dismounted and drew a line in the sand to indicate where the race was to start. From here she sketched the circular route of the entire race; it was to end at the east gate of the garden. The donkeys lined up. Jummo mounted her steed. At the signal to start, he took a step backward. The other donkeys rushed forward. People on the sidelines laughed and mocked the girls with hee-haws.

The girls understood at once the tricky move Jummo had made. "Jummo's a cheat!" they shouted. Laughing wickedly, she rode her donkey straight toward the finish line, kicking the stubborn beast and urging him to move even faster than her heart was beating. All of sudden, when he got to the pond, the animal stopped short. Jummo sailed over his ears and splashed into the scented water, scattering rose petals everywhere.

The other donkeys were determined to finish what they started, no matter how hard their young riders protested. They took their time traveling the complete circuit to the eastern gate, riders giggling all the way.

Jummo surfaced. Her two braids, studded with pearls, sprung out from either side of her scarf. Her veil had been swept away, her face was scandalously exposed.

Sidi Wahdana had been bending over the edge of pond having a drink. He, too, had gotten soaked by Jummo's fall.

Where had the dervish come from? How did he happen to land at the edge of the pond? And what was he doing in this all-female paradise in the first place?

"Sidi!" Jummo said in a voice full of wonder, all the more wonder-struck since her lips were bubbling with rosewater. She started sinking into the lake of Sidi's waxy, bottomless eyes. Trembling as if possessed by a reckless spirit, she knelt in the shallow pool. She opened her hands in a gesture of prayer, cried out "Sidi Wahdana!" cupped her hands, scooped up a drink of rosewater, and slowly raised it to the dervish's lips. With every drop he sipped, she felt closer to him, for it was her self she was offering.

Sidi picked up a trace of her wild scent in the water. He came closer. Bending nearly double, every muscle in his body strained and tightened as he stretched toward her cupped hands. He felt the fever-heat in her fingertips. He gulped and gulped again and he gulped again and again, licking the pillows of her thumb pads; he sucked the soft rose petals sleeping there.

The softness of his touch stunned Jummo. Her whole body was submerged in rosewater, numbed by it. But she never lowered her hands—they hung suspended in midair, totally at the mercy of the blind dervish, to be used by his lips.

In the space created by her abandon, his blind eyes grew wide, then widened more as he fixed on her face. She felt certain he was seeing her—yes, blind he truly was, yet truly he was seeing her.

Under her absent-with-pleasure gaze, his eyes assumed the color and shape of emeralds. This was the first time Sidi's eyes had ever been green. No, never before had they been this color—never green, everyone was absolutely sure of it—not even by accident, nor because of some mistake—no, no, emerald green had no place at all in the legend of Sidi Wahdana.

"Your eyes are the green of an emerald green hill," Jummo said. "Do you see me, Sidi?"

A garden bloomed in Sidi's eyes, engulfing her. His answer was as alive as only human pain can be: *"Ya hai, ya hai . . .* You who are alive, you who are alive . . . "

She surrendered every surrenderable thing to his energy.

She wasn't aware that the other girls had returned; she hadn't seen them circling the pond with their eyes glued to her. The sharpness of their laughter broke the spell, shattered the out-of-time instant she'd been wandering in.

When Jummo stretched out her hands toward the dervish's head, his turban fell off, exposing for the first time his seven shoulder-length braids. With each of her fingers she stroked the braids, so glossy, so sinuous they felt like living things. She tugged. His bony body fell forward into the water and sank. In one continuous motion Jummo jumped on his back and bounded out of the pond, splattering petals and rosewater all over the tiles.

The other girls didn't notice Sidi's emergence. One after another they threw their sweaty little bodies into the pond. Of the vanishing dervish not a trace remained, no evidence at all as to whether his apparition had been real or the product of the girls' overheated imaginations. They said nothing to the grownups, and the incident became a reverie buried in their shivering hearts.

Later that day, still dewy with rosewater, Jummo joined the other girls at a lamp lit banquet. Nara cast an appraising eye on her daughter. Jummo was showing no interest in the meat delicacies. She sat there idly nibbling raw lemons sprinkled with salt.

"You'll give yourself terrible heartburn," Big Ruby warned.

One of the old ladies leaned toward Nara and whispered, "Lemon juice can scald a girl's cherry. And once that happens, no man in Mecca would even think about marrying her."

Jummo replied to Nara's wink by setting her lemon aside and tasting a few slivers of green almond, which she dipped in salt.

Night fell, the lute music grew louder. The passionate singing of a Yemenite slave named Maliha inflamed the campfire. The spirits of the roses filled the air, mingling with an ambery fragrance that seemed to originate in a world far lovelier than this loveliest of gardens. Hips and bellies shimmied in the firelight, invoking Sidi's spirit, summoning him, imploring him to rise.

The only one who didn't take part in the dancing was Jummo. She withdrew to the darkest corner of the garden. There, in the hollow of a lemon tree's trunk, she lay down and pressed her swollen hands against her cheeks, recalling the soft incandescence of Sidi's lips.

The darkness all around her was populated by shadows, by hazy figures and apparitions of strange creatures who were on such intimate terms with darkness that they and the night harmonized a song of their own shadowiness. These creatures, Jummo thought, are quite capable of walking out of this garden, right out from between my legs and into the Unknown, closing the door behind them.

The shadows took the shape of Sidi Wahdana.

The earth shook and sent a trembling into her toes. It was perhaps the heaving of infinite worlds, the same worlds revealed by Death to those who long to see beyond life, to envision the Unseen. Jummo knew at once that she was capable of penetrating the darkness and following Sidi Wahdana. As if answering her thoughts, all the trees growing in the Unknown came closer and peeled back their bark, allowing Jummo to slip inside—to slip inside, that is, the Animal living and moving inside the trees. This was the same fierce Animal that had flowed from Sidi's lips into her body and her soul.

The Animal roared and raced through her veins, deafening her. Helpless, she surrendered to the waves of animal energy till she could stand no more. The creatures shed their skins. She blinked, closing her aching eyelids against the darkness. The creatures re-skinned themselves, veiling their spirits. Jummo opened her eyes.

There was a fire.

The campfire's brightness blinded her, it was the sparkling of the ferocious Animal, scattering everywhere. It raced through her body, consuming her.

She hopped out of the hole in the trunk of the lemon tree and walked toward the circle of people dancing around the fire. "This fire is a cooler fire, Jummo," she said to herself, moving reluctantly forward, seeking the warmth of the women's circle. She sat down, hugging herself, resting her chin on her knees, losing herself in the party noise and the soft tapping of the dancers' feet.

Nara nudged Khadija. "How unlike Jummo—she's so quiet tonight."

Khadija replied without taking her eyes off the flame-light dancing on her granddaughter's forehead. "If a girl goes astray, it's because she gives in to seeing things the way a man does. When a girl leaves the straight and narrow, she's chasing a man's mirage. Hannah's getting married, so now Jummo wants a *qreen*, a mate.

Nara studied Jummo for signs of the dangerous longing described by the old woman. Jummo kept staring into the fire, seduced by the conversational ups-and-downs of the flames.

An impressively ancient woman named Shara (she was said to be a hundred years old) butted in: "The way that girl rests her head in her hands, she's certain to look old before her time. If your daughter keeps on this way, resting her head in her hands and wrinkling her cheeks, her teeth will fall out and her hair will turn gray before she knows it—and before she finds a mate!" Old Shara raised her hands and recited a protective verse from the Qur'an directly into her wrinkled palms: "*Salam qawlan min Rabb raheem*—May the peaceful words of the God of mercy protect us." She wiped her hands against the coal-black hair on the sides of her head.

"Make sure Jummo keeps busy," Khadija whispered to Nara. "Too much time by herself, a girl starts thinking about her invisible mate. Nobody in our family has ever been very successful at leading the solitary life."

Khadija pointed at Ayten, a lovely Turkish girl, and asked her with a wink to wake Jummo from her reverie. Smoothly, like moonlight (Ayten means Moon Body), the Turkish girl slipped into the circle of dancers. She stood there, shining, between Jummo and the visions Jummo was seeing in the firelight.

"This is our dance," Ayten said, and without giving Jummo time to object, she tugged her into the circle of beckoning dancers. Ayten's body spoke a frankly sensuous language. Stutteringly, Jummo tried to follow her.

Nara caught the beat and started dancing wildly, skipping around Jummo and Ayten. The other dancers backed away, surrendering their places to the three main dancers, especially to the mesmerizing Nara. Dripping with rose-scented sweat, the young girls circled the inner circle, a planetary system of worlds whirling around worlds, closing on the moment of Creation itself; every dancer a demigod scattering life with each twist and turn.

Yellow strands of smoke rose from the fire like spirits lively enough to suck human souls up into their heat. So many quiet sparks.

Good Lord, my friend—you *are* curious, aren't you? You triggered the firelock and sent the map's incense flying for help. When I did my best to respond, you ran around asking about Ali, the lamb slaughtered under my window. Didn't I warn you that ringing a false alarm with the Rescue Map would shorten its life? You said that shortening the life of a map meant nothing compared to jeopardizing a living soul, that nothing was so crippling as snuffing a life, etc. For all your interest in Hannah and the splendors of her wedding, you remain more concerned about the suggestion of human sacrifice (little Ali?)—which kept you up all night worrying after reading my reply.

So what would you like me to say? When you bring up the subject of little Ali, you're getting close to the subject of our secret weapon.

Listen very carefully: Whenever someone entered our courtyard, we'd give him a name before welcoming him; in other words, we started by imprisoning the newcomer in a name. Once we were certain that the letters of the name had bridled him with an identity, we'd start feeding him, fattening him up for the slaughter.

How could we manage to go on living without being tethered by the rope of a name and all the control a name implies? We were brought up to believe that names are our essence. And Paradise, as everyone knows, is populated by nothing, no images at all, nothing but names or essences pulsing through Heaven, taking on unimaginable shapes. So it is written in the secret book, *Hadia al-Arwah, or The Souls' Guiding Light in the Land of Absolute Delight.*

I see you now. I know your name. You are not an infidel. You are not my friend.

You are Hassan al-Basri.

Why you, Hassan? Why should you be the one I tell my story to? What can I possibly say to Hassan of Basra, the celebrated character from *The Thousand and One Nights,* the finest goldsmith in all the Seven Heavens, a craftsman so masterful he can coax words from dumb beasts, whole paragraphs from inanimate objects—the only man crazy enough to get himself kidnapped and almost murdered by the wizard alchemist Bahram just so he could steal the secret formula for turning base metal into gold? How can I tempt a legend like you away from yours castles, your queens, your princelings, your Underworldlings? How could I tempt you with a story about today?

I could rush you, I could swarm all over you with words (maidenly words, of course, weightless as rain). I could attack, I could retreat—who knows? Just don't expect mercy. Innocents are completely pitiless when we choose to be.

I know your name, Hassan; I see you now. You are my rival, my confidante. We are each other's instruments.

10. Eyes, Buttermilk, and Bad Hair

Hannah could be quite jealous when it came to her husband, my father, Mohammed al-Maghrabi. For his part, my father was a man fiercely devoted to animals and their musical serenity. Hannah's soul gravitated toward plants, birds, and cats; Mohammed al-Maghrabi was enamored of larger mammals such as rabbits, donkeys, sheep, and mountain goats. This polarity defined the atmosphere of our home.

Ali, our little lamb, was the circle of safety, our trusty blade, the sacrificial blood regularly used to wash away from Hannah's doorstep any trace of the Evil Eye, disease, lurking demons, and geniis runamuk. There are those who think of blood as the sap of a royal jewel, but actually blood flows most naturally in a moat, and in this moat one can drown the wicked Netherworldlings who lay siege to the realm of human affairs.

Hannah was known to possess a discriminating eye or, as people used to call it, the Searchlight. She could see into the geniis' worlds, share their secret lives and uncover their covert activities. Hannah's Searchlight exposed the Netherworldlings circling around us, attacking us from within and without. She could see right through us. "Your lava is overflowing," She'd say when our foolishness got out of hand. She'd give us a sip of the buttermilk she kept in my father's leather bag, which was inscribed on all sides with verses from the holy Qur'an and God's greatest name.

Ordinarily the buttermilk was effective in quenching our volcanoes and cleansing our red-hot inner selves of their satanic streaks. But when some outside influence made us rebellious, my mother's Searchlight could see that we were being attacked by geniis, in which case she would resort to the remedy of isolation: the veil. This kept us sheltered from any and all incursions of wind or light. She allowed nothing but her Searchlight to enter our room. Her eye was always on the lookout, examining our hair for signs of lice left behind by Underworldlings.

Me especially she would take hold of, gripping me between her thighs to contain my trembling, and crowning my unkempt head with braids, three on the right side, three on the left, seven on the back, trailing down my neck and shoulders. She believed that arranging my hair, or at least organizing its disarray, was as good as cutting the assault ropes used by the geniis who were attacking me.

But the older I got, the more I let my hair hang loose. I let it grow wild. It flew every which way, all the time, leaving the air around me heavy with the scent of amber. I just could not accept any kind of bond or bridle.

My hair is reaching for the topmost untouchable Heaven. It floats back down as lightning, electrifying my animal skin. Can't you feel it—my hair? The electrical charge gets more intense the more I let my hair hang loose, the more wantonly I toss my curls.

11. Ice Flame

The first donkey my father owned was a Yemenite bred in the mountains of Sunaa. It was brought to him by a *haji*, a pilgrim from Yemen who traded it to pay his expenses in the Holy Land. It was customary for Yemenite pilgrims to enter Mecca shepherding three to seven donkeys. The city's markets welcomed these beautiful animals, because they contributed so much to the grandeur of the pageants orchestrated by the sheiks and other wealthy personages. Donkeys were the monarchs of Mecca's endless pageants, carrying crowds of people from one neighborhood to another, all on their way to the Holy Mosque.

There were artists who did nothing but create spectacular paintings on the animals' long-suffering hides. There were craftsmen who fabricated ingenious devices that rang and tinkled and rattled every time the donkeys twitched. It was not unusual to see a donkey adorned with pagan designs done in henna, with silver rattles and charms, cowry shells, and stunning golden amulets. The effect of all this imagery and noise, when caravanning in a pageant, was charming; the donkeys were trailed by crowds of admirers, and there seemed always to be a pageant in preparation for some festival or other: a trip to the Prophet's city, a graduation ceremony for scholars of the Holy Book, the anniversary of the Prophet's birth, a marriage, a victory over evil, the birth of a child.

It happened that Haji Swayn, a pilgrim from Yemen, entered Mecca leading but one donkey, a female whose hide was pure white, white as quartz. He planted himself next to his beast and stood in the middle of the market, waiting for a buyer, surrounded by fellow pilgrims selling their herds as fast as they could display them. Before long the other pilgrims were on their way to the inns reserved for visitors to the Holy Mosque. Some had already started the ritual of circumambulating the Holy Mosque and reverencing God's holy name.

Haji Swayn stayed behind, invisible to the buyers and sellers rushing back and forth. Perhaps they were blinded by the she-donkey's whiteness, which was so uniform and unblemished that the beast might well have been an icon cautioning against the follies of polytheism.

All day long Haji Swayn stood in his spot. Nothing like this had ever happened, not in the entire history of trading Yemenite donkeys, whose remarkable qualities were the envy of the world. Haji Swayn stood patiently. The sun set. Darkness fell. The market was illuminated solely by the glow of the donkey's eyes, which the pilgrim had covered with a veil.

My father happened to pass by. The veiled donkey immediately caught his attention, and he wasted no time buying it. Mohammed al-Maghrabi never could recall how much he paid for that white she-donkey—probably quite a bit. Then again, it's conceivable he got a bargain, if one takes into account the pilgrim's weariness and his pessimism about being able to get a good price for such a weird-looking animal.

Mohammed al-Maghrabi adjusted his elegant turban, tucked in his hair, and hitched his strange new donkey to a post by the gate of the slave market. It was here that the course of life—the life of a slave, at any rate—took some very wild turns. Here a slave's life stopped being one thing and started being something else altogether, careening in all directions down strange roads in the Holy Land. My father hurried off to answer the call to evening prayer.

All the merchants and worshippers in the area were drawn like moths to the donkey's inner fire, which, under the veil of night, took on an irresistible glow. It was easier now to get a closer look at the brilliant beast and contemplate the energy that made it shine. Mohammed al-Maghrabi was inundated with many offers for the animal at prices that grew more incredible by the minute. But my father was enthralled by his snow-white beauty. All offers were declined. The merchants moved sadly on, muttering, fingering prayer beads behind their backs, and mourning the loss of such a splendid commodity.

After prayer, my father returned to our house on the slopes of al-Shamia. A great stone house it was, seven stories, each floor harboring a world unto itself. My grandmother Fatma Mosliya was enthroned on the seventh, or top floor. There she reigned as a queen directing every activity between the skylights on the roof to the guest quarters on the ground floor. There were those who assumed that she ruled the heavens above as well.

Daughters-in-law, cousins, and slaves were scattered all over Fatma's kingdom. She had twenty female slaves at her disposal, and all of them quaked in their sandals whenever Fatma appeared carrying the stick of smoldering firewood she liked to carry around. Her stick tolerated not the slightest deviation in deportment, whether in animal, humans, or household furnishings. Sometimes, when she was in a hurry to adjust the behavior of one of her subjects to the expected level of perfection, the firewood burst into flames. Grandmother Fatma was thought to have the most skilled slaves in the Holy City, and the most loyal. In recognition of the fact that she was rich enough to maintain twenty stylish households in an otherwise indifferently decorated city, she was known as the Mistress of Twenty Subjects and Twenty Doors.

The houses of old Mecca were remarkable for their roofs. The roofs of the better homes were constructed in three or four compartment or levels. A portion of each level was open to the sky. The open-air spaces were called *kharija*, the enclosed spaces *al-mabeet*. Their functions changed—sleep, family socializing, parties—according to the weather. The greater part of an average person's life took place in the topmost story. The kitchens were the exclusive domain of women.

It was late by the time Mohammed al-Maghrabi made his way to the top floor. Huffing and puffing, he hurried up the curving staircase to the kitchen. Each step was nearly as tall as a man, and trying to climb the stairs without making a lot of noise was strenuous exercise. The passageway itself was high and narrow, interrupted by oddly dwarfish doors that opened onto twisted passageways, some of them surprisingly high, or perhaps into a sudden turn that opened abruptly onto the open sky, or to some unexpected section of the roof ringed by stone statues of soldiers so stubby and distracted-looking that you felt the sky could sweep you right up, or the abyss might nip at your ankle.

Mohammed edged into the kitchen. His mother was stationed in her *mabeet,* her omnisciently situated headquarters, surveying the activities of the subjects in her vicinity. Mohammed stole a look at Hannah, who was busy with her evening chores: polishing the lanterns, trimming their saffron wicks, and stirring the embers under the kettles. She covered the flames guttering in the stove against the cool evening winds sweeping down from the mountains. The embers blinked, quivered, and crouched under the peaks thrusting massively against the heavens, each summit a stanchion in the barricade ringing the Holy City.

"I've just bought a she-donkey," Mohammed whispered to Hannah. "And a gorgeous specimen she is, a pure white Yemenite."

Hannah didn't catch a word Mohammed was saying, because Fatma was giving her a look.

Fatma scolded her son: "What do you think you're doing wearing your turban in our presence? You think we're your lowly subjects or something?! Get changed. Get going; dinner's ready." She applied an ivory comb to her thick silvery hair, parted it, and began braiding it.

Mohammed looked back at Hannah. "Yes, I bought a she-donkey—a fine specimen, a pure white Yemenite. The minute I bought her, there wasn't a merchant in Mecca who didn't offer me a bundle for her. She's tied up downstairs. If you'd like to have a look . . ."

The lanterns pulsed and twinkled. Fatma's *mabeet* and the kitchen filled with the scent of old-fashioned Yemeni incense. Hannah sensed it and moved instinctively, without hesitation, to gather in the scent of her mate, jealously guarding him against the Unseen, which was flowing through the room, invisible to every woman except herself.

Fatma smirked. "So you paid no attention at all to the bargains you might have had—and instead you come home trailing some . . . some *animal*!" She turned toward the lantern hanging in the archway, a gesture she was in the habit of using to highlight the perfection of her profile (her face would have looked good on a coin) and the striking ruby redness of her lips.

"I just couldn't part with her," Mohammed said. "She's one of a kind. The Prince of Mecca would be proud to own her."

With two thin threads Fatma tied a small triangle of cotton on the top of her head as a base to secure yet another head covering. She wound her braids up in a long *midawara*, cocooning them, and plaited the braids into a crown. Over this crown she draped her *mihrama*, a scarf of gossamer silk, letting it fall loosely over her head and shoulders.

She tossed Mohammed a heart-stopping look. "Was my own son hatched from an old trunk full of craziness and illusions from the Unknown? You should have left the beast for the auctioneer or the Prince. Like father, like son, I suppose—you escape the madness of dreams only to walk straight into the bonfires of grandiosity."

Fatma's scolding did nothing to diminish Mohammed's delight in owning the pure white she-donkey. He turned to the young ladies of the household—Rida, Hannah, and his niece Khairiya. "Wouldn't you like to have a look at her? Just wait till I hitch up her saddle and arrange the silver rattles."

"Dinner first," Fatma said impatiently. "Better to see the beast in daylight, tomorrow morning. We're not going to waste the whole night staring at the hide of a white donkey like a bunch of crazy Yemenites."

That night, between Hannah's thighs, the white she-donkey displayed quite a bit of spirit, fire even. Hannah took turns riding it, barebacked, with Khairiya. It was on this night, for the first time, that the donkey felt a rider on its back, and it was for the first time, too, that the white beast surrendered his back to the women's heated play. The slaves watched wide-eyed, transported back to lands long forgotten—to Hindustan or Pakistan or Turkey—to homes where once they'd been free and whole as fire or wind.

Such madness was inconceivable in al-Maghrabi's house without the support of Dumboshi and that ringing laugh of hers. Her laughter was propelled by fierce internal combustion, by a hurricane roaring in her heart. It stormed under our skin, took our breath away. When she laughed we felt she was laughing in *our* chest, with *our* breath, laughing for all of us and bestowing her special sense of joy on every heart within hearing distance.

Even the white donkey, prancing through the halls, got caught up in Dumboshi's laughter. When she stroked the animal's hide it went crazy and started dancing the holy dance of a dervish, forgetting everything but her rider's electrifying touch. The black shadows of her snowy shape jumped and swayed from wall to wall, from ceiling to floor, till at last Dumboshi dismounted, dazed, still whirling, lost in the murky excruciating ecstasy that only true riders know.

When the snow-white donkey was not occupied with one of Mohammed's outings or taking part in a festival, the three young women of the household spent their time decorating her with silver rattles with square amulets at their centers. The amulets were inlaid with Tihami miniatures. Inside the miniatures were tucked little pieces of yellow paper, and the papers were inscribed with talismans in some half-forgotten language. The inscriptions were passed down from owner to owner, none of whom had ever dared to remove the contents of the amulets, much less inspect them.

The young women, however, managed to decipher a few letters of the talisman. With these letters they spelled out the name Ice Flame. They laced a nametag around the donkey's muzzle and set the animal free to roam as it pleased through the streets of Mecca. So Ice Flame wandered around rattling and advertising her presence by means of the talisman's baffling inscription. Even while she was standing at the foot of the hill, right next to the Holy Mosque, the clattering of her hoofs carried all the way up the slopes of al-Shamia.

The fancy neighborhood on the hill bubbled over with news of Ice Flame; everyone had something to say about the strange beast that al-Maghrabi's daughters were so enamored of. All the women were dying to stroke the back of the Yemenite genii (for so the donkey was regarded). Ice Flame cast a mighty spell over the fashionable homes topped by al-Maghrabi's house, whose sandalwood dormers taunted the ambitions of those who lived lower down.

None of the Maghrabi women would permit a saddle to come between her body and Ice Flame's. Saddles were implements of grandeur and solemnity used by men in public appearances. Naked animal skin, on the other hand, with its vital forces and volatile vapors capable of climbing the vertebrae and blinding the rider with wordless ecstasies—that was strictly for women.

But Ice Flame was fated to leave this female paradise. It was inconceivable that such a valuable creature—the donkey's diet consisted of a variety of almond known as the Prophet's Almond, which had to be especially imported—could be entrusted to the care of females. Inevitably there came a buyer, a water-rich sheik from another neighborhood, who made an offer that Mohammed al-Maghrabi couldn't refuse. This sheik proposed to buy Ice Flame and sell her to a pilgrim heading north, making it unlikely that she'd ever been seen in Mecca again. Mohammed al-Maghrabi was left with her rattles, which never stopped echoing on the slopes of al-Shamia.

12. The Peaceful Flood

The afternoon that Mohammed al-Maghrabi left with Ice Flame for the sheik's neighborhood, Fatma relaxed for the first time since the donkey had invaded her domain. An unaccustomed silence alerted her to the fact that the animal was gone forever. In its place there was an overwhelming feeling of loss and sacrifice. Fatma sensed a soul being stifled somewhere in the boards that framed the house, the same boards that had creaked and groaned all during the donkey's days of residence.

Fatma did something she rarely did on a Friday: she closed the shutters on the dormers, and when Hannah appeared with afternoon tea she sent it away untouched. She settled into a shadowy corner, hiding in the dimness. Her slave Tronja followed, sitting on the edge of a stone bench.

"Why so sad, mistress?"

"Oh God, Thou Generous One, Thou Guide, mayst Thou instruct Mohammed on this holy Friday to get rid of that she-donkey!"

"Friday has a secret hour," Tronja said softly, "when every prayer is answered. "Oh Generous God, let this be the hour, and may my mistress's prayer be answered."

Fatma relaxed and stretched out over the damask cushions, dangling her legs so the loyal slave could massage her feet.

"Listen, Tronja—the angels of the house just breathed a sigh of relief at the donkey's departure!"

Tronja sensed that a great burden had been lifted from her mistress's shoulders. "God preserve us from visitation by all evils," she said, eager to know more about her mistress' worries.

"Yes indeed, God preserve us!" Fatma said absently. She fell into silent contemplation of the shaft of light falling on the shelf where her china was displayed. The light beam slithered further across the room, pressed against the door of her Indonesian incense burner, and pried it open.

"Did you notice the eye on that she-donkey?" Fatma said finally. "God preserve us—the eye of a ghost it was, if ever I saw one. God knows I felt squeamish just being around the beast, and whenever I passed it in the hall I lowered my veil and covered myself with my *abaya* for fear of being exposed to that eye."

"If I wasn't afraid of upsetting my mistress I would tell you what I saw in that eye."

"Don't get me going with your mumbling, Tronja!"

"The eye of the dervish . . ."

Startled, Fatma cut her slave short: "Sidi Wahdana?!"

The shaft of light faded abruptly. The door of the Indonesian incense burner clinked shut.

The night of Ice Flame's departure, Mohamed al-Maghrabi's house was at peace for the first time since that sunset in the slave market when he first struck the bargain to buy the beast.

Hannah slept deeply, and in her dream she led the women of al-Shamia to the old house with the *nabk* tree, the home she'd left behind, deserted, when Sheik al-Baikwaly moved to his grand new quarters. There, at the entrance to the narrow street, Jummo met them. They spent the rest of the night competing about who was the best at climbing the *nabk* tree, and sipping nectar from its fruit. Midnight found the women perched on the boughs like buzzards decked out in leaves shaped like fantails, with modest coverings for the ankles.

Hannah went on ahead, Jummo followed. They came to the top of the great tree on the summit of Quayqian, Mecca's tallest mountain. Enthroned on high, the daughters of al-Baikwaly picked *nabk* fruits, tossed them in the air, caught them between their lips, and poured the juice into Ice Flame's mouth. The saturated she-donkey liquefied . . .

. . . and began spouting from the rocks of Quayqian, flowing like a great flood tide, swamping Mecca's roads and streets. The Nabk Flood swamped the valleys of the Holy Land with juice the color of royal robes. Against this crimson flood, the stark whiteness of the donkey stood out like a meteor that kept raising its head to get a glimpse of the *nabk* tree. The animal's flanks heaved. She licked the girls' faces and wrinkled her snout at the sound of *ouds* strumming the tunes of yearning and bitter memories that signaled nightfall in al-Baikwaly's house.

Mohammed al-Maghrabi got very little sleep that night, what with all he had to go through trying to tug Hannah away from her nightmares about the Nabk Flood, which were all the more inflamed by the fingers of the celebrated al-Kayal plucking the strings of his *oud*. This famous musician performed every night in al-Baikwaly's quarters. He was a maestro of heartstrings, a mover of hearts, much sought after by the most exclusive concertizing salons in Mecca.

Regarding the story about the she-donkey, I must tell you that if Hannah was expert in deciphering the animal's language and complicated secrets, it was Jummo who could plumb the pit of its heat and fire, where secrets and disguises counted for nothing. In the depths of the donkey's being there was a wild driving force that scattered whatever stood in its way.

13. Raised on Mountain Goat's Milk

Dumboshi took my mother's first male child under her wing. My grandfather al-Baikwaly had named him Nabee Jan, which is a real Khazar name. Dumboshi loved the name and wouldn't countenance any attempt to modernize or soften it to suit the tastes of Mecca's elite or the fashions of lands beyond the holy circle of Mecca (which, as it turned out, stole him away later in life). Dumboshi was happy to indulge the boy's every whim and tolerate his interminable tantrums, which maddened my father, Mohammed al-Maghrabi, who came to believe that the domain of his in-laws—al-Baikwaly's household—was purposely organized to spoil his son.

Nara smothered my brother with love. Sheik Baikwaly was his Ring of Solomon, the instrument that granted his every wish and made his dreams come true. Dumboshi, on the other hand, was always finding some way to get Nabee Jan to rebel, stirring his fires and causing all kinds of storms in the otherwise tranquil atmosphere of our household.

The alliance between Dumboshi and my brother started at an early age, before he was weaned, in the first two years of his life. In those days my father was basking in the pleasures of having his first male child. Earlier on, he'd enjoyed being the father of Joman, the crown jewel of his progeny, a sensitive, slender girl whom he pampered extravagantly. He used to bring her gum Arabic from Taif. She liked to chew it while waiting for him in the upper story of my grandfather's house on the slopes of al-Shamia. Even before she knew how to speak, Joman knew how to wait for his gifts, sitting patiently on the windowsill of her grandfather's room overlooking the sanctuary of the Sacred Stone. From there she could watch the road that climbed the hill and, further down, the Holy Mosque, while she waited for her father's striding shadow to break the hypnotic rhythm of pilgrims ritually walking in sacred circles, monotonously counter-pointed by casual passersby. For hours she sat there, lulled, memorizing the circumambulating humans, the gazelles, and the rainbow-feathered pigeons; memorizing, too, the prayers of humans, geniis, and animals, and contemplating many other things in her curious world, the countless wonders that never stopped ascending toward her sandal-wood window.

Mohammed al-Maghrabi always managed to bring her something surprising, despite the heavy burden of responsibilities he'd inherited from his father, whose sudden death left him in charge of a kingdom of women. Mohammed was the only male descendant in the al-Maghrabi line, so all family responsibilities fell to him. He wore his burden lightly, fascinated as he was by the newborn girl, the first of his progeny to survive. (My mother sacrificed five children to the Angel of Death in order to save another five for life. Those of us who survived were, first, Joman and Nabee Jan, then myself and my dark older sister Krazat al-Yosir, and Daj al-Layl, my youngest brother, the final grape in our family's cluster.) My father couldn't abide male spirits, with their tyrannical shrieking and warlike posturing. Whenever Nabee Jan started crying, he left the house to wander on the slopes of al-Shamia and waited for the boy's wailing to subside.

Nara took his clockwork-regular returns as the occasion to remark, in a critical mumble, "His *qreen*, the stud that inhabits his head, can't stand a partner!" Meaning that my father's twin of himself, his preferred self-image, couldn't bear to hear the voice of another male in the house.

Everybody believed that my father's *qreen* would emasculate and banish any male rival who happened on the scene. So they made sure to smother my brother's whimpering and tuck away his infuriating cries in a remote corner of the house. Yet Mohammed al-Maghrabi—at least in those moments when he was not afflicted by the variable moods and whims of his *qreen*—was devoted to his male heir. He worked hard to scaffold a temple of masculinity for the boy and reinforce the lad's own moods. In this regard Mohammed was quite resourceful. For the child's nourishment he procured a mountain goat from the wilds of Taif.

The shepherd who'd raised the goat explained in doctorly tones: "This wild beast would never have been tamed at all, much less touched by human hand, if it hadn't been for the years I spent living the life of a monk by the Falls of al-Mosul in the Kara Mountains. This splendid creature was raised within earshot of the Falls, listening to murmurings and gurglings that swarm through the mind like the sweet chanting of geniis. Such are the songs that the monkeys and other animals of Kara drink, purifying their milk and tenderizing their meat. It is the most energy-giving of foods."

Dumboshi took a special interest in the wild goat's milk and its mouth-watering ginger fragrance. She would sit watching Hannah milk the animal, the sweet-smelling liquid filling bowl after bowl. Dumboshi gulped it like a wild woman. As soon as my brother was able to take a few steps, he began toddling after the goat, sucking at her long swollen teats, allowing no human intervention to come between him and animal's milk, and resisting all attempts at weaning. (Let me assure you that no male takes lightly his passage through this particular bottleneck of life.) It was this early, satisfying suckling that confirmed my brother's fondness for Kara and the geniis of al-Mosul, and made Dumboshi his ally when it came to unpredictable behavior.

People began saying that the goat's milk filled my brother's veins with water and made them run with sparkling rubies rather than blood. They said the milk made his veins weak and porous and left him in danger of bleeding to death. "Al-Maghrabi feeds his son on milk from al-Mosul. It's turning him into a wild creature from the Falls. You know they way the waters murmur, and how the murmurs fade away till they vanish."

So Hannah took extra care to shelter her son from tiredness or minor injuries. He grew up wild, with a wild thing's ravenous appetites and a great talent for compassion.

14. Buckets of Gold

My father insisted, tenderly, on calling my mother Hanani. Hannah, her original name, gave way to this term of endearment and disappeared altogether. For her part, Fatma Mosliya gave in to her nickname only when age quenched the flames of her firestick and she had to hand over control of the household to her daughter-in-law and Khazar rival. At that point it became imperative for the old woman with the silver braids to make peace with her daughter-in-law. The marvelous braids stood the regal lady in good stead, thickening with age and gradually taking on a fiery sheen, reflecting the broad range of her feelings and sorrows, and ending up braided with rose petals and leaves from the *nabk* tree, anointed with oil of camphor, and arranged at last on either side of her bird-thin body when she was laid to rest in her white shroud. The long, graceful braids were blindingly vivid evidence of the beauty that had captured the heart of Sheik Abdul-Hai al-Maghrabi, and led to her enthronement in his kingdom of twenty slaves, endless conspiracies, and joyful musical gatherings.

The pitcher full of gold pieces fell and scattered its contents at my mother's feet. The suddenness of the accident obliterated everything except a memory of her wedding day, when she was showered with silver riyals.

The pitcher was one of many discovered by Hannah in the abandoned coal bin in Fatma Mosliya's sky-lit *kharija*. Startled, and frightened at having exposed hidden treasure, she buried the pitchers deep under the enormous chunks of coal, erasing their location from her memory. Years later, when she laughingly mentioned the pitchers to my grandmother Fatma Mosliya, they accused each other (with the utmost courtesy) of lying. The incident ended with Fatma Mosliya jokingly calling my mother a *baraja*, the most opportunistic kind of miser, one who makes use of whatever falls into her hands, recycling every piece of junk and hoarding every conceivable object, money most of all. My mother accepted the nickname in good spirits and consigned the incident to the stew of experiences that were better left unstirred. She never mentioned it again—except for the day, long after my grandmother's death, in the presence of Mosliya's favorite daughter, Aunt Rida. My father, hearing the story, jumped to his feet.

"Oh yes, I know all about those gold pieces," he said, "stacks and stacks of them—I counted them the night my father died." He went on to describe how Mosliya gathered up the gold pieces the night after Abdul-Hai Maghrabi's funeral. "I can still see my mother quite clearly, wiping hot tears in her *midawara* and digging up the mahogany trunks buried in the vault of the house where my stepbrother Salih died the year before. Her eyes were frighteningly bright. She didn't look any of us in the eye, she looked nowhere except maybe inside herself. She just went on excavating while we were listening to Sidi Wahdana's recitation of the verses about

Supreme Kingship from the Qur'an. Then she let out a wild, half-stifled cry and uncovered three beautiful boxes that had been buried in a trunk in a corner of the vault, under the blind arch over a sort of *mihrab* or prayer niche that was dug two steps lower than the rest of the damp floor. The boxes were perfectly square and made of ebony padded with mauve velvet, each box no wider than a hand. The blackish mauve was breathtaking. The stacks of coins flashed a weird gold light around the dim vault, especially on my mother's face. The coins were stacked in endless rows, side by side, top to bottom in each box. Mosliya wiped away the last of her tears and poured the stacks into a bundle and made me carry it upstairs. Our house went quiet, as if watching us. We came to her *mabeet*, her private room. She hid the bundle under her sleeping *mistaba*, with this warning: 'Your other stepbrother, the one who'd swipe the last crust of bread from out of your mouth—he'll be here at daybreak.'

"I understood only that she was hiding the gold against the days of famine that were bound to come. On this note we buried the bundle and actually forgot about it, or dropped it from memory, amid all the feelings of loss that followed Abdul-Hai's disappearance from our lives. We underwent a drastic change of roles and status when the great stone house surrendered control to the domineering Fatma Mosliya."

Generally speaking, the women of Mecca managed to live longer than the men, whom they delivered to early graves in the cemetery of Maala. It seemed death was in collusion with the women. They recovered quickly from grief and acknowledged this enduring fact of life: "Males were meant for death. Death calls not so much for grief as for dethroning one sultan and enthroning another."

My grandmother, Fatma Mosliya, was enthroned in the kingdom of the great house on the hills of al-Shamia. She wasted no time sorting out the destinies of her subjects. My father she ordered to leave school and go to work to maintain the family at the level of affluence to which she aspired. She scheduled the marriages of my four aunts and put Mohammed in charge of selecting suitable in-laws. Concerning Rida, the youngest and her favorite, she was very possessive. "Rida is my death shroud's vow-knot!" she proclaimed. By which she meant that Rida had been selected to live a maidenly life while waiting on her mother till the day she died. Later on, when Fatma Mosliya's hold on life weakened, she loosened her grip on her Shroud's Knot and made it her business to select a husband for Rida. She chose a burned-out husk of a man incapable of kindling her daughter's desire—or even of giving her incense, let alone burning it.

In a lofty tone tinged with awe, my father continued telling his story about the stacks of gold coins. "Once, when she took me to the printing house in Ejyad to work as a typesetter's apprentice, I asked her about the hoard of gold. My head was full of dreams in those days, and Ejyad had a magical hold on me. Ejyad was the mountain whose boulders gave birth to great steeds, and as I worked in this awesome landscape, I kept seeing the bits of type slip out of their slots—they looked to me like endless herds of horses being weaned. I was lost in a heaving sea of ink and desperately wanted out. Then I remembered the hoard of gold. But Mosliya turned a cold eye on my questions. She told me the gold had just barely covered the expenses of marrying off your sisters. So that was the end of the famous gold that was supposed to save our family. I doubted not a word of what she said and went obediently back to being an ink slave. I really had no choice except to struggle alone in the sea of ignorance, moving from one job to another trying to rebuild the family's name and fortune."

In the course of talking about the pitchers hidden in the coal bin, my father realized for the first time that he'd been deceived, and he finally understood how gullible he'd been to believe that the vast hoard of gold had simply vanished like quicksilver.

The day of my grandmother Mosliya's death, her slave Tronja closed all the doors leading into her ground-floor quarters in our new house, which my father had built with his own hands. My grandmother's corpse was still lying face down in front of the door to her room, pale as wax, where Ezrael, the angel of death, had greeted her just as she was on her way to get help. The angel watched while Tronja rummaged around in her mistress's room, and then, halfway up the stairs to the top-floor quarters, Ezrael came upon Fatma. The last thing she saw was the flash of Sidi Wahdana's white pupils, which soon began to blacken.

"He is *One!*" she prayed. Fatma lay in Ezrael's grip, in her last throes, but she would not permit Sidi to put into her mouth the invocation *No*

God but Him, Mohammed is His final messenger, nor did she allow him to anoint her soul, which had risen, rippling, to her throat.

By the end of the night and the conclusion of the Angel of Death's visitation, Fatma Mosliya was utterly alone. Her slave sank into a nightmare from which she was unable to wake until dawn, hours after her mistress had passed away. Of all the household's twenty slaves, Tronja was the only one who, after being granted her freedom to travel, made her way back to her mistress. Tronja had chosen to return and spend her last days with Fatma Mosliya.

Now, keeping a discrete distance between herself and her mistress' corpse while she rummaged around in the room, Tronja discovered three beautiful ebony boxes, wrapped so carefully in my grandmother's white head-coverings that they seemed to be taking a nap. Tronja wrapped the boxes up in a bundle, the very same bundle that was to play a role in the incident of the vault on the night of my grandfather's funeral in the house in al-Shamia. The boxes never left my grandmother's trunk. Tronja, the loyal slave, left our house forever, taking the dark secret of the treasure to her grave on Hindi Mountain.

15. Wartime Economies

"The only thing my mother liked about Hannah," said my father, "was her nickname, Baraja. My mother was the first to call her that."

My father never tired of ridiculing the alliance between the two most important women in his life. It was an alliance based on shared miserliness. My mother knew how to keep a secret and she had a gift for turning a few coins into a fortune. She was certainly not a spendthrift. We never actually saw her spend a cent, despite the oath she swore the night she first gave birth: "May Thou, oh God, help me never to let any of my offspring languish in need, and may I never see their hands lowered to beg." It was a vow she reverently observed for ever after.

As for Hannah, she kept everything, from bits of bread to passionate winks. She allowed not the smallest crumb of enthusiasm or good will go to waste. The style with which she hoarded life's miscellany heated my father's desire for her.

Her store of oddments included grim, endless stories about starvation. "The year of the invasion by the al-Modiyena . . ." Al-Modiyena were the authoritarian easterners who'd once invaded Mecca, and whenever Hannah spoke of this event, she conjured up the image of Khadija, her grandmother, gathering Sheik Baikwaly's daughters and the neighbors' girls and hiding them from the soldiers who came knocking on the door. Once the young women were safe in their hiding place, she set about scouring the roofs and pigeoncoops, scavenging for discarded crusts of bread and millet seeds. She scrubbed green fuzz off the moldy bread and kneaded it in soft balls before putting it in the children's mouths. When last piece of bread was gone and not one crumb remained, she cupped handfuls of Zamzam water into their famished mouths, for she lived in the belief that, as she put it, "To those who are hungry, Zamzam water is bread, to those who thirst, it is drink, and for the sick it is medicine. Zamzam is whatever you believe it to be—a medicine, a perfume, a banquet."

Buoyed by that belief, they survived their passage through the lean months that afflicted the Holy City in the wake of floods—whether the flood be of rain or of blood shed in battle.

During the incessant wars that washed over Mecca, the young men of the city often took refuge by disguising themselves in women's clothing or by hiding in water tanks. These strategies saved many lives over the course of the city's long history. Mecca's wars were female things, waged against whatever males happened to be around. The female wars swept up every young man, even some under the age of ten. The conditions, strategies, and military hardware of these blood-floods changed over time, evolving into a ceremonial camouflage precisely suited to the barren deserts where they took place: the white head-sashes bound with red-spotted headbands, the fashion for wearing no underwear . . . and always the mirages, great gushers of them—these came after looting the houses of the rich—and the precious pearls heaped in piles, to be exchanged for heaps of flour. Defeated, angry, the people of Mecca were given to muttering: "Back home, in the rocks of Twaiq, these easterners can't tell the difference between pearls and snake turds."

16. The Infatuated Messenger Boy

Nara whispered loud enough for everyone to hear: "Hannah is lucky Sidi Wahdana appeared the night she reached puberty, she's lucky she outlined her eyes with that white amber kohl of his. It's a sign of good luck—the pupils of Sidi's eyes are white amber. Except when they're black, that's when he brings death."

Nara and Big Ruby, the wife of the Sheik of the Textile Merchants, were in secret communication. Many bolts of fabric were delivered to Nara and her daughters to be sewn and embroidered and turned into dresses, *jubbahs*, turbans, and traditional hats, then sent back to Big Ruby to be sold. The typical Meccan *keffiyeh*, or simple headdress, would go in looking plain and come out looking gorgeous, embroidered with golden boughs, interwoven with leaves of white silk, or ornamented with Syrian tassels—whatever struck the girls' fancies. This entire enterprise had to be kept secret from Sheik Baikwaly, who was too proud to acknowledge any commercial activity on the part of his daughters.

Big Ruby engaged Mayjan, a trustworthy young man from a respectable Khazar family, to act as a messenger between her establishment and the house of al-Baikwaly. Mayjan was on the chunky side. It was a simple matter to hide things in the folds of his flesh; tiny rubies, for example, could be tucked away in the dimples of his chubby chin.

Mayjan liked to sit on the bare ground of al-Baikwaly's courtyard under the *nabk* tree, squirming on the sharp pebbles and picking up whatever jujube fruits Jummo deigned to toss his way from her throne high up in the boughs. There he would sit, patiently separating the bundles of fabrics, never taking his eyes off the glowing, vaulting rainbows he saw when he looked up at Jummo. He clenched his jaw. He yawned. He tried to relax. His dimples dribbled warm rubies.

Jummo dashed in to snatch a *keffiyeh* and hide it in a bundle of fabric waiting to be dyed. She spared him no trick in her repertoire, mean or playful; his only response was to become more infatuated. Jummo and the Khazar lad found themselves splashing in a puddle of infatuation, and she couldn't resist inciting his passions in small but effective ways. When it came to extracting little pieces from the smitten young man's store of fabrics—a triangle here, a square there—she exhibited the artistic talent of a pagan. She was able to combine them all into beautiful quilted collages that covered the boy from head to toe. She had a positively witchlike gift for making Mayjan lovely *jubbahs* and *keffiyehs,* all stitched together with threads of gold.

Every Friday morning Mayjan emerged from al-Baikwaly's house clad in sun-bright patches that added to the luster of the rubies puffing up his cheeks. Down Mecca's streets and alleys he glittered, attracting to the astonishing splendor of his person the stares of eyes peeking through dormers. Every Friday he walked through the city glowing with an intense inner passion until he come to the Holy Mosque, ready to hear Friday's sermon. He made his way to the Zamzam well and washed in the holy water, drenching himself with images of al-Baikwaly, Sheik of the Zamzam Water Carriers, and reinforcing the dominating spirits of his daughter, Jummo. Mayjan uttered not one word until he heard the call to prayer, at which point he set aside his vision of the Sheik's daughter and gave himself over to prayer, inspired by private amber spirits.

17. The Factory in the Hidden Well

"My mistress Yaqut Khan"—Mayjan always referred to his mistress, Big Ruby, in the most formal possible way—"she specifically said that Dumboshi is not to touch this particular bundle." Mayjan was lawyerly in conveying the warning to Jummo: "It is for the son of Naeb al-Haram— the wealthiest man in Mecca. The entire neighborhood of al-Qatari will join with the people of al-Osaka to celebrate of the graduation of Naiab al-Harem's oldest son. He has completed his studies of the holy Qur'an in the school of the Hanbali imam in the Holy Mosque."

Big Ruby organized her shipments according to the skills and efficiency of al-Baikwaly's daughters. The rush jobs, the ones that called for little in the way or patience or perfection, she usually assigned to Dumboshi. Commissions from wealthy and demanding clients she gave to no one but Hannah, whose hands she could count on to work until perfection had been achieved. Again let me emphasize that this entire enterprise took place under Sheik al-Baikwaly's unsuspecting eyes, and under the protection of the god of the Old Well, who was living in disguise amid the well's ancient rocks, sipping the energy of the Khazar girls and drawing upon the long-dead fabrics, in effect turning them into maps showing the way to resurrection.

Do you know that I can draw the tiniest details of the place as clearly as if I'd lived there—without ever having seen it? It's a mystery to me how I managed to get inside a well so closely guarded, and buried in the deepest chamber of my mother's memory. Did I enter through the door of a dream? It is all a figment of my imagination? One way or another, in I went, through a tiny door or narrow window at the rear of Nara's living quarters. The well was dug into the rocks. I memorized every sodden animal skin lying there, every hank of hair on every piece of skin, and the gown made entirely of feathers (a treasure all by itself) that you, Hassan, had hidden from your beloved genii wife. Clever rambler that you are, you used every trick at your disposal to hide that gown—which, if I but dared to spread it out, would fly me up and over and under the whole Arabian Peninsula.

Maybe it was coincidence, maybe it was humble magic, but it happened that Nara discovered the well slumbering under her daughter's living quarters. She immediately grasped the significance of the innermost rocks—it was from these very stones that Father Adam's flesh had been formed. Every fissure of the rocks, polished to near-translucency, reflected images of strange creatures. In their pitch-black hearts the rock mirrors stored forbidden scenes; these scenes they spilled into the girl's open hearts and splashed over their intimate parts.

The old well lay at the center of my grandfather's mansion in a wing called the House of the Nabk Tree. Its location had been forgotten long, long ago. Once the living quarters had been built, blocking the entrance to the well, there was no way in except by the tiny door or the narrow window above the stone bench at the back of the room. On that bench Nara used to spread her little prayer rug to rest or pray on, and supervise her daughters in their tasks of mixing colors and dyeing fabrics, a complicated process that took place inside the well. She sorted the dyeing herbs and improvised combinations of herbs and nectars to achieve new rainbows of colors. Hour after hour she sat sifting safflowers and dried pomegranate skins, calculating how the colors would look when fixed. Meanwhile, inside the well, the three girls waded barefoot in satanically vivid colors. Their pants, hiked up to their knees, were decorated with gold-embroidered poetry.

Every second of the lives those Khazar girls lived was drenched in their all-night vigils in the hidden well. Its nooks and crannies gazed in lust upon their bare legs, their naked arms, the guileless glimmering in their eyes. Their legs glittered.

What's wrong now, my friend? Your letter arrived with a frown on its face. You sent the Rescue Map's incense asking for help again!

You didn't really give yourself enough time before surrendering to despair. You moan, you whine, you play fast and loose with the story about my grandmother and the well, tossing words into the fire, erasing lines wholesale, even editing out a demon by the name of Rainbow. Such things, according to you, don't belong in a story about Jummo. You take liberties with the agreement we made at the start of our correspondence. I'm not about to renege on the rights I granted you, but can't I persuade you to listen to a little more about the well? Just let it be what it is—a brief theater for the girls' dyes, blank patches of cloth and skins transformed into glorious suns that rise to play starring roles in the life of Mecca.

You may go now, closet goldsmith—go and bend and forge and hammer and wring and flex whatever words you like. Shape your story, arrange your *objets* till you find the shape that gives you peace and contentment. Sidi Wahdana seduced you into playing his role. You are tempted, aren't you, by the thrill of killing, or conferring life, merely by glancing at my words.

The map's incense, by the way, also attracted the attention of my dark sister Krazat al-Yosir. She came to me burning incense she'd concocted from the feathers of my own genii. Krazat had fallen under Sidi's spell, too. Listen to the coquettish dying fall in her voice when she flirts with him (*Oh Sid-eeee . . .*), all the while burning incense to bring him out in the open so he can seduce still more of Mecca's women. She's getting him set to drive us all crazy and monopolize the story. Just listen:

"Oh SID-eee! Can't you feel how much vitality there is in this Sidi of ours? Have you got any idea how much sheer life there is inside him? When he walks down Mecca's streets, can he stop for a drink, can he nibble a piece of bread? He is molded from the energy pulsing through our city. This supreme sort of energy exists to be touched. My hand trembles at the thought of touching him. Let your words come closer. Touch him."

Jummo's laughter rattles the leaves of the *nabk* tree. She snatches the pilgrim's bundle. With pilgrims' fabrics she goes wild, embroidering them any way she likes, using unlikely combinations of dyes, sewing snatches of this and that into *jubbahs* and *keffiyehs,* and sending them all over the world. They return to Baikwaly's daughters telling horror stories about pilgrims' journeys, wild yarns about the wonders of the incense roads, about lands where the sun is ignorant of sunset.

Peacocks strut between the stones of the well and its drying pits, pausing only to scratch around in the holding tanks dug into the walls. Nara keeps watch, sitting on her prayer rug waiting for Sheik al-Baikwaly to make an appearance, dozing now and then, waking to pour another cup from the teapot that never runs dry. She sits timelessly, dozing, sipping weak Khazar tea sweetened with barley sugar. The girls go on wading in the Henna of the Unknown.

Nara dreams she's a perfumer, a pharmacist, a magician who mines yellow dye from the gallbladders of living creatures—green dye from irises blooming in the Empty Quarter's Sea of Quicksand (known in the fabric trade as Umm-As-Smeem), from which no swimmer has ever returned; blue dye from enormous whales inhabiting the hills of al-Soman. Black she milks from the eyes of the girls of al-Nowaria, whose eyes are famous for their dazzling whites and deep blacks.

18. Jummo's Alphabet Game

Mayjan, the Khazar messenger boy, shuttles between al-Baikwaly's daughters and the pharmacist's shop carrying fabrics rare as rainbows.

Al-Baikwaly's daughters spread them out in their well, splashing the stony udders of the wall with inks from Yemen and sketching images of plants and animals from the mountains of al-Sorat. They're producing clothes for foreign pilgrims and local worthies who frequent the holy circle of the sacred mosque. The red waxen seals on Mayjan's cheeks melt and dribble into Jummo's dyes, which are looking bloodier by the minute. To all of this Sheik Baikwaly is oblivious, convinced that his daughters are dutifully studying the opening chapter of Qur'an, the chapter titled "Concerning What?"

Jummo is expert at hiding Mayjan's name in anything she embroiders, whether it be *keffiyehs* for pilgrims or *jubbahs* for the leading men of Mecca. Everywhere he turns Mayjan comes face to face with his name cunningly embroidered on *keffiyehs* worn by worshippers walking in ritual circles around the shrine of the Sacred Stone, their minds dissolving with God's praise while they recite the Qur'an. Mayjan is touched; indeed he is shaken to the core, and when the *keffiyehs* venture out into the streets and alleys, he feels his soul has been splattered across every dormer and teak window frame in the city. He is possessed by a voice that pursues him wherever he runs or hides, captured by the electricity of the serpent coiled in every *keffiyeh* and *jubbah,* striking at him with red-hot fangs.

Panting, rigid with anticipation, he arrives to pick up the girls' finished work. He carries the tied-up bundles all the way to al-Hajla Road, clutching them to his chest. He sets them down in the shade of the mayor's house and frantically starts searching for his name, secretly and endlessly improvised upon, in Jummo's bundle. Always Jummo surprises him, tucking his name away in some unlikely place. She might, for example, magically blend the letter M in the weave of the *keffiyeh*'s star-spangled border. Or she might wrap up the M cocoonlike, so that it seems a belly button around which the *keffiyeh* twirls like an orbiting body. Or, maliciously, she might tease the spirit of the letter J and send it writhing and twisting like a snake disguised as the contorted crescent moon.

Mayjan is captivated by Jummo's unpredictable talent for arousing M to the highest pitch of ecstasy, wringing from it every last story and strange creature it's trying to hide. (Letters, as everyone knows, are pathways, that is to say, singular orbits in which unimaginable creatures lurk, and it is our task to explore the miraculous worlds they trace.) Mayjan suspects—he *knows*—that with every twist of her thread Jummo is calling him, not to say confusing him, by drowning the M in a sea of fabric and inflicting the J with thirst, until he can feel her thirst inflaming him to the point where he feels about to burst. From every *keffiyeh* he passes on the city's narrow streets, the plaintive calls of the letter Y leap at him, their yearnings flickeringly reflected in the water-spattered paving stones. (Despite the desert heat, the streets of Mecca are generally peaceful and cool, with water constantly trickling in the cracks between the gray pavers.)

Mayjan cannot grasp the depths of the letter game Jummo is playing with him. But he is enraptured by its pleasures, even though they are more than he can bear. The more Jummo delves into the secrets of his name, the more he feels imprisoned, especially when she gets a grip on his *alif*, the master letter-root of his body. When her fingers close over his *alif*, it becomes aroused and grows in power, its force spreading up and down his spine as if constructing something. Or tearing something down. Jummo is the master of Mayjan's *alif*, and *alif* is the master of his body.

19. Mayjan's Pilgrimage

He spends a few nights in his cabin high on Mount Hindi meditating on the mysteries of his name. "This name is *alive*," he tells himself. "It is a key to the puff of air responsible for my birth, the vagrant breeze that gives birth to us all . . ."

Mayjan is young enough to assume that everything that happens is his fault. And because he has such a great need to be lord and master of himself, he has always believed, ever since he left his mother's knee, that he should never expose his true self. The result is that he's cut off contact with people who try to reach him. "It's too late for regrets," he assures himself regretfully. Every day he feels more acutely how dangerous Jummo's hold on his name has become, and he realizes his chances of escape are getting slimmer.

Mayjan recalls the circumstances of his first trip to the Holy Land: The very first thing his mother did—he was seven at the time—was to slip off his name and hide it in the lining of his belt, where the letters arranged themselves in the semi-abstract shapes of flowering basil plants. In preparation for his difficult journey to the Holy Land, his mother insisted that he use a *nom de pilgrimage*—Qurdash. He became totally submerged in the disguise sounds of Qurdash, and virtually no trace of his true identity remained.

His mother especially wanted to be sure that her understood the danger of losing the sprig of basil in his belt, for it contained the sounds and spirits of his real name, Mayjan. Her parting advice to him was stitched into the lining: "The spirits of your name are your throne, and the bier that will carry you to your grave. To these two treasures are attached your ancestors, and your descendants as well. If you squander your true name or give it away, you will end up lost, a plaything of strangers and people of no substance, a wanderer in foreign lands, without the freedom to seek and follow the destiny that is your Holy Land. Do not reveal Mayjan to anyone until you come to the Holy Land, till you sit in the lap of Ishmael. There, and only there, can you be named again, and then you will be able to hear your true name in the divine presence, in God's own home, without any veil at all."

Mayjan was too young to grasp the meaning of this advice. He knew only that he was carrying a treasure in his belt and that it had something to do with the name Qurdash. He stayed in strict disguise all through his journey, never permitting any of the seven letters of his real name to trip on his tongue, nor even to linger in his mind. Many roads he traveled, with many caravans, and he went by many names, though mostly he called himself Qurdash.

He arrived safely in the holy city of Mecca. The first thing he did was unbutton his belt and release the name Mayjan. He believed he was following his mother's advice, but in fact he was about to be taken captive, in the Holy Land itself, by a woman with homicidal tendencies.

One morning, shortly leaving the house of Sheik al-Baikwaly, Mayjan found himself in the low-lying neighborhood called al-Hajla, encircled by children wearing gold-embroidered *jubbahs*. Mayjan, a simple lad from

Khazar-land, was too busy rummaging about in his knapsack looking for *keffiyehs* embroidered with his name to notice he was being surrounded. The children scampered around him, snatching his *keffiyehs* and old-fashioned knitted hats, draping the garments over their heads and galloping off on their hobbyhorses toward their homes. The children shrieked, their horses whinnied. Mayjan tripped and fell. He sat helplessly on the ground, watching his name embroidered across the *keffiyehs* on top of the children's heads. He took momentary comfort in the way the fireflies stitched into his *keffiyeh* just barely concealed his name.

A sharp clap came from the upper windows of the mayor's house. The ringleader of the swarming children understood at once that this was an order from his mother to stop fooling around with the stranger's stuff.

Every Friday from then on the women of al-Hajla sat at their windows watching and waiting for Mayjan to appear with his bundles, sneaking looks at the melancholy Khazar lad hunkered down on a doorstep, rummaging through his bundle of *keffiyehs*. Whenever he took out the one embroidered with his name and wrapped it around his head, they read the story emblazoned on it: the tale of the Khazar lover who flew away on rapturous wings and vanished, leaving not a trace behind. In Mayjan's body language the women could clearly read Love, which set their hearts a-quivering and their minds a-fluttering. Many a somber Meccan sunset they whiled away speculating about the charms of Mayjan's nameless lover.

"Foreigners are strange," one of the women remarked. "All the young men are head over heels in love with mermaids who swim in their way-faraway seas. Take this young man, for instance, the one with the moony face—he's totally obsessed with one of those notorious embroidery girls. Every Friday afternoon he sees her face in a *keffiyeh*."

"No doubt about it," said another woman, "he's possessed—God preserve us—by Bism Allah al-Rahman al-Raheem. Yes, the geniis have dazzled him with their scribblings—they look like hen's scratching to me—or maybe he's been hypnotized by one of her fancy stitches. Who knows? Either way, he might as well be blind when it comes to females of the human kind. So please, for God's sake, let's just keep the kids away from that damn bundle of his."

In the upper window, the mayor's wife clapped her hands again. Each time she did this, a child returned some portion of Mayjan's bundle. The last to obey was the mayor's son, who circled Mayjan in a final display of bravado, singing, *"Here comes the lady falcon, the big bad bird! Where's she coming from, coming from, coming from . . . "* approaching, closing the circle, till he stood directly behind Mayjan and deposited the last of the *keffiyehs* on the messenger boy's head.

Mayjan felt the magical M burning into his forehead, and in a flash the letters of his name were branded on his temples. He adjusted the *keffiyeh* and strode through Mecca proclaiming the urgent sense of oneness that drove him on, the perfect unity of the Ms and Js of their two names, Mayjan and Jummo.

20. *Candy Love*

It was you, my friend, who sent your curiosity to root around for more information about the secret of Mayjan and Jummo. This secret was buried during their lifetime and it's never really had a chance to resurrect itself, or catch its breath. You should know that I don't have much to say about it, since most of it was smothered by Nara's silence and Hannah's and Zubayda's winks. Love is a woman's possession, and about a woman's property there is no discussion, never.

Most of the details would've been forgotten if it hadn't been for Joman, my older sister and heir to that particular female memory. Joman had little patience for my earnest interrogations. She might sketch a hazy scene here, an incident there. Yet she spoke as an eyewitness, even though most of Mayjan's story happened before Joman was an itch in my father's backbone, and she embellished her stories with so many tiny details that it seemed she was inhabiting Jummo's own memory. But let's not forget that it was Jummo and Jummo alone who lived those brief moments that were snatched by memory from time.

◆   ◆   ◆

Three knocks on Sheik Baikwaly's door: recognizing Mayjan's rhythm, Jummo hurried to let him in. He stooped through the low archway. He was knocked off-balance when Jummo grabbed the sweet-smelling package attached to his tattered belt, which he'd fashioned from an old python skin. He gasped when her hand groped his waist; he gasped when she jabbed him to get him to let go of the package. He bent down and tried to hide the package under the *nabk* tree. He never took his eyes off Jummo, who was already climbing the tree and munching *fofuk bijawa*, a candy of incendiary sweetness made from ginger and burnt sugar.

Nara pounced on the bundle, searching for Big Ruby's instructions. Mayjan, wholly intent on the burnt sugar and ginger on Jummo's tongue, was deaf to Nara's questions. Every time Jummo pursed her lips and licked the candy, his heart fluttered. He tasted the sparks of sweetness her tongue was tasting. Her tongue was licking his spine, her tongue was an animal lapping his heart, her tongue . . .

Jummo sensed some lowly creature looking at her. She reprimanded him with her stuck-out tongue; he fell back. His eyes clouded over. He shuddered at the taste of sugar and fire; he staggered under her tongue.

When he came to, Nara was scratching one of God's names on his forearm with her fingernails. "Peace be with you," she said. "Now move—get going. Come back Friday."

Nara's glare was intended to make Mayjan pull himself together. This he tried to do because he didn't want Nara to see how far gone he was in the throes of passion. If she did, she might resort to veiling her daughter. (In Mecca, quarantine was the preferred method for dealing with serious illness and infectious diseases.)

Mayjan scoured the market of al-Masa'a for the finest sweets from the Yemenites' stalls. He tied a bundle of them to his waist to serve as bait for Jummo. He ran straight to al-Baikwaly's doorstep, thinking only of the spot where he'd tied the package of candies. The location varied: sometimes he tied it around his waist, sometimes around his neck so it dangled over his heart, and once he tied it around his right bicep—each time a new target for Jummo's touch. He deliberately chose his most vulnerable spot to guarantee that she would touch him as deeply and dangerously as possible. Jummo was like a hawk; she never missed her prey, and her talent for teasing the mortal limits of Mayjan's senses was masterful. She was instinctively aware of the power she held over her disciple. She reveled in that power and the authority it conferred.

21. Mother's Suffocation

You surprise me. I'm baffled by your insistence on writing, when all you really need to do is rest after years of searching. You quit your craft of goldsmithery for humansmithery. You fashioned a flesh-and-blood lover endangered by wild storms. Actually, the storms were stirred up your lover's willfulness. She was a wench, that one, always exaggerating the distance between the two of you just for the sake of having love problems to analyze.

Let us pray, let us think, let us sigh. No matter how closely we examine our images of extinguished loves, no matter how tender the light, they remain obscure. They only make us feel more acutely the chasm between this world and any other conceivable world, and agonize over the gaps between the various worlds we experience at different stages of our lives.

For instance, there will always be a gulf between the blue house we lived in so many years ago in Taif and the sternly shapeless modern houses we live in now—between our rootless contemporary home and al-Baikwaly's house with its *nabk* tree, between all these dwellings and the great mansion that came later. All the originality is gone now, and the grandeur. That's why I prefer to go back to the *nabk* tree house, or to my father's house, or to the blue house. Whatever we lived through in that blue kingdom had the cast of blue to it—the soothing blue used by my mother to deal with the problems flung at her by the bloody claws of raw experience. So poised Hannah was, never down, never depressed. Even when my father tried to suffocate her she came through with remarkable serenity. Even if she were to have died in the pit of oppression, she still would have glided serenely to the cemetery, casting her calming spell on us, soothing our hearts.

There you go again, interrupting me with brittle questions: "What kind of man would dare strangle his wife? Or burn her?"

Permit me to satisfy your curiosity with a disturbing story.

Wintertime in Taif meant fire; winter summoned fire like an icy temptress.

We went camping often, tracking the cold weather down wintry roads, trekking wherever the paths led us. We pitched our tents by the sides of roads as crooked as dropped strings. We kept the icy winds at bay by setting our campfires in a roaring oval, like Bedouins drawing circles in the naked sand so they could sleep undisturbed by scorpions. We arranged our circles of fire in the ocean of boulders covering Mount Hada. Our flame army—blue soldiers, green soldiers, red soldiers, purple soldiers; pale, colorless soldiers, too—patrolled the against the cold, which dared not shatter our consecrated circle.

Inside our ring of fire we sat, shivering not because of the cold but at the thought of scorpions who might be wandering in the winds, waiting for an opening in our fire-fortress, ready to bridge the flames by hopping on one another's backs, forming a spear made of wind and poison to break down our barricade. We held our breath while the winds howled, pummeling us like a solid thing, clutching at us, whirling, wriggling with the energy of baby scorpions riding on their mother's yellow back, subsiding for a moment while we grabbed onto one another in mimicry of the baby scorpions' clumsiness, feigning helplessness so they could ride in on the shell of their enormous mother's scorpion-wind.

So there it was—can you still see it?—the deadly thing itself, the instinct to slaughter, the rider and the ridden driving one another to destruction.

In such a primal, virgin environment there was no quarter given, no room for half-measures. Here all creatures were bound to push the limits of their natures—the way you pushed on to the outer reaches of your Never-Never Land, the Isle of Waq al-Waq.

No matter how far I lead you in other directions, you always come back to the victim's story.

It's true, my father was passionately in love with *nabk* fire, with the heavenly scent of smoke from the *nabk* tree. I remember every fire lit in our blue house in Taif. My father would bring huge braziers into the room where he spent the night with my mother, kindling their passion, rhyming their caresses with the rise and fall of the fire's glow.

In some dim way we children lived those rhyming couplets, too—at a distance, of course, from behind walls and locked doors, in a hazy dream, dark and chilly. We were imprinted with my mother and father's private tempos, high-pitched as Heaven (and as deep), just as their rhythms were tuned to the vagaries of light and shadow and the sudden intrusions of children. We woke in the middle of the night, hearing nothing, seeing no further than our noses, sensing only a ripple in the darkness, feeling The Unseen squirming deep inside us, frightened and excited, lurking under our mosquito nets and listening to our hearts thumping, knowing there was some spot, some central spot in the universe that was excruciatingly awake, spiraling up and up and up to its shattering point.

We pressed our hands over our hearts to keep track of the heaving in the fabric of the world, following its every movement, watching for our chance to break into the rhyming couplets as their rhythm grew more frantic. It never failed: we cried out at the crucial moment, disturbing my father and mother and their immaculate fire.

It was in Taif, far from Grandfather Baikwaly's house, that my mother's suffocation took place. My father had extended his stay in our summer house to enjoy the peace and coolness of the mountains. Grandmother Nara kept wondering where Hannah was.

When Scorpio came to dominate the heavens, and still Hannah failed to appear, Nara began to grumble. "Libra's breath chills standing water," she said. "When Scorpio rises, it's time for old folks to sell their ladders and buy wool blankets." Which meant the end of mild weather in the mountains of Taif, no more evenings spent on the roof. Scorpio's appearance in the sky was no laughing matter.

One night when Scorpio rose high, my father arranged for a long session of rhyming couplets (or "making the Khazar beast"). The door to my parents' room was shut.

Mother and father were nearly asphyxiated by wood smoke from their braziers. It was a miracle that father woke up and managed to stumble outside. Mother remained unconscious.

At dawn, my mother started floating back and forth across the low morning sun like a kite, tethered only by the string of our belief that she would never leave us. She continued to soar through the warm, windless afternoon and into twilight, never landing. We cried more tears than the waterfalls of al-Mosul. My father's sturdy constitution enabled him to come down to earth sooner. He staggered around in a feverish trance.

Soon there appeared grimly serious people carrying dark little bags. The people inspected my mother's sleep, then disappeared and reappeared with pills, with shots and ointments and lotions and potions, in endless attempts to retrieve her from her unreachable flight.

Sunset veiled the sky, brought her down and deposited her in our helpless hands, weak and semiconscious.

A shadow moved in the gloom, a slender shadow with seven braids. It passed in front of the braziers before falling across my mother. It stared at us with stark white eyes, then disappeared.

"*Bism Allah,*" Grandmother Mosliya said. "The arrow of God's name has struck."

She tried to keep us occupied. She set about measuring the bolts of white cotton my mother was going to be buried in. Spellbound, we started helping her, measuring, cutting and counting the precise amount of winding cloth till the shrill, slicing sound of it—*shhuuurrrt!*—echoed in our bones. At some point during this professionally detached chore, our younger brother Daj al-Layl went limp, wrapped his weary body in the winding sheets, and fell asleep. Nabee Jan, our older brother, leaned over him and wept, breaking Grandmother Mosliya's concentration. She flew at us, her face a sharp, angry triangle. She swept us up and set us on the window seat. Her steel-hard eyes dried the tears on our cheeks.

"Now listen," she said evenly, "your mother is dying. And if you don't start behaving, you'll find yourself wearing casts and splints—we're going to have to break those stubborn bones of yours and reset them." Her voice cut like a speechifying wind through the icy blasts rattling the windows.

◆　　　◆　　　◆

After Mosliya's threat we were relieved to see my mother breathing softly, pacing around shadow-like. She gathered us up, sheltering us from the old woman's designs on our bodies, which were already crooked with fear.

We never forgave my grandmother for what she said, even though we never quite understood what she was saying. Certainly she hadn't meant to hang the sword of death over our heads just for the sake of making us obey. Mosliya was not evil. She was old and lonely, she wanted power. We read her as best we could with our young eyes. Hers was an aging, elegant body inhabited by a lonely soul, though she was always with us; the family never left her alone. We moved from one place to another as one unit, from which Mosliya was absent only when she chose to be. The inventory of her soul included our house on the slopes of Mecca, her twenty female slaves, and the gold boxes she flipped open the night of my grandfather Abdul-Hai's death. They lived in her, and she lived in them. These objects were her life.

It must be clear to you by now that whatever happens, whatever the intention, all roads lead to the victim, to the killing and the sacrificing. Yet the idol behind the sacrifice remains masked. There is no hammer, no chisel, no words that can bring its shape out into the open.

But roads have a will of their own. Roads can make up their minds to follow routes planned by mere mortals like us, though we lack your tools of survival, Hassan. How I envy you your Invisibility Hat and your Scepter of the Seven Genii Kings, not to mention the Flying Red Roman Vase that can fly to safe harbor over stormy seas, through desert heat and shrieking winds. We haven't been lucky enough to inherit the cleverness of geniis who've spent centuries transforming their secrets into musical instruments that can tune all times and places to perfection.

You can see me now, can't you, wandering beside you on the road to our faraway Taif? Of course, you can—you're a master of the faraway—and how far away is Taif compared to your Isle of Waq? Or compared to the distance I keep between the two of us to make room for this story? Don't forget—I warned you at the start—I've been threatening to scatter you to the winds. And scattered you would truly feel you if I disclosed the real *my* of my secret.

22. Death and Games

In the holy circle that is the city of Mecca, darkness rules even in the courtyards where lamps burn brightly. Midnight drinks deeply from the dark mountains ringing the city.

Blackness prevailed over my mother's children, claiming the first five of them, one after another, till the cold volcanoes relaxed their grip on the city and my mother's tree of life sprouted five living children to replace the ones she'd lost. Which is to say that things worked out equitably for the descendents of al-Maghrabi: five for the blackness of Sidi's eyes, five for the whiteness.

The name of the first child, Hiyat, means "life." She was premature, and a septet, meaning that she lived seven days, just long enough to experience the ceremonies celebrating her birth. Every member of Mohammed al-Maghrabi's family—including some deceased ancestors, from great-grand-grandfather Ahmid to uncle Salih (and, of course, Sidi Wahdana)—attended the climactic celebration on the seventh day of Hiyat's life. In the sunny sitting room of the grand house they witnessed the conferring of her name, and they watched when the name of God was whispered in the infant's ear, imprinting the holy sound in her little mind.

"He that is Alive . . . new life . . . old life. . . ." Everyone heard the illustrious dervish invoking The Unknown, and everyone picked up his cry, calling out the baby's name: "Hiyat . . . Life . . ."

Her sputtering newborn vitality they left in the hands of fate.

Death carried her off gracefully.

The Septet is still sleeping peacefully, just as she was during the celebration of her seventh day, buried under the floor of the great hall of my grandfather's house, wrapped in her satin head-covering embroidered with pearls and gold. They lowered her in a sort of giant sieve, shaking it to rid her soul of bad luck, and laid her to rest amid the clicking of pebbles and mortar.

Mohammed al-Maghrabi couldn't bear being separated from his firstborn, not even by death; Hiyat was buried under the floor where later on we all would play, to be lulled by the mansion's intimate noises and the bustling of its busy days. There she will lie forever, changeless under jet-black flagstones of Yemenite onyx.

We passed those carefree days with cowry games. Our neighbor Sindiya was an expert at deciphering the twists and turns and shapes of female cowry shells—she was the next best thing to a fortune-teller. A twist to the right signified smooth sailing; a turn to the left meant rocky roads ahead. A diagonal ripple was a sure sign of surprises, and more surprises. (There is no way to read fortunes using male cowries, for the obvious reason that it is not possible to entice fortunes to take an interest in male cowries, because the blindness that afflicts male shells precludes the possibility of their providing a stable platform for fortunes when they descend from the Great Tableau, upon which, since before the birth of Adam, all human fates have been inscribed.)

My grandfather Abdul-Hai did his best to break up our fortune-telling sessions and shoo away "those fortune-snatching females," as he called our readers of fates. "Fortune telling," he said, "prevents the supplicant's forty prayers from entering the first door of Heaven. Since our prayers have seven Heavens to travel to, what will become of us if the first door is shut in their face?" He convinced us that whatever took our attention away from God would one day lead to misery and devastation.

So Hiyat slept, sheltered in the cool ground, sharing the smallest details of our lives, counting each cowry shell, every click-clack of our marbles.

The female cowries did not rest until they'd driven Hannah away from al-Mosliya's fort.

"Her first-born was a girl," Mosliya said. "So she's been riding her steed backward." In the parlance of Mecca, where everyone believed that husbands were beasts to be given their freedom (albeit beasts who could be tamed by expert hands), this meant that Hannah had her husband under control. But Hannah's sweet disposition could not dispel the increasingly warlike atmosphere in Grandmother Mosliya's household. And so the branch had to break away from the trunk: Mohammed al-Maghrabi left his family's home and bid farewell to the verandas overlooking the Holy Mosque for a succession of houses scattered across the hills and valleys of Mecca.

23. Hannah's Miscarriage

"The miscarriage took me by surprise while I was washing at the sink . . ."

Hannah bent over and let the river of blood run down between her legs. It mixed with the silvery ash-water used by the women of Mecca to clean their men's white clothes.

The night before her miscarriage, Sidi Wahdana visited Hannah in a dream. He appeared standing by the door of her *kharija,* her sky-lit room. When she made a move in the direction of the brazier in her *mabeet,* her private room, he blocked her way. She stood facing him, not knowing what to do. He reached out with his left hand. Bewitched, she extended her right hand. Sidi took it. Hannah made a fist. One by one he pried her fingers loose, first her middle finger, then the ring finger, then the forefinger. Each finger, as he loosened it, turned into a green bird. The birds flew up and hovered over Hannah's head till she was crowned with a green-birded crown the likes of which had never been seen by human eyes.

Sidi contemplated her crown. "Ridwan's courtiers . . . " he said at last, referring to the angels guarding the gate of Paradise. With his forefinger he pointed to Hannah's crown. The five birds soared straight up into the sky. The amazing thing about their flight was that they never broke formation; they maintained, as if mounting a ladder, the perfect circle of the crown. They disappeared from Hannah's sight. She lowered her gaze. Sidi was gone, vanished into a small green vent in the floor of the *kharija.*

When Hannah looked more closely at the vent, she saw five chairs lined up next to a gate made of emerald, a gate so toweringly tall that no eye could see all the way to the top. Hannah couldn't help noticing that the sides of the gate were embossed with circular letters arranged in repetitive patterns, the letters constantly turning in on themselves and assuming new shapes. This made her dizzy.

She looked away to the five chairs. They were made of solid silver and inlaid with pearls, and each chair was crowned by one of the five green birds that had sprouted from her fingers. The birds were chirping with a rhythm that blocked the beating of her pulse. She gasped.

Mohammed al-Maghrabi shook her awake in mid-gasp, rescuing her fibrillating heart.

At dawn she approached the bucket of ash-water with a feeling of apprehension. She couldn't put her finger on the source of her fear, though last night's dream was fresh in her mind. Her eyes scanned the room for the little green vent.

She used a cup to scoop more ashes into the water (the ashes, after soaking overnight, were heavy). She poured the infusion into the basin and when she sat down to start washing, she noticed a black shape clouding the clarity of the ash-water. She dipped her hand into the water and when she lifted it, a substance she took to be ashes escaped into the sink. Her middle finger brushed against something alive in a jelly-like way. Startled, she drew back her hand.

She remembered the touch of Sidi's hand on her hand, first on her middle finger. Dismissing her fear, she picked up her husband's turban to wash it. When she looked again into the sink, the black cloud had taken on the exact shape of Sidi's eye, and it was weeping and glaring at her with dark intensity, its tears seeping into the ash-water. His eye kept crying, kept staring at her.

Sidi disappeared as suddenly as he had appeared, and the water ran clear again. Hannah resumed washing. When she dipped her hands in the water, a shiver ran through her, down to the pit of her belly. A spasm of pain wracked her. Blood flooded her thighs.

She waited calmly until she'd discharged the last shred of fetal matter. She resumed her washing. She stood up to hang the wet clothes in the *kharija*. She didn't lie down in bed till she'd finished her domestic chores.

Her husband discovered the clot of congealed blood between her legs.

The scent of amber filled the house. Only then did everyone understand that a miscarriage had taken place, and that a fetus had been washed down the drain of the house on the slopes of al-Shamiya, all the way down to the great well called Yakhoor.

"The third miscarriage took me by surprise," Hannah said. "I was performing the ritual ablution for dawn prayer. I grabbed the silver water tap on the sink dug into the wall and I pushed. The placenta just slipped out."

Hannah reached down and with the tip of her finger she probed for the fetus's sexual identity. The male organ stood like the crescent of the moon.

We buried all our dead in the great hall of our house, under flagstones of Yemenite onyx. No fetus or short-lived baby was allowed to leave the family or go to the cemetery. For us the period of pregnancy extended from months spent in my mother's womb to years spent in the womb of our earth. And whenever, in order to remind us of Death, Dumboshi chose to walk across that dark spot at the very heart of the great hall, we could sense the babies crawling around underground and suckling the milk of our soil.

Dumboshi insisted that there would come a day when our brothers would be reborn into a clan made of red clay, and from their clay we would fashion vats to cool our water in. I have no idea where she cooked up such scarecrows, but she scattered them all through the stories she told whenever she took a mind to cross our grand hall, causing the Yemenite flagstones to quake under her steps and the delicately interlaced lines of white mortar smear across the onyx stones like the whites of cracked eggs. Again and again she insisted that the flagstones were about to hatch; any day now we'd be hearing their baby chicks clattering across our roof— which made us prick up our ears whenever the servants made our beds in the open-air *kharija*. We lay down with our hearts tuned to the flagstones at the center of the hall, waiting for the first clink to be made by our approaching clay-brothers. But the night sky over our house always pressed us back to earth.

Our brothers did appear, though—in the cyclonic shapes of shocking nightmares. We awoke in our snow-white mosquito nets and nuzzled against my sister Joman, begging her to hold us tight, to hold us forever. She spent the night gathering us in her warm, thin arms.

After Hannah's fourth miscarriage people began spreading a rumor that the cause was to be found in a curse written in ancient ink buried beneath al-Maghrabi's doorstep. Fingers were pointed in the direction of Mosliya, at those too-candid eyes of hers, and even at certain women frequently seen on Mecca's verandas (all of them in fact smarting with jealousy at their Khazar rival, Hannah), not to mention Zainub Kabliya, the pretty neighbor girl who sat by her window plucking her aloe-wood lute and singing:

> *Drink your own water, don't offer me sorbet;*
> *No God-fearing lover would water me that way.*

24. Death's Child

Sameer was conceived. Hannah brought him to full term. The day he was born, the house went wild with joy. All rumors of ancient talismanic inks under our doorstep were erased.

Sameer survived. By the first day of the Year of Ababeel's Birds, he was crawling. The Year of Ababeel's Birds commemorated an ancient Ethiopian king named Abraham who invaded Mecca with a horde of elephants and dusky soldiers only to be defeated by birds that swooped down and bombarded his army with smallpox. Shortly after Sameer turned two and was about to progress from crawling to walking, those very same birds were sighted over Mecca picking off several prominent citizens.

Hannah could not help noticing in Sameer's expression a resemblance to Death's Child, particularly in his eyes, which were so wide and penetrating that they seemed not to look at things, but into them and behind them, to gaze into The Unknown and cut a trail to what lay beyond, as if obeying an urgent command issued from the depths of his soul.

"Sidi's eye . . ." Hannah muttered. "Yes, this is the eye that can drown whole oceans full of people and stones, the torch that can incinerate any wall, can reduce the blindness of barriers to rubble."

She stifled her nameless fear (she was doubly afraid that naming it would bring it to life). She became acutely self-conscious about her forefinger, the finger Sidi had used to shape her circle-crown of green birds.

Death's Child, clad in his diaper, followed her with his eyes wherever she went, keeping her under surveillance, scrutinizing every move she made in the exquisitely finite space-time inhabited by mothers and their children. Hannah, herself endowed with an eye like a searchlight, caught little glimpses and overheard little things that lead her to believe more and more each day that Sameer was looking out onto a Time different from the time she could see and that he was destined to look only briefly on the days of this time, this ordinary here and now, and that he would move on, though before he passed away no detail of their life together would escape the attention of his piercing eyes.

Death's Child kept his eyes open all day long. Never once did he let his guard down or close his eyes, not until his gaze came to rest on the face of his father, for on his father's face he saw the whole world struggling. The rhythms in the rise and fall of human striving, the lows and the highs—all these he read in his father's face. He learned what there was to know about the fine line separating birds and human beings, the porous border between blood and water. He missed nothing, certainly not the smallpox that was wandering from house to house, filling the cemeteries, offering no truce.

Hannah's forefinger became terribly swollen; it was as if the Smallpox Demon had taken up residence in it. Her awareness increased of Sameer's knowing eye—which, even without smallpox, would have been enough to carry the child away. Indeed, Sameer's extreme sensitivity would have killed him outright had it not been for a neighbor lady named Qatana. Qatana came to the house and took Death's Child in charge, cradled him in her arms and singing lullabies while he looked up at her, studying her face and what lay behind her face. His knowingness pierced her like a hot iron.

"What's going on, Mosliya? Your children are so hot-tempered! The older ones are hot peppers, the little ones are ginger." Qatana gasped, and as she did, her Evil Eye hit the child, though she was not aware of it.

The moment she left, a bird dropped the lethal seed on Sameer. Pustules of smallpox broke out on his face, then spread over the rest of his body. Hannah, calm as a stone, continued to nurse him, pushing her nipples between his blistered lips, patiently waiting. Milk . . . pus . . . the life force of Death's Child oozed away. His soul, his full-of-life soul, dribbled all over Hannah's breasts and arms.

He waited for his father to make an appearance before taking his leave. He looked one last time into the shadows, sucked one last tearing suck at Hannah's nipple, and died.

Hannah felt his final suck from head to toe, in every vein and nerve and fiber of her being. She fainted.

She remained unconscious during the funeral ceremonies. All the sheiks of al-Shamiya trudged down the slopes to the Holy Mosque. Sameer was the first of our dead to be buried in al-Maala, our city's cemetery.

You might well ask, what all this has to do with Dumboshi and the conspiracy that ended up paralyzing her? May I reply that this is not just one story but a way of life that is being laid bare?

I might also say, by way of justifying my digressions, that every page contributes to a clearer picture of the conflicts in Mecca's households, and that all of this helps explain the conspiracy against Dumboshi. I could, of course, resort to any number of rationalizations, but in the end they amount only to mumblings designed to conceal a secret.

Because I can't imagine how our exchange of letters could explain the steps leading to murder. I will not offer you a redeeming motive, I will not explain these interruptions in the story. I will not claim that there is a plan behind these confessions, because from the beginning I've never understood why Hannah chose this time and not some other time to talk about her three miscarriages and the two children who died so young. She said she could still see them in her dreams, all five children coming to meet her at the Gate of Paradise, carrying silver pitchers brimming with heavenly water from the River al-Salsabeel. Whenever Hannah slept she saw her children walking across dunes made of pearls, their feet reeking of musk and camphor, the perfumes of death (in Heaven, the dead wear Heaven's scents). They waited for her at Heaven's gate, flickering like lightning, famished for the sight of her.

I can feel my mother's warmth even now, in the deepest part of me. I can still see her sitting in the hot sun telling us funny stories about her life while she embroidered pillows for us, her five surviving children of this world. Pillows to dream on.

The instant she heard the summons to afternoon prayer, she put aside her needle and thread to concentrate on the muezzin's voice. She repeated every word of his call, clearly enunciating God's praise and her submission to His power and will. She puffed air into her palms and buried her face in her hands. She raised her face to Heaven and wiped her cheeks. Once she was certain that the echoes of the muezzin's call had entirely died away, she picked up her embroidery again.

"If I kept on embroidering during the call to prayer," she told us, "it would make holes in the silver pitchers in my children's' hands in Heaven and they would be running back and forth like crazy birds with water splashing all around, never reaching me. Because every stitch I make while the muezzin is calling makes a hole in my children's' pitchers, and in the pitchers carried by the angels in Paradise."

As for Jummo—from the day she entered al-Maala cemetery to the day of her resurrection, she would be what they call a "chopped-down tree"—there would be no miscarried child with a silver pitcher to meet Jummo at Heaven's gate. The only thing waiting for Jummo would be the verses she used to make maps and locks and gates and colonnades that sometimes opened to greet her and sometimes blocked her way into The Unknown, into regions no eye had ever seen, no heart ever dreamed. Nothing and no one but Jummo's own self (and Sidi) awaited her in the afterlife. She and Sidi were as one—Sidi whom she created with her words; Sidi who, for all we knew, could be a merciful rain or a punishing torrent.

"Did it hurt a lot, losing all these babies?" my sister Krazat al-Yosir asked after the call to prayer.

A shadow of sadness, an agonized blankness, clouded my mother's face. She recovered immediately and glanced at my father, who looked worried. My mother never, not even in extreme pain, lost her mastery of the ways of love. "Oh, someone punched my pillow," she said, smiling almost coquettishly by way of translation: yes, she had suffered losses, yet she still had many of the things most precious to her. "Except for the unbearable thing . . . " her eyes said, " . . . losing our prince . . . "

Her illiterate eloquence melted my father's heart and made him fall even more deeply in love with her. "Oh yes," he told us, "in those days people came and tried to provoke me, tried to turn me against your mother. 'Hannah is like a cat,' they said, 'eating her children.'"

Mohammed al-Maghrabi, the son of a falconer, understood that his freedom was subject to the will of his falcon-mate, and he knew that she didn't fancy releasing him yet. Every word she uttered was nuanced with a mixture of desire and threat, a skill that made Mohammed worship her as if she ruled the heavens over his head. This man came from a line of scholars whose arsenal for doing battle in this world included poetry and sacred scripture, but little else. And this was a primitive, powerful woman who captivated him, humbling him with honey sweet as the honey from the mountains of al-Shafa.

But Jummo, she was not gifted with honey. Jummo's gifts were candor and fearlessness in confrontation. Whatever crossed her mind found its way to her tongue without moderation or qualification. Tranquility had no attraction for her. She had no patience for fudging the facts, she made up her mind in a flash.

25. The Face on the Floor

Mayjan climbed toward his tin shack on Mount Hindi, close to the encampments of Turkish pilgrims to the Holy Land. He pushed through the crowds of white-scarfed Turkish girls, peeking at him through their palm-leaf shutters. Oblivious, he moved on, totally absorbed in digging up and turning over every stone on the mountain. He was looking for bits of onyx, the valuable ones with pale pink veins—these were the stones he would use to sculpt his vision. The Turkish girls giggled and winked and looked at him looking at the ground. He disappeared into his shack. They stood at a heartbroken distance and sighed.

One evening a pretty girl followed him all the way to his shack and peeked through the window to see what was going on inside. She saw the Khazar boy standing still on the threshold, not proceeding into the bare room. His eyes were fixed on the floor, studying the spot where he was about to kneel and pray, the exact spot that would come in contact with his forehead. By the dim light of the lantern dangling from the door, the girl was able to make out an image on the floor, a face made of onyx tiles, incredibly lifelike. The face was gazing rapturously into Mayjan's eyes. It was pale, especially around the temples. There was a hint of roses in the color of the lips, so blushingly vivid that the Turkish girl was certain she could hear them breathe a sigh that blew against the cheeks of the young man standing transfixed on the threshold. He was staring so intently that he seemed, even at his scrupulously maintained distance, to be licking beads of rose water from the lips of the mosaic.

The girl knew nothing about Jummo—otherwise she would have understood at once whose face was pictured on the floor. She was so astonished that she forgot how bare the shack actually was, and she focused on the rainbow rippling across the walls, spreading a banquet of colors in a design as firmly circular as a seal or a ring. The door, she noticed, was covered with a curtain fashioned from a *jubbah* that had been patched with bits of red and blue fabric. The entire shack was curtained with clothes Jummo had made for Mayjan from the cast-off clothing of rich people. Mayjan had made a point of not folding any of these handmade clothes; he'd hung them all up. The cabin pulsed with flaming hot colors.

The Turkish girl shuddered. She understood now that the Khazar youth came here to feed on the energy of the fabrics' colors while he worked at perfecting the miraculous mosaic face of the woman he loved. This lad standing on the threshold—he was bewitched, mysteriously bound to the animal force of the creature pictured on the floor.

Something snapped inside the Turkish girl. She ran off mumbling to herself, not looking back, tripping on the hem of her robe. When she reached the safety of her own shack, she sat down in a corner and clutched herself to cover her shivering for fear it would betray the things she'd seen in the shack . . . in that dream.

Mayjan made a rule, whenever he came to the shack, of taking off his shoes at the threshold. He worked on the face with bare hands and toes, adding a tile here, a tile there, reserving the blackest Yemenite onyx for the curls tumbling over Jummo's forehead. They took his breath away, her curls did, like the flowing mane of a fast horse.

Once he'd finished working on the curls, he was wracked by serious coughing spells. Mayjan was tubercular, but he insisted on spending night after moonlit night refining her neck, exaggerating its backward-leaning arch more and more until the sheer vitality and grace of the image made him go weak in the knees.

He was never satisfied. He ended each nightly session by doing a little more work on the eyes, polishing them to a high luster, letting the lightning in them strike his heart, knocking him out. He stretched out naked across the face. It flamed like the face of an ogress, cackling and scowling, then swept away like a meteor.

Mayjan's performances infiltrated other dreams taking place on the mountain. The Turkish girls became uneasy. They sensed a blazing thirst emanating from the Khazar boy's shack and they feared it might consume them all—people, plants and things—leaving not one thing of value that could be used to barter for their beauty. The fair-skinned Turkish girls commanded high bride prices.

Every night Mayjan fainted across that trap of a face—every night but Thursday. Thursdays he raised the lid of the trunk, the only proper piece of furniture in the room, and uncovered an ancient musical instrument: a lute made of aloe wood, shaped like a triangle and strung with ten doubled strings. Whoever made the instrument had gone to considerable effort to decorate its face with beautifully embossed symbols from many of the languages that used to be spoken in old Khazarland.

Mayjan tuned the strings and played music of intoxicating intensity. The lute came alive in his hands; he had only to touch it lightly and music poured out as lavishly as water over pagan waterfalls. Every Thursday, when the lute appeared, it would lend some of its fragrance to the mosaic on the floor, diffusing the glow of the face with clouds of aloe incense.

The uncovering of the lute was followed by the appearance of stars in Jummo's eyes. Mayjan was convinced that the onyx eyes of his beloved knew all about the ancient origins of the ten-stringed lute. Yet there was no other lute like it, neither ancient nor contemporary, and only Mayjan could make music on it; only his fingers could flutter like dove's wings on its strings and climb up and down the stepless ladder of its scales. The melodies he played were magically passionate, flowing like wine across the mosaic face.

Mayjan lay down and stretched out and rested his head across the throat of his beloved. His fingers raced over the lute strings, strumming sweet tunes, faster and faster and faster, never stopping, faster still, never resting till Jummo's face began to soften and swell with life, full to overflowing, and she began with a cooing whisper to whisper the most secret secrets of her heart into his heart.

The mountain calmed down.

Mayjan's snoring mingled with the chirping of crickets and frogs and the hissing of giant reptiles thought by untutored people to be merely mythological. The stones of Mount Hindi and the human beings sleeping there slumbered with a sweetness that echoed in their inmost hearts till the rising of the new day's sun.

On the night that Jummo fell sick with fever, Mayjan withdrew once again to the solitude of his shack. He brought along bags of unhusked wheat, and he spent the night scrubbing her onyx face with the grains, transferring their vital energy to the face. By sunrise all the husks had worn away from the grains of wheat; the golden seeds were bare.

The Turkish girls watched Mayjan reciting the sunrise prayer on the bare earth in front of his shack. As he was finishing his second repetition of the prayer, a flock of odd-looking birds entered his shack through an open window.

The sun climbed high in Mecca's sky. Mayjan went inside and started rubbing the husks of golden wheat against Jummo's pale face. Her pallor gave way to a glow. The smell of fresh clay and overripe wheat hung in the air.

At sunset Jummo's fever crested. Her skin cooled. Amber-colored beads of sweat sparkled on her breasts and arms.

Dawn of the following day: Mayjan was at al-Baikwaly's house, rapping on the door with his three familiar musical knocks. He sat down and waited under the dripping *nabk* tree. Nara slipped her warm loaves out of al-Nabk's oven. Mayjan inhaled the motherly scent down to his knees.

Shortly thereafter he took to visiting the eunuchs who served as custodians in the Holy Mosque. From them he obtained leftover essences of aged aloe wood, of musk and camphor (these scents were used to perfume the holy Kaaba, the Sacred Stone). With these supplies in hand, he hurried off to the onyx face of his beloved and set about polishing her features and pouring amber on her lips. He watered her and he drank from her lips. Their energies mingled.

26. Jummo's Vigil

It was the time of the year when people pitched tents in the Saraf Valley, near the grave of the Prophet's widow, Sitana Mymona. There were no green fields in the Valley of Saraf and no buildings of any kind; it was a barren plain crouching at the foot of low, shapeless mountains. Rocks and the occasional thorny shrub stood listlessly, half-listening to things no human could hear, straining to detect the prehistoric sighs and voices that had haunted the place ever since the day the Prophet's widow was buried there.

Still, this celebration was something to look forward to, and al-Baikwaly's daughters insisted on making an excursion to the campgrounds, which lay a day and a half from Mecca in a cheerful community of colorful tents. Meccans believed that the best way to pay one's respects to the dead was not to grieve but to celebrate life as it might be lived just for the joy of it, and to shower their joy on relatives, loved ones or strangers who happened to be lying under the ground. Thousands of people beat drums through the night, sang songs in time to the snorting of their camels, and recited poems in praise of the Prophet. The days were filled with races, sacrifices, and stunt-riding.

The women of Mecca had a tradition of paying extended visits to the graveyards. They pitched camp and hosted parties and gave lavishly to the poor who followed the winking lights of their caravans, streaming in from the surrounding valleys and deserts, having popped up, it seemed, from the earth itself in anticipation of the rain of gifts and happy times.

Wealthy people pitched their tents close to the grave of the Prophet's widow and the small white mosque that stood next to it. This inner circle was surrounded by banners from poor neighborhoods in the Holy City;

each contingent had its own gaudy flag. Everyone sat around small fires of tamarisk twigs and told tales of the Unknown.

People kept streaming through the mountain passes. Inevitably, the banners of the poor crept closer to the tents of those who were well off, and before long the widow's gravesite was engulfed. Day surrendered to darkness, the chanting grew louder, the rich watched the poor take off their clothes and improvise shelters from their rags.

Those who'd lived long enough to have learned a few of life's secrets were fond of saying: "Nighttime in the Valley of Saraf is a mysterious creature, never touched by the paw of any earthly animal, never breathed upon by mortal breath." The old ones knew that it was wise for the women of Mecca to start singing as soon as night fell and keep singing till midnight. Then their tents went quiet in submission to the mysteries surrounding them.

The ladies of Mecca vied with one another in erecting tents of the greatest possible splendor. They connected the walls of their tents to form a network of open-air walkways, a web of reds and yellows arrayed in a vast semicircle across the desert, all facing east to emphasize how eagerly they awaited the nightly celebrations.

Nara's tent was one of those pitched closest to the widow's mosque. Jummo visited every night under cover of darkness. She would stand with her back to the arched gate leading to the *sahin*, the open courtyard, which in turn lead to the grave and the mosque. Over her shoulder, she could feel the courtyard widening in front of her. Off to her right she sensed the dome of the mosque, small and white, as if left high and dry by a rain of little white buildings. To her left stood the imposing colonnade; she dared not look at it. There were soldiers made of white stone stationed every few feet all around the roof.

Jummo waited as if expecting a guest or the start of a mysterious performance. She didn't have the slightest idea what might happen in the darkened arena of white stones. She knew only that whatever came to pass, it would answer her urgent need to achieve a sense of peace, or to witness the unveiling of a momentous secret.

She was powerless to withdraw from her nightly vigil. When the fires guttered down and the singers hummed themselves to silence and the cooks and their helpers and the camel drivers drifted off to sleep after a day of nonstop feasting, she heard the call. It drove her out of her tent and summoned her to come and wait by the white colonnade. Who was calling her so insistently?

During her long vigils at the gravesite (how odd, she thought, such finely chiseled edges on something so ancient), she came to feel a strengthening bond between the Prophet's widow and herself—between the widow's grave, rather, and herself. The grave knew her, it had been expecting her. And Jummo could read the grave's mind, she could see all the things it secretly saw.

Night after night she came, night after night nothing happened. Tomorrow everyone would leave the valley. All the tents would be pulled down and the camel drivers would come with their wagons and canopied carriages to carry everything and everybody back to Mecca.

That final evening, just as night was falling, a caravan entered the camp. It was scarcely more than a chain of camels and it was attended by a lone camel driver taking up the rear.

They approached gracefully enough, the way camels generally do. But they looked nothing like the sort of camels used for carrying passengers or freight. For one thing, they wore no saddles and carried no bags. Their bellies were enchained with amulets and silver. They were ornamented with skins to which jangling cowry shells had been attached, and blankets of brightly died braided wool with silver tassels. As they came closer, it became clear that the necklaces they wore were very like those used in heathen ceremonies. Their ears had been snipped like camels that had taken part in one of those pagan rituals where they were set free to roam as pets of God, as creatures consecrated to the Almighty. Certainly that was how they walked, with the easy sway of free beasts, strolling aristocratically ahead of their driver.

The driver was recognized the instant he entered the camp. Everyone from Mecca knew him—or thought they knew him—by the bewitching way he sang to his beasts; he sang in the style called Saba. It was a pleasant sound, soothing as the wind it was named for. Listening to his heavenly songs, looking nearly drunk on his melodies, the camels glided drowsily through the camp in front of their master.

Slaves were dispatched to invite the camel driver to the nightly banquet and celebration. He sent them away. "No pilgrim should accept invitations to banquets," he said. "If he does, he will end up being tamed by luxury; he will be unfit for travel in the deserts of the Holy Land." When they sent him a juicy leg of lamb, he refused to touch it and had it conveyed to the poor people camping out in the passes.

He glanced at a she-camel, the only one with full udders. She was trailed by a young camel with a speckled coat remarkable for its black-and-white patterns. The driver kept his distance from the she-camel until her baby drank its fill of milk. Then he came up and stood beside her in the dark, tugging her swollen udders. When the milk pail was full, he invited some of the poor people to share it. They passed the bucket around, standing shoulder to shoulder with the driver. No one thought to look closely enough at him to determine who he actually might be. Everyone was bewitched by the bucket and the trace of ambergris in the taste of the milk.

"There's nothing like amber for promoting life and vitality," the driver said. "Be sure to encourage your children to drink this wilderness milk. Truly, there's nothing like it for bringing things back to life."

The sheiks of the poor people tasted the wild ambery milk and pronounced it better than ambrosia. They ordered everyone to drink as much as they could.

The campfires were dying—all but the driver's, which flared up and came alarmingly close to the widow's gravesite. Jummo was there as always, standing in her customary spot under the arches, her face rubied by the flames reflected off the mud puddles. She stared at the thorn bushes and dust blown about by the stiff wind.

She sensed movement . . . something unseen. She drew her *abaya* tighter and listened. The movement stopped. There it was again, directing her eyes to a polished flagstone on the gravesite. For all the nights she'd kept vigil here, she'd never noticed this particular stone.

The more she looked at it, the clearer its contours became. There was a suggestion of boldly drawn lines. She kept looking. The lines began to shape themselves into two wild gazelles, darkly beautiful. Directly in front of the gazelles, right under their noses, an almond tree was growing. The wind picked up. The gazelles began to sniff the almond blossoms. In

Jummo's wide-open eyes, the inanimate was turning into the animate—into moving, living things.

She realized, without knowing how it had happened, that she was down on her knees. She stretched out her hand to touch the gazelle's dewy snout. The branches of the almond tree clattered, the gazelles bolted. She trembled with ecstasy.

"Alive . . . alive . . . you . . . gazelle. . . . " She shuddered with pleasure. She jumped to her feet, and in her haste she collided with someone standing right behind her.

"*Dustoor?*" he said. "May I pass by?"

Dustoor is the most respectful, humble, yet determined way of saying "excuse me." Typically, it is used by a stranger asking permission to enter a forbidden area such as the women's quarters or the realm of geniis.

"You . . . alive . . . "

She shivered in sympathy with the vibrating voice.

Suddenly Sidi asked, "Are you running away from life . . . you . . . alive?"

She clenched her jaw and looked shyly at the ground. "I saw a gazelle," she said, "and it was . . . the gazelle was grazing on stones and . . . and the stones were shrouded . . . it was death."

He held out a bowl of milk. She stared at his hand in fascination. She could keep looking at the curve of his fingers forever and never take a drink.

"What are you afraid of, you-the-alive? To drink is to drown?"

"I'm afraid I'll die of thirst." She reached for the bowl and brought it close to her face. She inhaled the sharp scent of amber. The aroma swept through her.

She felt a tightening in the overarching curve of the night sky: the starry blackness was bending—was being bent by the eye of the camel driver. As he raised his head, looking higher still, all she could of his up-turned eyes were the whites of them.

"You-the-alive . . . " he was saying. "The widow's gravestone is merely a gathering place, a beam of shapes beyond understanding. Mystical. As the milk—the milk is a single beam of light."

Jummo focused the blackness of her pupil on the white of his eyes. She was trying to understand, but the effort was making her dizzy.

"Sidi," she whispered, "I ache inside. I yearn to fly away, to feel free in the light, in the dark. I don't ever want to come back."

He stretched out his hand as if to pick her up. "You are here. You may stay here. You are alive. And free to live."

The she-camel snorted, calling its baby. The baby camel was lurching around in the dark, utterly lost.

Sidi began to sing like a drunken dromedary, gathering runaway souls to himself, retrieving escaping spirits and corralling them all in the perfectly circular enclosure of animal nature.

Jummo felt the scuff of an animal scampering between her feet. She winced at the suddenly bitter taste in her mouth. Her soul was being incinerated; she was turning into a gigantic reptile. The serpent's scales rippled, tightening on her humanness, sucking her soul away and rendering empty the substance of all animal and mineral things. She became a heavy shadow—a dim, drifting assemblage of barely living things.

The shadow extended itself in the shape of giants encircling the Holy Land. The giants clambered up the silk curtains covering the Sacred Stone of al-Kaaba and soared like a fountain in the sky. The scent of basil and other earthy smells whirled skyward, sweeping everything along, crowding the arch of the first Heaven of the seven Heavens. Heaven shut its gates.

Jummo felt Sidi's arms tightening around her. One tug was all it took to bring her back to earth. Thunderstruck, she fell down exhausted. She was caked with frost.

"Heavy curtains of cold, horrifying floods . . ." she said, her teeth chattering. "And layers and layers of hailstones . . ." She squinted through her lids, brittle with frost, and looked into the white of his eyes. Sidi wrapped her body and soul in his encircling heat and held her tight till the warmth returned to her veins. She lost track of time; she had no idea how long she stood there, shivering with cold, shuddering with heat. At last her trembling subsided.

"You-the-alive traveled to your death?" Sidi asked.

Jummo studied the whiteness of his eyes, looking for traces of the ter-rible heavenly tide, the great flood of the dead ascending to Heaven. "Is it time for me to die? Is this the hour of my death?"

"How could you ever be frightened after your soul has traveled to what lays beyond this world? To death."

"Who are you, Sidi?"

27. Choosing a Twin

"I am He—if you like. And if you don't like, I'm not He."

He lifted his arms from around her. She collapsed, tranced unto pa-ralysis, on the flagstones. For what seemed forever she lay there, resting her head against the low wall around the grave. She heard him moving. She arched her head back in imitation of the graceful way he was standing above her, embracing the darkness. He was the One-Who-Is-Alive—cast in amber, the pitch-black amber of night circling him, closing on him.

"If you are going to take my soul away from me," she said, "then darken your eye with kohl and pluck it out and put it right here, on this stone." Her voice was hoarse with the effort of trying to reach him from her subservient position.

He lowered his eyes and turned to leave. His glance fell on her body loosely draped across the gravestones.

"Alive, Alive, Alive," he said, washing her in whispers. "There is no living except in the everlasting flood. Your body is like the river that runs one way—to the Sea of the Eternally Alive. Here—look!" With his fore-finger he drew a circle over her head. "Look, between your eyes is the seal of the star called al-Risha." He drew a round seal between her eyes. Then, with a finishing flourish, he reshaped it into the tail of a fish.

"When the Fish appeared in the sky," he said, "the earth opened up like a heart falling in love. It is time now for the net to be cast, for the hermit to roam free in the wilderness, and the pearl in its shell to come to full size. In you, Jummo, lies the wellspring of energy and determination; in you is the dawn of abundance, the fruits of the apple and pumpkin.

You are the season, you are the reason, for planting palm saplings. It is for you to accept the fate of the Fish Star, but you must leave all human fates behind and dive deep into the river that flows behind all rivers, into the river that is fed by heavy inner rains, whose flow is full beyond measuring. In that river you will find your self, the source of your life. The Pleiades will follow you and place a crown on your heart, a ring on your finger, an anklet on your leg, and a wink in your eye. But these things will double your solitude and make you more lonely."

Jummo was doing her best to follow his fortune telling, but the fish-tailed ring on her forehead kept troubling her. The fish, the circle, the star—whatever it was, it turned into the letter H, which confused her still more. She stiffened. She tried to stand up.

"Don't ever turn away from my black and white," he said sternly. "There is no other way. You must stay true to the infinite versions of your true twin-self. Always remember: we have arranged for this self to accompany you and serve you through the Time of All Times and the Place of All Places. We will make the animal that is your body even more beautiful, and your beauty will become part of our self.

"And if you choose to follow my black self, he will take you and show you what no eye had ever seen and no ear ever heard. But beware; this black self is a tyrant. He takes no lover to his heart, not till he's ruined the temple of her body. Because for him there is no way to eternity more certain than ruining the body of his lover. With my black self you'll never get beyond destruction. That's the way it will be if you submit to my twin; that is the way it will be unless you put aside the whims of the body and its idle passions.

"But I am his white twin, and my way goes in the opposite direction. I am the easygoing twin. I am yours as long as you are mine, and along this road I will appear to you in many shapes, though you will never mistake me for anyone else. Whenever and wherever I appear, you must drown with me—be one with me, come so close to me that there is not a hairs-breadth of space for anyone to come between us. Be me.

"You will have no more chances to choose after this; this is a turning point that won't come again. Here, now—this is the time for you to decide your destiny. Look. Look again. Think and think again before you make a move: it's either me or my black twin. Or nothingness. Bear in mind that you may fail, you have a free hand.

"My twin is a blacksmith. It's his nature to bend things and shape them according to his desires, so they'll open whatever door he cares to open or enclose whatever he cares to enclose."

Sidi turned away. Jummo was stirred by his half-mad, off-key passion. She was scared to the bone. Something inside was gathering strength, urging her to get closer to him. But she recoiled.

When Sidi had finished speaking, he pointed to her eyes, turned, and walked away. She followed blindly at his heels, running barefooted, stumbling all the way to the foot of a cliff. He raised his hand, signaling her to stop: Don't follow!

She hesitated. Disobey and follow? Obey and retreat?

This was holy ground, and the ground was shivering with indecision. Clumps of ambergris were strewn all around. The she-camel and her baby had followed Jummo. The young animal was nuzzling its mother's legs, trying to nurse at the amber-spouting udders, and when it moved to lap up the amber milk that was trickling over Jummo's bare toes, Jummo was filled with a rippling pleasure so intense she had to shut her eyes. When at last she was able to open them again, she saw no sign of the baby camel. She heard only the gurgling of the pleasure deep inside herself, going on and on and on . . . and deep.

The camel driver had vanished too. There were those who suggested that he might have disappeared into the dome of the mosque by the widow's grave; others were certain he'd buried himself under the flagstones. By dawn there was no trace at all of his herd of camels—not unless one took into account the camel songs echoing faintly in the temple of Jummo's body.

She ignored the hectic preparations for departure. She wandered around the camp, soothing herself with songs in the style of al-Rasd, humming lullaby-soft melodies that were used to put babies and other restless creatures to sleep. She understood that from now on her nights were going to be long. She decided that she might as well give voice to the beauty of the dark hours, because she knew that nighttime, like animals and certain people, preferred to keep its true beauties hidden.

Everyone returned to Mecca. Everyone except Jummo, who stayed behind meditating on the seal of the Fish imprinted between her eyes. The ineradicable Fish and its rivers were telling her to shed her skin and follow their course.

She began to spend more time listening to the rustling of the river of mirrors in herself. She made a conscious effort to slow down and listen for sounds of the Alive deep within. There were times when she could feel Him in the fathomless reaches of her spine. And when she went out into the world, she could feel the River flowing all around her.

28. Hungry Graves

Jummo, draped across a limb high in the *nabk* tree, was surveying the world below. From this perch she saw people and things differently; she saw all beings as rivers. Hanim, her father's cat, was one of the wildest rivers and he ran like a torrent, never resting.

Jummo just watched, taking no part in the running around below. She watched her sisters Hannah and Zubayda pick up yellow *nabk* leaves from the pebbles in the yard. She watched Nara fussing at her crude oven, slipping the Khazar dough inside every morning, slipping the loaves out every evening. The plump, puffy bread was called *kolja*.

Jummo's watching was a thirsty drinking of the motions made by the lives being lived below her. The *nabk* tree was her observatory and the observatory was a fountain from which she drank the energy of all living things. She was always thirsty. She was thirsty for the quickness and liveliness she'd felt when Sidi touched her. She thirsted for the threat that would sweep her away.

So she sat up high and watched whatever happened to be crawling around on the earth below—earth, that enormous cemetery full of gaping graves eager to swallow her time. This world is nothing, she thought, nothing but open graves swallowing a slice of time here, a little piece of someplace there. Nothing keeps as busy as death. Nothing is so alive.

Yes, the walls of the *nabk* house were an observatory towering over a huge gravesite. Even the *nabk* tree where Jummo was perched—it was a grave, a spiraling-up-in-the-air sort of grave that devoured this time, this place, this light, breaking it all down into predictable patterns of black and white.

Jummo liked to watch the birds breathe and she liked to watch the naked little animals poke their snouts in the air and test the safety of the yard and she liked to watch the water carriers crossing and crisscrossing the alley, delivering cans of water to all the houses. True, water was colorless, but like the invisible Animal that seemed always about to overwhelm her, it carried all colors within itself. The essence of water implied everything that everyday water was not.

She watched, as if for the first time, the milkmen working in the dairy next door. She sneaked in between the cows and petted their snouts and breathed their hot living breath. She cupped her mouth around their nipples and felt their heat and energy and the energy of the milkmen's hands. The nipples, swollen by the cow's hulking soul, dribbled on her lips.

She watched the *nabk* tree for hours on end. She could imagine nothing more fascinating than the tree, the way it sprang from the flesh of the Animal that was the earth—the tree itself an animal in hot, full, skin-to-skin contact with the earth and the Animal, the inner animal that looked solid enough, but solid in ways that suggested incessant, invisible running. Jummo, in an effort to unite herself with this running, spent hours trying to fuse her body with the flesh of the tree. Sidi had shown her the trace of the River that was in every creature, and these traces of the River, all of them, cast their shadows across Jummo's body as she, a new river, came to inhabit the tree.

"The girl is possessed," Great-grandmother Khadija confided to Nara, who was wearing a belt fashioned from a silk shawl and leaning toward the vat where meat pies were crackling over a roaring fire.

Jummo could read the worry in the twist of the women's bodies. Her great grandmother was practically a cripple, and every Friday night her mother recited strengthening prayers for her legs in the hope that she might not have to stagger down the path her mother had taken toward paralysis.

"Ever since I gave birth to her," said Nara without looking up, "Jummo's been susceptible to the Evil Eye. I keep hoping she won't laugh, because laughter is what attracts that kind of evil." It was clear from Nara's tone that she was taking great pains to keep the fear that was her constant companion from overwhelming her. She took a wooden stick studded with nails and punctured the puffy faces of the meat pies, freckling them.

"You better hurry up and marry her off," Khadija said. "That's the only way to block the road that the devil's taking to steal her body and soul."

Under the *nabk* tree, scarcely an arm's length from the cooking fire, Khadija lay down and napped a cripple's fitful nap, dreaming all the while of the devil scuttling crabwise down the winding road to her great-granddaughter.

Nara dipped one hand in salty water and sprinkled the piecrusts. She stuck both hands, bare and still dripping, the drops of water sizzling now, into the oven, and crammed the pies against the red-hot walls.

"Lots of suitors have been approaching Sheik Baikwaly," she said, "but he doesn't know who to accept or who to send away. The sheik's blinded by what he reads about her fate in the stars. All his readings are contaminated with warnings, by shooting stars. How can anyone expect us to hand our flesh and blood over to such bad omens? It's clear from the omens that she's possessed—this is a fact. Whatever possesses her has mixed up the tracks of the stars and turned the reading of her fortune upside-down. The only thing to do is put our trust in God's Mercy. Tonight is the night of mid-Sha'aban; we're coming up on Ramadan. Next month we'll be fasting, but tonight the waters of the Zamzam well will flow like curdled milk, and the Book of Fate that shows our family history and the fortunes of all living people will be redrawn. Give Jummo a drink of bitter Zamzam water and pray that her chances—her luck in heaven and on earth—gets better."

Nara looked down at the flames licking the piecrusts. She looked up at her daughter curled up in her observatory high in the *nabk* tree. Her eyes clouded over with worries she couldn't define.

"God knows, grandmother," she said, "I'm so afraid for her if . . ." She drew back, not daring to finish the thought. She reached deep into the oven and picked out the first of the red-hot pies.

"Put your trust in God," Khadija said sternly, alarmed by the despair in her granddaughter's voice. "Trust in the Capable One, the Generous One."

29. On the Nature of Angels

Jummo developed a knack for seeing invisible creatures wandering around the house. She could detect their presence in the wink of lantern, in the creaking and popping of antique wooden trunks. The porosity of old wood, it seemed, was conducive to viewing the Unseen.

Whenever she saw a lantern wink or heard a trunk creak, Jummo said: "They are asking permission to come in, the good geniis and the angels." When she said this, her little friends laughed to shake off the panic plucking at their sleeves.

"Angels appear in the wink of an eye," Jummo explained. "It's like they come out of our own heads, like they have little homes in our heads, and the minute we open our hearts and minds to them, they flap their wings and come out. Would you like to see your angels?" Jummo extended this invitation in all seriousness to Hannah.

The cook's daughter interrupted: "We all know that Hannah has an eye like a searchlight. She can see anything you'd like her to see."

"This has nothing to do with your searchlight, Hannah," Jummo said. "It just so happens that whenever God's name is mentioned, angels appear." A pigeon cooed. "Did you see that, did you notice the way the light flickered? They are here among us, right here, with their wings so big and so many of them you can't count them, all over the *nabk* tree. The birds can see them because birds can feel the heat of energies that we can't see, and their yearning makes them fly in circles."

Jummo's girlfriends shuddered. They raised their heads to the flock of circling birds.

"Great God!" she said. "Did you see that?—how the leaves of the *nabk* tree are trembling, it's so crowded with angels."

Though the girls pretended not to care, they huddled close so they could stand together and face the invisible spirit taking on flesh right in front of their eyes.

"When the spirits appear," Jummo said, "I hold tight to the nearest stake I can find, or I hang on to an anchor or something, because the angels are strong as the strongest rivers, each one is a big fountain shooting straight up, whirling around and around, and when you see one it's like a door opens to some place you never even thought of before and everything that's in the way gets swept up in the current and all I have to do is just take a peek at the doors or one of the angels and I'm gone."

30. The Name and the Body

Nara was bending over a bowl of ash-water, washing her long braids.

Jummo said: "Nara's not your real name, right?"

Nara bent lower and scrubbed the ash-water into silver suds. "My uncle Abdul-Khaliq—may God preserve him—he's the one who took care of me when I was a nameless child. He raised me, he gave me the name I have now." Then, with a surprise more stinging for having been postponed, Nara straightened up, shaking the crown of silvery bubbles on her head. "How did you know about my name?"

Jummo had a secret answer: it was the vision of Nara's animal's soul, a definite tint, a halo all over her body. Directly behind her shoulders, another color lurked like a bright shadow.

"My original name got lost while I was traveling and moving from one country to another," Nara said. "I gave my name away, I offered it up as a sacrifice in gratitude for reaching God's holy land."

All the people in Jummo's life, they were growing on their names the way a pearl grows on a grain of sand irritating an oyster. But Nara's name was the name of a stranger, a shadow hovering over her nameless shoulders.

◆　　　◆　　　◆

Let me ask you, did you swim inside the Animal that was revealed to Jummo? How did you manage to lift your head above the waves and gulp the air that saved you? When the running waters of her Animal drenched you, did your arms, your eyes, your teeth, your heart—did they stretch and grow?

Jummo was possessed by what she was able to see of the Animal, the great Animal that runs through all of us, as it runs through the earth, the oceans, the heavens.

Don't say a thing, please, not a word. Be quiet or it will drink your voice. Don't move, it will drink your movement. Clutch your Animal to yourself, tightly; touch your true love, the lover as true as the day you were born, the day Scheherazade and I gave you life.

Jummo shifted on her high-altitude tree limb. She watched Hannah and Zubayda dusting the house and sweeping the damask curtains and the Persian carpets. This special housekeeping, a happy event in itself, was being done in preparation for the celebration that followed Ramadan, the month of fasting.

The fasting sapped Jummo's energy, Nara thought, casting an eye on the carpets that hung like limp rainbows on the clothesline in the yard. Jummo's lack of strength was a great worry for Nara—that and the way the girl kept avoiding her chores around the house. She had nothing to do, it seemed, but make excuses for not doing things. *Standing up to her, though, is like standing up to a flood. She seems so weak, but one wrong word and she explodes.*

Swat! The carpet rainbows scattered into brilliant galaxies of dust.

"What kind of husband would want to own such a lazy creature?" Great-grandmother Khadija asked out of nowhere. "Just look at her lounging way up there, loose as a string, dawdling all over the place, oozing from cot to bed, slinking from one branch to another."

Jummo was worn out by the vitality of the Animal that had been cast into relief by her fasting. She was experiencing its lethal energy. As her body grew weaker, the swiftness and force and freedom of the river rushing inside her became more than she could bear. It swept her down, deep down and far away into times long vanished, into a place of primordial simplicity where creatures shed their skin and exposed their hidden light, their elemental, everlasting bodies. Experiencing life this way sapped her strength, leaving her at once exhausted and excruciatingly alert to what she was seeing. During the final ten days of the month of fasting, her dreams, ordinarily quite vivid, became even more inflamed, propelling her to a sky in the Seventh Heaven, as far away as possible from the First Sky—precisely the sort of banishment she'd always feared. In her dreams she rose higher and higher, escaping her worn-out skin and rocketing away from her own river, changing into a symbol, penetrating the Tongue of Light, entering the essential, the eternal body, the Thunderbolt.

For months after each of these interpenetrations, she felt sick, as if her river, feeling absolute freedom, could not stop struggling to escape all limits, to pass the point of no return, reaching for the dawn, that ultimate display of the mystical body, the body capable of being every shape, every stone, every fire, every spark, every body.

31. The Heiress of Wise Royan

"So where is she, the heiress of Wise Royan?"

There is in Egypt an ancient book called *Kalila Wa Domna*, a book of philosophy, intended to impart wisdom. It is written in the language of animals, all the characters are animals. It borrows a story from *The Thousand and One Nights*, the story of Wise Royan:

Wise Royan came to cure a sick king whose illness had resisted the ministrations of all his doctors and magicians. Wise Royan said to the king, "I will cure you without any medicines or ointments, and without the least effort on your part."

These words cast a spell on the sick king. Wise Royan fashioned a ball. The king played with the ball till he broke into a sweat, and after this little game, miraculously, he was cured.

The king appointed Wise Royan his adviser, which caused much annoyance in his court. The chief minister convinced the king that Wise Royan was actually a menace to his throne. Royan was executed, but not before delivering a letter to the king. The king read the letter and fell dead on the spot. It was a matter of chemistry, not magic—Wise Royan had written the letter in poison ink. This was king's punishment for betraying the man who'd saved his life.

"So where-oh-where can she be now, our little heiress of Wise Royan?"

Enter Great-grandmother Khadija, moving slowly after her long absence in Arafat, where she'd kept herself very busy performing the rituals of pilgrimage. She'd succeeded for the third time in overcoming her paralysis. She'd cured herself with a combination of sheer will and religious devotion: fasting, ritual sacrificing, and many other ceremonies that pilgrims take part in. She was walking slowly to enjoy the new energy coursing through her legs.

Jummo stayed up on her tree limb, smiling down on the world but not deigning to descend. Her great-grandmother's glance climbed the tree. The tilt of her brow suggested she was resigned to the fact that Jummo was never going to leave her observatory.

Khadija glared theatrically in Jummo's direction, then turned to Zubayda. "Just look, will you? Jummo's about to fall on us out of the sky like fate. But I'll tell you one thing: there's nothing that'll cure laziness like talking about getting a man. Burzanjiya's fine young son is looking for a bride . . ."

Zubayda giggled, then gasped, smothered by Khadija's steel-armed hug. Jummo, light as a leaf, fluttered down from her perch, ran around behind Khadija, and started counting her great-grandmother's few remaining black hairs. "Tell me grandma, what would you say if I gave Wise Royan's ball to you? I'd have to do it before you lost your dark hair, because that's your last chance."

Khadija pulled Jummo against her breasts, engulfing the girl (she seemed to have a slight fever) with her strength and serenity.

"Dividing up Wise Royan's inheritance, are we?! Then who's going to cure you without medicine or ointment, or effort on your part?" The old woman glanced at Jummo's face. On the girl's throat she noticed an odd-looking shadow. Khadija knew she was looking at a miraculous sort of twilight, an omen of sacrifice.

That evening Khadija picked up her rosary-bead recital of Scheherazade's stories. The girls, along with the new son-in-law Mohammed al-Maghrabi and his sisters and the neighbors' little girls, all sat around in a circle, enchanted.

"This one is a story of a thousand and one tricks for avoiding misery and tiredness," Jummo announced. "In this story the power of the word is stronger than the power of the executioner's hand."

Mohammed al-Maghrabi leaned toward Hannah. "My brother Salih was bewitched by *The Thousand and One Nights*," he whispered. "Scheherazade stole his soul. He would hide her book in one trunk or another rather than face my father's anger. He traveled all over the world following her. Finally he died rather than give her up. After his death my father looked all over for the book and burned it."

"But I . . ." Jummo hissed, " . . . I am the victim of my master Shahrayar, Scheherazade's husband." She bit her lip. "He killed me . . . he slayed me with his charm. If my great-grandmother only knew, she'd burn me alive."

Zubayda pinched her to silence. "Great-grandma Khadija? But wasn't she the one who showed you *The Thousand and One Nights* in the first place?"

Jummo was instantly defiant: "The girls in great-grandma's *Nights* are shut away and locked up without the keys. But—may Allah preserve us—there are thousands and thousands and thousands of keys to the locks in *The Thousand and One Nights*."

The girls giggled. Khadija brandished her fan, swatting Mohammed smartly and putting an end to the uprising.

Every night, while Sheik Baikwaly's sitting room was filling up with musicians and their instruments, Great-grandmother Khadija curled up with the girls and told stories, braiding her own tales with Scheherazade's, squinting into the darkness and "reading" to the girls as if from an open book. The moment Khadija's recital came to an end, Jummo, convinced by this time that she was the embodiment of Scheherazade, rushed off to her private place under the *nabk* tree. There she sat, thinking very hard about the word *was.*

Was, it seemed to her, was a fast-running stream, and on its banks a whole kingdom of incredible creatures came to life. The images created by *was* dropped down on top of other things, and *into* them, making more things, which led Jummo to the following conclusion: *Scheherazade didn't so much mate with her husband Shahrayar as with her true self, her animal self.*

Suddenly, as if in response to this insight, she became aware of Sidi standing near the fast moving word *was.* (Actually, he was leaning against the trunk of the *nabk* tree.)

Formally and very softly, Jummo said, "*Dustoor,* Sidi. I beg your pardon . . ."

Sidi called to her as from a great distance: "Tell me, You-who-are-alive, how was the kingdom of words created?"

Confused, Jummo peered into the darkness, searching for the exact shade of darkness particular to the spirit who had addressed her. When at last she spoke, her voice had a husky darkness of its own. "The Animal of this World gave birth to the kingdom of words, Sidi. And from this Animal Scheherazade took shape, too. Her words ran up and down the Animal's spine, and this running water made her pregnant, so she gave birth to children, to royalty, and to timelessness."

Sidi's smile flashed in the dark as he completed her thought: "Look for the key word—the secret of *will* and *say.*" Jummo tuned every sense at her disposal to the deafening echo of Sidi's words. The volume of his voice never diminished, and stayed with her all night long; the only respite coming when great-grandmother Khadija started telling the story about the baggage carrier and the three girls. From that story Jummo stole a word, carried it off, and packed it away. She tugged at the edge of the *mihrama* covering her head. She sorted and rearranged the words in the phrase *Kan Ya ma Kan*—Once upon a time . . . She bent forward and braided a fold of the *mihrama* into her hair. It became a knot tied in the coat of an animal, constantly pulsing with life. Jummo couldn't imagine the day when this shiny braid might lose its luster. And her hair *was* getting longer, growing incredibly fast. Nara was worn out tidying it up all the time.

"May my eye go cold upon you," said Nara. She prayed that the incandescent envy she felt for Jummo's hair would cool off, sparing the girl's tresses from ruin. "Yes, yes, may my eye go cold upon you . . . and besides, your hair breaks scissors like I'm cutting links on a chain." Nara laughed, finished combing, and replaced the *mihrama* on Jummo's hair as quickly as she could, so her envy wouldn't find a way to sneak up on the treasure and do it real damage.

32. The Cure

He came for her during the last month of the holy time, when hunting and killing were forbidden. Jummo was sitting on a stone bench washing her hair, her braids cascading to the ground. "Nightfall" this was called, because of the way it covered a girl's body like night. All of Nara's girls had nightfall hair. Washing and scenting the nightfalls was done according to inviolable rituals, assisted by the all the women of the household and their inventory of Khazar ointments. At the conclusion of the ceremony, all participants nodded solemnly.

When Sidi appeared in the yard, Jummo was sitting on the stone bench with her hair falling to the water basin on the ground, where Nara was kneeling, scrubbing the thick locks with ash-water.

"*Dustoor,*" Sidi said in his most courtly voice. "I beg your pardon, you-who-are-alive. Please, may I enter?"

Zubayda was scooping water into a bucket from a basin built into the wall. At the disembodied sound of Sidi's call, her spine went stiff.

Sidi materialized on the bench next to Jummo. For what seemed ages, Nara did not raise her head. She scrubbed Jummo's hair so hard for so long that her fingers got numb.

"*Dustoor,*" Sidi repeated. "You-who-are-alive, please let me in."

Jummo bolted upright. The ash-water splashed over her robe, pasting it to her curves like the giddy paints of an artist who worships his model more than his art. The air in the yard twitched. Jummo's eyelids drooped as if she were falling asleep. She felt strangely rested, utterly at peace. With great effort she opened her eyes and looked at him.

"Sidi, the secret was revealed to me." She spoke with an air of satisfaction, like someone who'd just completed an urgent mission. "The secret appeared to me in the shape of an animal and it was escaping from one of Wise Royan's vaults. I made a fist around the secret and then I could feel it racing through my whole body."

"You-who-are-alive, you opened the vault!" Sidi said. "And to you the secret was returned!"

Jummo was elated. "And I tied it up in a knot in my *mihrama* and I played with the ball just like Wise Royan says you should and it was a cure for the sickness—no medicine, no lotions, no effort at all. Are you pleased?"

He bent his head and said only, "You-who-are-alive, God is alive."

Jummo was beside herself with happiness. "It was very small when I found it, but so tightly packed you could tell that *everything* was inside it: the desire to get well without medicines, the mysteries of the formulas from Greece and Persia and Rome and the Arab lands and the essential secrets of their medical arts and philosophy and astrology and healing plants. Are you pleased?"

"Alive, alive, God is alive! *Dustoor*—please, may I go now?"

33. The Husband

A few days after Sidi's visit, Sheik al-Baikwaly's family moved out of the house with the *nabk* tree. A little while after that, in defiance of dire warnings by the fortune tellers, Jummo's fate was tied to a young man named al-Neyabi. This husband-to-be was a dull-looking, pockmarked gentleman of no astrological consequence whatsoever, so there was hope that al-Baikwaly's daughter might somehow be able to free herself from the misfortune foretold by contradictory stars, disorderly entrails, and other auguries.

In the course of getting ready for the wedding ceremony, while she was removing her *mihrama* in order to replace it with a modern bridal veil, Jummo touched the knot she had recently tied, the knot that had cured her. She was overcome by a crushing feeling of loneliness. She closed the door to her *mabeet*, which ordinarily stayed open to the sky all night. But she had despaired of Sidi's coming for her, so now she closed it. For the past month or so, the period during which a bride-to-be was expected to prepare herself for her mate, Sidi had stopped appearing to her, and the sound of his call—*You-who-are-alive*—had faded.

On the eve of the wedding, in al-Baikwaly's new house in the ravine known as al-Hajla, a wind-blown loneliness buffeted Jummo's heart. But since she was by nature a happy and light-hearted young woman, she consoled herself with the thought that she would be going to a husband who would release her from the exhausting currents bullying her body. This prospect made her feel not only light-hearted but light-headed. Yet there was nothing she could do to make herself forget the knot. Underneath it all she had the vague feeling she'd broken a vow whose terms she couldn't quite remember. This made her feel even more dizzy with loss, anticipation and dread, until she was living in a trance and holding onto the knot, the one solid, unyielding thing in her life, as firmly as she could.

34. The Fruit

So as you can see, my friend, the secret treasure of Scheherazade's (and your) stories fell into Jummo's possession. The word-knot became embedded in her. And out of that knot grew my urge to talk with you, to tell you all about my Khazar aunt.

You sent me an ivory box. In the letter that came with it you said, "Receive herewith a gift from the elephants whose tusks grow like the limbs of great trees. Every night at sunset and at moonrise, you must switch the pieces of black ivory with the white ones."

I discovered this box of yours sitting in my lap. A box of feathered moments it was, full of images so light and buoyant, images of commonplace intimacies, images of hours, a rosary of ordinary, happy days. For a moment I thought you'd given me a dress made of feathers, or some such treasure you'd hidden from the geniis.

When I pried open the lid, the ruby-fruit of a *nabk* tree fell into my mouth. For a whole month I could taste its sweetness spreading inside me: from the first rising of the crescent moon to its veiling, the tang of your blood-fruit gave me no rest. I could feel the tree you picked the fruit from—this silencing gift of yours that came so close to ending the story before the veils were raised and the scenes began to show what shouldn't be shown and say what shouldn't be said. It turns out that even you, my friend, are afraid of words.

This *nabk* fruit you sent to keep me company—here it is triggering another memory, a glimpse of Jummo:

Mayjan was sitting on a carpet of *nabk* tree leaves, surrounded by embroideries, basking in Nara's hospitality. At Nara's signal, Jummo raced for a pot of sugarless Khazar tea. In a flash she returned with the golden pot and held the china cup over Mayjan's head. She held the pot way up high as she poured, not bending over, but arching gracefully, like a cobra ready to strike. Mayjan looked up and smiled open-mouthed at her silhouette curving against the sky. Jummo, with a sideways wink and a wicked flutter of her long lashes, pretended she was about to douse him with boiling water. Steam rose from neck of the pot. Steadily, slowly, lazily, from throat height to breast level, her left hand descended, further and further, to belly level, closing on his mouth. She touched the gleaming gold spout to his lips, she placed the cup of tea in his hand.

When Mayjan snapped out of his trance long enough to ask for more tea, she surprised him by plucking a plump, blood colored *nabk* fruit from its hiding place in her mouth and dipping it, saturated with warm spit, in his tea.

He did not just drink the tea, he got drunk on it. With fingers, eyes and nose, caressing it all day long with each taste bud on his tongue, he played with the forbidden *nabk* fruit. He walked around the city thinking about the fruit, the fruit, the fruit, only the fruit, resisting with superhuman fortitude the too-human urge to sink his teeth in its bloody flesh, until finally the sun set and the darkness of night fell across al-Akshaban, Mecca's two greatest mountains, and Mayjan allowed his teeth at last to close around the fruit and sink in, surrendering his soul to its heavenly juice, drowning in it.

Jummo continued to torment Mayjan with an artistry that could only be called masterful. Her sisters, Hannah and Zubayda, acted as co-conspirators, increasing her power by making no mention of it. Nara remained oblivious to these goings-on, or perhaps she simply neglected to notice what was better left unnoticed concerning the play of animal passions in her circle of virtue, her no-man's land, her free zone.

35. The Genii Cat

Zubayda, al-Baikwaly's youngest daughter, whispered: "Like geniis' daughters, that's what they are . . ."

Zubayda was being very careful to keep away from Hanim, the cat, because if she stepped on Hanim's tail, even by mistake, the arched gateways of the geniis would give way and open under her feet and she'd get lost in their hypnotic, hollow-sounding songs.

In the evening, Nara liked to hum songs about the geniis while Hanim the cat, with something between a meow and a purr, did her best to harmonize, and the candles guttered low and the lantern glass gathered soot so thin and fine we imagined it was delicate lace. Only my grandmother Nara and Hanim the genii cat stayed awake, dreaming a waking dream of a male descendent, of a son, an heir for Sheik Baikwaly. This was the unattainable dream that haunted his house.

Tell me, did you happen to see this cat, this . . . this creature? Did you see her discard her fake fur and dive into the river to take a bath? Did you count how many bubbles surfaced from this cat-who-wasn't-a-cat? Which genii-king did our cute little Hanim turn out to be?

When Hanim first appeared in al-Baikwaly's house with the *nabk* tree, she had no name and she was virtually bald. Sheik al-Baikwaly adopted this sorry-looking stray, feeding her tidbits of meat, little wads of amber, and generally fattening her up on superior attitudes. In the guise of a golden lion with eyes of rarest turquoise, she reigned as the queen of his private quarters. She became his favorite, his shadow, spending the night in his rooms taking part in the celebrations, shooting dice, dancing with the Khazar boys, strumming strings, driving the nighthawks crazy, and abandoning herself to the incense and the music, especially to the sad twanging of the sitar. Hanim never strayed far from Sheik Baikwaly's right hand. The turquoise stars that were her eyes stayed fixed on her master's face, attentive to his every thought, his slightest whim, occasionally soothing the souls of his friends (or aggravating them), guiding the evening toward its conclusion and preparing for the call to dawn prayer in the Holy Mosque. Hanim acted as the maestro of all activities, including the Sheik's moods, ushering his needs through doors leading to their satisfaction and banishing whatever he found tiresome or displeasing. She became the most pampered pet in the entire Meccan valley, a cat whose status approached the sacred. She was regarded as a blessing from God, able somehow to unlock the towering doors of wealth. Everyone took care to make room for her next to the Sheik wherever he was overseeing the distribution of water from the holy well of Zamzam to the city's neighborhoods and houses. People believed that some portion of the turquoise in Hanim's eyes was dissolved in every pitcher, every vat of water, and that the blessing associated with the turquoise would seep into all the houses and creatures who used it.

Hanim was apart from al-Baikwaly only during prayer time, when the Sheik, his hands still moist from ritual ablutions, left the house and made his way to the Holy Mosque. Hanim trailed behind, accompanying him to the end of the street where the *nabk* tree stood. There she would leave him to walk alone through the Valley of Abraham to the vestibule of the Holy Mosque. She stayed in her spot awaiting his return. And when she saw her master coming back, she jumped up and dashed through the crowd to meet him, scampering through the Sheik's entourage, between the legs of the horses jingling with shells and silver ornaments.

Sheik Baikwaly was not one to court the angels of sleep. He slept hardly a wink; in fact there were times he slept not even that much. When clouds of weariness gathered and blurred his vision, he would stare off toward the horizon, fixing his eyes on some high, distant point and letting his soul drift away in that general direction, and as it ascended, soaring invisibly from sky to sky, all the way to the Unknown, his soul would shed its burdens, one at a time, while the Sheik's body remained posted by the gate of his house until his soul returned feeling much lighter, and refreshed with the vital energy of meteors.

So Sheik Baikwaly did not sleep, and Hanim was his companion in constant wakefulness. She would meet her master way off on the wrinkled horizon and ascend along with his soul, much to the astonishment of his guests and the young women of the household, who regarded the Sheik and his cat like a couple of stone idols or shrines whose aura was as mystifying as their acutely felt absence in the Unknown, and only grew more powerful when they returned to bestow on their beholders and the Sheik's premises (already quivering with welcoming vibrations) an energy that was sometimes hard to bear.

When my grandfather passed away, each of us inherited a share of his energy. We also inherited the talisman he used to recharge himself; not one shred of his vitality was lost or scattered among strangers. Until the day he died, Sheik Baikwaly continued to wear his fur mantle and leather vest, the uniform of the water carriers, though he had long ago stopped being a water carrier and Sheik of the Water Carriers. But he held on to the cherished title of Sheik and handed it down to us, dripping with the secrets of Mecca's hidden springs, which modify their spirits and sweetness upon entering the sanctuary of Zamzam. The hot springs of Zamzam regulate the water to a temperature that is just right for healing and give it a golden glow that satisfies hunger and refines the sensitivity of the soul.

Sheik Baikwaly insisted that Hanim share his meals. From his own hand he fed her bits of sugared barley soaked in amber syrup. (This was his favorite snack; he maintained that it stimulated body and soul, and awakened certain physical powers which otherwise lay dormant.) For all the attention lavished on Hanim, and the way the girls kept talking about it, the cat never aroused the least bit of jealousy in Nara, though the Sheik showed his wife no special consideration, and as for the privilege of sharing his meals, that was a rare event. Whenever they went off to the orchards for a picnic, the family's sense of direction and domestic perspectives got all mixed up. The Sheik himself started the confusion by removing his turban and displaying his brilliantly polished bald scalp, hitching up the silk belt around his waist, spending most of the day helping the slaves light fires, and preparing his favorite Khazar delicacy of oysters with slivered carrots and quince. All class boundaries and veils were dropped when we went to stay in the turquoise tents by the pools at Majin or Nowaria. There were no sheiks there, no veiled women, only boys and girls splashing through streams and well basins under the swaying shadows of palm trees and trellised roses.

Nobody could say what really went on between my grandfather and Nara. Now that they're gone, I sometimes ask Hannah how the Sheik ever had time to be alone with his wife. But she keeps avoiding the question or issuing the absurd kind of denials appropriate to family secrets ("Sheik Baikwaly was never alone with Nara—never!")

Husband and wife spent no time together alone? May I inquire how we came into existence—as the result of some freak electrical accident?

My sister Joman laughs. "Every morning," she whispers, "Nara would arrange her robe very primly and go down and sweep up the Sheik's rooms and polish that hookah of his, the one with the reddish water—bubble-bubble-bubble, all day and night, don't you know?—then she'd come right back up."

"That was in the olden times," says my mother, who makes it her maternal business to know what every whisper is about, "in the dawn of time." She turns away for fear that my persistent questioning might cause the Sheik himself to materialize. The family prefers to remember him as a creature exempt from human needs and foolish desires.

"Zamzam water is for whatever you drink it for," Jummo whispers. "Maybe we're descended from Nara and Zamzam."

36. Water and Gold

Tell me, my friend—is there some spot among your stash of jewels where that olden time, with its meticulously filled-in calendar and the people who lived its hours and seconds, might be hiding? If there is (and I certainly do think there is), please be so kind as to satisfy my curiosity: Look among your jewels for Sheik Baikwaly, look for him while he's trembling, shuddering, lost in his Nara.

It was plain as day: Nara moved the way a pleasured woman moves. She spread her happiness over our picnics, she was the life of the party, the soul of our celebrations. Wherever she went, even her shadow shed brightness. Nara's body . . . her body enclosed an infinite spring, replenished from a source that never ran dry. This was what helped her, right till the end, overcome her attacks of paralysis; this was the resource that gave her the strength to come back glowing with life, ready to dance again. Even her lips, distorted by strokes, regained their voluptuousness, their inviting roundness. Right after she died, when her body was laid out on a wooden plank and her skin had the pallor of a corpse on the way to the cemetery at al-Maala, her lips glistened like rubies.

Still, there remains the question of where and how and when her little inner rivers nourished her. And why didn't we sense the seepage and gurgling and heaving of her waters, we who never missed a single, sweet-sounding tingle or tremor in any of the paradoxes that go into making a private life in this world? How could we have missed the intimate *where* of my grandfather?

My grandfather, by virtue of being Sheik of the Zamzam Water Carriers, became the refuge of refugees. His work was founded on the principle of supplying Holy Water to everyone who passed in or out of the Holy Circle around al-Kaaba. In this place, charity was the rule. Anyone who entered the Holy Circle was entitled to be a water carrier. This provision functioned as a safety net for hungry foreigners and homeless people, for anyone in any sort of jeopardy. My grandfather welcomed the newcomers by assigning them to look after the water pitchers and the *tazzas*, the copper drinking bowls. Clattering along with these items, the apprentice water carriers lurched through the Holy Mosque, distributing Zamzam water all day long. At night the Sheik paid each worker enough to sustain him. It was a nonprofit enterprise. The way my grandfather ran things, each émigré pilgrim made a living, and he made it by calling out to those who were thirsty, with a pitcher strapped across his shoulder, another pitcher in his left hand, and a stack of bowls in his right. During my grandfather's administration of this charity, there wasn't a single homeless student who didn't learn to work like a professional.

In Ramadan, the month of fasting, my grandfather and his men took over and used the Zamzam well to dispense water to the fasting multitudes throughout the city. The Carriers spread out across Mecca leaving a pitcher of water on every doorstep at sunset, and another at dawn. When the sun began to rise, there came a moment (some people called it a deadline) when there was just enough light for devout eyes to distinguish between a strand of black thread and a strand of white, and that was when everyone stopped eating. The clay water pitchers stood on all the doorsteps like soldiers armored in straw, filling the air with the perfume of Zamzam.

Throughout his life, Sheik Baikwaly strove to free himself and his family from the lust for gold. The vast amounts of money that passed through his hands never seduced him. Still the gold kept coming, Heaven only knew from where. It fell on him like a battering rain, not a merciful one. Al-Baikwaly's policy was to give away any surplus. "Money is the root of all evil," he insisted. "Money is sinful. And to nourish it with our tears and with our daughter's flesh—that is the greatest sin of all."

The women of the house with the *nabk* tree were weaned from gold even before they were weaned from milk. In short, they learned to live without regard for money.

Nara was convinced that Hanim was responsible for afflicting the Sheik with this peculiar attitude toward gold. The cat, she felt sure, was an operative dispatched by the Unknown to confuse and bedevil the water carriers and test the integrity of their intentions in giving away precious water to complete strangers.

The water carriers, because they were men of honor, truly devoted to their task, were entitled to cross over into the Luminous Worlds, mysterious realms that were generally regarded as hazardous to ordinary matter and the well-being of the material world. It came naturally to creatures who found themselves incarnated in one of the Luminous Worlds to become preoccupied with getting and having, with owning and ownership. From there it was a short step to wanting to enslave others and owning many slaves.

This, according to Nara's line of reasoning, was why Hanim shadowed the Sheik of the Zamzam Waters so closely, for it was the cat's mission in his mortal life to make the Sheik aware of the vast amounts of money that could be made from the wells under his supervision. Indeed, this water was perhaps the most ancient form of gold. It trickled down from sacrificial ceremonies and seeped underground to become the Holy Water coursing through God's Holy Land, dark subterranean layers of liquid stacked over other subterranean layers, darkness upon darkness upon darkness, fermenting into a potion that enhanced the soul's talent for uniting with the Eternal Self.

It was from this darkness that Hanim arose, intent on winning disciples and making confidants out of the hardheaded water carriers. Over the course of time she came to win the hearts of many Meccans, and she helped advance the interests of her allies, whose ambitious plans often bore a resemblance to the prayers they said while swigging their pitchers of Zamzam.

37. Caravan to the Unknown

In the dimness of pre-dawn, Hanim led Sheik Baikwaly through the ravine called al-Hajla. The cat paused to scratch the ground. The muezzin sang the call to dawn prayer, the lanterns of al-Hajla stopped clinking. The only sound was the pensive patter of slippers making their way to the Holy Mosque.

Hanim gave the Sheik a hard look, cat to master, transfixing him with her turquoise eyes. He knew he had no choice but to follow her. Halfway through the ravine, she came to a halt and started digging with her claws. The Sheik heard a jingling sound, blended with the snort of a camel. He spun around, expecting to see a passing caravan in some distress. The scratching of the cat's claws matched the tempo of the jingling and the camel's snorting, and the orchestration of these odd noises sounded like the gold coins clinking on the delighted ground, which fairly jumped for joy, like a pampered pet.

The entire ravine—the colonnaded walkways, the dormers, the marble soldiers standing guard on the roofs, the narrow alleys between the houses—everything went dead quiet, straining to hear who or what could be coming out of the ground and making such a commotion.

Suddenly the Sheik understood that the noise was coming directly from under Hanim's paws. He inclined his head (he was wearing a gold-embroidered turban lined with white silk) and started digging with his own hands, attempting to pry away the mask formed by clumps of earth. The snorting and jiggling grew louder. The head and neck of a camel emerged. The camel's mouth was spouting gold coins.

It is written, for those with the courage to read such things, that in olden times a martyr-prince of Arabia took refuge in the ravine of al-Hajla during one of the constant wars between rival kings, and that he buried his enormous fortune here before being hacked to death by his enemies. Sheik Baikwaly was privy to this secret. The gold-spouting camel was deliberately put in his path by a caravan traveling to the Unknown. The caravan's route, however, was severed by the slashing of Hanim's claws, and the result was that the caravan was obliged to pay tribute in order to pass through Hanim's territory.

Sheik Baikwaly would later describe the caravan as being unmistakably regal in appearance. The camels were carrying *howdahs*, or litters, decorated with gold brocade and precious stones, and the litters' curtains, studded with rubies, glowed a red more intense than ordinarily seen by human eyes. Yet the jewelry-weighted curtains were so fine, so sheer, that the Sheik could make out the beautiful women sitting behind them. The women, who were slaves of Netherworldlings, appeared to be made of gems that had a life of their own, for the Sheik could also plainly see, beneath their coruscating skin, bright flames flickering where their hearts might have been.

Hanim scratched the earth insistently. The Sheik, just as insistently, recited protective prayers. Their duet persuaded the leaders of the mysterious caravan that the wisest course of action would be to avoid a fight. So what happened was this: the sheiks from the Unknown decided to sacrifice their most valuable she-camel and send its gold-stuffed gorge to Sheik Baikwaly as a sort of peace offering, with the understanding that the Sheik and his genii cat would grant the caravan permission to go on its way.

Because this incident took place on land my grandfather owned, he had firsthand knowledge of the convoluted route the subterranean caravan had followed. He therefore felt an obligation to spend the gold from the camel's mouth on the construction of a seven-story house with a seven-sided dome, directly above the invisible underground crossroads. (To me the house was a lookout tower for scouts from the Unknown, and on the roof, I imagined, they plotted the safest routes by which to send their merchandise and launched their signal rockets skyward.)

Once the Sheik made the decision to build the house, Hanim disappeared. The Sheik never bothered to look for her. He knew full well where she'd gone, and he was content.

38. The Well Is Sealed

I have no idea where the sun of our visions sets. And I don't know why the old times, with their family rooms full of joy, choose to hide themselves after sheltering our childhood in Mecca's Holy Circle. The Holy Circle owns me still. Which is why I keep cataloguing my sins and why the Khazars keep coursing through my veins. I'm obsessed by Mayjan, though I never laid eyes on him. He departed this world of ours long before I was born. There was a rumor to the effect that he drowned himself in the Zamzam well during the month of Sha'aban, at midnight on a full-moon night, when the Zamzam water fizzed and bubbled with the work of freshening people's fates and rescheduling the dates of their deaths.

The night Mayjan drowned, precisely at midnight, while the Zamzam well was gurgling and overflowing with fates, Dumboshi was betrothed to a certain Ma'moon al-Neyabi of the Qashqar clan. Well, there did come a time when Mayjan was gone. Perhaps he only changed his name, a trick that became something of a fad among young people as Mecca entered the modern age. I can still see him sitting under the *nabk* tree. Whenever a cold wind blows in Mecca, I crouch against the chill and dip into my mother's memories, taking whatever I find about Mayjan and sitting down to write. Writing shelters me against the overwhelming memory of Mayjan, of his name. The name alludes to the essences of water and of geniis. You may recall that *Meya* sounds very close to *mya*, the Arabic word for water, and *jan* is the same as the word for genii. So, *Meya-jan* . . . water genii.

He touches me. I can feel him, I can see him holding up the soggy water bags from the well in my grandfather's old house and dousing me, soaking me, drenching me, drowning me in time, in the years of my family and my city, drowning me in the Infinite that keeps me afloat but accepts no excuses about sickness or failing strength or the charms of oblivion.

Our well was permanently sealed the day al-Baikwaly's family moved from the house with the *nabk* tree to the seven-story house in the al-Hajla ravine. That was the day the porters carried off the box containing the secret maps of the Khazar sea—the final touch that sealed the awful emptiness inside the house with the *nabk* tree. The living rooms were empty now, hollow. A few specks of amber fluttered high in the speechless archways, in the alcoves and in our secret hideaways, erasing the images of what once had been, preparing the house for everlasting abandonment.

Suddenly Nara remembered a tattered fur piece she always wore while embroidering on chilly nights. She climbed down from her *howdah*. The camel snorted, stretched his neck, and turned his head trying to get a glimpse (or a bite) of the beautiful white Khazar woman. Jummo laughed, fighting her fear and infatuation for the animal.

Nara didn't wait for the camel to settle down. She hurried back inside the house and ran under the arch leading to the curiously empty living room. She rushed to open the tiny window by the stone bench in the corner. She gasped. The window looked out on a cluster of boulders on Mount Quayqian. She could see nothing at all of the old secret well and the seven spigots built into the wall. She could smell not a whiff of the dyes' strong odor, no scent of the embroidery or stylish clothes that used to fill the ancient stone room and gave it the warm scent of life. There was no trace of the wise-looking old stones, nothing but drab volcanic rocks staring dully back at Nara's dumbstruck face.

She returned, fur-less and belief-less, to the camels and the *howdahs*. Were all those happy nights of working and watching real? Did they really happen by the well? Was there a well at all? Those maidenly nights, illuminated by virginal visions, were they true? And did any of those visions trickle down into her daughters' embroidery and their rainbow-colored fabrics?

Nara ran headlong away from the well. Jummo fainted. Fear shivered the knees of the camels and the porters and the camel drivers. The Sheik's daughters were petrified. "This is no mere sickness," the camel drivers agreed. "This is a magic spell!" The evidence—the glint of fear in the camels' eyes—was incontestable.

When Sheik Baikwaly's attempts at reviving Jummo failed, he knew she'd been ensorcelled. He gathered her up and tucked her limp body inside Nara's *howdah*. She was transported to the towering new house for treatment. Nara's heart dated the day of their moving from the house with the *nabk* tree with Jummo's bewitchment and the strange disappearance of the well that meant so much to her daughters. The well meant more than words could say to the women of Mecca; the well knew their most intimate secrets. The well was female. What was its source, where was its end? The family moved. I wrote and wrote and wrote. I kept looking for the well.

39. The Love Potion

The day before Sheik Baikwaly's move from the house with the *nabk* tree, Mayjan was stricken with anguish and pain. He had spread himself so thinly in his dreams, he was so profoundly lost, that being awake was becoming a straightjacket. He went to his uncle, Sonbok the pharmacist, to ask his advice about hunting gazelles. Fire or arrows, what worked best? Clearly, the lad was terminally lovesick.

Sonbok, Sheik of the Pharmacists, had adopted Mayjan when the boy first arrived in Mecca and saw to it that his ward rose to a respectable standing in the Holy City. He addressed him as nephew and secured for him positions in a succession of crafts and professions with the idea that he would one day come into an inheritance of pharmaceutical skills and become Sheik of the Pharmacists in his own right.

"Pharmacy and perfumery," Uncle Sonbok maintained, "are the crown jewels of the trades and crafts. The only way for an apprentice to get ahead in this business is to set sail in the world and get all the experience he can in the arts of design and color craft, and study the interlocking graphs that chart the simplest lines while implying the subtlest harmonic relations; to make himself familiar with numerical calculations, the blending of mathematical values one into another—all things, of course, turn out to be transformations of zero and one—not to mention paradoxical equations, and so forth. When these essential skills have been mastered, it's time to move on to the study of rhythm and tempo in material things, and the variations in texture between animals, minerals, glass, and artifacts made of wood. And so forth."

To make sure that everything went smoothly with his nephew's education in the mysteries of nature's elements, especially with regard to their transformative powers, Sonbok sent the boy to study with the Sheik of All Trade Sheiks. Mayjan got experience in trades of all kinds; he went from working in a store that sold general merchandise to working with master inlay craftsmen to laboring on construction sites and doing carpentry, including carving intricate scrollwork on dormers. From his experience with the art of inlay, Mayjan developed a familiarity with shells and ivory. He came to know intimately the harmonies of these materials with precious metals such as gold and silver, and with aromatic woods of high quality. He concluded his studies by working with the Sheik of the Textile Merchants, where he learned about designing and making fabric from raw material through each stage of manufacturing. He became especially fascinated by the natural-looking textures of fabrics that mimicked flowering plants and the patterned skins of animals.

As for the love problem at hand, Uncle Sonbok prescribed seeds of nutmeg and opium poppies, with instructions that the seeds "be crushed and ground till they emit their inner fire. You'll be able to see it—a seed of black fire. Now take this flaming seed and mix it with a fresh date, and wad everything up into a ball and give it to your lover to eat. She will fall unconscious. For forty days she will sleep the sleep that is kin to death. This will put an end to any connection between her and her clan. Her clan will surrender all claims to her and set her free from slavish family devotion—the same as when we sever our ties with those who have died. Then—and only when this has been done—will the death-sleep leave her, and after forty days she'll come flying back to your nest, wherever it may be. The trail to the nest will be marked by the husks of the nutmeg shells, and your lovebird will follow this trail all the way to her new home with you. And don't forget to spread some nutmeg husks on your doorstep, so the bird will be sure not to miss you."

That night, while Jummo was sleeping, Mayjan sprinkled ground nutmeg on her jugular vein, on top of a dark mole she had. He mixed the ground nutmeg with seeds of opium poppies so that the inner light of the nutmeg seeds came forth and mated with the seeds of oblivion.

At the stroke of midnight, Jummo's cheeks twitched. She sighed a shuddering sigh and winced. Mayjan knew that the seeds of long, deep sleep had taken root.

At dawn on the day of Sheik Baikwaly's move, Mayjan stood waiting at the end of the alley holding a little ball of kneaded date fruit and the mixture of seeds. This was the ball that contained the angel of sleep, the spirit of the bird. As soon as the Sheik went off to morning prayer in the Holy Mosque, Mayjan crept toward the house with the *nabk* tree. He rapped three times. Jummo opened the door just a crack. Speechless, Mayjan held his breath. He tweezered the date ball between his thumb and forefinger and tucked it between Jummo's laughing lips.

Jummo's lips were hot. Mayjan rubbed his thumb and forefinger together, astonished by the hot wetness from her mouth. She closed the door. He put his fingers in his mouth, tasting her heat. The sensation of her heat and her wetness echoed in his senses for all the rest of his living days.

Mayjan spent the next forty days walking around and around al-Baikwaly's towering new house, keeping his eyes on the dormers of the seventh story, hoping to glimpse his lovebird on the wing. But Jummo, who was getting used to her elegant new surroundings, and to eating elegant breakfasts spiced with cardamom and served on fancy brocade, had developed an immunity against feathers and the urge to fly. Thus, despite the nutmeg talisman, she didn't leave the seventh story and she never made her way to Mayjan's opium-furnished nest.

Nara noticed the Khazar lad pacing outside the house. She also noticed the date balls dunked in their pitchers of fresh Zamzam. (These were the pitchers set on the doorstep every morning by the Zamzam Carriers, who were loyal to Sheik Baikwaly.) Before long, the entire household sensed the ominous plot directed at getting al-Baikwaly's females to grow feathers and fly away, and then to separate Jummo from the airborne flock. Consequently, the Sheik's trusty water carriers were forbidden to leave the Zamzam pitchers on the doorstep. One of the water carriers, an eager apprentice, was recruited to carry the pitchers all the way up to the seventh floor and hand it directly to Nara, whose hands could be seen reaching from behind the enormous oaken door at the top of the stairs.

40. Mayjan's Fortune

Big Ruby's apartment was the most luxurious in all of Mecca. Her benches were inlaid with rare shells from Syria, and on the benches lay damask cushions, red ones and white ones, authoritatively arranged. Sandalwood incense drifted through the sandalwood dormers, perfuming the living quarters and Big Ruby herself, mistress of all she surveyed.

She was fond of spending her evenings sitting by the window watching stories unfold in the *souk* known as al-Layl, the market just below her house. Sometimes she turned the other way and simply looked around her living room, letting her eye come to rest on, say, one of the archways studded with cowry shells.

The women slaves of her husband, who was the Sheik of the Textile Merchants, knew that their mistress could hear all secrets, secrets of the land as well as the sea, in the cowry shells. Many of these secrets had to do with dervishes who fell in love with geniis from the Unknown. Big Ruby liked to combine these tales with the stories of travelers she watched passing through the market under her window.

It was sunset. She was reclining invisibly in the shadow of her dormer. She sensed a faint movement in the archway of the entrance to her room. She opened her eyes and tried to focus on the mirrors that hung like glittery shoulders on either side of the door. She glimpsed the shadow of her young helper Mayjan, standing on tiptoes, hesitating. She couldn't help noticing the boy's lips; they were trembling and dripping ruby-red blood. She was shocked to see him so distraught. She signaled him to come closer. He remained fixed in place, as if clinging to his reflection in the mirrors by the door and drawing strength from his twinned image. Or maybe, thought Big Ruby, it was the image of his *qreen*, his mate.

She sat up and took hold of her *mihrana*, the head covering she'd tossed on one of red cushions. She wrapped her dark hair in its whiteness, and waited to hear what the young man had to say. Mayjan kept standing there in silence. Big Ruby walked over and sat down on the bench nearest the door, not more than an arm's length from the lad, though the distance between them was a world of perplexity.

"What's bothering you?" she asked. "What brings you here this time of night? You finished your assignments for the day, and it's time you went home to your uncle." The lad remained tongue-tied before Big Ruby. She repeated her question: "What's the matter with you?"

Mayjan unfastened his belt. It was made from the pale green skin of Great Basil Python, the Reptile Queen of the Khazar Sea who had ruled during the epoch before the great flood. He tossed the belt to Big Ruby. Looping and twisting in on itself, it looked utterly lifelike. Big Ruby could not take her eyes off its beauty and the glow emanating from the skin, which looked like a light from ancient times. She undid the gold buttons that fastened the gown around her neck, took a deep breath of the Python's basil-like scent, and lost herself in contemplation of the belt's magnificence. The skin was richly variegated, mottled like the surface of an ever-changing river. She stared at the torrent of patterns.

"This belt comes from our ancient seas," she said, sighing. "But I shouldn't let my eyes enjoy its basil shade of green. I shouldn't keep staring like this. Because if I do, my awful childhood on the shores of Khazar Land will jump right out of these waves and whitecaps that I'm seeing."

She raised her eyes to Mayjan. She seemed a lost little girl. All the grandeur and sophistication of her status as wife of the Sheik of the Textile Merchants had deserted her. The mirrors in the room reflected only the skinny little body of a poor child. She no longer even had her regal name, Yaqut Khan. She was just a homeless waif, nondescript, of unknown ancestry, with no place to go, pitied by travelers who took her up and put her down in the Holy Land, where good luck finally caught up with her and enthroned as a queen amid silks and beautifully furnished rooms.

The layers of silk hung loosely on her now. Years of luxurious living in Mecca had not succeeded in peeling away the quivering coat of nervousness that came from years of living on the road. Every pilgrim to the Holy Land wore the same coat of fear, more or less.

Big Ruby looked hard at her girlhood in the mirrors. She looked at Mayjan, especially his face. She looked back at the mirrors. She looked at the belt, and in a small voice she asked, "What would I do with a work of art like this? Or should I say, what can I do for you?"

Mayjan ripped open the lining of the belt. Seven gold pounds spilled out, rolled across the floor, and tried to make their escape into the patterns of the Persian carpet. Mayjan ran after them, recaptured all seven pieces, and deposited them in the palm of his mistress's hand.

"This is my inheritance from my grandfather," he said. "I intend to use it as a dowry for al-Baikwaly's middle daughter."

Big Ruby's eyes widened. It took her a moment to steady herself and take in everything the boy had said, to weigh what he wanted.

"But you are so young," she said with a sad smile, "to bind yourself with a chain like this. We are speaking here about real bonds, about lasting alliances, and you haven't even shaken off the dust from your first adventures yet. You and al-Baikwaly's family are worlds apart. Between you and his daughter there is a difference in standing as tall as Mount Thor."

Mayjan shed the one tear he had anticipated shedding. "Al-Baikwaly would acknowledge this inheritance." His voice was breaking up. "He wouldn't turn it down."

"How did you manage to get yourself into such a mess, young man? Sheik Baikwaly acknowledges only the sons of the finest families, the most important families. You're a nice boy with fair prospects in trade.

But before you get to a certain level in the society of this city, no sensible father would risk his daughter on you."

"But if you cast a spell on her with that red necklace of yours," Mayjan said, "it can be arranged so that no suitor asks for her hand, not until I do become somebody, and then she can be mine." The boy's voice, reciting his well-rehearsed plan, took on the bright rustle of leaves on the *nabk* tree at al-Baikwaly's old house.

And the red necklace around Big Ruby's neck took on a wicked shine. She tucked it between her breasts and buttoned up the gold buttons on her gown. It was a very old necklace made of blood-red cornelian with spots of green at the center. These green hearts conferred certain magical powers known to be effective in influencing destiny. The necklace could, depending on the whim of its mistress, bring good luck or bad. It could keep a woman from conceiving, prevent a girl from getting married, or inflict paralysis on a perfectly healthy adversary. Whenever Big Ruby entered into negotiations on her husband's behalf, she always wore her cornelian necklace, and she always came out on top. As her husband, Sheik of the Textile Merchants, grew to be a very rich man, the cornelian necklace became famous for unlocking the door of good fortune, and locking it.

"What genii or demon has possessed you?" she asked. "You are deluded, young man. I'll say it again: You are too young to even ask about getting connected to Sheik Baikwaly's family. You expect me to make my best friend Nara's daughter a prisoner of love! A beauty like her! At the most marriageable age! Nara doesn't deserve that; the only thing Nara deserves is contentment and good luck and happiness."

Mayjan shuddered with despair. His rosy cheeks turned sickly yellow. He ran out of the room, leaving his seven gold pounds behind.

Big Ruby unclasped her fist. She spent some time savoring the coins, flipping one golden beauty after another. On the face of the first coin she recognized the monogram of the Khazar emperor, and on the second, the royal scepter ascendant, flanked by the emperor's eyes. She realized that she was holding in her hands a fortune too vast—and possibly too dangerous—for moneychangers even to estimate. She stuffed the coins back inside the pale green belt and buried the belt at the bottom of a trunk under her bench.

She went to the window, reclined in the cool shade of her dormer, and lost herself in the stories unfolding below, in the lives of the amusing characters down there, those little people everlastingly crawling from one kingdom, one state of being, to another.

Mayjan ran, ran, ran. He kept running until he came to the shop of his uncle, Sonbok the Sheik of Pharmacists and Perfumers. What tormented the boy most of all was the fear that Big Ruby would stop using him to deliver the messages she was always sending to al-Baikwaly's house, preventing him from seeing Jummo. During all the time he worked for the Sheik of the Textile Merchants, Mayjan had always been able to sense the compassion his wife felt for him. He knew that she knew how lonely he felt in the big city, menaced in by mountains all around. And now he knew that she was going to put an abrupt end to his agonized dreams and strip away his dangerous illusions.

His uncle greeted him with a knowing eye. Mayjan skinnied his shoulders and tucked himself away in a shadowy corner of the shop, nuzzling the bundles of medicinal herbs, mostly dried *nabk* leaves, that were going to be sent to the house with the *nabk* tree. From their scents he extracted visions of funerals, of coffins draped in perfumed fabrics. He struggled with all his might to maintain the patience needed to outlast his loneliness in the Holy Circle of Mecca.

When darkness fell, Sonbok rolled up the awnings and left Mayjan to himself. The boy's eyes grew heavy. He slept. The barricades of waking sense collapsed: the meaning of the house with the *nabk* tree, its *intentions,* changed suddenly from funerals to scenes of the house made whole. Mayjan was flooded with realer-than-life visions of the loving house loving his lover.

He stayed under the *nabk* bundles for three whole days. Sonbok diligently ignored his nephew's existence and avoided the chore of dealing with his amorous distress. He went serenely about his business, adjusting the flames under his bubbling alembics, stirring ointments, filling prescriptions to ease difficult births, and distilling elixirs and spirits that might wash the pain away from a young man's wounded heart and lend it wings again.

41. Mayjan Drowns

Another month, another crescent. Sheik Baikwaly was gone for good from his house with the *nabk* tree.

Mayjan, having abandoned all hope of ever returning to the lost paradise of the house with the *nabk* tree, pushed his way through the crowds toward the Holy Mosque.

"Oh Sheik, if you see to it that I get married, if you will permit me to select a wife from your lovely, warm family, I will work for you as a water carrier for the rest of my life."

Sheik al-Baikwaly looked around, searching for the author of this bizarre request. His gaze fell on the young man standing directly in front of him, arms courageously folded. He studied the boy, sizing him up, evaluating his bloodlines. It took some effort to credit the dark fuzz over his lip as a mustache. Cheeks quite pink, though; not at all impoverished, no . . . These calculations the Sheik filed away for future reference.

"Well," he said evenly, "if one still has a few bunches of grapes on the vine when one grows up . . ."

"But I am already a man of independent means, sir. I'm master of my own life. And in a year or two I'll be master of my uncle's and my grandfather's trade as a pharmacist and perfumer."

"Another crescent . . . two perhaps—in a month of so we will give our blessing to the suitor standing first in line. Girls are not at all like grain, you know—no, not like grain at all—girls can't be put on the shelf for seven years and stored against famine."

Al-Baikwaly left without saying good-bye. He hurried across the colonnade and the gravel-covered yard. He arrived, in full stride, at the Zamzam well. The tranquility of the well took him in its arms. He exhaled a deep angry breath. He lowered his lips to a vat of fragrant Zamzam and drank, submerging his beard, his face, and the better part of his chest in the perfumed peacefulness of the holy water.

Mayjan went to a corner of the Holy Mosque where the followers of Sheik al-Hanafi were studying their lessons. He sat down and listened to the students recite the verses of al-Ana'am, forgetting the burden of

Mecca's social codes, blissfully oblivious to professional responsibilities. He leaned against an alabaster pillar and dozed off. The latticed shadow of the sanctuary's lantern fell across his face.

The verses of al-Ana'am followed him into his sleep. These lines of the Holy Book tell how people put the bliss of animals to good use in their own lives, for beauty and nourishment. Some of the pigeons who made their home in the mosque flapped overhead, reading Mayjan's dreams. In his dreams the verses appeared as omens of good fortune washing over those for whom the scriptures were being recited. The pigeons soared and whirled, dipping their beaks in the rainbow arching through the mist of sacred words.

Mayjan woke with a start, jumped to his feet, and rushed to his uncle's shop in the al-Moda *souk*. There the spirits of the house with the *nabk* tree reignited the fire in his heart, intensifying his agony. He ran around in circles, not knowing what to do or where to go. Predictably, he returned to al-Baikwaly's big house in the al-Hajla ravine. Around and around the house he walked, but after awhile he found his way to the shack on Mount Hindi, the shack with the onyx face on the floor, which increased his pain still more, driving him back outside the shack, where he staggered blindly through clusters of pretty Turkish girls, seeing nothing but the image of Jummo, which smashed him like a thunderbolt, which propelled him back to his uncle to ask for a remedy or cure, something to mute the thunderbolt and temper his pain.

"Her star is higher than yours," Sonbok advised gravely. "She will burn you up."

Mayjan paid no attention to this warning. He began using elixirs and ointments to incite visions of Jummo, and dangerous visions at that—like the dream he had of her staring at him with dark, bloody eyes, her hair glistening like blackened silver soaked in water pure as the well of night.

Wherever he turned, he sank deeper into the dark, bloody eyes until he had no recourse but to escape her spell by reciting al-Zalzala, the verses of the Qur'an in praise of earthquakes, until all traces of the traveler who once was Mayjan were erased.

◆   ◆   ◆

Until, that is, the day of the announcement that Ma'moon al-Neyabi had been selected as Jummo's husband. On that day Mayjan went to the shack and planted his feet right in the center of the flaming onyx face. From the mosaic there came a breeze, a spirit so happy and light-hearted that it blew the weariness away from Mayjan's body.

The fresh skin laid bare by the breeze was hard as stone, and Mayjan, like a stone, was swept by a sudden flood down the slopes of Mount Hindi, past the dome that covered the Zamzam well, directly into the vestibule of the Holy Mosque, where he was deposited in Ishmael's Lap—the heart of the Sacred Stone itself. Here his prayers were sure to be answered. He stood up directly under one of the Zamzam spouts, no more than an arm's length from dozens of trembling water bowls. A Yemenite water carrier was giving a drink to a pilgrim from Africa who was so terribly thirsty that as he sipped he shuddered with relief, spilling his water, which trickled away in a thin rivulet and formed a puddle under the spout, as if begging to be picked up. Mayjan knelt down on the stone to drink, skinning his knees. The smoldering passions inside him, lured by the illusion of cool depths in the puddle, jumped into the water.

Like a shooting star he fell. He drowned—in the very Lap of Ishmael, in the Zamzam well—right before the eyes of the African pilgrim.

Thereafter the powerful fragrance of Mayjan's spirits blended with the earthy incense that was stirred into every drink of Zamzam poured in al-Baikwaly's house.

42. A Woman's Madness

That was the year of the great flood in Mecca. It was known as the Onyx Flood because it pounced on the city out of some dark nowhere, bubbling up from the navel of the universe and spouting in all eight directions of the compass. A great harvest of water, having ripened in secret, suddenly erupted, sweeping away everything in its path. Donkeys, chickens, sheep, the statues of soldiers guarding the rooftops—all sailed along on the floodtide with a grace and serenity that might almost have been called lovely. People remarked that the great majority of the victims were males.

The flood raged on and on. The sight of so much water aroused the city's animal spirits. Sidi Wahdana was observed riding the waves and shepherding swept-away cattle with cries of *You-Who-Are-Alive!* until finally he disappeared along with the flood, just as if he'd never existed.

The hot wind called al-Simoom blew stiffly. The sun shrunk the glistening puddles.

The citizens of Mecca awoke to find that the waters had left behind millions of shards of onyx, carried in from the rock-strewn hills surrounding the city. The streets were littered with fiery stones so brilliant that there was no need for lanterns; midnight seemed bright as noon. But the cobblestone alleys were shadowed by grief, and in the house of Sheik al-Baikwaly mourning ruled, skulking in its teakwood dormers.

The flood was followed by a time of astonishing prosperity. Women's eyes took on a breeding shine, the number of marriage contracts soared, souls were bound together, gifts exchanged, and celebration was the order of the day. Married couples became lovers, the insinuating sweetness of *raski* raisins lingered on everyone's lips, all citizens shared in the city's high animal spirits. Never before had the Holy Circle of Mecca seen so many happy nights.

Then people's eyes began to twitch, and their healthy gleam flickered. Among the women a sort of madness took hold. The flood of water was followed by a flood of talismans and amulets. There was a surge in demand for the traditional healers called Sadas, who specialized in treating disorders of body and mind. The Sadas kept very busy writing prescriptions and casting spells to save whoever could be saved of Mecca's women.

The madness invaded the house of al-Maghrabi, my paternal grandfather. My cousin Khairiya suddenly became fearless to the point of insanity, and ran out into the street without her veil. Taking off the veil on a public thoroughfare was a sure sign that Khairiya had taken leave her senses.

She ran wild till they caught her and wrapped her in my father's blackest *jubbah* and locked her up in a lightless room on the top floor, the one furthest from the street. There she stayed until the arrival of Sayed Hassan al-Sheik. It was then that Khairiya's story took its famously redemptive turn.

Sayed Hassan waited in the doorway. He did not cross the threshold of al-Sofa, which is what the old ones called the narrow doorways to every room in Mecca's ancient houses. The entranceway was dank. It opened into a darkness tinted by the faint scent of frankincense. Sayed Hassan waited and listened. The spirits in this place were quite sensitive, easily offended. He'd sent his own servant spirits on ahead to secure safe passage. He stood there for a long time, naked to the guardian spirits. Then he moved. Rather, he exhaled a long breath of acceptance—of his being accepted—but he did not step inside the room. He sucked up some of the silence and stayed where he was. Then he left.

He came to a halt on a plank of teak flooring embossed by triangles outlined with antique copper nail heads. He uttered his first words: a command to shroud the mirror on the left side of the door.

"Don't let her see the wild look on her own face," he advised Khairiya's mother Safiya. "If she does, the madness will get to be a habit, and she'll never be rid of it."

He left without laying a finger on the veiled woman. He didn't so much as brush against any of the ancient, distinguished looking stones that made up the walls of the house.

Sayed Hassan called for a pitcher of bubbly Zamzam. He placed the pitcher next to his prayer rug in the small sanctuary reserved for his use in the Holy Mosque. The next day, at dawn, the pitcher of Zamzam overflowed with protective verses from the chapter of the Holy Book called al-Baqara, The Cow.

Mohammed al-Maghrabi brought the pitcher back to his house, where the healers sprinkled the veiled woman with a few drops of Zamzam before any attempt was made to remove her clothing and bare her insanity. When the first drop of water hit Khairiya, the dark *jubbah* trembled as if the spirits that had taken possession of her were struggling to escape. When the second drop hit her, her reluctant body hesitated and she started speaking in tongues, or in some indecipherable, nonhuman dialect.

All the pigeons and women in the house froze like statues. Gradually, as the water kept pattering on her, Khairiya quieted down.

The first part of her they dared to uncover was her left arm. (Because the veins of the arms are the most direct route to the heart, the Sadas call this spot "the heart's abyss".) On the arm they hung an amulet of onyx so vibrantly black it looked alive. The pendant was the size of a thumb and was wrapped in strips of wild camel hide.

When they unveiled Khairiya's face, it was pale and lifeless as cloth bleached in turmeric. Safiya pried opened her daughter's lips and gave her a sip of Zamzam into which had been stirred the verses of al-Baqara, including the key protective verse *al Korsi*, or The Throne. The instant the spirits of these verses reached Khairiya's heart, she stood up on her own and her features regained their composure. The turmoil in her soul turned into a yesterday.

The onyx amulet stayed with her just long enough to do its work, gradually dissolving and disappearing into her skin. The wild camel thongs disintegrated. At this point Khairiya was ready to love a member of the human race, and fall in love she did, with a Sada gentleman from Indonesia whom she met while picnicking in Qarwa, a lovely orchard in Taif. They met while he was resting under a peach tree and watching her as she walked toward him, unaware that she was being watched. He stole looks at her and tucked the looks away in his heart. Khairiya had a distinctive arch to her eyebrows, and this arch grabbed the gentlemen's soul and pinched it, and from the spot where his soul was pinched, poison spread throughout his body. Yes, poison it was, or perhaps the flame of a shooting star. Or perhaps just some vast emptiness.

He fell into Khairiya's love. When at last she noticed him, his chest filled up with her love and his love overflowed into her.

What transpired was this: Khairiya was shielded from the onyx amulet re-veiled, so to speak, by marriage, and saved from possession by geniis by becoming addicted to human love.

So Sheik Baikwaly hurried to veil Dumboshi by tying her in marriage to Ma'amon al-Neyabi, thus sparing her from the trouble of dealing with floods of madness and the capricious moods of onyx. Or so he thought.

43. The Marriage Dance

On the seventh day of Jummo's wedding celebration, Sheik Baikwaly threw a party for his in-laws. Huge tented pavilions were erected on the sides of the ravine, bonfires were lit. Khatim al-Hijazi, the maestro of *majroor*, sang the heavenly music he'd made famous in the Sorat mountain range. Some people said he played a drum covered with the skin of a sea-*houri*, or mermaid, and that the slightest tap on this drum would summon up echoes of treasures drowned in the Kolzom Sea, which in olden days was the name of the Red Sea. In al-Hijazi's songs people heard echoes from Kolzom's grottos, the shushing of waves on its coral reefs, and the murmuring of exotic sea creatures:

> *Don't send me away, I've come so far.*
> *You ladies from Safa, you know me well.*
> *Al-Madieq's flowers—how sweet they are,*
> *How beckoning—welcome me home!*
> *Your kohl pencil feels at home*
> *In the shadows under my eyes.*

Wearing an unusual silver headband (Sheik Baikwaly's wedding present to her), Jummo the bride moved like a queen through the crowd of guests, eyes aglow. People couldn't stop looking at her. She danced to the beating of drums pounding in the gaudy tents, danced in a trance, danced to music no one else could hear, wherever in the world they might be, wherever the music might be coming from. The aching strains of an aloe lute, with its ten doubled strings, hung in the air. Each strum of the lute raked the bride's taut nerves; she danced and danced and danced and danced, careening through the other dancers like a bird who'd just had her throat slit. It was the first time that one of Sheik Baikwaly's daughters had danced herself unconscious.

Jummo, tranced, looked up at *al-sohail*, the brightest star in the constellation Carina. So high, so high above . . . she lost herself in skies that others could scarcely see, though the skies bewitched them, too, for Jummo bewitched them when they looked back down at her.

Out on the street, in the pavilion where the men had gathered, there was a feeling of unease, as when animals sense the approach of a predator or a natural catastrophe.

The heat that was roaring inside Jummo, her insatiable smoldering heat, was making the air around her uncomfortable. She ran to an alcove in the living room and flung herself down on the blood-red cushions. They cast a ruddy glow on her cheeks. She was a woman on fire. She pawed the cushions, frantically searching for a place to extinguish herself in their checkerboard patterns of white and red.

She got up and started dancing again. Hannah and Zubayda hovered around her. Hannah watched her daughter's limbs quaking. Jummo whispered in her sister's ear, making sure that nothing she said reached her mother-in-law, who was sitting in the center of the alcove. "A man makes a whirlwind. His whirlwind enters the woman's belly. From the belly, the whirlwind rises and makes clouds in her head."

Zubayda squeezed in between the bride's whispers and Hannah's laughter. Jummo continued in a lower whisper: "I don't know how I'm supposed to surrender to the touch of this Ma'amon al-Neyabi. Truth is, he just doesn't move me."

She threw herself back into the crowd of twirling dancers and didn't sit down for the rest of the party.

Khatim al-Hijazi beat his drum till the mermaid skin took on a shine. Moaning, tapping, he sang . . .

> Zaïd plays with passion's night messengers . . . wa–he–nah.
> There's a reed in his hand
> And he's crowned with a black headband . . . wa–he–nah . . .

◆   ◆   ◆

By the end of their honeymoon (a crescent honeymoon, of course), Ma'amon al-Neyabi felt dipped in honey. But Jummo was gagging on the taste of sour apples. "There's no hope I can ever feel anything for him," she informed her sisters. "No hope whatsoever."

The fact was that she despised the bridegroom, the *green* who kept battering her without being able to incite the pleasure-storm she expected to seize and shiver her spine. "There are storms inside him, but they're tame—just little waves. He doesn't know how to open up or how to take me into him."

Jummo went on complaining with her usual inventiveness. Then, turning her attention to Hannah, she became sad.

"Tell me, Hannah," she asked, "how does the storm open you up—how does it swallow you up? Does one storm follow another? What about Zubayda? Is it really like a hurricane with her and her husband al-Kashkari? These little hurricanes of mine—they're so awfully safe! Ma'amon al-Neyabi's got a blind spot in his soul; he can't even begin to see me."

Jummo never tired of finding new ways to describe her disappointments and define their exact shapes. With her it was an art form. (As perhaps it is with you, dear friend.)

It got to the point where she was paying morbid attention to her feelings. To al-Sharifa, who was treating her condition with amulets, she confided: "There are certain souls who are so locked up that even the locks that lock these souls have locks of their own. My soul wants . . . my soul wants desperately for currents to flow between his soul and mine. I want to ride up high, I want to fly. I'm crying out to him, but there's no answer. Instead of helping me burst happily into flames, he's crippling my soul. How can you get close to someone without uniting with them? And what's the point of uniting if it doesn't set off sparks? Besides, how can you get close to someone who doesn't set your soul on fire and get your body all worked up? He can't even get my fire started. His body is blind and deaf and dumb. He doesn't feel a thing."

Three more crescents came and went. Now it was the groom's turn to start complaining—about cold weather and stiffening in his joints. He squeaked so loudly every time he moved that whenever he reacted to his bride's caresses, the household was treated to a concert.

Ma'amon al-Neyabi's mother and sisters, who took after him in meekness of manner, picked up his refrain of complaints. There was nothing he could do to silence their wailing; his sister, a widow, felt that her children had been doubly orphaned by her brother's troubles.

Sheik Baikwaly dispatched spies to assess the newlyweds' domestic situation. A Yemenite servant, the one with chronically bloodshot eyes, returned with this report: "I saw my mistress Dumboshi, she was a wax candle-doll. And master Ma'amon al-Neyabi couldn't bring himself to touch the wick of the candle. As it were . . . "

The Sheik appreciated the Yemenite's cleverness, while deploring the clumsiness of his symbolism.

Finally, six crescents after her wedding, Jummo bolted like a wild filly. She returned to the house of her father, al-Baikwaly, and steadfastly refused to listen to any suggestions for patching things up proposed by go-betweens.

"Al-Neyabi has fallen under a magic spell," she said, her voice teetering between laughter and anguish. "He's been bewitched by that bewitched witch of a cat, Hanim."

Zubayda laughed, shattering the veil of composure that Jummo wore even when her expression bordered on wildness. Tears streaked Jummo's cheeks and dribbled down her cleavage. Seeing her tears, Hannah went white.

White . . . who else's eyes were white?

Dumboshi broke into hysterical laughter, which became contagious— everyone in the room got caught up in cackling. Breeze-blown curtains scuffed the windowsills. *"Aman ya rubee aman!"* Nara muttered under her head covering. "May God save us all!"

"Believe me," Jummo continued, "the top half of him—he's just a pig in human skin. And the bottom half—it's made of stone. What am I supposed to do every night—rub my body like a grindstone against that boulder of his?"

Zubayda interrupted with a loud and rather nasty version of an old proverb: "Don't try to fool me with false promises of red meat. Just let have my own little lick of the grindstone, thanks very much—I'll be the mouse in the butcher shop—and sleep by myself, even if it means the death of me."

Nara, who seemed wholly intent on dissolving a lump of sugar in her light golden tea (and she never drank tea with sugar), listened politely to her daughter's stories of escape from domination by men. But she never for a moment even entertained the possibility that Dumboshi, for all the fire in her temper and iron in her soul, could thrive in a relationship with a man. She conveyed her opinion with another proverb: "The bread men crave is a fire eaten by someone on fire."

The debate about the finer points of combustible passions and pig- and stone-ology went on and on till the tears welling up in Jummo's throat turned to stones themselves. The three women discussed every intimate detail of their lives. Wounds were exposed for all the heavens to see, and the heat of the wounds was cooled by the sweet sighs of compassionate friends. As for cleansing and healing these wounds, that was left to time and Mecca's sun.

44. Divorce

Toward the end of the seventh crescent, al-Neyabi arranged for a special place, a sort of den, where he could claim his bride and confirm her un- conditional surrender to him once and for all. The bridegroom was pre- pared to use the full force of law, if necessary, to take Jummo.

But Sheik Baikwaly put a crimp in his plan with a letter delivered by one of his Khazar messenger boys. When al-Neyabi opened the letter, its directness struck him dumb. (Indeed, he was so taken aback that he failed to detect the miniscule green particles on the paper, which blurred his senses and robbed him of his free will.)

In the name of all that is decent, the letter said, *set her free.*

For the first time since the campaign of threats and go-betweens began, Ma'amon al-Neyabi appeared in al-Baikwaly's quarters. He took a seat. Sheik Baikwaly sat in the middle of a circle of sheiks. These worthies, along with the Imam of the Holy Mosque, were present as witnesses.

Dumboshi's fate was pronounced in one word: *Divorced.*

The Imam of the Holy Mosque wrote out the document and the Sheiks sealed it with their signatures.

Jummo broke into trilling, soul-wringing cries of joy that shook the seventh floor of the house on the ravine. Her shrieks confirmed her fate and gave it a coating of sadness and grief.

Let me assure you—in all the years he lived among us, no one found any hard evidence of magical literacy on the part of Sheik Baikwaly. If my grandfather had some special talent in this arena, it must have included a talent for invisibility, because it never assumed a shape we could see.

My older sister Joman, who was the custodian of my mother's secrets, always accompanied mother whenever they traveled between Mecca and Taif. On those occasions, when our household spirits got upset and my father's authority was thrown off balance, it was my mother, the illiterate, who took refuge in letters. She would sit down and with Joman's help she'd fill an entire page with observations about figs and olives and the hailstorms we sometimes encountered in Taif. When they came to the bottom of the page, Hannah signed off with what amounted to a call for help, which Joman wrote down in oil of camphor: *qilin bitta ish*. In their secretive Khazar dialect, this meant, approximately, Do something! or, Write something down! To Joman's and Hannah's way of thinking, such writing—or whatever it was—was a magic formula, a message in a pagan tongue obscure to my father, intelligible only to the person to whom it was addressed; namely, Sheik Baikwaly.

Qilin bitta ish was the key that caused Sheik Baikwaly to appear whenever help was needed. Immediately after one of these distress calls, the Sheik would appear out of nowhere and strut around the house dispensing peaceful spirits, who made short work of the soldiers of Satan, the forces of alienation and abandonment between lovers, and the agents of war and hate. With Hannah ensconced safely on her throne once again, and with her star ascendant in my father's skies, she would resume her role as the shaper of my father's backbone and sculptor of his heart.

Sheik Baikwaly would spend the night and the following day in his daughter's house, then make his way down the Kara mountain range, passing by the pilgrim site at Arafat and the springs at Zubayda, arriving in his quarters and settling in with his books and musical instruments, and catching up on accounts with his staff of Khazar boys.

My mother insinuated herself into my father's inmost being with the determination of someone who was getting help from adepts of the Unknown, from masters of the arts of passion and joy, from experts who knew how to lead a lover along and how to control him with love. Always, in every move she made, in everything she did with my father, even when she had to fight against the soldiers of hatred and alienation, she maintained the aura of a queen—secure, protected, waited upon. The idea of her losing a battle, of coming in second, was out of the question: such an eventuality was beyond imagining—was, for my father, a path more foreign than the farthest roads in the Kingdom of Waq, where not even the Sheik of the Zamzam Water Carriers dared to tread.

One might say this story is clear proof of the power of talismans—remember the powdery green dust on the letter? On the other hand, when you examine the awful emptiness Dumboshi experienced in her marriage, you would be forced to entertain doubts as to its efficacy; you would in fact have to question the whole concept. What, you might ask, was the point of the talisman's work? And where exactly does one find soldiers of lasting peace and reconciliation? Dumboshi used to insist, "No soldiers, no matter how powerful, could do a thing to change how clammy his skin was, or how cold I felt in his arms."

We do know this much: whenever Dumboshi was at war in her soul, Sheik Baikwaly would come along and touch her between the eyes with the gemstone in his ring, the one with the magic cipher inscribed on it, as if branding her, and she would get a few moments of rest. And when certain basil-scented spirits attacked Dumboshi and she fell down the bottomless well of delusions, Nara went out behind al-Baikwaly's back and procured amulets from inventories stored at the houses of the Sadas, where sacred scriptures were routinely used in treating incurable cases. Nara gathered up all the amulets she could, attached them to Jummo, and waited for peace to descend upon her daughter's troubled spirits.

45. The Undomesticated Pearl

We once came upon a forbidden scene taking place in one of the lower rooms, just above my grandfather's room. All through my life, that lower room has haunted my dreams.

Jummo was wearing a thin gown. I can't find the means to describe just how her arms looked, all circled with gold. From wrist to shoulder, bracelet upon bracelet upon bracelet of the bulkiest and most precious gold doubled the width of her arms.

Nara and my grandfather Sheik Baikwaly stood in front of her, performing the ritual of the Kennah. My grandfather turned around to get the Kennah ready. He took a bowl out of the cupboard, stooped low over the brazier, sprinkled some ashes in the bowl, took a deep breath, and recited verses and names into the ashes until their spirits spread their wings, leveling the surface of the ashes.

Nara handed him a piece of sheer cloth. This he wrapped around the sides of the bowl, bunching the ends at the bottom. He carried the bowl over to Dumboshi while reciting scriptures about opening up and relaxing. With the mouth of the bowl, using a circular motion, he stroked Jummo's belly, sketching in ashes on her smooth, shiny skin, which was covered only by her gossamer gown, until at last the young woman let go a gasp—more like a blast of heat, it was—and my grandfather held up the bowl to Nara and showed her the ashes, in the center of which, like the nacreous shell of a snail, lay an eye staring vacantly back at her.

"The Evil Eye came out," Nara murmured, confirming Jummo's fear of being possessed.

"Here come the spirits of the gold," Jummo said in a confidential whisper, "the ones the Sheik warned us about!"

She sparkled when she moved, arms bristling with bracelets, wrists swollen with their weight. Some of the gold melted and seeped through her skin, into her veins, turning her blood to molten gold. I watched her standing there, shining, clinking, clanking, brightening, veins throbbing and glowing.

Jummo loved to undress in the dormer of the room overlooking Abraham's Valley, the flood plain that spread out over the tangle of lowlands near the Holy Mosque.

Her hand was quick on the gramophone. *Adani danat*, songs from Yemen, rattled the rafters. She sang along, her neck veins pulsing, flexing the magic formulas tattooed on her throat. She held up an arm loaded with bracelets and amulets tied together with strips of hide from wild camels that had been sacrificed for this very purpose. She turned around. The low, streaking sunlight penetrated her private parts, illuminating them. She tilted her upper body, shifting the bracelets against the thongs tied just below her shoulders. She stood like a spear slicing the air.

Bending down, she started wrapping herself in a sheer robe and rubbing her skin with a bit of ointment she'd tucked between her sandal and the toes of her right foot (this was the point of entrance favored by geniis when they want to gain access to the human body). She perfumed herself with a mixture of pungent amber, tannin blossoms, and saffron. She massaged the triangular spot at the base of her spine, gathering the energies stored there. She took a wad of royal jelly and quickly molded it into the figurine of a bride whose curves were a miracle of passionate artistry.

Joman was sitting in the back of the room admiring Jummo's aura. Now and then she'd get up and heat a thimbleful of oil to refresh the lantern of her aunt's body. Much as Jummo appreciated the warm oil—Joman was very clever at using only sunlight to heat it—Jummo also made use of Joman as a sentry, for Joman was sharp-eyed enough to keep even Netherworldings from spying on the healing sessions.

Fumes of heated saffron, swift as hail clouds, hissed up Jummo's legs and slithered back down, subsiding, seeking hidden openings, pathways to her soul—there! under the arch of her right foot, where every nerve, every feeling could be touched, every sensation controlled. Like a candle sputtering inextinguishably in a flood, Jummo stood glowing in the dormer.

Despite being protected and anointed with talismans, silk, and essential oils, she could not avoid al-Neyabi's contagious fluids, which had been flowing into her for seven months now, long enough for his germs to incubate. She could feel his fluids branching across the triangle at the base of her spine. She was teetering on the brink of exhaustion, but just when her strength was about to give way, the amulets rushed in to build new barriers, finding ways into her intimate parts and lending grace to her curves. She was thriving, actually—defended by an army of amulets who'd pitched camp on her aura, drawing strength from her loveliness. This protective force increased in blackness till her neck and her waist and the bracelets on her arms were branded with it.

We have no exact information as to how long Jummo kept trying to wash away al-Neyabi's infectious fluids. We do know this: the day that her divorce decree arrived in Sheik Baikwaly's quarters, she acquired the look of someone who'd been released from an ancestral sin. She rose purposefully and lit the flame under a pot of water. When the water came to a boil, she poured camphor into it, then just as purposefully she allowed the vapor to suffocate the pigeons perching in the balustrades of my grandfather's roof. Three of the pigeons sneezed, four fell dead on the street. Jummo immersed herself in the haze of camphor steam as if preparing her body for its funeral. When all the camphor had boiled away, she rinsed her hair and her tender parts with a distillation made of *nabk* blossoms.

All through the day Dumboshi kept calling out to the African women who passed by the house. She invited a group of them upstairs. They buffed her skin with infusions of lemon and powdered cowry shells, chattering all the while in several languages. (Cowry shells mixed with lemon is a powerful exfoliant, useful for removing scales from fish and tattoos from human skin.)

The next day, and for seven days afterward, Jummo brewed ash-water, leaving the ashes to soak overnight on the roof so they would absorb the energy of the stars, and washing with them in the morning, lathering herself from head to toe with silvery suds. When she'd completed her seventh bath in ash-water, she washed once again, this time with mud. Seven crowings of the cocks, seven morning prayers—seven dawns watched Jummo's nakedness, sheltered only by the muezzin's call to prayer. At last her husband's scent was gone, and her privacy—her self-possession, really—was restored to the secret parts of her body.

Again Jummo took to inviting the African women of the neighborhood up to the seventh floor, and again they bathed her in a mixture of lemon and cowry shells and unintelligible tongues. From bits of white ivory and black amber beads, the Africans made pretty things, which they attached to her eyebrows and eyelashes, to her braids, her tongue, her nipples. When Jummo caught sight of herself in a mirror, she burst out laughing and said, "Ah-hah—my freedom bath!"

So she emerged from her divorce pure as virgin bride, a pearl utterly undomesticated. It was as if she'd never been pried from her shell.

46. The Late Lover's Massage

It may interest you to know that anyone who happened to find himself in the vicinity of my grandfather's open-air roof was likely to be distracted by the charms of a naked woman flitting between the stone soldiers guarding the parapet. My grandfather was not so much interested in constructing private rooms as he was in increasing the amount of *kharija,* or open-air roof spaces with views of the sky and the streets. From his one-floor house with the *nabk* tree he came to his tall house in the ravine with visions of a vast *kharija* with many, many mirrors and dormers. These architectural preferences led us to believe that he was expecting the arrival of a bird from Khazarland, a great sea bird who would soar across Samarkand and the four rivers of Eden, come to roost on our roof, and lay golden eggs. The creature who did arrive, amid a rush of wings and the scent of basil and the flash of amber in water, was Sidi Wahdana.

Mayjan appeared in the seventh floor living quarters. Jummo had just completed the postdivorce waiting period, during which she was forbidden to marry. She had already made it clear that she would under no circumstances entertain the possibility of a reconciliation with al-Neyabi.

She caught a glimpse of Mayjan walking through a cloud of benzoin incense. "*Bism Allah!*" she gasped. "My God! Mayjan has returned from drowning?!" Something Nara once said came back to her: "If a person takes his own life, he can't enter the isthmus that separates life and death, where the dead must wait till their final resurrection."

Mayjan answered her thoughts: "Mayjan would never be allowed into the isthmus because his soul is attached to Jummo."

Jummo could not understand his words; she understood only the overpowering fact of his presence. She saw him as an idol made of rubies. The idol knelt in front of her and started bathing her. He took the little toe of her right foot, lingering over it and swabbing it with lotion brewed from nutmeg. Jummo's arms and legs began to feel heavy, drugged, as if she were about to faint. The nutmeg-tea bubbled and turned black as amber. The essence from which the potion was brewed had been mixed with oil of amber, and with sap from the Persian Mummy Plant, an herb much sought after by wild gazelles when they needed a remedy for broken bones. To this Mayjan added the spirits of the verse that goes *A lam nashrahu lak sadraka . . . wa ilâ rabbika fârughabu,* the scripture that speaks about cleansing the soul of its agony and returning to God in prayer.

With these ingredients he massaged her arches, then went up to her ankles, where he traced little circles between her black-beaded anklets, then higher up her legs, stroking the backs of her knees, settling there until the spirits of the verse had communicated everything they had to say to the bends in her knees. The nutmeg salve oozed over her thighs and her navel. Her spine was electrified by the verse *wa rafa' nâ laka dhikraka aladhî anqada zahraka,* We lightened the burden that was bending your back. The nutmeg melted into the base of her neck. Her skin started to peel—the tarnished veil, that diabolical mask of whiteness, simply fell away, leaving Jummo bloody and bruised, as if she'd been set upon by leeches.

For an entire week she stayed in bed, afraid of exposing herself to any geniis or malevolent humans who might be lurking about. She kept to her room and waited for Mayjan to reappear.

This time he didn't touch her. Instead he wrapped his basil-scented spirit in a bundle and put it under her belly.

On the morning of the Saturday following Mayjan's appearance, Jummo rose from her bed completely healthy and clean. Every last trace of Ma'amon al-Neyabi had been eradicated from her body. She emerged from the experience a new woman, a woman made of onyx.

Perhaps it was this skin of onyx that was responsible for turning her into stone. Whatever the cause, it will come as no surprise to you that I am anxious to discover who or what cast the spell on Jummo, turning her to stone and confining her to bed during the prime of her life.

47. The Private Lives of Sea Creatures

"Hannah kills with silence," people in our family used to say. "Jummo kills with sheer volume." Indeed, her voice was louder than al-Srsar, the gale-force wind we likened her to.

Al-Neyabi, the luckless man who had entered Jummo's world and got captivated by her ringing laugh, put himself entirely in her merciless little hands. His complete surrender amounted to a kind of displaced dying that Jummo found repellant. That, along with his smallpox-scarred complexion—"cheeks engraved by Ababeel birds," was how she liked to put it—nourished a deep, all-enveloping hatred in her.

Al-Neyabi, being dull as death and therefore oblivious to Jummo's feelings, spent his nights gorging himself on her body. She curled tighter and tighter around her inner core, which remained closed to his advances, with absolutely no way in.

"She leaves the basket full of groceries hanging on a nail on the back of the door—just leaves it hanging there all day long, never lays a finger on it. Doesn't move, doesn't do a blessed thing. She lets everything go, she waits for him to come home from work so he can start cooking and cleaning up the mess; that's what she calls it, the mess—meaning the children in his family, like they're invading her part of the house."

Nara was complaining to Sheik Baikwaly about her daughter's professions of hatred, which, in Jummo's mind, entitled her to mistreat her miserable husband, who never uttered a word against her. "And if he wasn't so wild about her," Nara concluded, "he would've sent her back to you long ago."

What al-Neyabi's urges built up, Jummo's hatred knocked down. In the end hate triumphed, sending Jummo back to the house she'd only just left as a gorgeous, glowing bride.

The family physician did his best to explain to Sheik Baikwaly how even a marriage of many years can come to grief when torn apart by hatred and lust. He added: "On her lower back, there is a network of nerves. These nerves have gotten knotted up with strange fibers, and they're spreading. She may have contracted a disease by sleeping with someone who had syphilis."

Jummo's face clouded over. She thought back on al-Neyabi, on the image of his diseased body planting his sickness in her. So it had been there all along, that nameless thing, that towering barrier between the two of them, keeping him from opening up, smothering her heart and her senses. She could see it—a flock of Ababeel birds, the legendary carriers of smallpox, flapping down his spine, swooping through his body, then on to hers. She felt so defenseless; there was no protection from these birds.

The physician wrote several prescriptions in an effort to stimulate Jummo's natural resistance and get her to fight the death creeping up her legs. But she was somehow detached from it all, absent, without the energy to fight or rouse herself or even postpone her collapse. It was as if all along she'd wanted only to be a tree that never moved from where she stood, never wanted to be burdened by any chores or responsibilities other than keeping pensively still in her place, her time. For all her flare and quickness of temper, there was always in Jummo the germ of something that wanted to die while she was living. Certain instruments were never made to play in concert, certain instruments were made to make solo music. Maybe Jummo's nervous system was one of these.

Our neighbor Safiya was fascinated by this talk of musical instruments; it seemed to shed light on the secret ways of her own body.

"He comes and goes, my husband, in and out, he's got all the right moves, he's a virtuoso at it, the way he rubs me, gets me all hot and stokes my fire. But my feelings—he doesn't even come close. I'm lying there, all right, but I'm far, far away, somewhere way out at sea and the waves are tickling me, shipping me off me to the Unknown, to the pastureland of sea creatures. I'm sailing along just like we used to sail with my father when we were little children, when we lived like we were sailing for all eternity. Those were the days when people liked to go to the mountains, but we took our holidays in tents, on sandy beaches by the Kolzom Sea, outside in the fresh air. At home on the water, moving and bobbing along—that was the only language my body ever really spoke. When I got splashed by a wave, it felt like I was going under and I'd never come up and I'd be lost forever in the infinite world of strange creatures and colors and shapes and sultans and seahorses.

"Want to know how I learned to ride a seahorse? I hugged its mane and pressed against it and I became one with it, so the seahorse thinks he's the rider instead of the one being ridden, and then we swim free, wriggling up and down, up and down, all at once, so I'm riding on a sea-horse the way other kids swing on swings and I'm playing hide-and-seek in the coral reefs. My father was very careful to teach us how to dive and ride the waves without taming them, and so now I feel that every instrument other than the sea is tame and boring and doesn't have any real beauty, not the kind of beauty that moves.

"I dive deep. My husband finds me asleep in his arms. Eleven years of marriage, my instrument isn't responding, there's no vibration between mine and his, and whenever he comes to take me, all he finds is me cold and asleep. I pity him, really I do. Maybe I pity myself, too—I don't know."

Everyone had some comment to make about Safiya's confession, an objection to raise, advice to issue, another drop or two or three in the overflowing bucket of passion (not to mention the tiny teacup of amorous artistry). Not one of the neighbors could refrain from playing the maestro of passion and using her mastery to show off the artfulness of her instrument. But how many instruments hid their frustrations and dared not put their disappointments on display . . . well, for every candid confession, there came a rebuke from the listeners. Whenever anyone summoned the courage to speak up, the other women reacted as if it were their job to punish her. "The marriage bed is a bottomless pit," they agreed. "The mirrors on the bedroom walls shouldn't be allowed to share their reflections just so other people can have something to gossip about."

The neighbors' comments were many and varied, but as long as Safiya was doing the talking, all their remarks were vicious, though her grievances were politely packaged in the form of a mythical sea creature (granted, her imagery was temptingly transparent). Perhaps Safiya chose that particular creature the way she might have selected a piece of cloth to cover her nakedness. Maybe *she* was a sea creature.

Which may have been the case with Dumboshi. The wounds she suffered as a result of responding to her mate may not have been an expression of her death wish so much as an expression of her desire to run free with the wild animal that held the reins of her being. She was married for all eternity to that being, that nonhuman presence.

48. Medical Opinions

When Zubayda got married, Jummo became the queen of my grandfather's household. No longer was there any thought of the house with the *nabk* tree and the endless conversations we used to have there, the words ebbing and flowing with every breeze and shifting beam of light. The easy dialogue between us and the Unknown came to an end. The giddy parties were over, too, and the singing and the embroidery sessions and Khazar girl-gazelles' races to the top of the *nabk* tree.

The Sheik of the Zamzam Water Carriers fell under the sway of a woman who endured life as a hostage of fate. One day when my father came to visit him, he found his cheeks wet with tears.

"Jummo baffles me," was all the Sheik managed to say. This man who was so adept with talismans admitted his utter helplessness in dealing with the tangled talismans of his middle daughter's heart. It was the one and only thing al-Baikwaly ever complained about in his whole life, he who had such a long history of standing up to life's crises, who bore his burdens so resolutely, who put even his sufferings to use as patches for the rips in the Water Carrier's jacket he wore across his shoulders; never stumbling, never giving up, never letting his athletic frame tremble or bend, never giving in to sickness. But the puzzle of Jummo's mysterious illness—this came as a terrible burden, and it bent his back.

One of the many healers who treated Jummo recommended that she pull herself together and get a *qreen,* someone to mate with. "It is precisely the arbitrariness of such an action," he explained, "that could effect a cure. It would becloud the talisman that keeps making her turn away from life and shun its complications. There's nothing like a good strong shock to pull you out of a state of withdrawal from life and its little tasks, especially nothing like the self-interest of a mate—now there's a thing that would take a mother's mind off her own baby. And as for a woman and her demons, it will certainly make for a distraction. So get a mate for your daughter, a wild one, one of those half-genii, half-human hybrids. Marry her off."

But Dumboshi, with amulets circling her arms, waist, and throat, withstood all assaults and thunderbolts from the wild. Whenever a suitor came calling, the amulets shivered and rattled and clanked, shutting her heart in his face and sending him away disappointed.

Needless to say, the Sheik of the Zamzam Water Carriers obtained · a second opinion by consulting his own special agents of the Unknown. This private assessment of the situation confirmed what the healer had already told him: "Whenever a woman curls up in her own fire," the agents reported, "she turns into a fire boulder. Are you familiar with fire boulders, Sheik? You do know, of course, how the things of this world, when they are destroyed, are in fact consumed by fire, which is air and light. Fire boulders, on the other hand, are concealed from human eyes because they have the power of absolute destruction. Fire boulders lurk all around us, passively assuming the shapes of ordinary formations. Until something or someone comes too close. Then the victim vanishes without a trace—leaving nothing, not even the slightest scent or crumb of ash, to testify that it ever even existed. In short, sir, you have no choice but to marry her off."

It came naturally to Jummo to keep her fires to herself. Even when acting spontaneously, she never lost sight of the equations by which she calculated her actions, and which ensured that none of her brilliance, not a single one of her impulses, would ever be wasted. What most concerned her, and what she devoted most of her energy to, was maintaining a balance between the many fires in her arms and legs, the object being never to allow crowding or bunching up of the fires, which could lead to paralysis and eventually to decay. She permitted no interruption of the rhythm that sustained her creative force—no excessive flights of fancy, no mad fits, nothing that might dissolve her body and turn it into a mere luminosity that no one could touch.

Would you happen to know the secret location of the fragrant ember of Jummo's soul? Its actual whereabouts in her body, I mean. At what point did the ember become active and transform her from a woman into an untamed mare? (I myself have only lately come to know that its hiding place is in the heel.)

Jummo knew, whenever she got sick, that the fires had joined forces to conquer some part of her. At such times we would see her, knife in hand, lighting the brazier and stirring the flames with the blade, then getting down into a crouch, curling around herself while touching the blade, red-hot from the coals, to a spot on her heel. Every spot on the heel is actually a pathway to an arm or a leg or some other part of the body, and so it was that Jummo, with fire, touched and brought into balance every part of her body.

Sssssssh!—went the knife in the living tissue. Jummo cringed at the smell of burned flesh and basil. She exhaled, letting it settle into her.

It became clear that there was nothing to be gained by marrying her off to a *qreen* for the sake of curing what was inexorably becoming a bedridden existence. The fact was, she was already betrothed to the Unseen; she was possessed by It, owned by a sultan who was tutoring her in the ways of fighting fire with fire and teaching her how to contain her fire by turning herself into a fire-boulder.

Such was the image of Jummo that took shape in the minds of the people around her. She herself was bitterly opposed to any other way of life. The only image in her own mind was the knife and the hot coals—things she would never put aside for the remainder of her confinement.

Sometimes I wonder what it looked like, the thing that took possession of Jummo, daughter of the Sheik of the Water Carriers, whose wisdom and wiliness were not enough to expose the demon, much less defeat it. The Sheik went to his grave having abandoned control of his daughter to a strange sultan (or sultana), to the nameless ruler of an unknowable kingdom.

49. Naughty Girls from Nowaria

In Mecca, as I mentioned earlier, there were certain newborn babies who, because of their tepid temperaments, were called Children of Death. Other infants, those with lively personalities, were called Children of Life. Dumboshi, that noisy, eager child, was a Daughter of Life.

Her divorce from Ma'amon al-Neyabi in no way diminished the eagerness of Mecca's men to marry her. When her refusal to marry became common knowledge, all of us—children as well as grownups—put out the word that Jummo was betrothed to the spirit of the famous al-Muddah, the singer with golden vocal cords, the foremost artist of the Yemenite *danat*, which included all seven thousand melodies and lyrics from the Mihrim Valley in the Sorat Mountains. (Sometimes we suspected that Jummo's true love may actually have been none other than Sidi Wahdana.)

Or maybe it was you—maybe it was you who locked her up in the body of a genii, imprisoned her in a feathered gown, and kept her away from human contact.

Be that as it may, in the years following Jummo's Freedom Bath, the number of men seeking her hand increased. Many of them wanted to smash the rigid mold that had shaped her; some were widowers, or men grief-stricken for a variety of reasons. All came asking for Jummo to be their *qreen*.

Not even the professor known as Abu Sharrab was immune to her charms. Abu Sharrab was tormented by geniis from al-Nowaria. He became obsessed with having Jummo, this woman whose fieriness was the very insignia of the Nowaria Mountains.

Jummo was endlessly resourceful in finding new ways to tease him and turn him down. She neither accepted nor spurned his emissaries, leaving them dangling. Nor did she hesitate to make fun of Abu Sharrab in front of her women friends from al-Nowaria. The unfortunate suitor became famous as the Sultan of Fools, a ridiculous figure made all the more clownish because of his habit of wearing white silk socks even in Mecca's heat. (Abu Sharrab, his nickname, meant simply Sock Man.)

"Why would anyone want to marry this cocooned silkworm?" one of the girls asked with a wicked wink.

"Oh nonono!" said another. "Cocooned in socks? No, by God, we can't have anything to do with a character like that!" Everybody knew what the wink that went with "cocoon" meant.

Then Hamida, who was shrewder than the rest, suggested, "Well, why not settle for Sultan Cocoon? Then just wait for someone with a better-looking, uh, turban to turn up."

◆   ◆   ◆

I suppose it's only fair to tell you that everyone in Mecca knew that those girls from the mountains in Nowaria were direct descendents of the nymphs of Waq, the very same virgins who dress up in knights' armor and recline on ivory thrones too lofty to touch. These young women, who were related to Nara by marriage, lived in the mountains of Ejyad and al-Masafi. From this region, it was said, the Beast of the End of Time would one day appear, after which . . . Doomsday, the destruction of the world.

This circle of women and their leader, Hamida, were exempt from the authority of men by virtue of their ancestry. Their bloodlines, their roots, were believed to originate in Mount Nowaria's legendary rocks, in the Doomsday Beast itself. Their origins were intertwined with the fierce storms that howled like curses over the mountains. Whoever dared challenge or provoke these imperious ladies risked being buried alive under the molten lava of their wrath, or at the very least being hit by some nasty affliction. This was no legend—it was real, real as the women's rage when it struck the mountain like lightning, cracking dams wide open, unleashing floods that swept away things so carefully constructed by men.

It is not altogether clear whether or not these floods erupted as a result of nature's sympathy with the constitutionally defiant women. The association of natural catastrophes with women's volcanic tempers has long been a subject of debate. Some scholars maintain that since the women of Nowaria, by virtue of living so high up on the mountain, were closer to heaven than ordinary mortals, their prayers and maledictions may have been more likely to come to the timely attention of heavenly powers.

Whatever the spiritual geometry of the situation, the women of Nowaria did lay a curse on Mecca and its male citizens. "Beware of Hamida," they warned. "Beware of Hamida Khaja."

Khaja is an honorific designating a supremely wise and experienced leader of the Khazars. Khajas are feared and respected for their knowledge, which is so subtle and far-reaching that people regard them as omniscient. Even in death, it is not unusual for a distinguished Khaja to attract many disciples and students of the Unknown. These disciples assume responsibility for looking after the Khaja's descendents.

"Hamida is Khaja, Hamida cannot be denied."

"Hamida Khaja is quick to anger. Don't stir her ashes or you'll get burned, you'll get poisoned. Your mouth will turn around and you'll find it on the back of your head."

"Hamida Khaja—her kindness is the kindness of Radwan, the Guardian of Eden; her compassion is infinite. Her wrath is the wrath of Malik, the Guardian of Hell; her wrath is fire upon fire."

Anyone who dared to go against the Khaja was doomed, accursed by the Sadas. There was no husband, no neighbor—alive or dead—bold enough to try saddling Hamida Khaja. "She rides," the saying went, "but she's never been ridden."

Hamida was allowed to live wild, and she grew even wilder, carrying on however she pleased with the men of the mountain. But for all her ferocity, she had the charm and sweetness of Tobtab al-Jana, the Lawn of the Garden of Eden, the semitransparent ground of Paradise, which is confected of ginger and burned brown sugar. Hamida was merry as a ginger root, full of laughter and music. Wherever she went, dread and suffering departed, and the place would immediately be filled with happiness, by restless warmth and vibrancy. Her charisma extended throughout Ejyad and the mountains of al-Masafi.

People said she was descended from the magnificent strain of horses that were born from the boulders of Ejyad. Her *qreen,* or husband, testified that she was a winged colt from ancient times who rode the winds with him clinging ecstatically to her mane as the blissful couple galloped on and on and on to mind-boggling peaks of pleasure. The husband was perfectly content to submit to her mercurial moods; assured of happiness, he surrendered to one astonishing delight after another.

"Hamida Khaja—her mercy is the mercy of Radwan, Guardian of the Gates of Paradise."

Hamida took an interest in the welfare of every man and beast in her mountain kingdom, seeing to it that her followers and servants were made welcome in the households of Mecca. I remember quite clearly the way she planned her assault on our house, with its stairs twisting up to the roof, and the views looking out on the secret lives of our neighbors.

50. Bunnies in the Plumbing

Hamida came to our house at the beginning of every month along with her favorite son, whose wimpy name, Bunjaka, never failed to amuse us. When we heard her coming, we'd run and hide under the stairs and keep absolutely quiet for what seemed forever, waiting for her to leave. Of course, she knew what we were up to and she was very clever about finding ways to trick us into spending time with her darling boy.

Every crescent moon, she turned up with bunny rabbits to entice us. This only drove us deeper under the stairs, where we did our best to blend in with the patterns of knots in the wood, which looked to us like horses and the branches of flowering trees. Here, under the stairs, the bunnies had no power to lure us out into the boring world of the wimpy Bunjaka and his mother's honking laughter.

As soon as the door closed behind her, we sprang from our hiding place, grabbed the rabbits she'd left behind, and tried to make them mate in front of us. Though our efforts inevitably met with failure, the progeny of the purple-eyed creatures somehow did increase; before long there were enough little bunnies to completely clog the sink built into the wall.

We explained to my mother that the rabbits came dripping out of the faucet whenever we turned it on. "And see—our hands are dyed all purple from the rabbits' eyes because their eyes leak into the bowls we use to wash our faces off. And we've got rabbit whiskers growing under our noses. And they tickle us all night long."

We didn't stop laughing under our mosquito net till my father came with the whip-stick he'd soaked in water for seven nights. The sting it delivered was sharp as a scorpion's. The mere appearance of his scorpion-stick was enough to wither our rabbit whiskers—and our laughter, which still escaped our lips in occasional giggles. These muffled titters my father chose to ignore; otherwise he'd have been forced to loose his scorpion stinger on our hides.

The scorpion and the rabbits waited till sleep stole us away. In our dreams we chased the rabbits with stinger-sticks, while they rabbits changed into something between fish and the lavender-like shrubs we knew as African Rue. Our dream rabbits propagated into more rabbits covered with fish scales, not at all the sort of coats that Hamida's original rabbits would feel comfortable in. We worked hard at inventing ways of torturing the fish-rabbit-plants we dreamed about.

In the morning, my mother turned on the faucet in the sink, slipped a bowl under it, and waited for the rabbits to dribble out. We couldn't figure out how the rabbits kept making more rabbits. It didn't occur to us that they did their mating in private, nor did we understand that they were so prolific they had infiltrated the inner workings of the city's water system. Bunny rabbits started popping up in the wells and sinks of houses all over the Valley of Abraham. Certain people who were quick to blame pointed their fingers at Mount Ejyad, for it was clear from the rabbits' distinctive features that they could only have come from al-Khaja.

Finally my father discovered a crack in our sink, and he patched it with tar, so the rabbits' white fur would stand out if they tried to sneak through the crack. Uncovering the secret activities of the purple-eyed creatures severely diminished their vitality. The number of births declined. Their urge to breed weakened and their colors turned drastically pale. They began to respond when we invited them to mate out in the open, under our curious eyes. They flopped around like worn-out rags and limped miserably back to their spot in the sink, where later we found many of them flyblown and stinking. The stench of their decay was strong enough to keep birds from flying overhead for several days. The flies that buzzed in the bunnies' fur, we believed, were there to torture them even in death. The stink of defeat overpowered the surviving purple-eyed creatures, turning their eyes pale gray.

We lost all interest in the rabbits and turned to spending our nights watching our neighbor, a lady from Indonesia, who was an artist when it came to pampering her master with heaps of grapes and platters of candy, oohing and aahing all the while she waited on him. She was such an expert wifey that she used an iron filled with hot coals to smooth his satin *jubbah*—while he was wearing it. Night after night, before our very eyes, his skin became smoother and smoother until there was not a single wrinkle to be seen on his entire body. The man did not age, not as long as his beloved kept massaging him with spirits of benzoin. If a white hair appeared on his head, it was instantly darkened by a touch of coal.

We followed this drama with increasing avidity, until Dumboshi betrayed us to Hannah, who stirred from her customary unflappable state, knocked over all the mosquito netting we had installed on the roof, and forbade us to climb the stairs or have anything ever again to do with the endlessly fascinating things that went on after sundown.

She even kept us out of the room when the doctor came one morning with two nurses to treat my oldest sister Joman. He lanced a vein and gathered her redness in a bowl, which my father and mother passed back and forth with pained expressions on their faces, assessing and certifying the quantity and vitality of the blood, after which they authorized the committee of doctors and nurses to write out a Certificate of Virginity. The blood in the bowl, as if writing a certificate of its own, trembled and made long eyelash-shaped ripples. My mother stored the medical certificate under several wrappings, each one more un-openable than the last, until the night of Joman's wedding, when the document materialized during the final act of the marriage ceremony, and was presented to her husband.

It seemed wicked of my parents to make such a secret of this episode, forbidding us even to mention it, the implication being that it belonged in the shadowland of never-quite-fathomable female mysteries. But I do remember how, throughout the procedure, my father stood guard at the door and covered every crack just in case we tried to get a peek at what was going on inside. I still remember Joman's bare leg, the way she extended it, and I remember the color red. The redness remains in my mind.

It was only later that Jummo's laughter unmasked the nature of the medical procedure that had taken place under our noses. Not that she satisfied our curiosity by giving us a detailed account. "It's the sort of thing that has to be kept secret even from the girl herself," she said. "It can only be discussed by her *qreen,* her husband. So stop asking!"

To punish Jummo for this betrayal, we held a war council in which we decided to imprison her overnight in the faucet of the kitchen sink, to be released the following morning when my mother turned the water on to fill her washing bowl.

51. Sock Man Takes a Bride

"I am Khaja!" said Jummo with a laugh. "No one's safe from my Heaven. Or from my Hell."

Professor Abu Sharrab—Sock Man, if you will—became the victim of this spirited young woman. His real name has vanished from Mecca's holy circle as the result of certain actions by the women of Nowaria, or by the Khajas, or by a woman who passed herself off as a Khaja. We remember the victim only by his *nom de crime,* Abu Sharrab. This nickname originated in his obsession with covering his swarthy toes. It seemed the man could not abide darkness of any kind, especially not on his own body (which was odd, since even the mountains around Mecca are totally blackened by volcanic ash). Determined to cover his blackness, Sock Man went so far as to wear sheer white socks in Mecca's searing heat, even when al-Simoom, the hot wind, was blowing. And so it came to pass that he fell under the spell of certain women in Mecca, or of their geniis from Mount Nowaria.

Mount Nowaria is a woman. It is from the smooth white stones of Mount Nowaria that the most seductive women of Mecca's most influential families were formed. You can feel them, can't you, when you walk past their houses, calling out to you, so white and unyielding on the surface, so tender and inviting and hot inside. Sprinkle a drop of water on them and they'll hiss.

Abu Sharrab was consumed by the desire to unite one of their bodies with his. This longing was no mere garment he could put on or take off as he pleased merely to forestall the fate of marrying a dark woman—a woman hot as tar who sizzled when raindrops struck her, puddling on her ambery blackness.

He cringed at the thought of the inevitable blackness of his bride, and these thoughts bred more blackness in the blackness of his black nights. At the crack of dawn, he began whining about the loss of his pale-skinned genii from Nowaria. He shambled off to join the other men gathering on the street. In every place where the men sat down to talk, Sock Man left a melancholy memory of his yearning for his white Nowarian dream.

One day he happened to be listening to some Turkish musicians singing about the charms of Turkish girls: "Turkish delights imported from the land of the Turks purely for the pleasure of the masterful men of Mecca . . ." At that very moment the poor heartsick man caught sight of Dumboshi leaving our house on a morning errand. He was instantly smitten by the Turkish charm imprinted on the palms of her hands, which he glimpsed under the darkness of her *abaya*. He understood at once what had to be done: he went to my father and asked for his sister-in-law's hand in marriage, since Mohammed al-Maghrabi had assumed responsibility for the Khazar girls following the death of Sheik Baikwaly.

Dumboshi's reaction to the news of Sock Man's offer was typical: she burst out laughing. So shrill was her laughter that its echoes blew Abu Sharrab over and knocked him into the muddy well at Yakhoor, where the waters from Mecca's flash floods drain. Divers, specialists from Asia, had to be summoned to haul him out, half-drowned, soggy socks and all.

Jummo's ferocity frightened Abu Sharrab away from the lily-white women of Mecca and turned his attentions to the dusky ladies from the Nile Delta. By marrying one of these women, he was in effect choosing his place of exile, from which he would return for six months every year to lament the loss of his ideal Meccan woman, not to mention the nymphs of Nowaria, and, of course, "my little Paradise of Turkish delights." Then back to Egypt he went, to plant a seed in his wife's black amber, after which he started all over again, singing,

> *You called, we came—'cause we're sailors—yohoho!*
> *And come again we will, for as long as she likes.*
> *'Cause your sandy beaches are soft as a baby's bum,*
> *And we're waiting, just waiting for his return—*
> *Our hero, our gallant knight, our love—yohoho!*

. . . while Jummo, tapping her toes to the drip-drip of water echoing from a seductive somewhere, started dancing in her room, then danced downstairs, then danced out on the street, where she met up with other dancers from the neighborhood. Round and round she spun, jumping high when the other dancers jumped, her wide dress billowing like a flower suddenly

blooming, baring the ivory whiteness of her legs beneath the flower's cor-
onet. Her body was an emblem sketched with sap squeezed from Indian
aloe in light, quick strokes that mapped the route her soul might have
taken on its flight from her unconscious body as she escaped into the wild
skies of Nowaria.

52. The Temple of Provocation

A bird set on fire by my flame is flying your way. A bird-word, an ordinary word, entirely self sufficient, lacking nothing, certainly not exaggeration, when it announces "Something is torturing me. Someone is
torturing me."

You send my bird back with one crushing word: "Fly!" You send one word,
accompanied by an order: "Fly *her* away!" Tell me—are there aeries where
buzzards take refuge from the fierceness of the Nafud Desert and the ter-
rors of Suman Mountain? I need a place to hide from the details of the
vanishing world of once upon a time. Don't go pointing your finger at
me. Because if I wanted to, I could point my magic finger back at you and
you'd have nowhere to turn.

In the glare of Mecca's afternoons, when shadows turn to molten colors
that flow into the river who is Sidi Wahdana, splashing against his luminous crown—there, deep in the shadows Jummo would stand, laughing
out loud for the sheer fun of it, eyes ablaze with the fires of Khazarland,
like mischievous beacons confusing all ships and their sailors. In her short
life, Jummo never failed to notice a single one of the people or creatures
or things who wanted their passions to play an important role in Mecca,
that city so full of desires. I can't understand how her eyes, that used to be
quick as sparks, turned into fish eyes, frosted by death. Is it possible she
wanted to be frozen like a statue in order to hide the Alive that was pulsing inside her?

◆   ◆   ◆

Jummo sits by the window of her room in Taif, looking out on the orchard of al-Mathnat. She grabs her black silk veil and tosses it in our direction so we can hang it up to dry. The veil, which was originally transparent, has been washed with ash-water and soaked all morning in rosewater to ripen its blackness.

My sister Yosir and I fight to catch the veil, each of us grabbing a corner. The other two corners dangle behind the shutters on the window, where Jummo holds them tight. The rest of the veil bellies down like a rippling black bridge from the window all the way to the rose bushes in the yard. The three of us—Jummo, Yosir, and I—snap mists of rosewater from it. Jummo wants to go shopping later that afternoon, when the sun is lower, so we need to hurry up with the drying.

The veil dances and floats like dark waves in the air. We jockey for position under its wings and the cool spray of rosewater. Tingling from the mist, we roll around on the velvety basil leaves carpeting the floor by the window. "The soul's throne is made of velvet basil leaves," Jummo says mock-scoldingly. "The basil thrones keep the soul safe when it's coming down to earth." She laughs, taking pleasure in our pleasure. I know she wants to roll around on the rosewater-misted basil, too. I nibble one of the velvety leaves, letting it linger on my tongue, which breaks out in nipply taste buds. The hot-cool greenness bubbles on my lips. I can hear the buzzing of bees and the scuttling of scorpions under a vine.

The Bedouin brats (as Jummo calls the gardener's children) collide with each other as they chase the veil—by now it stretches across the pavement for several yards. The other children can hear the scorpions' scratching, too, and Jummo's laughter, and they catch her scent in the folds of the veil, which never loses her fragrance, no matter how many times we wash and iron it. I don't understand what any woman could possibly do with such an enormous piece of darkness, when all she needs is two arms' lengths to cover her face.

Jummo snatches it out of our hands. Moments later she and the veil reappear in a procession of women making their way to the market. They walk all the way down from al-Mathna's orchids to Barhat al-Gozaz, the Glass Square in the center of Taif, with us racing after them, hard on their heels, raising dust and kicking stones into the tidy vineyards by the side of the road. "Be careful, girls!" Aunt Rida shouts. "You'll upset the Nether-worldings and make them attack us!" Hannah shoots us one of her menacing looks. This is all it takes to let us know what we're in for when we get back home: the inside of our thighs throbbing in pain from Hannah's stinger—her thumb and forefinger mercilessly tweezering our flesh.

Hannah, Dumboshi, and Aunt Rida stroll from one small shop to another, escorted by a Yemenite servant. We run after the trays of *basbusa*, sweets made of wheat, milk and sugar, which the candy vendors (also Yemenites) balance on their heads, vying for customers with the Syrians who specialize in Nowaim—sweet cookies stuffed with dates. With sugar from the *basbusa*s stuck to our cheeks, we scamper between the giant rolls of textiles.

Now and then Jummo sneaks some candy from one of us, popping it behind her veil. The candy vendors try to steal a glimpse of her candy-sweet arm in the brief parting of the silk.

The only thing Dumboshi is really interested in buying is gold. She spends some time bargaining and comes away with a diamond brooch. None of us will ever see her wearing the brooch; she keeps it buried in her trunk.

Hannah goes through all the fabrics and picks out some hangings for us, white cloth trimmed with lavender. Later, scissors and thread in hand, we sit on the floor of my mother's room, spreading out the cloth and doing our best to cut and sew it. Three times in a row my I let the sewing machine needle slip and jab my forefinger.

"The idea is to get experience," my mother says. "That's how you get to be a master craftsman, an artist." *There's nothing like pain for polishing the gold of the soul*—this is her proverbial message. *You can learn from your mistakes.*

My stabbed finger and my mother's smoothly dispensed wisdom draws a laugh from Dumboshi. My wound, they agree, should be treated with a dab of lemony perfume. My sister, Krazat al-Yosir, volunteers to tie a bandage around it, which cuts off the circulation in my finger. *A little work never killed anybody. Hands too proud to work get dirty.*

My grandmother is lying on the couch gazing at the little pots of red vinca that have taken her all spring to plant. Every so often she gets up to pinch back a bud or tuck a leaf between her breasts as a guarantee of good health, generally ignoring us while we wander further and further astray in our forest of fabric. Dumboshi does keep an eye on us, though, but mostly she busies herself wrapping and hiding the enormous bolts of fabric she's bought. She doesn't fool us, not one bit. We know she's about to sneak off to one of her secret places, where she will invent marvelous new designs and embroideries in anticipation of her . . . of her what? . . . her marriage? Yes, of course—Jummo's marriage, yes. The marriage always expected, forever postponed . . . Jummo's marriage, yes.

We spend the eve of al-Mathnat, the orchard festival, sneaking peeks at the new satin dress she's made. It exposes a daring amount of neck and throat, and a bit of underlying corsetry. "Tomorrow," Nabee Jan says, "when they sacrifice the ram for the feast, they'll slaughter Jummo too." Joman, our older sister, pokes us in the ribs and tries to get us to stop gloating over the trouble Jummo is getting herself into.

Jummo stays up most of the night putting the finishing touches on the Temple of Provocation she's sewing. The wick of her lantern burns down, the last of its flame gutters feebly on the arched ceiling. She stands up and spreads the dress on the floor. She undresses. A few dark moles stand out on her lustrous skin. She is so beautiful . . . So beautiful, wriggling like a snake shimmying into her slinky private perfection . . . The satin slips down her torso. The light gasps. The lantern's wick, that lean horny old thing, stretches out full length so it can dance with her. Believe me when I say that on this night a *houri* flowers in our house, a maiden to rival the maidens your rival Sinbad boasted about.

The night we spent watching Jummo was a night spent lost at sea, bobbing on waves and peeking at mermaids from the River Waq. From where we stood, peering through a crack in the door, it seemed that Jummo was perfectly capable of spending the whole night wriggling from one skin into another while we, knowing only the relatively modest magic of the eve of al-Mathnat, shivered in a darkness so desperately enamored of Jummo that it scared us.

Nabee Jan gasped. We crouched stiffly in the triangle of light pouring from the crack in the door—not pouring, no—beaming, it was, and flashing from Jummo's curves as the satin slipped over her narrow waist. Every wick of every lantern in our country house leaned as far as it possibly could, holding its breath, straining to lick Jummo's gleaming, uptilted breasts with little tongues of light.

Sometime during this most mysterious of mysterious nights in Taif, Joman gathered us in her slender arms and held us close while the house went on shivering and the boughs of the quince trees outside bent low under the weight of their fire-yellow fruits. In the morning they found all four of us asleep on the floor, lined up in a row as if we'd been struck by lightning, just outside Jummo's barely open door.

This was enough for my mother. Buzzing with anger, she informed us that our spying forays were over. But that wasn't the end of it, of course, because we were determined to surpass all previous provocations and keep my mother buzzing. The very next Friday, we spied on Dumboshi and Qahtan, the handsomest of the Bedouin brats.

53. Jummo and the Bedouin Horse-Boy

My sister al-Yosir interrupts the story at this point, claiming that the tale I'm about to tell never took place, not unless one credits the alchemy by which a writer's ink can mutate into a bee, frantically zipping around and gathering nectar from the buds of dreams, from the blossoms of reality, from that slender isthmus that lies between life and death, from the Moment of Resurrection itself.

But it's true, absolutely true: we did walk at sunset through the orchard, under trees weighed down with mulberry and incandescent quince. We walked, we did, really; it was sunset, and the trees . . .

There was no one else around, only the gigantic shadows that kept revealing our hiding places whenever we tried to conceal ourselves behind the sky-high trees. We were hiding from the Ram, who did the seeking in our games of hide-and-seek. We took turns playing the Ram.

Have you noticed how a shadow gathers up the body that's casting it, then turns and lays it down in a long, relaxed shape, casting itself across the chaser and the chased? This was why all our attempts to elude the Blind Ram (in this case our older brother, Nabee Jan) failed. Nabee Jan loved to play the Ram; he was forever volunteering to chase us and dislodge us from our hiding places in The Unknown.

Jummo's talent for concealment and disguise was highly developed, so she was the hardest to catch. Round and round the Blind Ram turned, trying to catch the scent of her basil-soul, never succeeding.

Then, in the absolute stillness, we heard a low, pleading moan. It seemed to be coming from the well, from the bucket-chain on the waterwheel.

We had strict instructions never to go near the well after sundown. Sunset was the well's time to rest. Besides, the well could drown us in its moonlit lonesomeness.

That moan—ferociously human, fiercely musical—crisped the quince fruits and seared the leaves over our heads with the heat of its pleading. We bolted from our hiding places in the shadows and ran to the well. We were greeted by another shadow, the shadow of a mulberry shrub growing out of the well. This new shadow cloaked us while we watched, and we used every ounce of its stillness simply trying to see what we were looking at.

Jummo was bent over in an odd position. She had surprised Qahtan in the act of rolling up his sleeves and hiking his *shirwal* up to his knees.

The sun took its own sweet time setting. Qahtan, sleeves and *shirwal* rolled up, waded in the irrigation trench. The mouth of the well was rough and mute under his bare feet. A sheet of water from the late afternoon's irrigation gleamed and shivered like frosted silver in the cold wind whistling through the orchards of al-Mathnat. All of us—all things living and dead in the orchard—stood utterly still, as if blind, deaf and dumb, deciphering what was going on with secret senses.

Jummo's sudden appearance startled the young boy. He stayed where he was, feet planted in the irrigation ditch. His stillness attracted her. She draped her black silk veil over his wheat-blond hair. She noticed his hat, overflowing with ripe mulberries, lying next to the tree whose twitching shadows we were hiding in.

A sparkle spread across Dumboshi's face, like the sheen on fresh basil leaves, turning her cheeks green and giving her a woody fragrance. She set about staining the boy's skin with the mulberries. Around his ankles she drew a thin, blood-red chain that grew darker and darker from the sheer force of the mulberry bush's will; blended with wisps of blood-red darkness from the peaks of the al-Sorat Mountains and the icy water of the irrigation ditch that was trickling up Qahtan's legs. He got down on all fours, like a small flying horse, Jummo's black veil streaming from his head all the way to the treadmill where oxen were walking, turning the waterwheel.

Ever since we'd arrived in al-Mathnat, Jummo had been keeping her eye on Qahtan. She had ideas about turning him into a horse. The more we thought about his behavior and his looks, the more we became convinced that this was a plausible course of action. It was obvious that beneath his white clothes and the country-bumpkin hat he wore, there lurked a fine horse.

Jummo bent forward, raised her hands to her throat, removed the amulet brooch, and placed it like a crown on Qahtan's head. The big stone of the amulet blazed on his forehead.

Dumboshi stretched out on the cold bare well stones and started taking off her bracelets, transferring them to his ankles. She selected the darkest mulberries she could find, and with them, in light red stokes, on the backs of his knees, she drew a vine. The circles and triangles that shaped the vine, along with its mysterious specks of color, seeped into his skin.

Jummo broke into a song in praise of the Gazelle of the Valley of Saqeef.

On all fours the Bedouin boy stood, each of his limbs darkened by the blood-red patterns she had drawn. He seemed on the point of turning into the very animal from which his ancestors had sprung.

In his eyes Jummo glimpsed the whiteness of Sidi's eyes. The head-band slipped lower on his forehead. It was about to split apart and reveal the spirit that would turn him into a horse.

A Bedouin woman named Rabha walked briskly past the waterwheel and yanked the boy away from the talisman. With a shout she tossed the headband and the silk veil into the treadmill, to be trampled by the oxen. She departed with the horse-boy in tow, trailed by Jummo's dark laughter. Our little scene went limp.

From that day forward, the Bedouins of al-Mathnat would exchange the whispered secret of Jummo's secret by reciting the story of The Wicked Colt Who Kidnaps the Boys of Sorat and Turns Them into Horses.

As for reactions to my reporting this story—they varied from Hannah's furious buzzing to cautiously modified behavior on the part of Jummo, who stopped following the horse-faced boys of al-Sorat and applied herself to embroidery and sewing with renewed fervor.

54. Dream Strategies

Dumboshi enacted a new set of rules, The Laws of Locks and Disguises, whose main object was to keep herself hidden, even from Ezrael, the Angel of Death.

She established a policy of locking her door whenever she went into her room to work on her wedding garments. (Another reason for her seclusion may have been her increased interest in Sidi Wahdana's surprise visits.) As far as we were concerned, her secrecy amounted to an admission of guilt, though guilt about what, we weren't quite sure. Clearly she must have been committing the darkest of sins in her sanctuary—otherwise why all the secrecy in the first place? Needless to say, there was no lock or key capable of diminishing our curiosity. We hovered like flies around the trunks that Jummo traveled with.

She worked tirelessly to increase her collection of wedding finery. Whatever she came across in the way of odd stuff—precious things or throwaways, it was all the same to her—she stowed them in one of her trunks, but not until she had first tried out each item (more properly, the spirit or essence of the item) as an article of clothing or bodily adornment. Jummo was a woman always on the move, always alert, and she took great care to conceal the means by which she would one day capture the heart and soul of the ideal man who would pursue her till the end of time and beyond . . . into the timelessness she cherished more than the man.

Between us and the screen of secrecy that Jummo devised to nurture her dreams, there was a zone of undeclared war. We were fascinated by her secrecy and the illusions it produced, and we embellished them with artistic touches of our own. In her trunks we used to hide wooden soldiers, little knights whittled from twigs of mulberry bushes and fig trees. The idea was to lure Dumboshi away from her ideal man and get her to fall in love with one of the knights of olden days—in other words, to marry a dead man. For us, riding the crest of our naughtiness, nothing came more naturally than manufacturing noble knights. All we had to do was cross two sticks and there it was: a knight with arms wide open, eager to embrace his lover and plant a gallant kiss on her lips. Or simply play the scarecrow.

Strange, isn't it?—the vigilance, the hoarding, the waiting for vague dreams to come true. If Dumboshi had merely gotten sick with, say, smallpox, we'd never have been so interested in her ailment, not nearly so much as we were attracted by her dreaminess. In her condition we saw the human condition, a reflection of ourselves in a mysterious someone else. And as children we felt privileged to serve as messengers bringing news of fearful things to grownups who had reason to be frightened by their dreams.

It began to dawn on us (or perhaps I should say that gradually we came to accept the belief) that life—real day-to-day life, from beginning to end—is actually lived in the Garden of Eden. Along the way to the end, nothing ordinary or monotonous should be allowed to seem ordinary or monotonous, not until death.

There is no harm in injury, we felt, nor even in death, because bodily injury is the body's concern, and the body is capable of marshalling many resources and healing itself. Our confidence in this belief couldn't be shaken, not even by falling down and breaking a bone. It was more likely, when we did get hurt, that we'd have to face my mother's displeasure, and perhaps even punishment, since injuries were believed to be incontrovertible evidence of demonic activity summoned into action by our own recklessness.

There remains, however, the matter of mortal peril. Full awareness of the dangers of this world, and the disturbances they create, is accompanied by the onset of solitude or loneliness. Solitude is an assault by The Unknown. Gloom and depression are forms of siege warfare, savagely conducted by forces from the Unknown. For these reasons, women are inclined to join forces to fight against any tendency to retreat into solitude or isolation.

Dumboshi, the coltish Dumboshi, was an expert when it came to detecting the slightest symptoms of surrender to The Unknown. She allowed Joman, our oldest sister, not one second to live the life of a dreamer, much less wrap herself in daydreams. Jummo was rather vicious in the way she picked on Joman's fantasies, exposing them as nothing more than hot air, making a big fuss and talk-talk-talking about whatever other fantasies Joman might be hiding, jabbing at her desires, longings, dreams and private moments with a rat-tat-tat skill that was disturbing, until there remained in the dreamer's heart not a glimmer of inspiration, where once there'd been so many sparks.

Between Dumboshi and ourselves, a series of ritual maneuvers evolved, whose goal was to unravel the secrets and reveal the hidden agenda of creatures from The Unknown. This campaign dragged on until the day we succeeded in turning the attention of our rival, Dumboshi, toward something even more dangerous, to *The Thousand and One Nights,* to the torrent of stories we took to bed every night, to sleep, to endless visions in the flickering, fading light.

55. The Game of Tasting and Naming

Krazat al-Yosir, my sister, my dark *green,* has this to add:

My skin has turned amber-yellow. Grandfather Baikwaly orders me to wear the veil and stay in the *mabeet* till I'm cured, however long it takes. As sentinel of my sick room he enlists the services of a ruby the size of an egg—he appoints the ruby to be my healing stone, the medication that will clear up all my symptoms.

Nara is a dedicated nurse. She spends all her time flaming my body, painting it with the glow of the ruby-egg. I've never seen a stone anything like it, certainly never one that glows like it's alive. I get it in my head that this egg was laid by a rooster, and so I firmly believe.

The ruby dispatches its spirits into the yellow infection creeping up my arms and legs. Attacked by the ruby, the swollen yellow skin swells even more, then subsides and turns pale, and finally goes gray as cinders.

After every flaming session, I pass out and wait for my cindery skin to revert to its normal blackness.

This treatment goes on for a week. On the last morning I wake up to the strong scent of basil. From under my mosquito netting I watch Mayjan—needless to say, he is in violation of the sanctuary of the women's *mabeet*—sneaking around with Jummo, who has no business being in my room, either.

Mayjan is standing very tall, his red shadow entirely enfolding Jummo, while she rises slowly, gracefully, like a dancer, unfolding the whiteness of her embroidered *shirwal* and her sheer vest, whose gold buttons are strewn all over the ground, and she, as if straining to see something on the other side of the closed window, stretches her neck back so far, so wrenchingly, that it seems about to snap.

From his vest pocket Mayjan takes a piece of parchment made of multi-colored basil leaves (which reminds me, by the way, of the pieces of cloth that Jummo used to take when she was a little girl and sew into garments for Mayjan). On each basil leaf that Mayjan takes out of his pocket there's a drawing of himself sealed in wax. Light glints off the shiny basil, setting the *mabeet* aglow, filling it up with green spirits. Very slowly, Mayjan reaches out and touches Jummo's back, stroking the white line of flesh bared by the dress she's made. Hunching slightly, circling her, he places the basil parchment on the indented triangle at the base of her spine. When the parchment makes contact with her skin, it dissolves and turns into a tattoo and the tattoo starts rippling and the ripples spread across Jummo's back and wherever there's a wave there's a quivering and the quivering spreads to her neck and takes hold of the back of her neck, and it spreads to the cleft of her knees until her whole body begins to shake violently, as if protesting the theft of her most precious possession by the sultan in control of the tattoo, but the tattoo goes on showering the most intimate parts of her body and soul with its sweet rain and bits of its own soul, and Jummo goes limp like soft yellow dough, drawn out, long and lean, and speckled with drops of dew.

Mayjan tears open Jummo's bundle of personal things. He comes across a box made of sandalwood, which he opens, revealing row upon row of bottles full of fine perfumes, meticulously lined up from one corner of the box to another, and stacked with an efficiency so perfect that the manner in which the perfumes are arrayed is as breathtaking as their fragrance. The bottles are all thumb-sized, and nestled side-by-side like honeycombs in a hive. The inside of the top of the box is lined with feathers carved like ivory, and resembling thin sticks of kohl.

Mayjan begins the game: he lies down. Dumboshi lies down. Between them lies the box, the knots on its sandalwood bright and round as polished eyes. The lid, flipped open, looks like a chessboard, at once simpler and more cunning than the players sitting on either side of it.

Mayjan dips a stick of kohl in one of the brimming perfume bottles and tastes it. The fragrance of Taif roses rises from his tongue. Now it's Jummo's turn.

They go on dipping kohl-feathers in the perfume bottles and tasting the exquisite distillations of scent and sun and soil until the *mabeet* swells with wild presences from faraway mountains and valleys, even from the Valley of Noa'aman, rutted by lava flows, while Jummo lingers over each taste until she's able to tell, by analyzing the fragrance, precisely what it is and what place on earth gave birth to it.

"Myrtle . . . cyclamen . . . dianthus . . . musk . . . tulips . . . lavender from Nijdi . . . chrysanthemums from the Hijaz . . . hollyhocks from Hada . . . irises from Towayq . . . jasmine water from al-Sorat . . . jasmine . . . sweet basil . . . Ethiopian cardamom . . . tulips—again! . . . mastic . . . aloe . . . saffron . . . camphor from the Garden of Eden . . . "

Jummo has no idea who taught her the names of all the plants or who might have instructed her in the intricacies of their royal lineage. But name them all she does, on and on, and the *mabeet* feels even more crowded now, this time by words. The effect is to make the players of the Tasting and Naming Game feel light-headed, on the brink. An identical shiver runs through the two of them.

Jummo feels a wild rush. The tattoo on her back twitches, as if bubbling up. She turns her head and leans back, hoping that a fresh breeze might accept the invitation made by the space she's created between Mayjan and herself, and restore a bit of her sanity.

But his tongue takes her by surprise, leading her through new variations in the Game. Her tongue follows his everywhere it goes, licking places on his body that he licks on hers, each player nuzzling and teasing the green buds of the other's skin. She closes her eyes, the more intensely to feel the letters he's licking on her skin, tracing their ups and downs, veering with the curving strokes, anticipating the dots and accent marks. Letters teem on her tongue, her nostrils twitch at every scent. Each letter has its special perfume, its own ancient smell, an atmosphere of antiquity that keeps changing, twirling around and around without ever opening up. And every letter is surrounded by deserts, deserts, deserts—by labyrinths of deserts.

Trembling . . .

Trembling, Jummo feels Mayjan's basil-green essence pouring between her lips. He tastes of . . . what?—birds? Yes, he tastes of birds. Of water, too. And wind, a wild stiff wind pushing in, pushing in, in, in. Birds, water, wind—she's too dazed to settle on a single flavor. She's breathing hard.

He breathes, and he speaks to her in a voice more powerful and darkly shadowed than any she's ever heard. "These are the fires of the *nabk* fruits you used to suck on, the spit and fruit that inspired me. So it's your fire, your water, and I'm giving them back to you. The perfume in these bottles, it's just the taste of your own mouth." He goes deeper. "The rarest creatures of all are the ones who don't drink very deeply, but they make noise when they drink, a whistling sound."

His words settle on Jummo like a scent, inscribing themselves all over her.

"Drink!" he says. "And feel the mountains circling the Holy City. Cling to the stones, as you cling to me—fiercely." He repeats this over and over until finally he dissolves into her tattoo. Then, from the tattoo, his vanished limbs begin to sprout again, branching in the shape of basil buds, twining around one another, blindly overlapping, groping for the secrets buried deep inside her. "Feel the stones!"

Mayjan—the young man, the spirit, the vining plant—drinks her light, drinks her secret soul; drinks everything, veiled and unveiled, that is her, and he keeps drinking, the animal liquids gushing from his several mouths, spilling into places where she's sheltering the gazelle that is her private, truest self, driving her to seek refuge on the wild slopes of the mountains that loom above the Holy City.

Never have I seen, never in my entire life, anyone drink with such a thirst. It is a thing for the ages, this thirst of Mayjan's. On and on he goes, his thirst tentacling under her skin, and she's drinking, too, and running away, running like a desperate animal till she encounters (so it is in her eyes) a herd of gazelles on the top of a mountain overlooking Mecca. She runs into the wind and opens herself up to it and she widens her eyes and widens them more till their whites reflect eternity.

I see her floating in air, floating away, almost slipping out of the dormer's windows. I don't know why I cry out, but I do. I hear footsteps in the doorway. The gazelle is flattened against the ceiling of the *mabeet*. I can't help noticing, as if for the first time, that the ceiling is made of the clear oak, and that the near-white wood is inscribed with verses from al-Waqi'ah, the verses describing Doomsday. There is a crackling noise, as if not the wood but its whiteness is splitting. Mayjan vanishes. Jummo falls unconscious, crashing on the floor.

56. This Awful Hoping

That night Jummo became feverish and started hallucinating. Her eyes were still wide, very nearly popped out, and her forehead gleamed with sweat. She told a strange story that shocked Nara and made her feel ashamed.

"There was a morning," Jummo was saying, " . . . one morning when al-Neyabi didn't want to leave my bed. He kept trying to touch a spot inside me that was untouchable. It was a spot that not even I knew where it was, but in the end he had to let go, he broke away. I uncoiled. I stretched out, I sprawled all the way out into the courtyard. My little house, the little one-story house for the new bride, looked so tiny, just two rooms opening onto the dusty yard, with basil plants, twenty of them, all smooth and velvety in their little pots. I stroked the leaves like I was swimming in a sea of basil.

"Three dancing taps come rapping at the door. I just barely hear them, but I know it's Mayjan—and you know his taps, too, mother: tap-tap-*tap*!—and I rush to the door and I open it and Mayjan, who died so long ago, ages ago, and I've been losing sleep over him ever since, there he is standing at the door, my married door.

"This hoping . . . this awful hoping . . . this is why I open al-Neyabi's door, open my husband's door to another man. But Mayjan refuses to enter or say a word. He doesn't even breathe, he just stands there watching me with something like anger on his face. His face—if only you could see that face, mother—it's made of onyx, only it's totally transparent. Is it the face of death? The face of life?

"Mayjan keeps standing there, for ages and ages, it seems like—for so long, anyway, I feel like I'm growing old. I do get old standing in that doorway. All the neighbors see me standing there. He stretches out his hand through the doorway, across the space between us. His hand is clenched up in a fist, like a block of stone without any blood or life in it. I can't figure out what he wants. Then he opens his fist right under my eyes and I see the drawing, the picture of the ram, the same ram whose image used to scare us in the old well at the house with the *nabk* tree. The ram's got seventy thousand horns made of amber, of black and white amber. Mayjan's hand is hanging there in front of my face like a piece of stone and it's impossible for me to close the door. Now I can tell he wants me to follow him to where the ram grazes.

"Of course, Mayjan is dead—you know this, mother. It took him forever to die and forever for him to lie in peace and forever for me to accept that he was dead and forever for him to die and die and die and find his own destiny, find a fate of his own apart from me. It was him, he was the one who designed his own death by letting the distance between us turn into a kind of dying, and then he comes and announces, the minute he dies, that he's dead. It wasn't just him: on top of this, the Zamzam water carriers came and told me the news, too, every time they delivered some water, that he drowned in the well. So I couldn't really tell, when he came to visit me the morning after my wedding night, if he was dead or alive. Is this a dream? Am I awake?

"I look very hard at the drawing of the ram with its horns curling round and round like he's just about to catch me and I hold myself back. I realize Mayjan has disappeared. The door's just swinging there like a helpless creature, and the doorway's all hollow. My knees are wobbly. I can hardly think, only just enough tell my feet to walk back to my room, but my legs won't obey. I look around. Everything's quiet, completely still, like it's waiting for signal to do something—to breathe and come back to life, or just die and disappear. "So I shout: *Jummo is master of this place!*"

"Because for the first time in my life, mother, you're not in charge. This is the very first time you're not around with your rules and your eyes watching me and your daughters' eyes and your mother's old eyes. No—I'm alone, just me, I'm the master now, the absolute master. I'm the executioner's sword, I'm the bare neck of the condemned criminal. I'm the all-powerful dictator—me, in my dinky little house behind the cemetery of al-Maala.

"I can feel a charge racing through my whole body, and I'm dancing around in the dust of the courtyard, dancing so fast that little dust devils start twirling up to the sky. There's the smell of overripe basil in the dust and the smell makes me feel drugged. And then all of sudden the door in front of me opens wide and then wider and the road looks like it's going to jump in and pick me up and take me away. Without me realizing it, my hands are arranging my *abaya* and my veil and I'm all covered up and I start walking down a road I've never seen before but somehow I know it by heart.

"I come to the street that leads into the huge square of al-Maala. When I get to the end of the street, all of a sudden I'm floundering in the market-sea—birdcages, stages where people are putting on shows, sellers' stalls and tables, and most of all those perches, the ones that look like little armchairs, where they keep masked falcons sitting in a dignified circle around one great white Persian falcon, and on either side of them, left and right, there's flocks and flocks of pigeons from Qatafi, plus smaller ones, the Clown Pigeons, and local roosters next to Persian roosters, the ones with the long graceful necks and their funny white eyes, their eyes are following me.

"And there's Mayjan at the edge of the market. He's chirping to the goldfinches and waiting for me to turn up. He senses I'm coming. He wades into the market, into the middle of all the feathers and noise. He wants me to follow him. The African parrots are saying hello, greeting invisible visitors. A blue parrot is perched on an invisible gold minaret like an impossibly perfect statue of a blue parrot perched on a gold minaret and he keeps repeating the muezzin's call to prayer, tuning the muezzin's mortal voice to a pitch of incredible glory—*all glory to God!*—and the eyes of the other birds snap toward the blue muezzin bird, and the other parrots, drunk with their brother's call to prayer, slowly close their too-wise eyes in ecstasy, and the call fades away and the birds peck deeper into the hot red peppers and their eyes pop wide open, hungry again, sparking with the heat of their homes so many many deserts away.

"I give myself over to the commotion and let myself hear the strange vibrating voices of men cooing to birds flying overhead, cooing and whistling and reciting little rhymes and singing songs. Each sound they make is a way of steering the flight of the birds. The birds obediently bank and turn and soar and swoop back down to their show-stands to be sold.

"This is the bird market that's held in the square every Thursday. It attracts bird dealers and bird lovers from every quarter of Mecca and from all over the surrounding regions. Mostly Bedouins it attracts; they come with their new catches and they bargain and they take a lot of money back to their tents. You almost never see a woman in the market. People believe that the presence of a woman, or a woman's spirit, disturbs the birds' peace of mind. If a woman does happen to appear in the market, well, bargains and profits are gone with the wind. The sound of a woman's voice makes the falcons' inner eyes go blind, and the carrier pigeons are as good as blind because they can't follow their trainers' commands.

"Mayjan stops me. I see a pigeon strutting out of a big cage. It moves around the market like a king, nodding, looking at me with his right eye, then with his left—always give you lots of profile, birds do—never lowering his head to peck the ground, keeping me always in sight, the breeze is ruffling the thick feathers on his head, neck and legs. The feathers on his legs are especially thick—stirred by the wind and his strutting, they look like a team of little hedgehogs commandeered to carry his royal highness along.

"I jump when one of the vendors shouts, 'Close the cages of the Virgin Shiraz!'

"But the Virgin Shiraz pigeons are quicker than their owner's call for help. The priceless pigeons are flapping away after their leader, who's soaring with the wild confidence of a dancer, higher and higher.

"The dealer turns around just in time to see his whole flock up in the sky. They're still wild, they haven't been trained yet to carry letters and military dispatches. The hunters only recently brought them in from the swamps of Yunbua, near Medina. The Shiraz pigeons like to roost there to warm up during their long migrations."

"Their escape throws the market into turmoil. One of the men from Yunbua, the owner of the flock, he's running back and forth between his cages and the dowels the falcons are perched on, upsetting the tame birds and their trainers with his yelps and his pathetic cooing. The crowd is so chaotic that I can't get through, so I press up against the nearest wall, which happens to be attached to the house of the Mayor of al-Maala. I know the place well, I remember it from just last night, my wedding night, when it was lit up by lanterns for the marriage celebration. Only this morning, at dawn, the Mayor was receiving guests and greeting the Mizmar dancers and clapping when they sang their songs. Their songs were so sad.

"I arrive at the wall of the Mayor's house just when the cooks and their helpers carrying out trays loaded with honey and a thin, crunchy bread called al-Zalabyia—they're still celebrating the first day of my marriage. And the trays are sprinkled with rosewater as they pass down the road from al-Maala to the al-Hajla ravine, all the way from the south of Mecca to the north quarter, and the procession is proclaiming the tying of the knot between al-Baikwaly's line and al-Neyabi—and my future as a brood mare.

"I press against the Mayor's wall and wait. Mayjan shields me from the crowd rushing past. The flock of Virgin Shiraz pigeons is soaring in circles over al-Maala, nearly landing on the dormers but not quite, always swooping up again and sketching circles in the sky over the market. The owner has abandoned any hope they'll ever land.

"Mayjan steps away from the wall. He raises his fist to the sky and opens it. The pigeons respond by clustering and stalling and careening out of control. Then the birds compose themselves and arrange their flight in orderly squadrons. Some of the birds begin to fly in overlapping circles, and squares, and arrows, all aimed in the direction of the cemetery. Each pigeon lands on a grave and quivers for a second before taking off again, flapping its wings furiously, scattering feathers on the dormers and swooping back and forth as if carrying messages between the living and the dead.

"'From God we come," cries a Sheik of the Qatafi, 'and to God we shall return. What we are seeing here is a portent of death for the rulers.'

"The flock of pigeons soars up high, then down again, sweeping against Mayjan's outstretched palm, tracing arches on it with their wings. One after another, with an orderliness than is obvious but impossible to understand, all the birds make a pass at the palm of his hand.

"I stay curled up under the Mayor's dormer, watching what's going on and waiting for Mayjan to resume our journey.

"The astonished trainers whisper among themselves: how is it possible that this young Khazar has such skill, so much secret knowledge, that he's able to command the flight of wild birds?

"Mayjan takes three pairs of ring-necked pigeons and places them in my hands. I'm swept up by a nameless joy, by an overwhelming joy, I'm drowning in joy, the joy is taking hold of every fiber of my being. I need to run away. I try to respond to the question in Mayjan's eyes: *Yes, yes—it's me! It's me who made the Virgin Shiraz pigeons escape and fly away. Yes, I sent them flying, never to come back. I told them, Fly away, drown yourselves in the Sea of Fate. Do this in front of everyone in Mecca—including you, Nara—because all anybody can do is stand around helpless.*

"Their flying away set me free. I run away with Mayjan. I follow him. I've never felt so alive in my life. He walks, I follow. We get to the shelter of the canopies at al-Moda, where the perfumers and pharmacists sell their wares. Death takes us by surprise there, in the shade of the market stalls. We meet a funeral procession for the Sheriff's son. We shrink back. The coffin is being carried from al-Safa and al-Marwa, the streets where the mother of the prophets Abraham and Ishmael discovered the well of Zamzam where water had never been before.

"On through the market in al-Moda to al-Maala. It's an astounding thing to see, more lavish than a wedding celebration. To the people of Mecca it's a dream—a coffin followed by fifty riderless horses. The horses walk slowly, their heads down as if drugged by grief, and when they pass, their flanks tinkle and flash with tassels of silver and cowries shells, and gifts are tossed to the crowd.

"People say prayers for the dead man in the Holy Mosque, in the spot nearest to the entrance to al-Kaaba. Then they proceed to the cemetery, followed by the Sheriff's men, all of them rich, then by poor people and sick people, straggling side-by-side.

"The coffin, carried high on the kinsmen's shoulders, passes close by, dragging with it a crowd that ebbs and flows like a flood. No one dares step out against the tide, because everyone's frightened that death—the corpse being carried aloft—will snatch them away. I follow Mayjan and the pallbearers while they chant, 'Praise the One God, praise the One God . . .' Through the crowd I catch a glimpse of the green shroud draped over the coffin, a sign of the dead man's youthfulness, and I think how wonderful it must be to cross over into death so young, to exit life so full of energy. When I die, I want to be sure my coffin is covered in purple. Purple, yes . . . purple would be nice, wouldn't it?"

57. The Sacrifice

"Yes, it would. So I decide there and then that what I need to do right away is buy a roll of purple satin for my death shroud. Mayjan and I duck into a pharmacy—it's the shop of his Uncle Sonbok. Uncle Sonbok sizes me up and puts on his serious selling face. To get my attention, he strums his fingers across a package of aloe from India, but all the while he keeps looking out at the crowd and the big loud procession. We're standing in the middle of crates full of cinnamon and saffron and the green-covered coffin is coming closer and closer, shifting smoothly from shoulder to shoulder, passing over hundreds of silk *jubbahs* and tremendously tall turbans with tassels dangling halfway down the backs of the imams and the preachers. The tang of basil cuts through the strong, heady smells of saffron and other spices in different stages of ripeness.

"When I look up at the corpse, I can see it changing into a gigantic green bird. The bird takes off in the direction of Mount Mercy in Arafat—going against the intentions of the pallbearers, who are heading toward al-Maala, where they plan to bury the Sheriff's son next to the mausoleum where his grandfather lies.

"Flying behind the green bird are dead men and women dressed in satin *jubbahs*. They've been buried for a long time. But these are the Wise Ones, the carriers of the prophetic tradition, so their bodies are intact. The dead people are fascinated by the green bird; they follow him all the way to the caves on Mount Mercy. Meanwhile, there's nothing on the faces of the pallbearers to suggest that they have the slightest idea that dead people have left the sacred confines of the cemetery.

"The Sheriff's contingent stops at the front of al-Maala and starts unloading the camels and donkeys. They distribute silver coins and Ember Bread stuffed with dates. Every poor person (and every rich person, for that matter) gets a share of the handout, especially the date bread, because that's the medicine usually prescribed when death stings us with loss.

May God have mercy on the dead, somebody says. And somebody grabs a sack of food. *May God have mercy on the dead.* . . . The sacks are empty. People remember . . . *remember the dead, remember to pray . . . remember . . . mercy . . . mercy . . . pray for the dead . . .*

The cemetery is shrouded by prayers. Winged angels descend upon the crowd. More angels hover overhead. The angels have thousands and thousands of wings, exactly like the ones that light on the heads of pilgrims. They arrange themselves in neat rows so the prayers for the dead man can glide smoothly up to the Seventh Heaven, and the mountains around Mecca echo with the thunder of wings and prayers till the angels disappear.

"The Coffin Bird lends me its wings. I fly away, easily outdistancing Mayjan's long strides. We head across Mecca in the direction of Hindi Mountain. We climb the boulders. They're smooth and a little tricky— like those Turkish girls. I move along without fear. I have no regrets, no regrets at all about leaving home on the first morning of my marriage.

"Mayjan leads me to the crossroads where his shack is, and he sets me down on a rock shelf and disappears into the shack and comes back out carrying a bundle of cloth, pieces of cloth in all kinds of colors, and I realize these are the clothes I sewed for him when he came to visit the house with the *nabk* tree. Back and forth between the shack and me he runs, heaping up more and more clothes till I'm looking at a whole rainbow of them. I'm amazed—did I really do all that sewing just to get his attention? I'm getting to the point, looking at Mayjan bobbing up and down and the colors flaming, where I'm starting to see double—has he set the clothes on fire? Yes, he has!—the fire's burning higher and higher, he's tossing every last scrap of cloth into the flames till there's nothing left to burn—no color escapes his bonfire, nothing that was ever made or imagined.

"I can't take my eyes off the patches of cloth crackling in the flames. And the smells—the smells . . . Everything from the house with the *nabk* tree, it's all burning in that fire. You're burning, Nara. And there's lots of juice from the *nabk* fruits gurgling and spitting, and the smell is like roses blooming all over the slopes of Mount Hada.

"Mayjan and I are facing each other. The fire is tall, it stands between us. The mountain looks inquisitively at us. There are some curious passersby, too. But gradually they disappear. What do you suppose I find out at this point, Nara? That when fire touches colors, the colors melt and turn to pure light, and then there's no trace of the flames, and no ashes at all, not even a smudge.

"The colors dye me, and my *abaya* and my veil. Mayjan brings his face close to mine. My colors are reflecting on his skin and his skin is polishing my colors and we turn into one big colorful shadow and he says, 'Jummo has died. I've put away my anger and my grief at losing you.'

"His words make me shiver. They stick in my throat, they choke me, they bend my brain. In that instant, I pronounce my own death, and it's as if my death throes give him some satisfaction because he walks away and there's nothing left behind, not even my body, nothing but the shadow that Mayjan has polished and worn like an old coat and walked away from.

"We come to a cleft between two rocks. It's a cave so huge and dark, there's not a breath of anything alive. I keep going in total darkness and then in front of me there's some kind of shape, a form, and it lights up. It's the Ram, drawn on the wall that looks down into the bowels of the mountain.

"Mayjan's shadow falls across the wall and the rock sucks up his shadow, and it dissolves. It hear it dissolving, his shadow; it makes a hissing sound, very clear, like it's happening inside me. The Ram steps away from his wall and charges. When he gets two arrows' lengths away from me, he stops and stares hard at a spot on my forehead. I can feel the fire in him trickling down from my eyes into my whole body and it flares up so fast that I have to double over so I can stand the pain.

"The Ram looks hard at me, as if repelled by what he sees. He's saying something. He's speaking in Mayjan's voice. What he's saying has the force of a hot wind but it has no connection with any language spoken by man or beast. I recognize the sound, though.

"*You're covered by a veil as white as the feathers of a Persian falcon, and behind the veil is a knot, and the knot is more twisted than a peacock's tail. Your fate is the fate of a serpent, tied up in a knot.*

"'Mayjan,' I cry softly, 'You tied me up. And then you died.' My voice is fluttery. I'm stammering: 'M-m-Mayjan!'

"The Ram speaks clearly: *Mayjan . . . oh yes—he's one of the less fortunate dead. Because he's alive in me.*

"Mayjan left me something. Mayjan became part of the way I smelled. He haunted me, I could smell him every time I smelled myself, every time I washed, even when I felt sleepy. Late at night, when I looked out my window, I saw him running around in the gray darkness just before dawn, running with the processions on their way to pray in the grand mosque. He was so thin. He was invisible, really, and his invisibility enabled him to seep into what can't be here, in this life, or can't be at all—into The Forbidden. And here . . . his death, it tugs at me, and tugs at you. It's what made you bring me into this cave.'

"I feel emptied out, I feel drawn to the desire in the animal's eye. The Ram walks around behind me and I feel his snout sniffing up and down my back and he pokes up under my clothes and with his big rough tongue he licks the triangle at the base of my spine. One wide lick on my back—*tshshshsh!*—and I'm paralyzed.

"His breathing fills the darkness with the faint smell of amber and this smell triggers a hunger in me, in each of my senses. I'm thirsty for his sweat. I want to turn around but a breeze whips up from under my feet and blows over my head and it's as if the entire place I'm standing in is thirsty for the magic amber, too, and it's already started drinking it all in.

"The Ram circles around in front of me. He's wearing my father's *jubbah* and *keffiyeh,* and he's tossing his unraveled turban over his shoulder and he's looking deep inside me. His eyes are green . . . are black . . . they're asking me to know them. He speaks in a human voice, very deep:

"Don't take another step. There is no next step, there's only sacrifice. The one who was chosen, the first sacrifice, that is your child. You must never dream, you must not even wish, not for as long as you live, to have a child.

"I shiver again. I'm thinking I'm going to be sacrificed, right here in the dark. But he surprises me. He asks, *Where is the bundle of blood?* I know at once what he's talking about. It's the bundle of cloth that you, Nara, spent years embroidering—big round eyes you stitched on the rags, so big they looked thirsty enough to drink blood. And you took such care on my wedding night to spread the eyes over my bed so they'd be able to sop up every last drop from my . . . my one and only . . . my seal.

"Where is the bundle of blood?

"His commanding tone brings me back from my wedding bed. I'm holding the bloodstained bundle—stained with human blood—in my arms. His eyes dart back and forth between the bundle and me.

"I obey the order in his look—knowing you'd have done exactly the same, Nara. I spread out every damp piece of cloth, every rag with a big wide eye stitched on it—I spread everything out on the floor of the cave till finally, at my feet, there lies a circle, shyly perfect . . .

" . . . which transfixes the Ram. His eyes take on a bestial gleam. He bounds toward me. Seventy thousand black and white horns charge at me and send me toppling into a bottomless well. All the horns cluster into one huge fiery horn of black and white and it's digging deep, deep, deep inside me, penetrating to the base of my spine. There's a sharp smell of ambergris all over.

"Now I'm crumpled in a heap in the courtyard of my little house. My head is resting on the bundle, the old bundle of blood-red cloth, and its redness has seeped into my hair, it's redder now than if I'd dyed it with the strongest henna from Yemen.

"Nobody ever asks me about the bundle, not even you, Nara. I guess it just dropped out of your memory. Have you forgotten the ceremony where you spread it out in front of the witnesses?

"I cleared my head and dug a grave in the courtyard and buried the bundle there, in my private al-Maala, so that a bond would develop, a brotherhood between it and the rest of the dead. Ever since that day, whenever I dig it up, I find the bundle still warm and wet, still soaked in blood, looking and feeling very much alive. So it was, at least, till I got divorced and left the house. Now maybe if we dig it up, we'd find it still bleeding, fresh as the day it drank my blood. And Sidi's."

Nara knew that her daughter meant Sidi Wahdana. Which seriously disturbed her.

"It was when I fell down that he entered me," Jummo said. "It started in my back, the numbness, and it spread all over me. Sidi's numbness."

Nara recalled that her son in-law al-Neyabi had found Jummo passed out in her wedding-morning dress in the middle of the courtyard. The door to the street was wide open; anyone could have entered.

Nara secured the head covering around her hair and her face, masking herself, shutting herself down. She told herself that the things she'd heard were the hallucinations of a feverish invalid.

58. Heaven's Gate and the Heart of the Cat

You, goldsmith—did you ever test such metal in your oven? Have you ever tried casting a human being? Did you chip the mold with your chisel and douse it with your chemicals till its curves sagged the way human curves do?

Sidi was the master of this art and craft. He came to Jummo in every conceivable shape because he wanted to make her over as an immortal animal. The perfume game, for example, the Game of Smell and Lick I told you about—that's what eventually caused an eruption of the Absolute in her.

The perfumes came from plants that lived in secret places in Jummo. Every one of the hidden plants subtly announced its presence by means of a miniscule horn on one of the bumps on her tongue, or on the dark moles on her back—and especially by means of the warts on the soles of her feet, where a woman's fate can truly be read.

It was generally agreed that Hanim the cat disappeared shortly after he'd revealed the location of the treasures to Sheik Baikwaly. Having accomplished her mission, she simply returned to the Unknown where she'd come from in the first place. Now Jummo, who can't resist the sweet aftertaste that comes from telling a forbidden story, will tell you the secret she shared for so long with Hanim:

It happened just after the sun sank behind Hindi Mountain. From the Holy Mosque came seven calls to prayer, filling Mecca's holy circle with angels. I was holding on tight to a limb near the top of the *nabk* tree because I was afraid that the great tide of angels might sweep me away. The pigeons and falcons who lived in the mosque were making circles in the sky, playing their part in the great winged beings' song of praise that rang from horizon to horizon during the call to prayer. Whoever and whatever was moving in the holy circle, I saw them all gliding in one vast circle. The shape and sounds gave honor to the One Almighty God, while I, for the first time in my life, gazed calmly at the twilight, feeling no need to rush, even though I was about to get my period, which ordinarily would have made me hurry to finish my prayers in the short time before sunset.

"Sunset is a stranger," said great-grandmother Khadija as she led us into the room where we were to recite our prayers. "And strangers can come and go in the wink of an eye. You should never miss the chance to meet a stranger—or your soul could end up feeling lonely and cut off."

Khadija always said the same thing while shepherding us toward the room to pray. She wouldn't let us pray out in the open, in the yard. This was her reason: "Angels might shoot you with meteors if you dared to peek when they fly up to Heaven with your prayers. You, Jummo—look down! Now!" Khadija made use of the prayer-room's ceiling to shield us from the temptation of peeking at the angels while they ushered our prayers, along with the prayers of all the animals and minerals, to the sky of the First Heaven.

One twilight, I stayed on my limb in the *nabk* tree while the angels came and gathered up everybody's prayers—Great-grandmother Khadija's, mother's, Hannah's, and Zubayda's. I looked around very carefully, I looked twice, because I was convinced that Nara's and Zubayda's prayers would surely be wrapped in soiled rags by the angels and thrown back in their faces. If this were so, how could a hurried, mumbled prayer like mine be delivered to God? Great-grandmother Khadija and Hannah were always so sweet—they had so much patience; their reciting of the sacred verses was so refined, they could immerse themselves totally—physically—in prayer, giving themselves over with complete peace of mind to kneeling and bowing and submitting to God. They seemed to have all the time in the world, enough time anyway to ascend toward Heaven and look out over Heaven's Gate to gaze on what lay beyond, then come back down to earth. My spiritual buoyancy was very different from theirs: the moment I looked beyond the Gate, my lightness cut me loose, and I got lost. I never had, and I never will have, enough density—enough ballast in my soul, I guess—to bring me back home.

At one of those moments when the skies of Mecca were crowded with wings, I happened to look down, and what do you suppose I saw? Hanim the cat! She had left her post at the head of the alley where she usually waited for Sheik Baikwaly to return from prayer in the Holy Mosque, and she was looking up at me. When I looked back down at her, into her turquoise eyes, they merged into one great big eye, and from this eye a whirlwind spouted and caught me in its grip. I slipped down off my tree limb and landed right in front of the great big turquoise eye. In it I saw a strange sea where creatures made of pure turquoise were swimming around. There was a sky in Hanim's eye, too, a sky wide as an ocean and full of blue birds, and the blue birds began flying into my heart, filling me up with the sweetest prayers, but the words of the prayers were far, far removed from any sound anyone's ever heard or dreamed about; they were more like signs or symbols or squiggles drawn in sand or stitched into the cloth of a *keffiyeh*. The signs or symbols or scribbles or stitches were being written on the deepest fiber of my being, transforming me with their sweetness and freshness. I was filled with profound devotion, I became transparent. I felt a desperate longing to have more of the sweet fresh symbols, more of the spirits that had entered me and changed my body's basic codes.

Hanim shut her turquoise eye (or eyes, at this point) and trotted off to meet Sheik Baikwaly. I couldn't bear the thought of her getting away from me, so I reached out, grabbed her tight, and tucked her in the folds of my dress, where she stayed completely quiet, not meowing or even breathing, so she wouldn't give me away. I walked past Khadija and Nara, who were sitting down and reciting the final prayer of Complete Submission. I could tell that it was a struggle for great-grandmother to keep her pious concentration and not let her eyes follow me.

I walked across the room where the women were praying to the old hidden well and crawled into the pitch-black darkness, into the deepest hole in the rocks. There, nestled in the body of the mountain, I put my hand on Hanim's breast. It opened like a flower and the flower was oozing turquoise, the cat was bleeding an ocean of turquoise. The hot liquid drenched me, boiling with a heat unlike any I'd ever felt, wrapping me in its strangely protective authority. The heat was hot but it did not burn. It came at me like an aggressive ghost, reshaping me.

The cut on my right thumb, fresh from this afternoon—suddenly it was healed. And the pimples on my forehead cleared up. I felt my body straightening up, filled with tremendous energy. I dug my fingers into Hanim's' breast. With my bare hands I dug and dug and dug till my fingers touched her engine of nonburning fire. I held it in the palm of my hand, so small and compact it was, like a grape, but its drum-beat could be heard all over the holy circle of Mecca, drum-drum-drumming, pumping fire, and from my very own palm the fire was flaring up and my heart was drumming too. Every part of my body was one great heart, drumming, pounding. I didn't even realize I was closing my hand around the animal's heart. In the blink of an eye, it was in my mouth. My taste buds opened to it. From my tongue the fire spread out. I sank into a flame so huge I couldn't grasp its enormity—it was a flame not burning but flowing with a liquid fire almost like water. My body was gleaming, it was beautiful, breathtaking. The rocks of the mountain where the well was built turned into mirrors and the mirrors reflected my lightning—I was a bolt of lightning slicing and crashing in a whole world of lightning, and the other lightning bolts were beautiful, too, and they all came at me, and crowded around me. I passed out. My lips were blue when Zubayda came and found me. My chin and throat were blue, too. There was no trace of Hanim. She'd plunged back into the Unknown, her Unknown, in order to test us, I suppose, with a new variety of grape.

59. The Ring

The day Joman was to be married, Jummo let her have a look inside her sacrosanct boxes. Box after box after box Jummo opened. Musky odors rose from each one, and echoes of old melodies, too, strummed on an aloe wood lute. More boxes opened, and now there was the scent of old silk, the peculiar smell that time and solitude confers, the smell of a mysteriously pure substance smoldering somewhere in the far distance.

Jummo let Joman choose her wedding gift. Joman was dazzled by all the gowns; they were more than she could take in. She squinted at the hanging gardens of gold chains. And the dresses . . . some of the dresses were cut rakishly low, some trailed to the floor, and some, coquettishly, came only to the knees. Most of them were inlaid with brilliant beads and semiprecious stones from Khazarland, row upon row of sparklers edging the necks and hems and sleeves and folds like incandescent sentinels. So many points of light. . . . Joman staggered backward, then blinked and lurched forward again, grasping with an unsteady hand at a vest inlaid with agate studs.

"Yes, yes," said Jummo. "Agate chases sadness away." She spun Joman around. "The best thing is to wear it close to the skin, right on the skin . . . it's best worn *as* a skin, actually." She fastened the vest around Joman's breasts. Joman shivered at the scuff of the rough weave and the sharp agates against her baby-soft skin. Her senses were confused by the contrast between the warmth—the heat, really—of the weave and the deceptive coolness of the agate, which in no time at all had gauged her pulse and was beginning to sparkle, rather ominously, with a ferocious gleam. "No, there's nothing like agate for catching your mood," Jummo said, "whether you're blowing hot or cold."

The vest was actually an omen that would shadow Joman and eclipse her lucky stars. Stars rose, stars fell. Joman's fortune was a sieve; even shooting stars slipped through it.

"It isn't really my vest," Jummo explained. "The day you were born, Sidi Wahdana appeared, and he revealed a mark on your forehead, the seal of suffering it was. And he said, 'She is one of the afflicted ones. She will suffer in this life that mortals lead.'"

Joman was to have her share of misfortune. But it was not very long before Dumboshi's name, too, was inscribed in the great Tableaux of Fates, on the page where the names of those meant to suffer were listed.

Speaking of agate, Sheik Baikwaly visited me last night in a dream. He was sitting at one of his great banquet tables, on the right side. My sister Krazat al-Yosir and I were sitting on the opposite side, far to the left. The Sheik, in his peculiarly detached way, was totally absorbed in eating, the main course being oysters from Khazarland, his favorite dish. Suddenly his right hand darted into a drawer hidden under the table. He held up an agate stone, gripping it between thumb and forefinger. It was a flawless specimen from Yemen, compacted from the sweat of many years, the sort of stone that must have spent eons underground feeding on many varieties of subterranean life, distilling them in the darkness and heat of its lightless home. It was perfectly oval, no matter what angle you looked at it, and it was mounted on a silver ring expertly engraved by master Yemenite craftsmen. There was a hint of aggression in the perfection of the metalwork: the silver peeked shyly out from under the agate, rising a little up the sides of the stone, though never quite enough to compromise the excellence of the stone's form.

The Sheik raised his hand. The stone glowed with the wisdom of the ages. So weighty was its aura of knowledge that it almost toppled the Sheik's hand—and surely would have, if he hadn't made a deliberate effort to squeeze the agate tight, steadying it. He turned toward our corner of the table as if to ask a question.

Flabbergasted by the stone's presence, I deferred to Krazat al-Yosir. "It's yours," I said, obscurely convinced that she and I had made an agreement long ago stipulating that the ancient stone belonged to her. My main concern was to keep it a secret from the Sheik that this stone belonged to whoever happened to claim it. I wanted to convince him that Krazat al-Yosir was its undisputed owner.

Quietly but firmly, the Sheik rolled the ring toward us across the table. It rolled until it stopped right in front of us, and all the while it was rolling there was a look on the Sheik's face that said, Don't kid yourself—I know all about this stone.

It came to rest on Krazat al-Yosir's forefinger. I was startled to hear her deny any claim to ownership. She adjusted the fit of the ring around the base of her finger. She studied the stone, contemplating its personality and energy.

"It doesn't fit easily on my finger," she announced. "It just doesn't suit me."

I gasped. I did my best to convince her of the ring's unique properties. I insisted that her name was engraved on the bottom of the ring and that it had been waiting for ages and ages for her to claim it. I said there was a seal hidden in the ring. A seal of what? I had no idea. Then I thought, well maybe it's the Seal of Exaltation.

Krazat al-Yosir remained unconvinced. She removed the ring and set it down on the wooden tabletop.

I picked it up and I realized that it was not the same agate that had flashed in my grandfather's hand. Even more amazing was the sensation of the original stone, the one my grandfather had displayed, on the palm of my hand. It felt like it had been there for ages. It was identical to the one my sister had put down except there was a deep, indefinable air of antiquity radiating from the very depths of the authentic stone.

I compared the two. The newer one was mounted in silver, with a bit of filigree branching across its face. The silver of the ancient stone's mount remained decorously subdued at the base of the stone, never presuming to show off its own richness in competition with the crown it supported. I lined the two of them up on my left wrist, thinking maybe I might combine them into a bracelet, a fortress of precious stones.

"This is me," said Krazat al-Yosir, opening her hand and displaying another treasure, a square agate stone.

I'd never set eyes on anything like it—a perfect square enclosed by miniature colonnades of silver. On its right corner was engraved a *nabk* tree, the emblem of Khazar craftsmen in ancient times. The inscription looked exactly like one of the drawings and talismans that Krazat al-Yosir likes to paint on canvas.

Standing directly behind her was a Bedouin poet. He was singing a poem he'd composed about the absolute perfection of the square agate.

The Sheik of the Zamzam Water Carriers listened without raising his eyes to look at it. He could see it without looking: its shape was imprinted in the waters of the spring of Zubayda, which ran into the Valley of al-No'man, where most of Mecca's water comes from. In the image of these springs, in his mind's eye, there was also the image of the perfect square. All this I knew without words.

60. The Sheik's Funeral

"Leave it alone," Krazat al-Yosir said. "The buried treasures of the Sheik of the Water Carriers are none of your business. Why would you have a dream about the Sheik? Jummo's the one who should be in your dreams, she's the one who ought to be coming after you for telling her secrets."

My sister's teasing exposed a dreadful void in our correspondence, Hassan. I fretted about it most of the day. I realized I'd been using every trick I could think of to tempt Jummo back from death so she could tell me more secrets about how she actually lived her life. I wasn't so much interested in the time she'd spent confined to bed, nor even in her death. I wanted her to tell me whether she'd really died or if she'd simply deliquesced into another world unknown to us, we dim creatures who carry the freight of mortal bodies with arms and legs and all the rest of it.

But don't you think that the appearance in my dream of the Sheik of the Zamzam Water Carriers may be a sign that Jummo has accepted the reports of her life that you and I have been corresponding about?

Dumboshi on her prayer rug—this was a woman who never stopped praying, never stopped looking for the prayer that might save her, never stopped searching for the ideal form to proclaim the praise of God.

Always when she finished praying, she cupped her hands and raised them to her face, seeming to wipe herself off with her prayers. Jummo was like a bird, the way she started moving at the crack of dawn. She got up, glowing in the dark, and roused the entire household with her muttering and free-form talking to herself, ruffling our mosquito nets and our dreams.

Nothing soothes your melancholy, does it? You keep going back to the graves where the lambs are buried, and the little birds, and the grave of the Sheik of the Zamzam Water Carriers, and Dumboshi's—not all that many graves, really, but deadly enough to keep them living in our hearts, we heirs of the Zamzam water. Lately you've been after me to resurrect the funeral of Sheik Baikwaly. I'm as hopeless as anyone else when it comes to rendering the hidden depths of death. But I'll make an effort from the vantage point of the women's quarters.

Sheik Baikwaly died away from home. During the day there were reports from the delegation that had left Mecca to bring his body home: they said the Sheik himself had received the delegation and sent them packing along with the coffin, after declining to go for a ride in it. All through the long night we kept hoping that he'd come back to life. We simply could not believe that such a strong-willed man, such a fountain of vitality, would give in to the dictates of death—never mind that he was going on ninety years of age. Or nine hundred. To me he was made of the same primordial clay as Adam. As far as I was concerned, he could easily have had a hundred-year childhood and a thousand-year youth, without ever growing old.

Friday afternoon his body arrived at the door just as the sounds of prayer were fading away. This was first time the Sheik had missed the prayer he'd attended every Friday of his life in the Holy Mosque, his neighborhood mosque. His body arrived in the back of a truck, a suitable means of conveyance for someone who never thought twice about long trips over many roads. His legs were lying beside him. Evidently the stumps—his driver was tired, the Jeep overturned, the door sliced off his legs—had been bleeding all the way back to Mecca. They continued to bleed when he was laid out on the wooden washing table. Arrangements had been made to install the washing table in the Sheik's room overlooking the ravine. All the windows in the dormers and the balconies were thrown open, and the damask drapes and cushions and couches and the Persian carpets were stowed to make room for the washing.

The leading men of Mecca took turns performing the rituals. This was a day when not only the Sheik but also his entire household looked as if they were being bathed in waves of worry and confusion. Water ran down the stairs and splashed into the ravine, where it mingled with the trickle left over from the city's last big flood. Always in the Valley of Abraham there was some water flowing; that's why people had been living there from time immemorial.

The Sheik's body, though packed in ice, was warming fast in the sweltering wind called al-Simoom. The scent of *nabk* leaves filled the air, branching over death-pinched faces, some weeping freely, others stiff with shock. Throughout the washing, the women stood lined up on the seven flights of stairs leading to grandfather's rooms, waiting for him to wake up. Hannah's hot, quiet tears fell with a loving hiss into the crystal pond of the Sheik's departed soul.

Jummo's moaning crept between the legs of the men doing the washing, making more than one of them stumble. I never felt she was in any real pain. She seemed bewitched or hypnotized, looking out on the proceedings like someone blowing a horn so its empty brassiness would drown out mere whimpers of raw feeling. She held herself apart from the angels attending the washing rituals, yet she hovered over each utterance of God's name—*Bism Allah*—that accompanied every splash of water on the corpse.

They summoned us to kiss the dead man . . . to kiss the Sheik. The men folk vacated the room. How white it was inside! I couldn't tell whether the Sheik's body had been elongated by al-Simoom or if our eyes were being taken in by an illusion. His face was unveiled. His skin looked astonishingly clear and pure, there was a lifelike redness to it. A wide swath of cotton was laid across his forehead. He seemed to have fallen into a deep sleep.

I stood at the entrance to his quarters, going no further than the door to the bathroom. I made no move to salute him or say good-bye. I thought,

There's no need to say good-bye. So many times we saw him leave on one of his long trips, and we never kissed him good-bye then—so why now? We never presumed to touch this man who looked so solid, cast in amber he was. This trip he's taking now is no different from the trips he always took.

He went on sleeping. I kept thinking my haunted thoughts.

They made up the story of his death; it's just an exaggeration of the deep sleep he's sleeping. Where are the wounds and the broken bones and the bruises and the mangled flesh they keep talking about?

There was a smile on his face, a gentle smile with a touch of irony in it. He might have been expressing sympathy for the flock of women crying over him.

Hannah was the only one who dared lift the swath of cotton and look under it. A deep gash ran from one side of my grandfather's head to the other, laying bare his brain. This was the brain that once had moved with the assurance of an orbiting star, controlling the men of Mecca.

The women were required to leave so that the deceased could go to the Holy Mosque in time for afternoon prayer.

The coffin crossed the ravine toward the municipality of al-Shobaika and progressed through the Valley of Abraham on its way to the seven minarets of the Holy Mosque, going contrary to the direction usually taken by the flash floods. To me it seemed the coffin was being moved along by shudders of the Holy Land's prehistoric volcanic plates; it was being borne away from the seven visions, the Seven Pillars of Wisdom, on which the Holy Book and the Sacred Essence were built, away from the hallowed verses cooed by pigeons through an Eternity whose endlessness was compacted into al Kaaba, the Navel of the Universe.

When the pallbearers turned and headed directly away from the house, the coffin wobbled on their shoulders as if to say, stutteringly, *I want to go back.* The pallbearers understood that no dead man would want to go back home unless he'd left a loved one behind, or an orphan, or someone in great distress.

A few years before his fatal accident, Sheik Baikwaly had adopted a son. He'd named him al-Hosn, the Perfectly Beautiful One, intending that the name would bind the boy to his family and keep him from getting lost in Mecca's horde of unfortunates and unclaimed orphans, or falling in with the Mizmar Dancers, who ran around brandishing weapons, brawling, and getting into trouble.

The Sheik's adopted son liked his name and grew up unaffected by the air of melancholy that settled over al-Baikwaly's family after the girls got married and Jummo got divorced and came back to run the household. Al-Hosn was a trusting lad. He was receptive to the stories invented by Dumboshi and Nara to put the spark of life back into the stagnant atmosphere that shrouded the ravine after the great floods had subsided and all the bell-clanging and horn-blowing quieted down.

It happened that Sidi Wahdana decided to escort my grandfather to al-Maala cemetery before al-Hosn had reached the age of ten. (Ten, in Sidi's opinion, was the age at which the boys of Mecca ought to be regarded as adults.) The coffin bobbed slowly along through the Valley, amid the cries of mourners and the ebb and flow of the crowds, all the way to the Holy Mosque. There were those who claimed to hear a faint drumming coming from the heart of the coffin, like tapping on a wooden washboard. The coffin was clearly seen to shudder as it passed from shoulder to shoulder on the way to al Maala.

"Praise Him, praise the One God. There is no God but Him . . . " Fluttering its last flutter, the Sheik's shrouded heart escaped its shroud and bolted back home with the coffin.

We saw—the pallbearers saw this, too—how Nara caught up with the Sheik when he returned from his death and his funeral to retrieve his adopted son. He hoisted al-Hosn on his back—he wanted the boy to accompany him on his journey through the Land of Death. The Sheik was absolutely determined to take his son along, and he was not at all bothered by the fact that the boy happened to be sound asleep. He picked him up, still asleep, and hurried toward the door with the furtive energy of a soul returning to life in order to steal his own heart and keep it from breaking because of the separation that was bound to come. Nara struggled to drag al-Hosn off the Sheik's back. But the boy was glued here, his fingers sunk into his father's flesh like roots. He slept on, dreaming.

"Have mercy, Sheik!" Nara cried. "Leave the boy alone!"

The Sheik continued briskly up the stairs as if carrying a weightless package.

"Have mercy, Sheik! The boy's still young. Your road is too long!"

The Sheik was not listening. He was in a hurry not to miss his appointment with Death. He was racing with Time.

"Have mercy, Sheik! The trip you're taking now is a long one, and your women are left here all alone."

The loneliness in Nara's voice was an axe that split the Sheik's will to take his male flower with him to the grave.

Nara pulled al-Hosn away and clutched him to her heart and carried her load up the steep stairs all the way to the peace and security of The Seventh Heaven, as the top floor was called. She laid him down in the *mabeet*.

He woke up and started to cry. He stood by the dormer, clinging to it, calling out for the Sheik to come and carry him away again.

The boy's cries reached the Sheik in his coffin just as it was about to pass through the Door of Abraham in the Holy Mosque. The coffin shook and teetered on the pallbearers' shoulders. The chanting of verses in praise of God whirled through the air, lending the air enough substance to support the coffin by itself and giving the dead man enough strength to accept his death and depart in peace. The verses of praise severed the secret cords that every soul casts out toward the ones it loves. When this was accomplished, the verses took on the shape of a ladder or staircase so that the Sheik could put down his coffin and set his shroud aside and proceed upward.

Jummo watched the river—the bright river of glory—and the wings, the shining wings, that were leading the Sheik higher and higher, until he could be seen no more.

61. The Manuscripts, the Land, and the City

My grandfather was gone. His women were brokenhearted. All that was left was his house towering over the top of the ravine. It looked rather aloof now, though its turquoise-inlaid dormers cast a pleasant shade on the delegations that came to pay their respects.

The stone tomb of mortal time closed over the living spaces, over the graceful arches and the echoes of verses reverently recited, and on the many manuscripts relating to water that my grandfather had collected.

The house went through a succession of owners, all enchanted by its location overlooking the Holy Mosque. But none of them was able to tame it or change it so that it functioned as a modern house. In the end, they all gave in to its ironclad determination to be *waqf* property, a house dedicated to God, veiled in the Secret Ways, in the Old Time.

There was no shortage of profiteers interested in turning the property over. It passed from one to another while remaining essentially faithful to its original owner, the man with the soggy fur jacket that he wore like a second skin to keep him dry in a life full of leaks. That jacket, I suppose, is still locked up somewhere in the vault of the house, and is still regularly visited by floods, as are my grandfather's manuscripts, where Sidi likes to hide, deep in the deepest pages. New world, old world . . . as Sidi likes to say. Maybe it's from this hiding place that Sidi emerges when he's ready to collect his ransom of souls and living flesh, to gather up those people of Mecca who've scattered across other continents and forgotten him, or maybe assumed they could defer the debt they owed him.

I never did get a chance to examine my grandfather's collection of manuscripts, but the images came to me in a dream, and when I woke up I discovered that my soul had memorized the entire archive and I could recall every detail. The pictures served as proof of the existence of a kind of life that disappeared over the course of time, surviving only symbolically in the iconography of the city's official seal.

Mecca lies in a barren desert surrounded by volcanic mountains. To a stranger the land looks empty, devoid of life. Actually it is full of life. The life appears in formations that bolt and gush from the soil of Mount Mercy, up from the deep-rooted bodies of ageless beings. Because these beings spring from the Yolk of Time, they are even more precious (if such qualities can be thought of as measurable) than beings that grow in more fertile soils in other parts of the world.

The mud of the people of Mecca, as Jummo saw it flowing in the River of Glory, was blacker than an ebony rainbow, so black that one glimpse of it, one whiff of its fumes, and you knew that it had erupted from the gorge of a volcano. From sunrise to sunset, each time one of the five calls to prayer is cried out, the mud responds, making itself ready. The calls to prayer make the mud's secret flames flare up, creating harmonic vibrations that form a bower of peacefulness. The flames, pure and perfectly formed as young flames tend to be, can never be distorted or extinguished.

Consider the old women of Mecca—how astonishingly pretty they are. And the glow they have about them! The calls to prayer milk energy from all living things in the universe and they infuse its glowing milk into the Holy Circle, into the people who live there, and people just passing through, pilgrims paying homage to God's home, people who come there simply because they must *know*. The women of the Holy Circle seem always self-possessed, moving serenely through the pasturelands of the Hijaz and its complicated embroidery of beings and people, managing somehow to see stories in the chaos, accepting all fates. They fold the fabric of confusion for their own ends, catching the best-defended hearts in cleverly designed nets. They are acknowledged masters of the arts of love. These are women, after all, who can mate in the sacred pasturelands at any time of day or night and bear children who are capable of thriving in a world of endless thirst. Even in the heart of the desert, these women go on and on having children and passing on the code of survival. Their bones are the stuff of volcanic stones; no storm, no calamity is fierce enough to bend or break them.

In Mecca, in the afternoon, when the hot wind subsides, people go up to their *kharijas,* the open-air rooms on the roofs of every house in the city, and relax. This is where you will find stories of love braided with other stories of love, the plots getting richer and wilder, blending with clouds of steam rising from mint tea and green tea, from red tea, cinnamon tea, ginger tea, and tea of anise. For every sensation the soul can feel, there is a corresponding brew to stimulate and enhance that sensation; for every symptom of love in distress there is an herb with curative powers. Cloves are effective for arousing passionate feelings toward your lover.

Cardamom puts an end to lovers' quarrels and reconciles the warring parties, no matter how deep their hurt or how vicious the disagreement. For sheer expansiveness and abundance of potency, the perfumes of Asia are more powerful than clouds. (It should be noted that the clouds over the Valley of Abraham and the adjoining valleys are darker than average, owing to their high perfume content.) The valleys are interconnected with mind-boggling intricacy; it's as if they were incised on the parchment of a great book we happen to be walking on, unaware of the deep currents pulsing underfoot.

On the cover of a manuscript I once saw an image like this, drawn in my grandfather's own hand—a map of all the valleys filling the entire cover. The page quaked with the force of the floods implicit in the topology. The one and only time I saw this map was at night. I was walking in my sleep, descending the stairs in Sheik Baikwaly's house. Wherever my dreams led me, I followed, filling in the outlines of faces and moving effortlessly from one species of time to another, soundly sleeping all the while. It was my favorite thing, walking in my sleep. Every morning someone found me on a different step, where my most recent dream had left me.

One night an overpowering presence yanked me out of the middle of a dream. I opened my eyes and saw the Sheik standing in the doorway to his quarters, watching me in my sleep, and I also saw—the image seemed to plummet into my vision—the manuscript. I immediately committed its cover to memory. The Sheik reached down and picked me up. I saw nothing more of the manuscript, not a single page, and I had no idea how it vanished, or where it went. I knew only that the Sheik was carrying me upstairs to the *kharija* and I was gasping for breath and his broad chest was tenderly crushing me and I could feel the hot strength of his body and finally he deposited me in bed.

The cover of the manuscript comes back to me now. It's made of skin so smooth it feels alive, and on the skin there is drawn a map of the knotted valleys that intersect beneath the Sacred Stone, al-Kaaba, the home of God. There is one thing about the map that haunts me more than any other, and that is the outline, drawn in blood-red ink, of the valley where the men who died in Mecca's endless wars are laid to rest. This is the valley of al Noa'aman, the Valley of Blood, and from here I can trace the lines through Mecca's geography and biogeography all the way to the mouths of the waterways that branch into cracks and streams that become finer and finer till they infiltrate the wombs of Mecca's women. Every child of this land bears within him the blood of ancient wars—their lives come from the stream that flows from the Valley of Blood.

It is at sunset that these blood-lives make their presence felt most forcefully; at sunset their yearning provokes a response in the blood of people living in Mecca. They light fires. It is the sweetest time of day. And in the springtime, when there are so many weddings and so many thunderstorms with lightning, people know where to look to find the life force, because more lightning means more births, more babies to swell the stream of Mecca's history.

62. A Dark Side of Sidi

Why am I gushing like this? I really don't know. I feel on fire with longing for the mountains around the Holy City. The mountains that stand out on the seal of the city, they are more than an emblem—they were my grandfather's heart and sinew. You can smell the emblem, can't you?—its scent is still sharp and fresh. One look at the seal and the memories are good as new. It was my father's wish that I would one day know this seal and understand how it bound us to the Sacred Stone—though he added a warning: "Mecca banishes bad people." Which was meant to silence our grumbling about al-Simoom, the ferocious wind that takes such delight in tormenting the desiccated skin of the Holy Land and its inhabitants.

No one was safe from the dark side of Sidi. There wasn't a household in Mecca immune from human frailty and gross mishaps, not even from homicide. These misfortunes, in their infinitely variable forms, swept over the city in waves. Killing became a sort of hobby with the princes of Mecca, who were always at one another's throats. There were all kinds of killings, for all kinds of reasons. There were princes who murdered for amusement, others who killed for profit. Some killed to sow confusion and sever family ties. There were those who killed to keep people in line, there were those who killed to make room on the lower rungs of society for the greedy and ambitious. There were those who committed murder for the feeling of release it provides. The result was always the same, but the motives were so infinitely varied as to suggest that, in the final analysis, there was perhaps a kind of innocence about the act itself.

My grandmother was fond of telling this story about my paternal grandfather, Abdul-Hai:

"He was a religious man, and a wise man, a man of moderation. His model in life was the balance scale. Balance, he believed, should be the goal in everything we do, even in our dreams and idle fantasies. Weakness of character, giving in to grief—these traits were not acceptable in a well-balanced personality.

"Abdul-Hai had a son, Salih, by a wife who had died. Salih was a footloose young man; no home, no country could hold him very long. Not even his lofty status as the scion of Mecca's most distinguished and wealthiest family could keep him living a life he regarded as dull.

"Salih had a habit of walking out of our house in the neighborhood where people from Istanbul lived and disappearing down into the alleys and side streets for days or weeks on end. He'd lose himself in the foreign quarters or in the desert, then pop up out of nowhere, each time more changed—braids dangling down to his shoulders, sprigs of basil tucked behind his ears, the soles of his feet covered with magic formulas and occult signs tattooed in henna by nymphs from the Valley of the Great Flood and the Little Flood, which lies on the way to Taif.

"Salih came to be possessed by the spirits of a certain palm tree, which was itself possessed by geniis. The state of exaltation typical of this kind of possession lent an exceptional sweetness to his lips; he had only to utter a few words and everyone instantly fell in love with him. Wherever he went in his wanderings, women threw themselves at him. One word from those sweet lips, their hearts were his. It became an affliction, this talent for attracting women, and there was a certain kind of woman, wild by nature, who came his way as naturally as thirsty mares galloping to water.

"This loose behavior upset Sheik Abdul-Hai and put a wobble in the exquisitely balanced scale of his self-composure. He made it his business to adjust his scale by trimming the excesses of his son's style and attitude. At the rising of each new crescent moon, Abdul-Hai took his son and his special scale into the vault of his house, the secret vault with the dark heart; it was a gloomy, locked-up dungeon without a shred of sympathy for wandering souls. In this vault there was a stick, a sort of ruler, that functioned as an aide in measuring certain calculations made by the scale, and as a rod for discipline. The father beat his son till the roads disappeared from the soles of his feet.

"Salih wandered through our house overlooking the gate to the Holy Mosque known as al-Ziyada. He walked around aimlessly, like a blind falcon, till the henna tattoos faded and the spirits of basil blackened his feet, and then he heeded the old pagan call and ran away without looking back, putting Mecca far behind him—for him the holy city was a place of rules and scales and whipping sticks. Again and again Salih got locked up in the vault, and every time he ran away he took one of the roads going downhill from the Holy Mosque (rather than uphill toward the mountains). He'd spend at least a month, a complete course of the moon, gathering to himself the wildness of the Hijaz, the entire Fertile Crescent from Syria to Jordan to Lebanon.

"He was a lost soul. His intangible self had been stolen by ghouls, or by people who looked as ghoulish as he looked lost. But always there was about him the scent of perfume so extraordinary that people took it for a magical substance. Wherever he went, whatever tales he told to express his torment, he spread the pagan perfume. One night—he spent most nights with Tronja, the slave who slavishly served him with the perfumes of her own passion in the hope of setting him back on the path that normal people take through life—he confided his secret to her:

"'I was hypnotized by lutes strummed by the daughters of the ghouls,' he whispered. 'The lutes were wild. The ghoul-daughters played notes as high as the highest, most dazzling kingdoms. There were no rulers in these kingdoms, no wizards, no restraints. The lute playing was wilder than the conjurings of sorcerers, and the sound of their strings was so free that locks broke open.'

"Tronja controlled her passion long enough to inform her mistress, Fatma Mosliya, about the lutes. Fatma Mosliya embellished the tale for

Sheik Abdul-Hai, with special emphasis on the lutes' facility for inflaming the passions of the women of Mecca.

"Sheik Abdul-Hai learned all he needed to know about ghouls by studying the effects they had on their victim—the way they would pounce on him in a calm moment, driving him wild; the way they changed how he saw his surroundings, making everything look monotonous and crimping his brow with resentful wrinkles. People called him Mister Misery, this unfortunate casualty of the ghouls and their lutes.

"Accompanied by the wisest and most influential men of Mecca, Sheik Abdul-Hai would sit by the window in his room looking out on the Holy Mosque, totally focused on the streets below, waiting for a glimpse of the familiar figure, sniffing for the scent of basil curling around the dark corner outside his room.

"The last time Salih returned, Sheik Abdul-Hai welcomed him with more than a hundred lashes of the whip. All the hennaed lines were blotted out and the last whiff of basil was extinguished. The Sheik sealed the door of the vault, leaving his son inside to find repentance. But when the door closed this time, there was a gleam in its dark-as-ebony tamarisk planks that said 'closed forever.' Twenty devoted slaves managed to sneak in with water and fresh warm bread, but Salih refused to take any nourishment and wasted away. When the guards broke in and examined him, it was clear that his soul had deserted its temple. The corpse smelled of dark basil kneaded in amber. Evidently Salih had survived his confinement for a surprisingly long time by feeding off the scent of perfumes that my grandfather (with the help of unidentified denizens of the vault) had spent his whole career accumulating.

"The Wise Ones and other people with keen insight saw Salih's spirit fleeing down the slopes of Mount al-Kaaba, penetrating the darkness inside the curtains covering the Holy Stone, then ascending through each of the Seven Heavens. Finally he emerged from a crypt that was surrounded by an impregnable ring of vaults and disappeared in the company of Sidi Wahdana, whose entry into the house was witnessed by all the slaves, male and female, and by the Zamzam Water Carriers making late-night deliveries in the neighborhood.

"New world . . . old world," Sidi said, and Salih followed, vanishing into a place between Heaven and earth, escaping the heavy hand of Sheik Abdul-Hai, leaving behind the music of the Valley of Abraham and its tributaries, and the geysers bubbling under al-Kaaba.

"A short time later, Abdul-Hai succumbed to a stroke. People said Salih had appeared to him while he was washing up for Friday prayer, and the vision paralyzed the Sheik. After this visitation, he never managed to get to his feet again."

63. Jummo Learns the Secret of Immortality

The rest of Abdul-Hai's children were mostly girls, an impoverishing circumstance that made it necessary for my father, his youngest son, to go into the printing trade. This made him a devotee of words and letters, which meant that he gave himself over to the task of imposing order on an alphabet that was essentially wild, and with this order he forged a record of the secrets of the city's life. Mosliya had a rationalization for why my father was tied like a draught animal to the waterwheel of letters. "Let him learn to deal with the knowledge buried in his grandfather's vaults. Once he masters the secrets in the vault, they will make him master of all he surveys, and he'll have no need to travel to learn anything. Go deep into the time of your grandfather, Ahmid of Morocco—you could find yourself in the ancient city of Fez, or soldiering in the army of Alexander, the world-conqueror with two horns on his battle helmet."

I'm sending you this letter from behind the seven domes of the seven heads of Dumboshi's sacrificial rams. These domes appear once a year, during the month of Rajab, and a pavilion made of saffron rice surrounds each one. Jummo carried on the tradition of sacrificing rams in honor of the Martyrs of Badr, who gave their lives fourteen centuries ago in the first defense of the faith against the infidels. The battle took place on the road between Mecca and Medina. The slaughtering of rams on the anniversary of the battle, though not an altogether orthodox practice, remained popular with women who believed that it contributed to healing the sick and subduing evil. It was a private ritual, practiced at home. The rams' heads were cooked with rice. Bread was soaked in the light broth brewed from the heads, and the meat from the rest of the rams was distributed to the poor. Jummo lined up the rams' heads in a long row stretching from one end of the living room to the other. (The carcasses had already been dispatched to charitable people who would see that they reached those in need, leaving the heads to play their role in the epic ritual taking place in my grandfather's house.) Dumboshi paced around and around the heads till the Angel of Blood lifted the Evil Eye and the Shroud of Weariness from her body. She continued pacing around the room, circling the animals' energy currents, sipping their souls, gathering their force and strength into the animal who was her self, rebuilding herself, straightening the angles and cornices of the temple of her body, bracing her arches, her colonnades, her towers, and her private alcove. She performed these rituals every year. Each sacrifice was a reaching out to the martyrs who had sacrificed themselves to reach the Infinite River. In Jummo the bodies of the martyrs were made manifest, and by cultivating echoes of the heroic lives, by listening to their courage—they had waded so terribly far out on the shores of Death—she learned the secret of immortality. By practicing the ceremonies of Badr and by studying other rituals relevant to mummification, Dumboshi came to the conclusion that it was possible to save the temple of the body from trudging down the road to death. She was entranced by the possibility of passing through the eye of death's needle, even though Ezrael, the Angel of Death, had never allowed any embodied soul or any material thing to pass through this difficult portal intact.

64. The Dancers

Say your prayers to Mohammed, pray to Mohammed, pray to Mohammed!
Everybody—pray!
You—flags of the armies, army flags—

Sheer force keeps you flying.
Hidri, son of Joma—Joma's son, Hidri—Hidri, son of Joma—
Why didn't you dance? Why not?

In a dormer looking out on the Sacred Stone sat the widow al-Ribeanya, singing softly, just barely breathing the words in a voice so husky, so rich, and so stirring that the women listening to her trembled each time her passion produced another note as light and sure and sparkling as dew.

Though al-Ribeanya was still relatively young, she'd spent a lot of time perfecting her technique. Her voice was an instrument capable of transforming mortal cries and moans into the cries and moans of anguished angels. The truly heartrending thing was that the huskiness of her voice never lost touch with her all-too-mortal anguish.

Al-Ribeanya had come up to Mecca from the Valley of Mohrim, near Taif. She came after the deaths of her four sons, who drowned, one after another, in a well in the orchard she'd inherited from her husband. The husband had perished in one of the hailstorms that occasionally struck the valley's orchards and swept on over the nearby mountains, which were cultivated with quince trees. He had gone out in the storm because he wanted to protect the only vine that grew in his orchard. When he attempted to cover it with a piece of sailcloth left over from Noah's Ark, the wind caught the sail and lifted him high in the sky, where the hailstones battered him, breaking every bone in his body. By the time the wind deposited him back on solid ground, his skin was blue. It got bluer and bluer and bluer. Finally he expired.

Hidri, son of Joma—Joma, Hidri's son—Hidri's son, Joma—
Why didn't you dance? Why didn't you, didn't you, didn't you dance?

The bracelets jingled on al-Ribeanya's arm. Ordinarily, this extraordinary woman sat imperiously enthroned on a bench at the end of a long carpet. Now she was lying on the floor. Since coming to the Holy Land, she'd taken a liking to wearing men's clothes. Whenever she paid a visit to one of Mecca's important families, she dressed up in a *thob,* the most fashionable men's garment. She wore it over an embroidered *shirwal* and a traditional vest. She also wore a hat brocaded in the Hijazi style, and on top of that she wore a tasseled *keffiyeh.* On her hand was a man's ring with an agate stone from Yemen; on her arm a silver bracelet forged by lightning that was known to strike in the vicinity of Salsabeel, one of the fountains in the Garden of Eden.

Al-Ribeanya's style was disturbing. She never failed to upset the decorum of the women's quarters, which of course were off-limits to males . . . except for al-Ribeanya. And whenever she lifted her voice in yearning for Hidri, son of Joma, the women winked and giggled. Some said Hidri was her oldest son, others said he was her otherworldly soul mate, her *qreen* from the Unknown. This Hidri, whoever or whatever he was, was a possessive lover whose jealous nature kept al-Ribeanya away from other men. He accomplished this by setting a ring of fire around her; potential suitors ran the risk of incineration.

Hidri made his presence known to the *sharifas,* the women adept in the dance called al-Zar. Al-Zar was more than a dance, just as al-Ribeanya's singing was more than music. It was performed by a *sharifa* who, because of her intimate acquaintance with the Unknown, and with the help of her genii assistants, could cure sick people and drive wicked spirits from the souls of those possessed. In exchange for a favor, or sometimes for the price of some preternatural form of payment, the *sharifa* would command the spirit possessing her patient to show itself. Then she shooed it away. Essentially, the evil spirit or genii would appear to the *sharifa,* chat her up and negotiate a price for his cooperation. While all this was going on, the afflicted person kept dancing, dancing, dancing as wildly as the spirit who was appearing to the *sharifa,* and at some point the patient collapsed, a sign that the noxious spirit had vacated the body of its prey.

Al-Zar was a great favorite with the women of Mecca, and they paid tidy sums to have it performed. Certain *sharifas* were famous for their mastery of the dance. Each one cultivated her special audience, who took tremendous pleasure in the virtuosity of their favorite performer. Women friends got together with the *sharifa*'s assistants to watch the performance, though not necessarily to be treated for possession.

Whenever al-Ribeanya was in attendance, Hidri would appear. The cream of Mecca's society also came. Fancy ladies brought their own ingredients for the ritual: henna marinated overnight in rose water, barley sugar, and benzoin for incense. Hidri manifested himself in the bowls of henna. The women got to know his charms in great detail, and they learned the most artistically satisfying ways of rousing his passions.

From the *kharija* of Sheik Baikwaly's house came a platter heaped with henna that had been soaking all night in rose water, along with barley sugar, cardamom, benzoin, and sticks of aloe for incense—covered with a sparkly topping of stars that had streaked overhead the night before and fallen into the tray.

Nara followed right behind the tray. She sat cross-legged in the dormer and divided the henna into three portions: one for the guests who wanted to share the dye, another portion for use on her own soles and palms, and a third for Jummo. Nara sat in front of Jummo, cross-legged again, and started dyeing Jummo's feet, decorating the sides with green paste. The fresh scent banished the Spirits of Blood from the room.

Through cracks in the shutters we watched as animals of legend took shape in the platters of henna, spreading out like cool, leafy boughs across the women's skin and all over their bodies (forbidden territory for all living creatures). Nara wrapped Jummo's feet in a black kerchief so the spirits of the henna and its colors could ripen and mellow in privacy. Jummo held out her hands, palms up. The green animals seeped into them. She closed her hands around all the animals' currents, taking in their spirits. By the time the ceremony came to an end, she was glowing.

Al-Ribeanya's voice rose: *Hidri, son of Joma—why didn't you dance?*

Dumboshi furrowed her brow. She had a firm policy of avoiding al-Zar, with its raucous singing and visitations by spirits of so many different colors and densities. She wanted no part of shortcuts to the Under- or Upper-World. She worried that her substance might get diluted, or that she would lose her way in the mazes of the Unknown.

"Dumboshi's star is light," Nara liked to say, insinuating that Jummo lived between fire and air; that is, on the cusp of craziness. It was common knowledge that light stars were composed of porous material easily blown away by a passing breeze looking for space in which to assert itself. So Jummo stayed away from al-Zar parties because the spirits, like passing breezes, hemmed her in.

Hannah's searchlight eye, on the other hand, resembled a watery star. On the placid surface of this star one could clearly see many weird and wonderful worlds. Hannah missed not a single move by the inhabitants of the Unknown in the house we lived in as children, and I suspect she saw some things they did even before we were born, too.

65. The Attack of the Jealous Geniis

The Pool of Majin was the takeoff and landing spot for all spiritual apparitions near the Holy Mosque. It was the portal for all the spirits who came by to partake of the energy produced by the concentric circles of devotion surrounding the Holy City. This energy was useful for casting spells and subduing unruly people. So it happened that whenever the Sheik of the Zamzam Water Carriers arranged for a Circumambulation to irrigate the visiting spirits with the blood of sacrificial animals—in other words, whenever he threw a big party for poor people, lepers, and dervishes—Hannah had to endure the stress created by these creatures from the Unknown, who had a habit, while attending the festivities, of appearing to her in their natural shapes, some of them quite astounding, and engaging her in lengthy conversations.

Only once did Hannah break her cautious silence regarding the actual appearance of the spirits, and that was the day she gave birth to my oldest sister, Joman. She lay veiled, under a mosquito net, with her newborn child. She had already cautioned the servants not to let the infant be exposed to any drafts, which might carry with them the invisible script of a destructive talisman, or expose the child to the meddling curiosity of earthlings.

On the seventh day following the birth of her child, the Sadas were consulted. Their recommendation was to replace the mosquito net with a Net of Joy, a net decorated with flame-bright satin tassels, fringed with ruffles, and hung with braids rather than the customary plain cords.

Shortly after the new net was hung, creatures from the Unknown paid their first visit. It happened toward the end of a Friday. For magicians Friday was a day of rest. The magicians' helper-geniis took Fridays off, too. On this day they had no spells to cast, no dilemmas to solve, no orders to follow up on. Friday was also the day when those who practiced black magic were free to do as they pleased; evil was released from all restraints.

It was on a Friday evening, then, that the ruffles on the Net of Joy began to tremble and smolder with mauve-colored flames. The air was filled with the acrid smell of burnt roses, which is the closest thing to the stench of burning human flesh. The dangling braids danced. Hannah felt the net contracting. The top was slashed open, and the net was pulled upwards, like a pointy arch, and on top of the arch there was an unlikely looking, wiglike mat of hair on top of a head that was making a lowing sound, moo-like.

It took Hannah some time to focus her eyes (or searchlights) on the visitor looming over her newborn. It was a female . . . thing, a cross between a lioness and a hyena. The hair on its head was a snarl of serpents stinking of wormwood. It went on making the mooing-lowing sound right on top of Joman, snake braids dangling, saliva drooling. At the sight of this beast, time stopped. Nothing moved. Hannah lay under the net. Its tiny tremors had ceased. Her lips were dry and cracked, she was unable even to move her tongue. A bird fluttered in her breast. The Verses of the Throne rose in her heart: *"There is no God but Him, He-Who-Is-Alive, He-Who-Is-Rising . . . "* Hearing the hymn to God-Who-Is, Who-Is-Rising, the lion-hyena-serpent froze. *"His throne holds sway over all skies and all worlds, and he keeps them all in his care, never tiring. He knows everything, he sees everything."*

At the sound of the letters of God's name that signify sight, the eyes of the earth opened wide and swallowed the demon visitor whole. It disappeared along with an entire flock of diabolical creatures, those evil shapes that change and change and change, never resting, exposing the deepest currents of our fears, creatures whose nature no tongue can tell and no imagination can begin to describe.

But the she-beast kept coming back, flapping her lizardly wings, dribbling greasy drops of wormwood on Joman's cheeks. These sudden eruptions of the Unknown suggested that the creatures of the Underworld wanted Joman for themselves and were conspiring to take her down to their dark kingdom. Why else would they risk exposing themselves to Hannah's searchlights and the shock of the Verses of the Throne? They kept coming, night after night, creeping out of the shadows, slithering from dim corners. For several years, whenever Joman's birthday drew near, they would reappear, hovering over her and mooing like sacrificial cattle bleeding from their slit throats, thirsty for the blood of the girl-child.

Sidi Wahdana put the notion in Hannah's mind that these denizens of the darkest Underworld were looking for a home in her daughter's slender body—that they saw her flesh as a wall they wanted to live behind. Hannah stood her ground against the fiendish visitations. As the hour neared midnight, they increased in frequency, in the intensity of their darkness, and in the volume of shrieking. She faced down the Unknown with little more than her illiterate's recital of the Verses of the Throne. She knew nothing of the Holy Book except for that passage in the second Sura, referred to as Umma. This was a time when women were forbidden to enter the world of letters, with its secret doors and seductive powers. The first chapter of the Qur'an was as far as a woman like Hannah was permitted to go. Hannah, my mother, mastered the first chapter by memorizing the sounds of the letters, not their bodies or the strokes that formed them or the way they flowed. Yet the letters, when she looked at them, revealed their true essence, their authentic energy, and she could see that they were capable of embodying and making visible anything one might imagine. And things beyond imagining. This was how Hannah, the illiterate, received letters into her mind, and how she learned them, and it was this illiterate literacy that led her to uncover the geniis' intentions toward her newborn daughter.

A delegation of geniis lay in wait for Hannah in her dreams. They captured her and escorted her to one of their underwater palaces. From there they took her to a kingdom constructed of precious stones. The jewels genuflected when the delegation passed by. The gems gleamed and glittered as they saluted their masters. Winged geniis lifted Hannah in the air. Her mouth was gagged and bridled so she couldn't say the Great Name; the mere sound of it could crumble the geniis' kingdoms and pulverize the ruins.

They brought her to treasure vaults encased in ice. In one of the vaults they showed her a bolt of silk with a fiery sheen to it. On the silk there was a throne, vacant and crumpled up. The geniis wrote—they wrote expressly so that Hannah the literate illiterate would understand—that the vacant throne was the sanctuary of the name Joman, which means the Pearl. The geniis accused her of stealing the pearl-name from the treasury of their King of Kings. The King of Kings, they said, had been cultivating this pearl in its silken throne with the idea of one day fashioning it into a trap to catch every beautiful thing that happened to pass by, every single thing of value, so the King would be able to take these things and exploit them for his own benefit.

It was a common genii strategy to hoard names they loved or feared. Names were the means by which they controlled human beings. Whoever or whatever had a name could find itself entrapped by its own name.

So Hannah came to the conclusion that names were traps set by geniis to ensnare creatures of all kinds. She accepted this theory as fact, but kept it to herself. We did learn, however, what the she-beast had in mind for Joman: she wanted to enter the child and consume the soul or essence that derived from the spirit of her name, then restore these valuable properties to the treasury of the geniis' King of Kings.

Following the long nights of warfare waged by the soldiers of the Throne, my mother described for Nara the shape of the diabolical visitor, the leader of the pack of hyenas from the Unknown. Hannah, because she was so determined to defeat her opponent, conferred the name Hyena on the she-beast. She had come to understand, as the result of her excursions to the geniis' treasure vaults, that the best way to beat the geniis back was to imprison them in names, then make the names known. Exposure was lethal to them.

The Hyena, the Shape with a Name, was handed down to the women in the family until finally it came to us, myself and my sister Krazat al-Yosir, the granddaughters who struggled to be worthy of inheriting the family legends, the stories that still haunt us.

66. The Dot

Joman's story made you skeptical; it opened even more doors of doubt in your heart. So tell me—what was it the geniis did to you? Did they make you fall in love with a woman, or was it just a word? Maybe you were chasing after someone who was nothing but a name the geniis took from one of their favorite songs, after softening it with the silk of their illusions, and all you could do was run like a maniac after the miracle that was only as real as you thought it was.

As for my own doubts—you never responded to them. You cast yourself as an innocent looking into my story with a dispassionate eye. You rushed to send us your Hat of Invisibility as earnest money, as down payment for your share of our inheritance. You wanted more than anything to be part of the same inheritance. You wanted me to gather up and send you, like little lambs all in an obedient row, more juicy tidbits about these women who were obsessed by letters.

Don't you understand that for Hannah the alphabet consisted of no more than seven letters, and these might as well have been folded up into a single letter—M—that as far as she was concerned was the beginning and end of all possible alphabets.

How could this be? After years of struggle, Hannah managed to pull together the letters of the first name of her soul mate, Mohammed. Then she mastered the letters of her own name, which she contrived to arrange so that she could capture the name of the one she loved. This is how she did it: she arranged the six letters of her name in columns within a rectangle she had built from the letters of her loved one's name. The letters of her name occupied the corners of his name, dazzling him out of the corners, while blocking any clear path of escape—diagonals, diameters, or radii. She arrived at the conclusion that M was the Queen of Letters (an important part of the proof was that her father's name was Mohammed). She became convinced, as a corollary, that the letter H signified vitality or energy. And D served as a protective seal for the male ego, sheltering men's secret vulnerabilities.

There were only seven letters of the alphabet as far as Hannah was concerned, and they had only seven possible combinations, of which she knew only two, being ignorant of the other five. The other five were the letters from which our names, the names of her five children, were composed.

Jummo, on the other hand, was a devotee of *The Thousand and One Nights*, which inspired her to subdue the forces of the letters, to read and know everything there was to know about every Night in the book.

Once, in a trunk that had been overlooked for years, my mother came across a veil. Though its color had almost completely faded, she recognized the green velvet Jummo used to cover her navel with so no one would come into her. Jummo believed that the navel was the gateway to her body, and an army could march right through it.

I watched while Hannah unraveled the stitches that held the veil together. Pieces of paper tumbled out, and on them were rows of letters in blue and black and silver ink. My eyes were drawn to the transparent symbols at the exact center of each piece of paper. Exquisitely drawn, their meaning uncertain, they were hemmed in by squares divided into shelves, and centered over a miniscule dot. I got exhausted trying to decipher the patterns of squares and curves stacked on top of one another, as if shielding the tiny dot at the center.

Here it comes now, the crescent moon turning its face to me. Zol-hidja, the month of pilgrimage, is upon us. My personal pilgrimage, my obligation, is the solitary struggle to decipher the secret locked in that spot, that little dot.

The crescent turns again. Very soon it will be Moharam, the month when hunting and killing are forbidden, and now the dot opens up for me and out of the dot comes a tongue full of sweetness that is the sweetness of the dot. I touch the dot, I lick it. The stale taste on my tongue dissolves when I taste the taste of Jummo and Sidi Wahdana, and savor their struggle to discover and master the essential word, the essential book.

It takes a while to master such a revelation. The possibly lethal consequences of unveiling these secrets—I set them aside for now. I hit on a plan. I will smuggle glimpses of what lies behind the veil to you. My hope is that by doing this we'll develop a pact, a secure way of working.

Krazat al-Yosir grabbed this manuscript and started making her own capricious changes. Without once consulting me, she mixed in harmonies, scents, minerals and spices. She uncovered Sidi's face from under heaps of abstract foliation—there, under the veils I'd covered him with so tenderly, was his warm flesh!

Then Yosir prettified herself, and on the tenth night of the forbidden month of Moharam she approached Sidi and starting exploring his body in search of more secrets.

It was a night saturated with strange winds. When it was over, Yosir bathed. She fasted for the rest of the day, the tenth of the month. At sunset she broke her fast and began dictating to me details about what was buried in the vault of our house on the ravine during the great flood:

Jummo was inside the vault in the house on the ravine, bailing out the floodwater, when she stumbled on a shadow lying down in front of her. She looked up at the east wall of the vault. She saw Sidi Wahdana sitting cross-legged in a secret alcove.

"Go away, Sidi!" she snapped in a startled whisper.

He turned and faced her. She couldn't tell, in the dimness, whether his eye was black or white, but she understood that he was signaling her. He motioned for her to look in his lap. She saw an enormous book there, opened up. For some time all she could do was stare at its ornamentation, a weave of circles and straight lines. The lines were bordered by stars and intricate flowers that took Jummo's breath away.

"It's my father's book! That cover of dark gray bark, the complicated ornamentation, like a work of engineering—I'd know it anywhere. How did you get a hold of it?"

"Eternal . . . Alive . . . " Sidi began. " . . . there is but one God. The One is repeated. He is the one, he is the reason, the whole reason, complete, containing it all—the one and the all, singular, plural, the shape of the letters of His name, their proportions, the way they link and emerge from one another, the way they live together—it is the subtlest composition, and the most balanced, everything in perfect harmony and agreement."

"You're talking about miracles," Jummo said.

"I'm talking about a miracle, yes—where the old world and the new are tight as true lovers."

Jummo half-understood. She pressed on. "I've always wanted to touch the ornamentation, it looks so alive. Would you let me?"

He took his hand off the book and motioned her to come near. She came closer, hands extended, fingers weaving prayers in praise of the ornamentation, fluttering in time with Sidi's chanting.

"Behind every veil, another veil," he said. "Alive, alive . . . God is alive."

Her fingers danced, she danced. She might have gone on dancing forever if she hadn't heard him say, "And you want to come in, don't you, You-Alive?" He opened the book.

Without answering his question, she came closer. Closer. She clutched the book. She felt its hot, racing breathing-breathing-breathing. Her eyes clouded over, and wandered. On one of the pages she saw a watery line, a miniature river twisting and turning and flowing on the paper. Her eyes followed the river to its source in a tangle of springs and tributaries. Sidi shifted the book. The river ran off the edge of the paper and disappeared, drowning in space. The page went blank.

Jummo gasped in wonder. "What happened to the water?"

"It returned to its source, You-Alive." He reached out to her. "Reach out, You-Alive," he commanded. "Open wide."

She gave him her hands. One by one he unclasped her fingers, exposing the dense map of creases on her palms. With his forefinger he separated her age line from her life line. He twisted them and tied them together at a precise, dot-sized point on the heart line.

"The dot," he said, "is the beginning, the origin of every thing that lives, or exists." From the dot he extracted a triangle. "This is a static form, completely still. But once you begin to build with it, it breeds shapes that can go on and on forever. You are a stillness, You-Alive, a stillness that moves and changes and grows." Again from the dot he extracted more dots aligned in the shape of a triangle. "A stillness that moves and changes and grows . . ."

Very softly she said, "Does my story end happily-ever-after?"

He nodded yes. "You uncovered the letter." She was startled to feel his hands tighten around hers. "Hold on, You-Alive."

"All I did was grasp the meaning of Amma, the first chapter of the Holy Book. If I could only discover the secrets of letters, what I'd really like to do is discover the secrets of *The Thousand and One Nights.* Because there's an animal sleeping in there."

"You are human. But you are not completely present in your life. Look—watch the river. Train your eye to follow the flow of words and you will have nothing to fear."

"So I'll have baby boys and baby girls and live happily ever after?"

"You will know pleasure, its true essence—real pleasure. The body, like a snake, can change its skin." He looked hard at her. "Alive, alive as a snake, live as a snake . . . alive . . . "

From his body to hers a quiver passed, and she tightened. The sounds of S and V—*sss*snake . . . ali*vvvv*e—hissed and shuddered as Sidi repeated them, and for the first time Jummo tasted true pleasure.

67. Of Bottles and Women

Sidi tried to rewrite Jummo's life to the tune of *The Thousand and One Nights*. Was it just a story Jummo fell in love with? Did the echoes of the story distract and confuse her?

To Jummo the illiterate, *The Thousand and One Nights* was a closed book. But some vague instinct—a seventh sense, I suppose—alerted her and drove her to watch us kids while we spent long hours pouring over one volume after another. She tilted her eyebrows at a suspicious angle each time our fingers turned a page.

No one could stop us from going down into the labyrinth of writing, no one could keep us from being captivated by the subject matter itself. Jummo tried and tried, but her attempts to hide the keys to the books and keep us away from the forbidden pages of the *Nights* always ended in failure.

Hannah regarded the manuscripts with great reverence and awe. She was, after all, the one who had inherited the worshipful dread associated with books and their mysterious powers. This was her inheritance from her father, the Sheik of the Zamzam Well, with its green dome and numberless channels and magical waters. She *belonged* to this inheritance; was a captive of her heritage, a slave to the paper it was written on. At the same time she held in her hands the power to unleash the parchments with their gazelle-skin bindings and metallic embossing, and all the words, words, words riding on their backs—she had the power to release them and let them invade our worlds and take us prisoner.

One night she was stirred out of sleep by water splashing and splattering in Nabee Jan's mosquito net. It wasn't very long ago that he'd been moved out from under our dark blue net because, so they told us, he was approaching puberty. The evidence, they further explained, was the gleam in his eye whenever he looked at a woman. He was immediately banished from our mosquito net, the Net of the Three Sisters.

Jummo, startled by the sound of water in Nabee Jan's new blue net, slipped out of her net and went over to his and joined us, the girls, who were standing around quietly watching the pond of Nabee Jan's life's story ripple around his bed. His lips were an alarming shade of blue. We were transfixed by the blueness.

Jummo took us by surprise, swooped down on the pond while the geniis' daughters were still playing in it, and shooed us out into the sunlight, which made it impossible for us ever again to escape into legends. Still, we had seen the geniis naked, and the feathered dress had been blown away. The vision, now forbidden, left us feeling more guilt-stricken than usual, and somehow skinnier. Getting caught, in this case, meant punishment by confiscation.

The thing a women fears most of all is the water of that pond, because this is where she wants to play and be free. But the pond is also a place where peeking eyes like to go—and being watched can arouse a woman. According to Nara, a girl could get pregnant just by being looked at. She could get pregnant if a bird pooped on her shadow, or if her scent got tangled in a rope swaying in the breeze. A girl is a magical, bulging, long necked bottle capable of catching giants and trapping them in her dark interior. The darkness of women is a trap for power. A woman, therefore, is the bottle of the proverbial genii-in-a-bottle.

Women, more than all other creatures, know how dangerous it can be to change from a state of repose and take on an active, assertive role. They understand that such a move can prove fatal, they know how a girl can drown in her own darkness. So they resort to diluting their darkness with occasional splashes of sunlight and bursts of noise, never letting the bulging, long-necked bottle get too absorbed in its own thoughts.

Parents try to solve this problem by arranging a marriage that is little more than a harness of hatred. They do this to make sure that their girl won't get seduced by diabolical values that might overwhelm her body-bond feelings. Above all, parents want the girl's body and feelings to stay intact, passion-proof.

Jummo fell into her own bulging, long-necked bottle, and the cork sealed her in. She never emerged. There was no way out.

68. Jummo's Thirst for Death

For years after she was dead and gone, Jummo, our heiress of Wise Royan, kept calling on my sister Krazat al-Yosir in her dreams. Always he came carrying a parchment folded in the shape of a triangle, and whenever al-Yosir opened it up, roses sprouted from the words, along with loaves of *kolja* bread and shady-looking animals with heavy udders ready for milking, and Jummo would announce, "This is a page from the book!"—meaning a page from *The Thousand and One Nights,* specifically, the page where the River Was was described.

This is where Krazat al-Yosir and I continue to dive, dream after dream, and this is where Jummo still rises, buoyed by the will of the rivers and currents, because of all the perilous turns that life can take, the path of Wise Royan is not invariably fatal.

"This whole planet is nothing but a graveyard," Jummo was thinking. "We moved from one house to another, but the graveyard stays the same. True, our new house was higher up, and its view was a wider panorama of the realm of death. But the house my father provided for us was just a tower looking out on a field of graves."

On the first day of the year 1400 A.H. (1978 C.E.), a man claiming to be the Mahdi, the savior of our world, smuggled coffins full of guns into the Holy Mosque, along with coffins packed with dates to feed his band of rebels. His snipers picked off some of our neighbors sitting in their homes.

Mecca shuddered with tanks, fighter jets screeched across the sky. The Mahdi and his men were carried out of the Holy Mosque in coffins.

Nara was petrified. Jummo didn't blink an eye. She tried to quiet Nara's fears. "There's never been a time," she said, "when the coffins haven't been in plain view right below our house. The difference now is that you can't help seeing them, and all the corpses heaped up in trucks. But what you're seeing now has been there all along."

Nara uttered the Name of God to rid herself of the indelible image of universal death. But she couldn't stop herself from counting what couldn't be counted—the infinite number of dead. She felt paralyzed.

Jummo couldn't take her eyes off the creatures crawling toward death on the slope below our house. She was a passionate observer of death; it was a taste she shared with Sidi. The two of them liked nothing more than to get one last glimpse of life before it vanished into the earth. The more she drank in the sight of death, the thirstier she become for another sip, and another . . . another taste of what it might be like to overrule the ultimate law of animal nature. The life force she saw in living people and things was not enough to quench her thirst.

"This dormer I'm sitting in," she thought, "or even this house itself— they've never been truly safe. It's all just a raft floating on a sea of death. It's a grave for all the little moments of my life, a burial ground of my thoughts and private feelings, a pit that swallows the River of Time running under my skin . . . as long as it does keep running in this Mecca, in this holy land."

A flash of light distracted her. The light became a smile dawning on her face, and she turned to the windows, bathing in shadows and light whose filigree informed her that the dormer was full of Sidi and his currents. Hungrily, he opened her whole being to the shadows. No—mortal lives, the lives led by living people—this was not enough for her.

"Nothing can quench my thirst," she said aloud, "except a drink of Sidi."

◆   ◆   ◆

Jummo in her observatory, observing: Every second she spends by her window is a bite out of the lives of the people and creatures passing below. She's watching Time grow and change. Her Time is a vivid creature of legend, a gigantic serpent licking, licking the energy of living things, never satisfied.

Time's insatiable thirst becomes an obsession with Jummo. She wants to take a big chunk of Time and put it inside herself. She wants to be Time. Because of this, she turns into a passive human being, the sum of all her latencies. She does everything in her power to forestall decay and death. She wants to make mortal time forget about her, pass her by, as if she were nothing but a birthmark or a tattoo on Time's shoulder blade. In this way, she thinks, she will be able to have more time, to gain more space in which to feast on the energy of life around her.

She becomes obsessed, too, by the fluid map she sees in the flight of birds. When the sun begins to set, she lies down in the *kharija* and looks up at the birds gliding across the sky on their way to their nesting places in the friezes. She watches the wings of soaring birds fold like prayerful hands. She watches the red shadows left by the birds in the vast openness of the Holy Circle's sky. She lies there forever and ever, drinking in the voices rippling and calling in the Alive, growing stronger.

69. The Cripple's Kitchen

Let me just tell you now, in the plainest possible language, that someone was responsible for paralyzing Jummo and confining her to bed.

Oh my God—all this smoke is suffocating me! You ignited the last bit of incense you had, didn't you?—on the Map of Living Skin—and you wrote a message begging for my assistance—I must send you a telegram identifying the culprit responsible for Jummo's predicament. Well, well, well . . . quite the little name-sleuth, aren't we?

Simmer down, friend. You and your incense and your couriers are trying to break up the story at the end of its telling—you want things summarized for you. If you think you can shut down what's left of Jummo, you've got another think coming. Every story wants to keep building and blabbing on and on, and this one is no exception.

You! Having you ever considered making yourself a prisoner in the world of women? Have you ever been curious about feminism? Did you ever get pinched between the mill wheels of history? Did you start taking an interest in women only to be baffled by our lives? Our lives . . . circling on themselves, round and round and round, like snakes swallowing their tails . . .

The same little circle of earth that great-grandmother Khadija paced on was paced on by Nara too, and by an endless succession of granddaughters. Could it be that Jummo was the only one who got away with not pacing that same small circle of ground, and didn't have to stand around watching history's water wheel grind her freedom to bits?

"I live in seclusion," you say, "in the Palace of the Three Sisters."

Oh? Or is it the Palace of the Seven Sisters?

Have you been seduced by the esthetics of history? Permit me to inquire how, in your opinion, a passive personality could get along with, much less get married to, an outgoing, assertive personality? The world in which assertive people are engaged mirrors the world of passive people, but each world stays in its own orbit, complete unto itself. Neither world can break into the other's orbit; neither can find a spot to pin a tail on the other.

Gradually, during her years of confinement, Jummo stopped venturing out into the ravine and its whirl of strange lives. She was content to sit all afternoon in her dormer watching what was going on below, and feeling far away from her self. Her body took early retirement.

"*Ka-te-lo Ya ob-be!*" cries the Indian vendor in a typically Meccan mix of Persian, Arabic, and perhaps Urdu. He's standing directly under Jummo's window, hawking yams from Yemen. "*Ka-te-lo Ya ob-be!*" Jummo sends her servant down to buy some. They're grilled, with yellow hearts bulging under purple skins. "*Ka-te-lo Ya ob-be!*"

Though the house on the ravine has become a cavern of oblivion, there are a few things still living inside. When Jummo's life slows to a crawl, the house follows her lead. In sympathy with her penchant for sitting in one place, things get simpler and smaller. The kitchen abides no presence but hers. The fires in the ovens look shyly at the ground, and all the dishes arrange themselves on lower shelves to accommodate their mistress, who is no longer able to stand. Jummo reigns over a kingdom of dwarfs: All the chairs are short, with seats only a few inches off the ground. They are made of polished ebony, like her old trunks.

From her bed on the floor she crawls under the south-facing dormer to the west entrance to her rooms, on to the narrow hall that turns right into the *mabeet*, then left to the kitchen, where she ascends her ebony throne and surveys, with the squint of a monarch, the low fire in the oven, the water tap ringed by a low collar to keep the dish water from running all over the floor . . . She moves closer to her bubbling pots. She is an accomplished cook, and she's always preparing some recipe or other for Nara and her African servant.

She has abdicated all responsibilities except for cooking and concocting elixirs and potions to promote healthy spirits. (In Meccan dialect, the words for cooking, *tarkeeb*, and concocting, *arakib*—"I construct," are related.) Jummo carries on in her cripple's kitchen until there comes a time when she is no longer able to leave her bed, at which point all responsibilities for running the household pass to her daughter-in-law Rahma, the wife of Sheik Baikwaly's son Hosn the Perfectly Beautiful.

70. The Watching Room

I see them clearly now, on the seventh floor of the house built on the ravine, Dumboshi on the right side of the room, Nara on the left, rolling cigarette papers, gluing them around the tobacco with their spit, smoking with exquisite intimate pleasure. Beside each of them stands a pot of light tea and a china bowl. No sugar. The bowls are so fine, so uncannily round, that it is a thrill merely to touch them. Their superbness insinuates that there is no greater pleasure in life than one long sip of their celestial golden liquid.

Nara and Dumboshi observe an elaborate ritual while preparing their tea, pouring it two or three times into the bowl, and returning it to the pot so it can continue to steep under the elaborate pot cover and achieve just the right ripeness of golden color and taste. Nothing compares to the taste of grandmother's tea.

(We never do get to taste Jummo's. She won't let anyone near her precious china.)

Nara and Jummo stretch out and sip their tea. Jummo breaks into song. Nara gets up and starts dancing, lightly tapping the floor and circling with regal slowness around her audience, Jummo. Nara moves as if drugged, dragging the foot that has just recently recovered from the stroke that nearly turned it to stone. Her dancing is earthbound; her body stirs the ground beneath her feet without disturbing the air. On and on she dances, on and on, always with the same lightness of spirit. The shadow of her youthful figure dances along with her, slithering from wall to wall, and the room becomes a kaleidoscope of dancers. Nara has the courage to let go and dance spontaneously in front of an audience. Only Nara is bold enough to display her body's vocabulary of seduction. She lets it all out. Her daughters inherit the same vocabulary; the body language of the Sheik of the Zamzam Water Carriers. But they dance only in a ritualistic way. The lighthearted dance—with grandeur—this is grandmother's specialty.

"Be careful, woman" Jummo warns with a laugh. "Your *bishdanic* is going to fall out." *Bishdanic* is not Arabic—it's Khazar slang, a code used by Jummo and Nara, and what Jummo is saying is that if Nara wears herself out dancing, her womb will drop between her legs.

My grandmother's womb dropped between her legs in its own good time. Every now and then it would announce its need for some seed. Her womb remained fertile till the day she died. Then she, along with her womb, was taken up to Heaven.

Jummo and Nara: two women in an observatory, observing. From the moment the season of pilgrimage starts, there is scarcely a second when they're not at their watching-posts in the dormers. All day long they sit, one in the dormer facing the Holy Mosque, the other in the dormer overlooking the ravine, and from these vantage points they provide each other with running commentary about the goings-on below.

All along the front of the house, from the corners to the main entrance, there is a sea of ever-changing faces, with endless eddies and undercurrents—all material for the sitters-in-the-dormers. And always in the dormers, the teapots and the teacups follow the ladies from place to place like loyal retainers.

China, more china, Jummo sings to herself. *Full udders . . . more milking . . . more feeding . . .*

Below, the story wheels, the wheels of life, keep turning and spilling more twists and turns. Some of the stories go on and on and move from place to place. Other stories go even further, beyond the range of the viewers in the dormers. One way or another, the watching is an art form that calls for a sharp mind and a vivid imagination. There are times when the briefest glimpse can patch a hole in a tattered story. Some little sound might be all it takes to fill in the gap in a story discarded long ago for lack of observable detail, or because the absence of that crucial detail had consigned the story to dullness.

"Aysha the Onion ran out of her house. Aysha the Onion bumped into the water boy and knocked him down. Aysha the Onion locked herself in her hidey-hole place for a whole month and then she came out and then she roamed around the well for a whole other month and then her onion sprouted from her chin, so Aysha the Onion has a stinky onion beard and it makes her cry . . . "

This was Jummo's and Nara's version of the escapades of an old woman named Aysha. They appended the Onion (*Basala*) to her name because Aysha had orange-yellow hair and frizzy whiskers that looked like an onion's wispy roots. They watched Aysha the Onion all the time. She lived somewhere in the jumble of big houses, or maybe in an abandoned lot, or a doorway, or a shack on the hillside behind the big houses.

Aysha the Onion got crazier with age. She had a way of popping up out of nowhere with her *abaya* draped over her head, but without a veil, exposing the yellowish fuzz all over her face. She was oblivious to the presence of men, and when one of them threw pebbles at her, she'd run away, splattered with mud, orange hair flying. There were people who swore they'd seen her going in and out of a dark cave—more like a hole, actually, in the side of the mountain—but in all the years Jummo spent watching Aysha the Onion, she was never able to solve the mystery of where she lived or how she managed to appear so suddenly. When she did appear, " . . . she'd be right where she wasn't a second ago—standing on the slope of the ravine, taking a long, slow look around, then walking all over, combing the dust with the hem of her *abaya,* which seemed to get longer as age and insanity shriveled her frame, till finally there was not a speck of dust left for her long black tail to sweep up, and the back of her *abaya* split into two enormous tearful eyes, goggling wider and wider each time she made an appearance, and one day the eyes swallowed her up and that was the last thing anybody ever saw of Aysha the Onion."

How stunted and limited our wild, childish imaginations were compared to the artistry with which Nara and Jummo nursed their stories and patched the holes in their plots, ushering the simplest, most obvious incidents toward a realm where they acquired the splendors of the Unknown. Whenever we entered the Watching Room, we were obliged to participate in the rituals of watching. We took a seat in one of the dormers, where we could see through the stories taking place to the north, east, and south (the west was blocked by the tall house of our neighbor, Mr. Musroor). From three points of the compass, the stories of our neighbors' lives poured in. Most of the plots were unresolved, of course, so it was our job to catch a glimpse here and there, or maybe just pick up the murmur of a name, to flesh out the actors playing their parts in the endlessly unraveling play, the steady rhythm of narrative that never stopped saying, *I'm talking, I'm talking, I'm talking . . .*

In the observatory we endured an ordeal by watching, an epic test of creative powers, the exacting enterprise of tracking the orbits of all the star-lives swirling around us, memorizing every detail and letting none of it fade away. Not till now. Nara warned us about looking into our neighbors' houses and invading their privacy, but we never could resist the temptation of a story that seemed about to burst with the sheer variety of life, and we never could say no to peeking behind the veil to get an idea which way the story might turn.

71. Torrid Ladies

Looking east, for example, we watched the comings and goings of many, shall we say, "torrid ladies" in and out of the Musroor residence. Every day at sunset, Mr. Musroor smuggled a few "torrid ladies" into his house. The rest of the evening he spent "opening the vaults of the vineyards and irrigating the grapes." This went on till the crack of dawn.

Jummo pulled the blankets up over our eyes. "You can't resist the Lord of Sleep," she told us, reserving for herself a private viewing of the saga of Musroor and the all-night revels on his roof.

Joman did manage to stay awake and tune into bits of Jummo's and Nara's commentary. When Musroor fell in love with a new woman in the neighborhood—this one came originally from the seaside village of Mustora—we were the first to know about it. He plied his new love with every gift imaginable, but in the end the only gift that could catch her was the gift-trap of marriage. At last, after securing her acceptance on his roof, he spent the rest of the night in her arms, "opening the vaults of the vineyards ... etc." But the scenes of actual consummation—of "taming, taking, and milking"—could not be seen from the dormers of my grandfather's house, because Musroor absconded with his lovebird to distant pastures—down to one of the lower floors, where, we imagined, he continued to "drink her wine" while veiling her charms in secrecy, so that not even Mecca's lofty mountains or the birds in the night sky were able to get a good look.

Every Thursday, the lady from Mustora paid us a visit. We broke out in a sweat trying to elicit details of the amorous strategies Musroor had gleaned from the torrid ladies. These tricks, we assumed, he'd taught to Mustora.

"When he comes to me ... " she laughed, " ... he *comes*. It doesn't matter if I'm smelling of onions or Anza root." Her eyes brimmed with a kind of pleasure we barely understood. Mustora narrowed her lids to dream-slits. We heard the crashing of waves in the distance, the opening and closing of the ocean's secret chambers.

We were the first to know, of course, when Musroor's hankering for the torrid ladies revived and his itch for variety returned. Mustora's sea magic and all the other wondrous sea-things she was made of were no longer of interest. In no time at all, Musroor went from monogamy to gamy-gamy-gamy. He exchanged the uniform of a faithful lover for the robes of a dervish woman-worshipper. Mustora's nights were shattered by waking nightmares of endless partying and singing on the roof. There were arguments, there were bitter struggles; the bride's heart was broken.

Are you familiar with the way a woman's satiny skin can turn dry and rough as wood? All of Mustora's mermaid smoothness, all the deep-sea richness of her body and mind, dried up. She turned into a stick of kindling, brittle and flammable. Insults sparked in her face, desertion stung her, jealousy attacked from all eight directions of the Unknown.

On the night when Mustora confronted the leader of the torrid ladies, not even the blankets that Jummo piled on top of us could keep us from hearing. The gasps, the shrieks, and shudders woke us out of deep sleep. We shared the watch; we took advantage of the adults' distraction to sneak into the dormer and spend the night watching Mustora and the torrid lady in hand-to-hand combat, their clawed fingers striking like snakes at one another's braids till their hair hung down like tangled rags.

Dumboshi burst out laughing. She'd gotten so absorbed in the battle on the roof next door that she'd forgotten where she was. She'd seen something shocking: Mustora running over to the lowest wall on the roof and getting ready to launch herself into the air and jump to the pavement below. Musroor, running just as madly, rushed from the festivities downstairs, where he'd been hiding, and stopped her before she caused an unconscionable scandal.

We went back to bed. Jummo whispered into Nara's blushing ear everything she'd managed to hear. Joman was the only one of us able to understand this report and only recently did she pass it on to me, when she realized I was actually committing Jummo's story to paper.

The leader of the torrid ladies pats herself on the lap, or thereabouts. "*This*," she says to Mustora, "I can't do anything about. It's your husband you ought to do something about."

Confronted by this egregious gesture of physical freedom, Mustora flies into a rage. She wants to die.

A few days later we see what looks like soldiers fighting on the roof. We see the vines from the vineyards on the lower floors twining up the stairs. We see Mustora grab many bottles and carry them across to neighboring roofs, out of harm's way.

Night after night, the dormers of all the houses in the neighborhood buzz with tales of the great attack. Mustora is the object of everyone's attention: "He *irrigates* you, you say? Your mind is gone, girl. What've you been drinking?"

In the dormers, secrets are piled on top of secrets. In the dormers, secrets are swapped and fingered and weighed by women wearing snow-white head coverings and fancy Syrian pants, and sipping endless cups of *sahlab* spiced with ginger. The dormers—these are the rooms where women live their lives, and die. These are the observatories where everything and everyone is seen, nothing hidden.

72. *Murder, Funeral, Marriage, Divorce*

We moved on to watching the wars waged by the daughters of our neighbors to the north, the battles between them and their older brother. The girls used the standard carrot-and-stick technique to tease him.

One day we saw this young man being carried into his house. Evidently he'd died while pursuing the object of his affections in some pleasure-land she'd seduced him into. His mother, Dublola, assumed he'd been murdered. She and the young man's five sisters yanked his widow by the hair, tossed her out of their little house, and forbade her to attend the funeral.

How could we possibly turn away from the sight of a mother shrieking over the body of her only son? Dublola wept; she tore at her braids, her head cover and her dress. She wandered around in her Syrian blouse and white vest, trailing the torn hem of her dress, circling around the *kharija*, screaming in her daughter-in-law's—her rival's—face: "He's a corpse now, a corpse that's got nothing to do with you, and you have nothing to do with him. He belongs to me, he's my treasure!" Between gasps, Dublola raised her eyes to our dormer and called out in a voice gone hoarse from crying: "Be my witness, Jummo! Sheik Baikwaly, be my witness, too!"

She was playing to an audience. She was fully aware of the eyes peeking from behind our discreetly closed, occasionally blinking shutters. Dublola and her five daughters knew from the start that their private lives were being observed by an Eye-on-High. They knew about it, they accepted it, they were comfortable with it, as with an old friend. What's more, they elaborated the details of their lives in order to cater to the Eye, to shock or amuse. They saw to it that their behavior unscrolled at great length, with the utmost clarity and candor; so that everything would be registered by the Eye-on-High.

If ever Dublola had doubts about which way the story should turn, she found time to consult with Nara on the top floor of our house. Entire afternoons she spent going over the disappointments that plagued her life, laying bare the most intimate details, and weighing every emotional trip hammer to analyze the outbursts, the tedium, the downright pointlessness of the play being performed in the theater below our window. As soon as she went back home, we hurried to the dormer to watch the next development.

The day of her son's funeral, Dublola was still showering curses on her daughter-in-law. The five daughters pushed the young widow out into the street; a handful of neighborhood men were rounded up to attend the obsequies. We watched while the mother and the daughter-in-law spun like tops, one in the courtyard, the other on the street, till the coffin was carried away, the daughter-in-law staggering after it like a madwoman, bareheaded and unveiled, all the way down the ravine to the market called al-Saker, where she collapsed. Then she too was carried away, and made to wear her veil.

Needless to say, Nara did not permit us to watch the washing of the male body, which took place in plain view in the courtyard directly below us. Her threats, along with our natural dread of the washing ritual, were sufficient to keep us from seeing what transpired with the buckets of *nabk*-water and the bare wooden table on which the body lay, completely naked except for the little piece of cloth covering his loins.

As for Jummo, she paced nervously, not daring to transgress on the taboo, that thin veil separating the sacred from the profane. She did have a dream, however, in which she joined the parade of angels descending from Heaven to claim the young man's soul. She clearly saw them removing his vital spirit from its body-temple. She watched the spirit crouching in the temple, reluctant to come out and be cupped in Sidi's patiently waiting hand. She saw row upon row of angels extract the spirit, one strand at a time, from the body's sinews and veins, and carry it up to the sky till the procession vanished behind the gate of the First Heaven. Afraid to follow any further, she woke up.

She did not watch the washing rituals the next day. The spirit had long since departed its earthly temple, and she wanted nothing to do with a vacated corpse. Later on, though, while the coffin was being carried across the ravine, she sat at her perch in the north-facing dormer, staring down at the *nabk*-water puddling like a blood stain in Dublola's courtyard. It refused to dry until sunrise of the following day.

We missed not one second of the festivities following the funeral. Crowded into the dormer, we counted the dozens of wooden platters heaped with rice, garbanzo beans, and *shushne* candies. *Shushne*—a mix of shredded pumpkin, raisins, cardamom, and almonds—the taste is still fresh on my tongue, along with the memories of so many funerals in Mecca.

(As I've indicated, the food served at the funeral was no different from food served at a regular party, except for the garbanzo beans and the *shushne*. Actually, the difference was more a matter of nomenclature than substance, since almonds were an essential treat at weddings, and raisins and garbanzo beans were mixed with cardamom and sugar to make sweets served at wedding celebrations, too.)

Following this death, new life entered Dublola's house: a man came to marry her youngest daughter. We watched the sprinkling of rosewater to welcome the son-in-law, the *qreen*. The groom, a widower, set one condition on the wedding: the women were not to dilute his grief with ostentatious displays of happiness. So the ceremony was quite dull. There was an orphaned air about it that piqued our expectations as to what might happen in the next act of the play—an earthquake, or something along those lines.

The next twist did not disappoint us. The groom underwent a sudden change of heart: he bolted and with a single word—*divorced!*—he rid himself of his bride, handing her back to Dublola, who had just gotten used to the comfort of having a new man in a family whose exclusive femaleness was beginning to get on her nerves.

"The bridegroom," she explained to Sheik al-Baikwaly, "is possessed by the spirit of his late wife. She's lingering on the Isthmus dividing life and death and scolding him for deserting her. He responds by divorcing my poor darling daughter. I beg you, Sheik, in God's name, help him get rid of his dead wife. Women of the Isthmus belong on the Isthmus. They should let our girls be with the men who live in the realm of the Known. Excuse me, Sidi." Dublola always concluded her litanies of complaints by asking Sidi's permission to continue on her way. My grandfather listened intently, eyes fixed on his turquoise ring.

It got to be a habit with us, whenever the word divorce was unsheathed to threaten the bride, to watch Dublola, cloaked in her *abaya*, emerge from her house and stride purposefully around the corner to my grandfather's house while we scuttled from dormer to dormer to keep her in sight, finally settling in the window overlooking the Holy Mosque. She disappeared into our house and secretly made her way up to my grandfather's quarters.

Whereupon our house turned into a war zone of silliness. Pandemonium rattled the rafters, frightening pigeons off the façade. The walls cringed.

"This is *dumboshi* mischief," Nara proclaimed. She was referring not to Jummo but to Mecca's cult of African magic. "Strange things are going on downstairs. Dublola paid us a visit today."

This pronouncement meant that madness reigned. Since we could not be held accountable for our actions as long as provocative spirits were loose in the house, we went berserk. We relished this blissful state of irresponsibility and moral incompetence. The Recording Angel had suspended, if only for a short time, his accounting of our misdeeds, just as he did in the case of those who were seriously ill or insane. We went wild for as long as the quill of the Recording Angel remained motionless, though Nara reminded us that our accounts were bound to be reconciled in my grandfather's ledger. Our understanding was that we could misbehave until the bride found a way to be reunited with her groom, at which time we would turn back into obedient drones—we and the shuddering walls and the flustered pigeons—and the Angel's pen would resume its task of noting our wicked deeds. Then our craziness—call it a vacation, a leave of absence—would be over.

We took several vacations before the bride exhausted her three chances at reconciliation and was obliged to return to her mother's house. The third proclamation of divorce put an end to the marriage. The groom rejoined his dead wife on the Isthmus and shortly thereafter the bride went there too—Dublola's youngest daughter died.

Again we watched the funeral . . . again . . . again . . . a dreary succession of sad ceremonies. We dedicated ourselves to watching the life people lived after death: the procession of platters fragrant with almonds, cardamom and ginger. Through all this Jummo sat in shock, never touching the tray of rice and garbanzo beans that had been left in her kitchen. Hope that she might taste something was abandoned and the tray forgotten.

The thing we watched most of all was funerals. Even in times of flood, with water rushing through the streets, what we saw were omens of death sweeping away the souls of Mecca's citizens. The sight of running water still brings back the eye of Sidi Wahdana and his parade of sacrificial victims.

73. The Task of Being Dead

The people of Mecca spent quite a bit of time preparing their processions to Medina, the city dearest to the Prophet's heart. With great solemnity they dyed the donkeys with henna and draped them in brocade. To put themselves in a suitably exalted frame of mind, people listened to the singing of the camel drivers, whose songs touched their heart of hearts.

The floods that came to Mecca would accept no other rituals. The floods came once every year, reliable as camel raids. The city responded graciously, surrendering a king's ransom in precious goods. The two opposites, water and death, became one in the circle of holy Mecca's ⵁ.

We never knew where the Alive might come from next. This instilled in us a sense of worthiness, of being competent at living side by side with miracles.

Al-Shobaika was the oldest cemetery in the city until it was dug up to make room for new houses and modern roads. But the graves, having taken on substance over the years, disgorged gigantic corpses. The Wise Ones and other sophisticated commentators maintained that these were the corpses of ancient kings, good rulers whose flesh the earth dared not eat because they'd been mummified by the verse from the Holy Book known as The Realm. The words of this verse neutralized agents of decay present in the earth. The corpses that rose from their graves were the bodies of wise and virtuous people who had traveled to the Holy City after their death so they could rest in consecrated ground. They came as pilgrims to perform the rituals of pilgrimage, then resumed the task of being dead in this land of ours neighboring the House of God.

When it came time for al-Shobaika to be moved, the good kings and virtuous people were disinterred and carried in coffins lavishly decorated on the inside and plain on the outside. Despite their modest facades, the coffins drew crowds of commoners and upper-class people on their way from al-Shobaika to the cemetery at al-Maala, where they were laid to rest at the mouth of a stream that marked the intersection of several sacred valleys. There they slept, in a spot where the waters that flooded Mecca would be filtered by their ancient perfumed flesh, absorbing and distributing their fates to people living in the vicinity of the Holy Mosque.

Every flood that struck Mecca claimed its tribute of living things and carried them away on its back—plants, animals, snakes, people—to the far shore of the Unknown. All we knew for sure was that no creature who traveled with the floods ever came back to tell tales of that distant shore. No one ever returned to tell us about life in the great beyond to which the flood delivered its passengers. No one escaped the tug of its dreadful tide; no one was heard to say, *Come on, take the next ride with me.* Not that there wasn't a next ride. There always was, and it always took the city by surprise, carrying off whatever lanterns it fancied from the Holy Mosque, as well as citizens known as Shepherds of the Secret—Mecca's true elite, the wealthiest people, the dervishes and the ascetics who'd consecrated their entire lives to serving the Sacred. The floods spared no one, not even little children who'd yet to glimpse life's true face.

Sidi Wahdana rode the crest of every flood, perched on a wave sprouting vegetables fresh from market, surrounded by bobbing camels, saddlebags bulging with fruit from Taif: clusters of figs, sacks of onions and leeks. Sidi always bore with him the scent of fresh earth and the perfume of living things, and his head was always tilted up, only the white of his eyes showing, and always he was saying, " . . . old world . . . " wagging his head slowly back and forth, never looking down, repeating, " . . . alive, alive, alive . . . new world . . . old world . . . " The whites of his eyes became even whiter, and from their sockets, at moments that came to be considered sacred, crystals of white ice seeped. When times were confused and tragic, they leaked pus. There was never a serious flood in Mecca when Sidi wasn't seen riding its back through the streets alongside the bodies of those who had drowned. With a silver bridle he directed the water toward the deserts and dark wells that lay at Mecca's feet. To the merchants in the markets, it seemed that Sidi Wahdana was making his way to their shops with the express purpose of checking their inventories and exacting a yearly tax to be paid to the denizens of the Unknown, who where the ones who'd instigated the flood in the first place.

When, after spending some time in Taif, we went back down to Mecca, my father was obliged to pay his overdue taxes. The flood came right on time, swirling around the foundation of my grandfather's house. It crested during a crystal-clear night, under a sparkling sky so eerily still that Nara had gone ahead and lit the lanterns in the *kharija* overlooking the minarets of the Holy Mosque.

We even had time to dance a few steps of the Water Carriers' Dance. Under the open sky we twirled, Jummo drumming on a tin box, Nara dancing and singing lonely melodies about being abandoned in the desert, the sort of song usually sung by homesick pilgrims from the Sudan.

The pigeons came out from under the eaves and flocked at Nara's feet, following the tapping of her toes with longing in their blinkless eyes. She turned and turned, her waist bound by a vivid belt, hair crowned by a white veil embroidered with violet flowers. All through the night we

watched the shadows fanning away from the lanterns, twitching, bewitching, brightening, darkening, rippling across the *kharija*'s lightly stuccoed
walls, warmer, warmer, warmer. We watched, breathless and amazed, as
the dancers' towering shadows stretched over the stubby walls and leapt
out into the darkness to twitch across the skin of the night.

A fragment of the dancing shadows must have broken off and fallen
into the ravine and woken up a spirit slumbering by the road. The fact was,
there wasn't a shadow in the city who could resist Nara's dancing—they
all joined in. When the shadows got tired, Nara sat down and gathered us
close, her sweat reflecting points of light on our faces. She started singing
in her not-quite-native accent:

> *Oh beetle-beetle-beetle,*
> *Mistress of all mistresses,*
> *Will you marry little-bitty me?*
> *I'll buy you lots and lots of dresses.*
> *Said Mistress Beetle: I'll go ask my Mommy,*
> *Cause my dowry's tucked right up my sleeve.*
> *Oh mommy, mommy—his eye's so big.*
> *But mommy, mommy—his head's so teeny-weeny!*

Mistress Beetle's refusal of one suitor after another—the cockroach,
the mouse, the ghoul, etc.—went on and on and on. The beetle's black
shadow lengthened across the walls of the *kharija,* crept through the air,
and slithered up the slopes of the great mountains, Khondoma and Abu-
Qubais. Every snake in the land came out to play with the creeping, slinking darkness.

The night was still incredibly calm. Nara bent low over the lanterns
and forged glowing anklets from their flickerings. One by one, she called
on us to dance with the jingling light, as she sang:

> *Ha qo-fa ya si ya si—*
> *I went down to the pond wearing six silver rings,*
> *And a blindfold round my head,*
> *And I found the cook still crying.*

I dried his tears with the tassels on my belt,
Then turned the belt around and dried his tears again.
Uncle! Uncle! Make my anklet wider!

She rattled her silver anklets, we rattled ours, and the stars overhead rattled, too.

The air in the ravine was frosty and utterly still. Nara arranged our "mosquitoes," as we called our nets. They were made of an amazing material that stiffened in the heat and shone like the sun on those rare occasions when frost descended on Mecca. The nets fluttered as if in private conversation with Nara, who knew that the brightness of the fabric wouldn't be enough to keep us warm on a night like this. So she revised our sleeping arrangements. We hoisted the beds on our skinny shoulders and went down to the lower quarters, where we spread them on the floor and went to sleep. My father went around opening the shutters on the dormers just wide enough for a breeze to ventilate our dreams. Nara, before heading back up to the seventh floor, took a quick look at Joman, who was standing in front of the beautiful mirror to the left of the door studying her face.

"Looking in the mirror is a dangerous habit," Nara said. "All this looking at yourself—it's tempting insanity. Mirrors are where the Netherworldlings make their home at night." She meant that creatures from the Unknown, the ones who inhabit the interior of the earth, come out at night and lie in wait for us in mirrors. Looking in a mirror at night, it's awfully easy to slip and fall down into subterranean layers where humans aren't supposed to go.

Joman had always been fond of mirrors and their bewitchments. Her skin was very soft, and on her face were fine blue-green lines shaped like a slender, branching tree. Joman's vein-tree frightened Nara. "The girl is susceptible to outside influences," she said. "Her blood flows very freely. One twitch of that tree and her blood will spill out into the air."

Nara paced restlessly in the little room next to where we were sleeping, not knowing whether to leave or stay. My father was restless, too, pacing as if trying to secure the perimeter around mother and us, around sleep itself.

Nara came in and hovered by Joman's shoulder. "Netherworldlings travel all the time," she said. "Every day when the sun goes down, they set out and move their huge pavilions and their horses and their music into mirrors in the human world. They stay there, singing and dancing all night long. Then, at the crack of dawn, they pull down their tents and go back to their underground kingdoms. And even those of us with search-light eyes—no, they don't let anybody see them in their silver encamp-ments—in the mirrors, I mean."

We all knew that Joman had her mother's searchlight eyes and we understood that such eyes could serve as portals to the Unknown. The unfortunate side effect of this inheritance—if the soul of the seer were not strong enough to frame her visions of other worlds in comprehensible hu-man terms—was madness. Or, if the seer failed to maintain her fluency in the babble of the Unknown, she could succumb to that loneliness that lies beyond all loneliness. Another possible side effect was blindness, which afflicted the seer if her insight was not disciplined enough to distinguish between life's shockingly quick changes from darkness to light.

Nara continued trying to impress her cautious wisdom on Joman's heart. Joman stared back at her with one eye while her other eye watched the Netherworldlings erect their enormous tents and slaughter their ani-mals and feast on goats with twenty udders and a thousand legs.

Nara moved decisively to cover Joman's eyes and forced her to lie down to the bed on the floor. Joman lay white as ivory in the midst of the damask-draped benches. As Nara backed away, she bumped into a table inlaid with shells from the Kolzom Sea. She didn't bother to look back at it. My father was relieved to see her go.

The lanterns in the room burned low. The campfires of the Nether-worldlings flared in the mirror. The scent of amber rose from the river of blood flowing from the animals they'd slaughtered for dinner. Beneath Joman's sleeping feet, a cup full of blood bubbled. My mother—she slept not a wink all night—saw it.

In the middle of the night, when the stars reached their zenith, a strange pattern appeared in the heavens, a curious arrangement noted by only the subtlest astrologers. Certain stars, taking advantage of the fact that people were fast asleep, extinguished the messengers that usually travel in the wind. From the general direction of the cemetery at al-Maala came the roar of a huge explosion, as if the underpinnings of Abraham's Valley had cracked open. The roar quickly became a thing of horror. Rain drenched the city, not just rain from the sky—great lashes of water seemed to spout from the rocks themselves. Rain, rain, rain from the Unknown, rain orchestrated by Sidi Wahdana, rushing through streets and alleys, pouncing on living things, sweeping them out of the shadows, out of doorways, ripping furniture and people away from the rescue ropes strung across the streets. No living thing was spared—all rode the tide. Finally the flood came, with its ten mighty horns, to the house of my grandfather, Sheik Baikwaly, where it stopped and rested briefly—not long enough for my father to finish gathering up his family and the contents of his household.

The roaring waters shook us out of our dreams and drew us to the dormers. People and creatures and things were bumping along with the tide. All ten horns of the flood, heaving and gurgling as if confused, crested at the house of the Sheik of the Zamzam Water Carriers.

Sidi Wahdana appeared, the whites of his eyes flashing in the dark silver torrent clutching the sides of our house. "Alive . . . alive . . . alive . . . new world . . . old world . . . "

Splashes of silver water—sparks struck by the flood's ten horns—drenched me as I stood at my post in the dormer on the fifth floor. It soaked into my hair and trickled down my back. All of us—everything, all at once—trembled.

The cold eye of Sidi the dervish wiped the protective talismans off the walls of my grandfather's house. Some of the talismans were smeared together, blended as if in brotherhood. Others were erased—tamed and subdued into the service of masters from the Unknown. Once Sidi felt confident that the power of the talismans had been neutralized, the ten-horned flood climbed skyward with a great roar, then crashed down, splintering the door to the vault and carrying off in one swoop all the treasures my father had accumulated during the years he spent in Taif, away from the Holy City. All our material possessions were carried away by the flood, including the furniture that had survived the trip down from the Kara Mountains roped on top of a truck, along with everything else we'd shipped from Taif through Arafat to the Holy Circle. It was Sidi Wahdana, after all, who had shepherded the whole load down from Arafat only to hand it over, in the end, to his fellow shepherds from the Unknown.

By the light of morning it was clear that we'd come back to Mecca in the same condition we were in when we'd left it years before—empty-handed. My father had embarked on a new life the day his father died. He'd paid his dues; he'd left Mecca and traveled long and hard down many lonely roads. The city, too, had dues to pay: the inevitable floods of water, the ensuing floods of blood—this was Mecca's fate. Over and over, on and on, till al-Noa'aman, the Valley of Blood, became swollen with the souls of martyrs to the flood, and the streets of Mecca were awash with the blood of camel drivers and warriors marching in endless parades honoring countless kings.

The name Zubayda was borne along by the flood and distributed among the women of Mecca. The first Zubayda, she was the one who bestowed her name on the spring that rises in the Valley of Blood and channels its water through crags and deserts to supply the Holy City. We drink from her name-spring today, we sip the waters that run through the Valley of Blood, the Valley of Souls Departed, carrying souls to Mecca, a city whose name has always, in all times, echoed with death—Mecca, this Dwelling of God fought over by armies of every color and creed, the throne-city that was home to God before it ever sheltered human beings, this city whose citizens look like they've been weaned on mortal combat and sculpted from the same rocks the city was built with.

74. Doomsday and the City

What do you want from our past? Does the past, like a star, shoot across the present and light it up? In the Holy Circle there is no separation at all between yesterday, today and tomorrow; no wall between Was, Is, and Will Be. We are them all. We are the everlasting rumbling of black boulders and volcanic rocks. We are the new world, the old world. We— women, especially—are the spring of Zubayda, and when the spring fills up and overflows and spills more water than Mecca needs, the builders build new buildings beyond the perimeter of the Holy Circle and we are pushed further and further out till we start to feel we've been exiled from our home, God's home.

On the outskirts of the Holy City there is an orchard called Jurwal. It is a place where exiles and visitors can feel at home. As for the heart of the city, it's been overrun by the usual mindless monstrosities of steel and concrete. We—those who think of ourselves as living water from the ancient spring—we keep busy in our parks and orchards pouring our substance into material things, and our souls feel so lonely away from the holy places, so abandoned, that in our yearning to identify with pilgrims, our hearts beat faster at the sight of strangers and our loneliness sprouts into sprigs of spiritual balm under Mecca's blazing sky, casting cool shadows across the desert wastes, and our branching shadows—the fruits of our spring water and our souls—grow tall and provide shade and comfort for people who travel all over the world searching for the locality that happens to be our home, and from this mixing of waters a new world is born, a new being whose blood is a rainbow of many lights, the rainbow of eternal renewal.

This was. This was the dream we lived until the water table dropped and the flow dried up and our line—the vintage wine from the Valley of Blood—came to an end.

Do you know how to subdue someone from Mecca, how to crack open his chest so invaders can snatch his heart? The same way people break up big rocks: You heap firewood on the victim's chest, put a match to it, and let it burn till the heat builds and cracks the rock. Then you go down into his secret self and make indelible marks and major changes to what's left of his innocence so it conforms to the image favored by your idols.

But his instincts recoil. He can't submit, not ever.

The people of Mecca, so the saying goes, are made of the same stuff as their mountains. So be careful. What you're dealing with is a boulder from Mecca, and written on this boulder are inscriptions in a long-forgotten language, and for this language no key remains, only a few faint hints of meaning in the faces, a certain tilt of the cheekbones of people descended from the tribes of Nowaria. Have I told you about Mount Nowaria? Did

I describe the way its white rocks climb out of the heart of Mecca like a frozen beacon, eternally ascending? This is the mountain that all the women in Mecca are made of.

Legend has it that if al-Nowaria ceased to exist, the earth itself would cease to exist. The Great Reptile would emerge from Mount Ejyad and whip the face of the earth with its tail, turning the planet upside-down and dumping buried bodies on top of living people, and the Reptile will become the one-eyed Antichrist and dive way down to the pit of universe, the lowest level of creation, with Doomsday slouching close behind.

We can infer, therefore, that the extinction of Nowaria's women would mean the end of men, too. I just might be the last of the women from Nowaria.

75. Nara Dies

Nara is dragging her paralyzed legs up and down the stairs in the house of the Sheik of the Zamzam Water Carriers.

"I can't lie down," she says. "If I do, the sickness will catch up with me. I'm so old, so weak—if I stop moving, I'll fall apart."

Though her tongue is also paralyzed, she keeps talking to my mother, keeps wagging her tongue for fear it will shrivel and die. She never stops, never gives up. She manages somehow to get to her feet. She starts walking around with steps as light as a young woman's. She never lies down. Eighty years old, she won't give sickness a chance. She goes downstairs to fill the Zamzam pitchers from a spring the Sheik has diverted into a cistern in the basement. She polishes all the lanterns so they'll be ready if anyone feels the need for old-fashioned illumination. With stubborn fluency she cultivates the increasingly obscure vocabulary of days gone by. Her hands shake. She picks up a piece of broken pottery. She polishes the clay pitchers, pats their bulging bellies, strokes their long necks, and smoothes their tails that terminate in spear points. When all these things have been accomplished, she turns to the huge vat she loves even more than us. She identifies with the vat. She *is* the vat.

There's an old Khazar proverb that goes, "While you're waiting for one vat to crack, a hundred pitchers will break and disappear." Meaning that it's often difficult for old people to die, even while young people are perishing by the hundreds. Over the course of many years, the neglected old vat on my grandfather's roof becomes Nara, or a symbol of Nara. By the time she starts to deteriorate, most of our pitchers have preceded her on the road to death. The stone soldiers on the parapets, she becomes one of them, too. She's very alone, though she is surrounded by pigeons and snakes, by the mountains ringing the Holy City. She pays scant attention to the pitchers, passing them by with a perfunctory wipe of a damp cloth. But with the vat she takes plenty of time. Yet she never goes to the trouble of polishing its bulging belly, which she leaves untouched for so long that it gets caked with grime and the grime cracks in map-like lines and she begins to wonder, *Where do they lead?*

The map on the belly of the vat is the mottled pattern made by the faces of all the people who have lived in the house for so many years. The pattern is formed by rings, one on top of the other, covering the vat from its pebbly bottom to its rim, layer upon layer of the faces and minor incidents that make up our lives, all etched on the surface of the vat.

Nara doesn't dare touch it, she doesn't want to scratch a face or risk peeling off a single incident. She leaves the faces just as they are, merely moistening the clay occasionally so it won't crack when al-Simoom blows hot. She is careful never to let the vat go empty. A puddle of stagnant water lies at the bottom even after she dies, lies there forever, going from yellow to green to black, immune to evaporation.

The vat still stands in the *kharija* of the house on the ravine, unbudgeable, unnoticed by the succession of new owners; stands there with a serenity and wisdom that elude understanding. Going up there again, to my grandfather's *kharija*, for another look at the grimy black vessel—the idea frightens me. I seem to know—I *do* know—that one look into the heart of the vat would bring Nara back to this strange, alien world, our new world. Better to let her rest in peace. No eye has the right to peer into her vat, her mirror, her pottery-twin.

◆　　　◆　　　◆

The temple of Nara's soul would have simply refused to die and leave the neighborhood of the Sacred Stone if Sidi Wahdana hadn't paid her a special visit one night.

There is a rumbling in the Holy Mosque. Death is dispatching corpses in the ravine below our house. Sidi outlines Nara's eyes with a special kohl she's never come across, not even in her dreams—this kohl is made from shadows cast by the Holy Mosque. She is granted a vision of the Holy Mosque, a sanctified image free from any taint of death or impurity. Her body, carrying the burden of each of her eighty-five years, surrenders to this vision of the old world and never returns to our new one.

Those of us who happened to live right next to the Sacred Mosque, we had truly passionate feelings for God's home. For us there is no other way, no other road but the road leading back to Him.

For Nara, existence was everlasting circumambulation in the court-yard of sacred serenity. Hers was the circumambulation of people turning round and round, made fragrant and healed by the spirit of Zamzam. Whatever worries or grim moods hung over the people of Mecca, their troubles would lift when dawn broke over the holy courtyard. The circumambulation of souls, the affirmation of brotherhood in the black stone of al-Kaaba, a deep, slow drink of Zamzam, a taste of water bubbly and warm from the sacred well—with these rituals, hearts were unburdened, worries dispersed, souls set free to fly again.

The extraction of Nara's soul takes three nights. Ezrael, the Angel of Death, is in attendance in my grandfather's rooms on the seventh floor. Nara is lying in bed in the corner of the dormer facing the Holy Mosque. This is the first time she's consented to be put to bed. She's semiconscious. We don't understand that she's dying. Hannah watches her mother's departure with complete composure. Ezrael, the angel of death, goes about his business of teasing her soul from the nooks and crannies of her body.

All during the three nights that Nara lies dying, she washes herself with invisible water trickling from invisible taps in the air above her head. She spends the nights endlessly performing the rituals of ablution and prayer. She recites verses and prayers never before heard by human ears.

Then she fasts from words, yet she continues to talk, moving her tongue in silent praise: *Al-lah . . . Al-lah . . . Al-lah . . .* praying, breathing the Name with her whole body, her hands and her arms and her legs a rosary of beaded praise rising with the scent of amber and aloe wood. At dawn after the third night, just as the call to prayer is being sung, she goes with Ezrael. The rosary falls back. She rests.

When the women wash her body, they discover the Great Name, along with images of al-Kaaba and its upper doors, tattooed all over her body. We ordinary citizens of Mecca know of only one door to the Sacred Stone, the one looking south, toward Yemen. But the tattoos on Nara's skin show pathways radiating from all parts of the Stone, and on every curve in every pathway, there are thousands of doors, like the openings in a vast birdhouse, into which creatures from the Unknown and pageants attached to Sidi's procession climb and disappear. The creatures approach the doors seeking refuge. The doors take them in. The doors lift them up. They ascend.

Tell me please—how is it that the heroes and noble kings of *The Thousand and One Nights* wander all over the high seas—man, women, slaves, freemen—and not one of them ends his journey bearing any trace of the River Was? Could this be why Scheherazade's wanderings among people and other wondrous things never come to an end, and why she never languishes in one land for very long?

Jummo fell in love with *The Thousand and One Nights* because Sidi showed her the waters of life that flow through the book. She came to see the value of metamorphosis, the glimmer of gold in every stone, the enchanted prince in every frog, the priceless diamond in the belly of every whale. The *Nights* taught her to look toward what lies behind things, to the Beyond, to pass over superficial impressions and look deep inside. Magic and rapture, she discovered, do not consist in stripping things naked. She learned instead to lie in wait. She dove down into what lies beyond, into the River Was. She turned into a dome, a bell jar, and under this dome she—the real Dumboshi—hid herself and lay in waiting. Just how deeply she went into the Unknown, we'll never know. Such speculation is best left to Ridwan and Malik, the gatekeepers of Heaven and Hell.

76. Jummo Dies

There is no clear, conscious decision to leave the house on the ravine. The move insinuates itself like a vapor into our hearts, into our lungs. There is definitely something in the air. It hangs over us, a cloud, perhaps a sword, steadily gathering weight and substance. Jummo senses it, but she has no idea when it may fall and lop off her head. It's as if the house has decided to sever the umbilical cord connecting itself to its inhabitants.

The only Khazar woman left in the house feels more and more lonely. A chronic chill seals her seclusion, her extremities take on a bluish cast. The Sadas prescribe a pilgrimage to Mina: ceremonial healing under God's tall sky above Mount Arafat.

By the time Jummo arrives at her tent in Mina at the beginning of the days called Tashrîq, most of the other pilgrims have already settled in. She can't exactly say what it is that's hovering around the tents and pavilions. They are trembling with watchfulness.

All pilgrims are watched by an unfelt wind, by an overarching eye that looks down from on high, sizing everything up, moving here, blinking there, guiding all souls toward the sky, selecting the ones who won't be tossed like chunks of raw meat to Satan and his diabolical minions. (After being imprisoned in Mina for four days, the demons will be stoned by the pilgrims.) Yes—the aura of sacrifice, that's what's giving things an otherworldly aura.

Jummo's tent is pitched on a ridge, giving her a view of Mina's crude market stalls, of the pilgrims singing hymns of praise, and of Satan locked up with his demons. All is motion, ceaseless motion. Jummo sits down and with the help of her rosary beads she begins to recite a litany of the spirits in everything that's moving. Down there, just below her, so many, many things are moving from hand to hand, from one mode of existence to another. Nothing stays. Nothing puts down roots. Nothing lasts. This frightens her: the constant movement of things suggests something else inside, a hidden self that propels all things, animal and mineral. Life lurks inside all things, that's what the movement keeps saying.

The hidden life calls to Jummo. She is the only one who sees the inner stillness. She alone is drawn to the still point—to the indivisible, vanishingly small essence of life cloaked in ceaseless motion.

Her first morning at Mina, she looks nearly as healthy and full of life as her old self. She even goes so far as to walk a few steps uphill along the crooked path leading to the tents where women pilgrims from Turkey are staying. She exchanges vague greetings with them in Khazar. They spend some time together kneading and rolling dough made of garbanzo beans and sprinkling it with sugar. They say good-bye.

It's still morning. Jummo's round face is gold in the slanting sun. She steps inside her tent—fresh sunshine here, too.

Sidi is standing with his back against the tent pole, watching her, enjoying the sprightliness of her entrance and the way she lights everything up. He has appeared to her many times since she was a girl. This is the first time she doesn't tremble at his unexpected presence in the here and now. She regards him with a nonchalance very like the lightness she used to feel with Mayjan in the house with the *nabk* tree. Sidi reciprocates enthusiastically; they share a moment of vivid silence.

They move. He joins her at the narrow slit of the tent's door, and they stand looking out on all of Mina. Ordinarily, the entire camp is packed with geniis—except for now, these four days of Tashrîq, when the Netherworldings desert the camp and occupy themselves elsewhere, leaving the pilgrims to perform their ceremonies of sacrifice, imprison their demons, and shed their sins.

Jummo thinks about how much sacrificial blood has soaked into this earth. She focuses on a cluster of women hunkered down in the middle of a herd of cattle that have just been blessed and pronounced ready for slaughter. She concentrates hard on the women. What she senses most of all is the power of the basil sprigs they're wearing, how their perfume overwhelms the rankness of the cattle and their hot breath.

The sun skids to the center of the sky, between the horns of the Gazelle. The necks of the animals are sliced open all at once.

The scent of living blood rises, becomes a red mist. The pilgrims, cleansed, catch their breath, and their sighs of release mingle with the strangled gasps of the dying animals, softening this darkest of sounds. The sky throbs with reds and greens, the insignia of animal spirits. The hunkering women exhale audibly, as if restored to life.

Jummo is fixated on how the women are moving their fingers. Her shoulders sag with the effort of watching them so closely, how their fingers flick in and out, weaving patterns of eternal movement. One pattern in particular takes shape, grows and grows. By the time the sun starts to set, the women are holding, it seems to Jummo, a bolt of satin, shiny and alive-looking, in their hands.

Without knowing how or why, Jummo discovers the precise word for this miraculous piece of satin. It jumps to her tongue. "A shroud!" she gasps. "It's dark, like a shroud!" She gasps again. The satin wraps itself around her, colorless now but unbearably firm. Jummo asks, "Who would have the nerve to die wrapped up in such a strong animal?"

Sidi hears her talking to herself. He moves to the moment where the shroud is about to float toward Heaven, gathers it up—it seems to be everywhere—then takes it to the tent. Jummo follows. She stands in the door of the tent, as if poised to run away. Sidi measures the shroud and rips it into pieces as long as his arm, saying, "From the Alive . . . the shroud of the Alive . . . " He spreads out seven pieces of satin on the floor of the tent, arranging them like the membranes enclosing a human heart. He gestures to Jummo, instructing her to step into the membranes, and she does, laying down on the shroud. The moment she touches the material, it floods with a dark red color, like the pulp of a pomegranate. Sidi stoops down. From the black half of his being seven drops of liquid spill on the right side of her head.

"I speak now the Sevenfold Verse of Light," he says. "I raise up all sides of your being. I enfold you in the seven folds of the verse, and this is what it testifies: Oh Lord of Lords, Ruler of kings, King of kingship, Master of all realms—may He bring light to your grave, may He shine on your face, may He illuminate the life you will lead after death."

On her forehead he outlines the spirits of You-the-One, and in that instant the Mighty All-and-One reverberates in every part of Jummo, merging her flesh with the verse of the Light. She lies naked, letting the lullabies of al-Rasd wash over her.

Sidi kneels beside her, lifting away layers of old life, bathing her without washing her, healing her, stroking her, veiling her. When he finishes fashioning her shroud in this way, he stands up and looks down at her, studying the Alive in her, and when he sees it, it takes his breath away, and Jummo hears the catch in his breath and she senses he's afraid. She starts shaking. Again he kneels and whispers, "No fear . . . there is nothing to be afraid of. From the Alive to the Alive, you are changing . . ."

But Jummo keeps shaking. Sidi tries to support her with dark strips of satin. He tears it into smaller strips and ties them around the vein that's throbbing on the side of her neck, ties another strip around her waist, around her insteps and the palms of her hands, and around her head, just above her ears—there he wraps a coral-red strip of velvet, pressing into her fading brain the soft soul of the velvet.

She skips across the sea. She swims with creatures of the coral reefs; she goes everywhere with them. She reaches up, she floats, she clutches a bit of driftwood. She sails like a ship with a fluttering dagger sail to the source of the Zamzam well, the well that flows and heals with holy salt, keeping the Holy City alive and healthy, coursing from all eight directions of the age-old compass. She feels so alive, pleasured beyond pleasure. She cannot die, death is an impossibility.

She speaks her dying words: *Horat Kafane, tala jinza wolo saqat, thai jai khala red min sawd fan, tala minni zafi fe sak lan wan si di.*

There is no language in which this means anything. Forgive her.

Forgive her.

She feels it: she crosses the Isthmus that lies between her body and authentic existence, between the flesh her mother gave her and the body-temple she had before she came to mortal life. She understands the Sevenfold Verse of Light.

77. Jummo Dies Again

We moved out of the house on the ravine a few days after the pilgrimage season ended. In her new house, with its cool, modern windows high up on the walls, Jummo continued to touch her body, to feel the dark red satin wrapped around her, and she spoke as if breathing the words:

"My shroud is hot. It's hot as a baby's funeral, hot as a miscarried fetus. My nipples are dark red crescents. My petals . . . my petals are the same, the same dark red, almost black. My openings are closed, it's over."

There are no dormers in the room where Jummo lies dying. Her wedding trunks, they're someplace else, locked in another naked room. Jummo lies down, gathering to herself the Sevenfold Verse of Light. She pierces the verse. She arrives at the *nabk* tree sequestered behind the seven thousand veils of the Alive.

Just today I was digging around in Jummo's trunk and quite unexpectedly I came across this dress. I have no idea what makes me keep returning to this ancestral trunk after all the time you and I have spent exchanging letters.

What dress? you ask.

Of course. Of course . . .

The dress was the last gift we gave to Jummo, and when we gave it to her she shocked us by sinking back into the animal she was. We got the dress from a river, one of the four rivers that flow from Eden into Earth. The river is the Nile. We thought we might bring the force of the Nile to her, we thought it might bring the animal in her alive again.

In the course of our travels, Krazat al-Yosir and I came to know a group of spiritualists who gathered together every night to communicate with the souls of the dead. They assured us that they were skilled in finding ways to move between the veiled world of the Isthmus and the world that mortals can readily see. *We make connections between the living and the dead,* they told us. They had looked into the eyes of those who'd crossed the Isthmus into death; they had mastered the talismans on both sides of the great divide.

The spiritualists worked hard to demonstrate the efficacy of their art. They succeeded in conjuring up an image of Jummo—immortal Jummo!—in the dormer of the house on the ravine. They claimed that her soul had never left the house, that she was still there, wallowing in the Alive, nourishing herself with the Alive.

The mirrors in the spiritualists' house testified to the intensity of Jummo's longing during her afterlife in the dormer. The language of the mirrors emphasized her loneliness, her devotion to Sidi's authority, and her worries about the troubles that were afflicting the Holy Circle. Dumboshi manifested herself in the form of a mirror reflecting every movement of Sidi the Glorious King, all the dying souls and all the gravestones in his procession.

While we were reading these signs, we noticed some of Sidi's liquid amber oozing from a cut on Jummo's waist. This we took as a signal to respect her privacy; we called for an end to the session. A cloud of incense enveloped the spiritualists. My black twin Krazat al-Yosir and I were convinced they had connected us with Jummo's energy, and we were deeply touched.

That very same day, however, the fragile wings of our hopes faltered: our memories of Jummo turned sad. We decided to stop experimenting and simply go back to Jummo to see what we could do for her. We were worried that loneliness might overwhelm her and put her out of reach. Every day of our lives since then, we've stayed connected to her by the umbilical cord of mutual longing and needs. It's an excruciating and unbreakable bond.

The dress we gave her, as I mentioned, is woven from running river water. I can still read the embroidery in the ripples. It was sewn by a village woman from Mount Toor, who told me, "T stands for the Tree of Love. There is no loneliness."

The old woman proceeded to put the finishing touches on her embroidered tree: branches made of old cowry shells. They were so exquisitely set on the cloth that they quivered in the breeze when we looked at them closely, and on the branches birds were nestling, birds with human faces, and there were suns and angels beaming thousands of sparkling wings and sunbeams on the tree. "Whoever wears this T," the woman said, "will never be lonely. Never—not in life, not in death."

When we gave the Tree to Jummo, she was already in the final stage of her confinement, which lasted for seven years. She looked hard at the Tree. She recognized it, I think, by its glow of great antiquity. She stared at it for a long time, crumpled the fabric in her hands, and murmured, "*Inshallah*—God willing . . ."

"Won't you try it on, Jummo?" I said. "Let the tree rest on your breasts."

"She can try it on when she gets better and gets out of bed," said her daughter-in-law Rahma. "Right now Jummo is in no condition to be encased in a dress like that."

"My wardrobe these days is nothing but torn old rags anyway," Jummo said.

We took a good look at her. Around her waist she was wearing a sort of sarong, and to cover her breasts there was a sash, or maybe it was an old shirt. That's all she wore in way of womanly adornments. It dawned on us that since she stayed in bed day and night for months on end, lying in the pool of light shining down from the little window high on the wall, the people who cared for her had gradually reduced the articles of clothing she wore so that bathing her and the rituals of purification would go easier. They bathed her while she lay in bed, confined by her paralyzed body, walking around her—circumambulating her, if you will—passing over what couldn't be seen or couldn't be touched.

Jummo's gone now. What remains is the Tree of Love, of No Loneliness. I like to think that the million beams of its thousand suns are warming her sleep in al-Maala.

The day we gave her the dress, we were surprised to see a huge emerald ring on her little finger. It looked like a man's ring. It was in fact the exact twin of my grandfather al-Baikwaly's turquoise ring, which was believed to have the power to control time, distance, and many other things. For a while, whenever we looked at this ring, we imagined that we were also seeing my grandfather's hand. Even though he had been dead for years, we still expected to see him again in his quarters and hear the water running at noon, as it did every day while he was alive. For years and years after he'd been laid in the ground, we listened every noon for the sound of running water signaling his midday ablutions. Now, not only did we hear the water running, but we also managed to see his hand wearing his ring.

Dumboshi had less than no patience anymore for wearing the gold bracelets she used to be so fond of, but she never took off the turquoise ring. Once every year she visited the gold market to keep up with the latest styles and usually she added a few items to her considerable store of antique gold bracelets. Her arms were always a-glitter, a riot of precious metals, even when she slowed down and her shopping urges acquired a more confident relationship with her spiritual powers. But finally she rejected all glittering things as false and foreign, irrelevant to the austerity she deemed to be the proper attitude for one who was awaiting the dawn of . . . who knew?

It was about this time, while Jummo's Animal was reasserting itself, that my black sister and I became adults and started participating in the story as grown women. You should know that Jummo, more than anyone else, was aware of the peculiar waters coursing through our veins. She knew all about the keys we were fashioning to unlock The Alive and the doorway we discovered that led to the River Be. The wilder we got, the more Jummo thirsted for sips of our personal animals spirits. Krazat and I rode the mane of our wild steeds on and on, never stopping in one spot for even a moment.

As soon as I felt the Alive, I understood Jummo's thirst. But I didn't dwell on her dilemma, I didn't trouble myself about her indecisiveness: should she do this, that, or the other thing? Should she go with the Animal or with one of its transfigurations? She wasted so much of her precious life just trying to figure out which way to go. This was the point at which we entered her life, and we left her in the same place. After all these years her fingers are still alive on my arm, clutching me, pleading for help.

The Khazar princess braids on her forehead have turned into weeds of white amber, sparkling like white firestone. The white fires tremble at the sides of her face, which the years have made perfectly round.

Her fingers dig into my arm, trying to get my energies to seep into her and give her the strength she needs to fight the stroke that has blocked one of the arteries in her head. The afflicted veins feed her slender torso, which has surrendered to Sidi and flops around as if trying to clear the way for health to flow once again into her paralyzed lower extremities. The stroke twisted her tongue, too. It is stone-heavy, it rattles in her mouth. Her speech is slurred.

"He wants me to follow him, Sidi does. Oh Zohr, Zohr—bring me a drink!" She digs her fingers deeper into my forearm. I'm seized by an unearthly fear. I can feel the snow-white flames of her hair jump on my back and set the small hairs of my neck on fire. Down, down, down the fire burns, lower and lower on my back. The white flames freeze me.

"I can smell Sidi all over this room," Hannah whispers. She stands up and walks briskly as if shoring up the space around Jummo, reciting the verses of Yassen from the Qur'an, shattering Sidi's hold on the place. "If she still has some life to live, Yassen will help her return to life. If not, the calmness of the verse will help her depart in peace." Hannah goes on reciting.

I can just barely pick out a few of the half-words rattling in Jummo's mouth. She seems to be pleading for a confirmation of some kind: "Is it time for me to die now? Get me a drink of amber, please."

I come close to help her swallow. She wraps her arms around my neck, hanging on.

She enters my heart. She curls up somewhere just above my stomach. Then she hops from my whiteness to Krazat al-Yosir's blackness, sucking the life and strength out of both of us.

Tell me, did you ever in your travels come across the River of Death, the river that flows upwards to where no mountain can reach and no bird can fly? Can you teach me how to rescue someone who's drowning in the River of the Alive?

"Hold me!" Jummo cries. "Hold me close to Sidi's sheltering basil! Hold me close to the lanterns in the basil! Hold me! Hold me close to Sidi's basil obelisk! Hold me close to the lanterns in the obelisk! Hold me!"

My arms are shaking like the wings of a bird being sacrificed.

Despite her condition, Jummo eludes death, though certainly not because I'm holding onto her. She escapes death because in Fate's Tableau it is not written that Sidi should accompany her on her final trip, not yet. She has not lived quite long enough to endure the ordeal of the Sevenfold Verse of Light. She has one more word, one more mark in the book of her life, to go. Seven little marks, seven more years of confinement in bed, seven years of diving deeper and deeper into the river whose tide keeps dragging her down. It seems she must accept her full measure of the Bolts of Light before the River veers in her direction and sweeps her up to a higher place.

As far as we can tell—to all appearances, that is—Jummo seems at peace with the new and unique arrangement she's made with life. On the surface she appears to be in great pain, while at the same time it's clear her inner life is ecstatic. As for her body—her body has nothing more to worry about than a tree does. As long as a tree gets water, it keeps on shedding leaves, growing leaves again, and sending its roots deeper into the ground. All this it accomplishes more or less naturally, invisibly, and in silence.

There is no one else on earth with Jummo's talent for living the infinitely patient life of a tree. Just when we begin to feel certain that she's organized her handicaps and ailments enough to keep death at a distance, just when it looks like she's become more like some immortal form of plant life than a mortal human, when she seems ready to share in the ordinary act of being, or at least partake in the appearance of ordinary existence, to behave as if she's cut from the same stock as everyone else—that's precisely when she's likely to stop, to freeze in place, and change from a living tree to a dried-up trunk to a fossilized column of coal. Jummo is capable of avoiding death and making a connection between the Eternal Was and the Eternal To Be, and this she can do with ease, without the customary pangs of birth and rebirth.

Dumboshi wanted to dig her own grave right in her own living quarters. This was her way of guaranteeing that her body would come back intact and immortal. A grave (so her thinking went) is the best spot to plant a tree, or a body you might want to resurrect. For seven years she inhabited that grave of hers.

How do you like living in the earth of Mecca? You wait. You watch how death lives in her, how it takes possession of her, and how—most amazingly—it seems to buoy her up. You use my words to keep on living, to fight off the inevitable putrefaction, but in the end there's nothing like dying, is there, to pique your interest in Jummo's inheritance. I can feel you now. You're alive in the darkness of the room, very alive. You are here, in the grave, completely present and alive as life can be.

Maybe it's time for the funeral. This might be the most fashionable month for funerals. Let me tell you, then, all about Jummo's death, from the final vision she had in this life to her genuflection in front of God's throne.

We are not in Mecca, we have moved to a city near the sea. It's just after dawn prayer. In her demi-sleep, somewhere between dreams and waking life, Hannah sees Nara getting ready to tie on a scarf made of basil sprigs.

"The Sheik and I are getting ready for Sidi's parade," Nara says. "The *nabk* tree will be our companion. He's such a happy person, the *nabk* tree."

Hannah wakes up, very upset. She wakes my father up and tells him to get ready for a funeral procession that's about to pass by. By the time the sun rises, she thinks, all this will become clear.

It's been some time since we came to the conclusion that death would overlook Jummo. So not even in our wildest dreams do we connect my mother's morbid anxiety with anything happening in Mecca, certainly not with the woman self-imprisoned in her own room, lying in the fading glow from a little window high up on the wall—the unique, the magical, the legendary Dumboshi buried beneath all her years of living, obscured by the towers and minarets of a city that, truly, overlooks her.

Sometime during the night when Jummo goes away with Sidi, she rushes into my dreams. She utters not a word, just scoops some pickings off a plate. ("Pickings"—the word strikes me, dreaming, as odd.) In the pickings I can read a silent plea: *Hold me!* But in a twinkling the dream sweeps her away; the last thing I see is her hands and the crumbs sticking to them. I feel helpless to reach out and rescue her from whatever or whoever's going to pay her a visit when morning comes.

When I tell my dream to Hannah, her face goes gloomy. Shortly afterwards, we hear the news of Jummo's death. The middle daughter, the liveliest child of the Sheik of the Zamzam Water Carriers, is gone.

The news is brought by a messenger, an Indonesian. His heavy accent sounds like the rustling of the boughs in the almond tree that my mother's been pruning lately; she finished just this morning, while al-Simoom was still. The tree was heavy with almonds, bunches and bunches of them, reddish in color. The Prophet's Almonds, we call them.

The servants are still busy picking them. The watchmen are bracing the new shoots so they'll be strong enough to bear next season's crop. The news of Jummo's death drops from a dark red cluster of almonds and lands on the Indonesian, who passes it to us, his accent baffling and nakedly abrupt, like the news itself.

"Momma Jummo . . . she got no serpent in this world no more . . . "

What? The worldly life of Momma Jummo is over?

There is a wretched irony to the Indonesian's language. Picture it: Jummo has no serpent anymore; her inner animal, her snake-essence, has made off with her soul . . . There must be some mistake. There *is* a mistake: the Indonesian, an illiterate immigrant, has confused our word for life with the word for snake. But his mistake is eerily precise: the certainty of Jummo's existence has slithered out of our grasp.

The image of Jummo lingering from my dream—her pleading, the pickings stuck to her fingers—deflates. The envelope of air in which her image stood inflates with her cry: *Hold me!* My arms go limp.

There is nothing to hold. There is only Jummo's corpse, wet after the ritual washing. I hold her. Krazat al-Yosir holds her. We hold her forever, in a time out of time. We hold on to the unseen, the vanished Jummo we love. We cling to a time that is gone forever.

How can a woman be one with another woman, the way Jummo wanted to be united with us? And why us, why Yosir and myself? Why did Jummo pick us instead of Hosn, al-Baikwaly's adored adopted son? What made her insist that Yosir and I be her close companions through all the years of her decline, during all the days of her scuttling across the floor and the endless hours of her wasting away in bed? How was it that she completely forgot about Nabee Jan? She appropriated his wildness and his aggressiveness for as long as she had the wit to get away with it. So why, toward the end, when she became utterly dependent, did she turn for solace to a nurturing version of womanhood?

There is another question I can't stop asking: when did Jummo really die? Can it be that her life in this world really came to an end one morning when she happened to be fifty-three years old? Or had she actually been dead all during her confinement?

I feel so guilty.

78. The Colt

When the page Jummo's time is written on flutters down from the Book of Fate, dogs start barking on the street in front of the house of the Sheik's adopted son. The barking is sad, incessant. The house knows, even its stones know, that Sidi Wahdana will be dawning with the dawn. The sun rises. The sun has not forgotten the forgotten room with the little window high on the wall. The room is heavy with the scent of basil. Dumboshi knows this scent; it is the scent that makes all Khazars throw their hearts away. The basil exudes calm, calm, absolute calm. Everything moves as if in a dream.

Time for mid-morning prayer. The stones of the house stretch, opening just a crack, admitting a visitor who knows precisely where he's going. There'll be no mistake, the body he seeks isn't moving. He sees the small flame shuddering, pulsing in its temple, its cage. He comes closer. He is calm, calm, perfectly calm. He walks around her, past each one of the thousand roots of her soul, and he wraps them in his wings, extinguishing her flame.

The shadow of Sidi's wings makes her body shake. Her soul sheds its mortal disguise and shows its true self: the young colt made of basil, with thousands upon thousands of translucent wings. Whatever the colt touches catches its breath, heaves with life. When she exhales, angels are born in the steam of her breath.

The angels stand in long lines to the right and left, arranging themselves in colonnades that start at the colt's lips and ascend till they vanish into the Throne of the Seventh Heaven. Between the angels runs a river like no river that has ever run. The river is pure motion. Whoever looks into its water, his soul is stolen away and swept up to the sky. This river runs uphill, silently, faster and faster, propelled by the soul of the colt. The colt dips her snout in the water, then lifts her head, and her wings splash light in all directions. The colt's energy is seeping through her hoofs and into the ground. Everything in the house comes alive, everything is about to burst.

Everyone sees Jummo shudder, though they cannot see the colt—for them the colt is veiled. Al-Hosn knows only that the basil has blurred his eyesight and tears are streaming down his face. He takes her shaking body in his arms. He cannot stop himself from shaking. His teeth are chattering. Something tells him that the room, the whole house, has gone into a trance, that in this place time has been suspended, and that Jummo is the epicenter of the trance.

Jummo lies still. All of her senses have left her except hearing and sight. Her body sleeps and while she sleeps she watches the colt and the colonnade of angels rising from under Sidi's wings. Her eyes are wider than they've ever been. She stares at it, at the beautiful, fascinating glow. For the first time in—how many years has it been?—she sees herself, and she is spellbound. She is going to Sidi, her Sidi. She understands now how far, far away her confinement kept her from Sidi and the Animal.

Her final words are: "What a colt I was! *I am!*"

On the hot wind of al-Simoom, rising again, there is the scent of basil. Now, for every transgression she's committed, for every cutting remark she has ever made, she does sweet penance: the scent of basil overwhelms her soul.

"Go away!" cries Rahma, the daughter-in-law. She's not quite sure whether she's addressing her husband Hosn or the Angel of Death or Sidi Wahdana. Rahma sees Sidi sitting on Jummo's head with his back turned to everyone but her. Evidently he's been there for some time. He's in the midst of dispensing the spirits of the Great Names and reciting the Verses of the Realm in a low, singsong voice very like a lullaby, soothing the death rattles in Jummo's throat. Finally, after making an effort to repeat the words after him, Rahma shouts, "Enough!"

Hosn, Ezrael, and Sidi snap to attention. Rahma is relieved by the instant restoration of quiet and calm. The room sighs with relief. There is a special sweetness on the faces of the angels when they rise with the fast-running river and vanish into the First Heaven, the entire assembly collapsing upward, the Gate of Heaven closing after them. All that remains are the Verses of the Realm soaring in a circle above Jummo's new resting place waiting for her in al-Maala.

Jummo the Colt is wrapped in basil and carried toward Heaven.

I am far away, far from Mecca, standing in my private place by the waves of a distant sea. I see two rows of angels parading across the Heavens, carrying basil sprigs, and now the veil descends, and I can't see the basil standing by itself, braced between the Hands of the King of the Throne.

"I'll get a doctor," Hosn says feebly. He rushes out of the room, making an escape.

The sadness begins to weigh on us. We can't find anyone to carry her out. It's up to us to carry her—myself, my mother, Krazat al-Yosir, and the female attendant who'll help with the washing. We squeeze against her. There is a firm dignity in her limpness. We carry her from the wooden washing bench to the shroud spread out on the ground. I don't know where I find the courage to wrap my arms around the naked flesh under the smooth cloth. All I know is I'm touching her. And I can feel her even now, her limpness pressing against my breast, weighing on my arms. She is still soft and wet, the wetness of the washing still stains my lap, still splashes on my neck. This is Jummo, she is here. I will always be carrying her body wet with *nabk* water, ready to be perfumed with camphor and anointed with *hanoot* of dried rose petals and basil. Always.

Krazat al-Yosir, pitch-black against Jummo's pale skin, bends over and writes two blessings on her cold forehead in pure oil of camphor. All of us want to get as close as we can to the temple that for so many years contained an Animal so wild, so explosive. There are so many questions we want to ask the powerful Serpent, the Alive.

The day of Jummo's funeral, no one walked in the procession through the valleys of Mecca except Hosn, the adopted son, and three helpful neighbors—not many mourners, unless you count our eyes watching the wagon that carried the coffin. There was a green dome on top of the coffin, green in honor of the color of Sidi Wahdana's vest.

When the procession passed through the neighborhood where so many flood victims had perished, the many-horned flood suddenly rose again from the Valley of Blood. But before it could reach the cemetery and tear up the graves, Jummo's earthly body was laid to rest.

Somewhere in the distance we heard the sad strumming of an aloe wood lute. We knew this sound: it was the double stringed, ten-stringed triangular lute, serenading us with its heartbreaking blend of sadness and joy. The melodies coated us like a balm. We were all alone, we women. It was our funeral, entirely female, conducted by Hannah with her usual serenity.

79. The Sin

Let's go back to before the funeral, to the cause of Jummo's paralysis. Who was behind it? Was it a man or a woman? In order to mourn her properly, we must return to the beginning of her confinement, before she left the house on the ravine. Who was it who climbed the stairs to the *kharija* and went up the narrow steps to the topmost *mabeet*? Who pushed open the wooden door that was always unlocked? Who walked across the darkened dormer where Jummo sat watching? Who crept up behind her and brushed the potion of amber and basil on the nerves of her lower back? Who allowed the poison to spread, day after day, till it crippled her?

The things that scare you, they scare me too. I get jumpy when a sharp knife comes close to a round loaf. It makes me nervous to think about the knife touching a shape so perfect.

How did the perpetrator bring himself or herself to do the deed, to sever Jummo's nerve endings? How could he or she have been so cold-hearted? How could they have distilled death into one prick of a pin, how could they ruin her Animal? How could they force her into the life of a cripple; how could they condemn her never to have a moment's rest except when the hot al-Simoom blew hard and calmed her down by whispering the desert's ripe secrets? How dare they lay a finger on the silky private skin at the base of her spine?

These questions will follow me into the coffin that Fate has made for me. Because I'm the only person who knows what happened, who understands the progress of Jummo's illness during her long confinement. Something happened. Somebody made it happen.

In Mecca we lived side-by-side with angels. On Friday, mother forbade us to do any laundry, because the angels might get dirty or slip in a puddle of water while they were delivering her prayers to Heaven. How, in a neighborhood such as this, could anyone possibly commit a sin?

I know I warned you not to go digging up Jummo's secrets. But I will tell you that last night, in a dream, she came to me from the Isthmus.

I was on the seashore. The sand was gold. I was bending over some letters I was going to send you in the next mail. Behind me, the sky was feathered with emerald light. I felt the flapping of a single wing next to my head, scattering my hair in spokes and setting it aglow. A square-shaped silver tray appeared, heaped with candies and fruit. Hannah came and sat down cross-legged to make room on her lap for the best pieces. Ordinarily Hannah was an abstemious person, but when it came to getting in line for treats, she could be terribly greedy. Actually she was one of fortune's favorites, incredibly lucky, always the first to get the most wonderful gifts, and the luckier she was, the more abstemiously she lived. In my dream, she was given the chance to pick the choicest items off the silver tray: she took two pieces of almond candy. One she kept in her hand, the other she placed on the hem of her spread-out dress. Picking at the almonds, she looked like a bird made of rubies.

Jummo approached from over my shoulder and headed for the almond candy sitting on the hem of my mother's dress. I stopped her by reaching out and breaking the seal on a bottle and pouring her a drink of amber-colored nectar. She drank the undisturbed sediment from the bottom of the bottle; it looked like crushed crystals of bloody ice. While she drank she talked about the people she'd left behind. She kept on talking even when she started choking on the flames—the amber nectar, having burst into flames, was spilling out of two glasses made of transparent silver, one on each side of Hannah.

"Why do you suppose Hannah poured such a generous drink?" she asked.

I was puzzled. I noticed that whenever we looked at the silver tray it had been refilled, out of nowhere, with peeled pomegranates. Then the tray turned into a spring spouting water and pomegranates—rivers of pomegranates, ice and grapes splashed on the tray, and we scooped them up and ate them.

Mayjan's shadow fell across the tray, which made the spirits of the rubies, recently centered on Hannah, blend with the silver of the tray. I called out Krazat al-Yosir's name, not wanting her to miss the extraordinary fountain in the tray. She appeared immediately, closing the circle of women around the tray. There were four of us, standing firm against intruders.

Yosir wanted me to pass her my silver spoon, but she already had a spoon as fine as mine. I encouraged her to take what remained on the tray, and be thankful, and she said, "The sweetest things lie deepest in the spring."

I heard a sound that told me to pick out my favorite from all the soggy fur skins that mother and Jummo used to wear when they worked by the well in the house with the *nabk* tree. I chose the wildest-looking one. (Exactly which one, and how wild, we don't have time to go into right now.) I tucked the skin under my own skin so it wouldn't be seen by prying, envious eyes. I knew it would stay hidden there till it came time for me to run away—at dawn, that's when I'd flee, after shedding my sins. Sin. I'm going to send my sin to you now, so you'll inherit its last smoldering ember.

Do you believe that we invent our own confessions along with the veils we use to cover them up just so we can appease the layers and layers of fate we can't see?

My father used to shake his head in amusement because there was nothing he could do to restrain Hannah's flights into the Unknown. My mother was a Khazar, she had no qualms about mixing the Unknown with the dough of what can be seen. My father turned away from her without saying a word. He never questioned the validity of her flights. He consoled himself by remembering the wisdom of Sheik ibn al-Qayem al-Jowzeya, the great researcher into the life of the soul after death: *In truth, the dead do visit us in sleep.*

On the seventh floor of my grandfather's house on the ravine there was a *mabeet,* and above the *mabeet* was the roof, which had three different levels, or *kharijas.* Each one, depending on its height, received more or less of the cooling breezes from the sea or the southern highlands, which helped temper the sharp light of Mecca's sunrise. Higher than all these levels there was another level, a smaller *mabeet.* This was the loftiest space of all, and it had a dormer that looked out on the street. This *mabeet* was a sanctuary. No one was allowed to go there unless he was a serious student, a devotee of higher things who needed to be close to Heaven in order to learn more about it. The only way to get to this *mabeet* was by means of a narrow staircase hidden behind the other roofs. The stairs were so dark that the seeker had to grope his way through tight spaces between various blind dormers and find his way by listening to the cooing of pigeons. In this passageway, even sunrise was dark, and there were places where the overhang was so low and the turns so tight that you had to proceed on hands and knees.

Not a single creature, not even a pigeon, was allowed in the *mabeet.* The seeker after truth was required to wash his face before entering. There was a bathroom just below the stairs leading to the roof. My mother used to clean me up there when I caught the Disease of the Tears of Birds' Eyes, which was what the daughters of Sheik Baikwaly called chicken pox. I was very small when the birds shed their tears on my skin. The baths mother gave me started with silvery water, and by the time she finished I was purple. She laid me out on a spotless silver platter and poured pitcher after pitcher of clear water over me, banishing al-Simoom from my naked flesh. Ointments that were oddly odorless and dull followed the bath. I was not permitted to come into contact with anything perfumey. Perfumes, because they were so personal, were believed to stimulate sore spots and contusions, causing them to break out and spread. "Don't go near her with perfume," grandmother Nara warned. "The spirits of the

Birds' Tears will get excited and run away with her. Don't let the perfume anywhere near her."

The idea was to dull my body down. When this was accomplished, I was transferred from the silver platter to something purple—in this case, to a purple sarong held ready to wrap me in. Wrapped up, I began to burn and glow like Mecca on fire.

Nara affirmed the correctness of this treatment: "The change from dullness to fever is just the right thing to burn away the disease, cut it off at the root, and keep it from spreading."

Under the burning rays of the noonday sun, ringed by stone soldiers on the parapets and lulled by the cooing of the sacred homing pigeons, my mother spent a lot of time in the *kharija* infusing my sarong with purple dye. She did this not just because Nara's prescriptions were generally taken as holy writ but because white was a color associated with death shrouds, and wrapping me up in anything white would have provoked unacceptable omens. Purple, on the other hand, was just the thing for little bride-like me, whose moon face the chicken pox was trying to violate.

The Birds' Tears dripped tiny round drops on my left breast. Peaceful and pearly they were at first—before the sores started burning and spreading and blistering everywhere. My tender skin was washed and washed and washed again with silvery water, and stroked by the marvelously soothing hands of my mother, drawing upon her inexhaustible supply of love and warmth.

The many roofs of our house assimilated this image of the Purple Me into the mysterious book of scenes they lived to witness: images of the birds, of the Alive, and of the prayers that showered down on us from the seven minarets of the grand mosque. We came of age in the Sacred Circle, where no hunting or killing was permitted, not even the plucking of fruit from a tree. We grew up with a sense of wholeness, of immunity from fear.

The small *mabeet*, the highest space among high spaces, was regarded as the only peak higher, in an absolute sense, than anything else. It was therefore the ideal place in which to commit the crime.

After Sheik Baikwaly died, Dumboshi used to seek refuge in the small *mabeet* during the holy months, leaving the rest of the house to transient pilgrims. From behind the shuttered dormer she watched the ground below, the world of humans, the shifting mosaic of blacks and yellows and reds and browns and whites.

One year Dumboshi stayed longer than usual in the *mabeet*, even though all the pilgrims had gone back home. Ordinarily she would have gone right down to her empty quarters on the seventh floor. This time she delayed, though it was only a matter of hours between the formal end of the holy month and the moment she went down to her rooms. Sometime during these hours, the Page on which her fate was written took it upon itself to enter the *mabeet*, where whatever happened happened.

I was walking along a street in the ravine dressed all in black silk, just skipping along, light as a bird flirting with the wind, teasing the breezes that kept trying to catch me. I came to the crossroads where a *nabk* tree stood, at which point the street forked toward our house. I noticed something snagged on a branch in the *nabk* tree, a piece of paper or a leaf. The way it was flapping, it seemed to be calling out for me to pick it off the tree—just like you, trying to get someone's attention to rescue you. Little boys were crowding around the tree plucking *nabk* fruits out of the dense greenery, jumping up and down in time to the bobbing of the branches.

As if reaching out toward the tree, my black silk robe fell open, exposing my purple sarong. I picked the piece of paper off the tree. On it were words written in white ink. The words ordered me to go to my grandfather's house and respond to Dumboshi's request—to her need—to be ill, to get another life, even if it meant death. Though I failed to recognize the white handwriting, the scent of amber rising from the letters reminded me of Sidi Wahdana, of his eyes brimming with whiteness. I dismissed my suspicion that the white words had been written by his eyes. The black silk robe tugged me back toward the street to my grandfather's house. (Three years ago Nara had left this house and followed Sheik Baikwaly to al-Maala.)

It was empty now, and no longer grand. Only Dumboshi remained. There was nothing else there, no one to interfere with my interpretation of the words on the paper, no one to equivocate about the meaning of the message. I had my secret instructions. I understood what had to be done, I alone. And you, dear friend.

Glossary

GENII: a creature from the Underworld. Often mischievous and malevolent, it occasionally intervencs in human affairs.

HIDRI: a male spirit who manifests himself when al-Zar is performed.

HIJAZ: the western, most settled part of the Arabian peninsula.

JUBBAH: a robelike men's garment.

KEFFIYEH: a headdress for men.

KHARIJA: an open-air space on the roof of a house, typical of traditional Meccan architecture.

AL-MAALA: Mecca's principal cemetery.

MABEET: an enclosed space on the roof.

MIHRANA: a head covering for women.

NABK: A fruit-bearing tree, probably a lotus jujube.

QREEN: In Meccan dialect, a soul mate or sexual partner.

RIKA: a heavily ornamented bridal throne.

AL-SHAMIA: a fashionable neighborhood in Mecca, overlooking the central mosque.

AL-SIMOOM: a dry wind that brings the desert's heat to Mecca in summer.

TAIF: a cool mountain resort region of Arabia.

UNDERWORLD/NETHERWORLD: a realm distinct from the world visible to humans, though sometimes there is interpenetration.

The Underworld is full of dangerous creatures and unpredictable phenomena.

ZAMZAM: the well in Mecca's central mosque. Its waters, which bear the same name, are said to have curative and prophetic properties.

AL-ZAR: a sensuous dance performed by women.